THE STONE MONKEY

THE STONE MONKEY

Jeffery Deaver

Hodder & Stoughton

First published in the United States of America in 2002 by Simon & Schuster
First published in Great Britain in 2002 by Hodder and Stoughton
A division of Hodder Headline

A CIP catalogue record for this title is available from the British Library.

ISBN 0 340 733993 (hardcover)
ISBN 0 340 73400 0 (trade paperback)

Printed and bound in Great Britain by
Clays Ltd, St Ives plc

Hodder and Stoughton
A division of Hodder Headline
338 Euston Road
London NW1 3BH

To those we lost on September 11, 2001 – whose only crime
was their love of tolerance and freedom and who will be
in our hearts forever

Author's Note

I'm including here some information that might be helpful for readers unfamiliar with certain aspects of Chinese life that are described in the book.

GEOGRAPHY Most of the illegal immigrants to the United States from China come from the southeastern coastal region of that country, generally from two provinces: in the far south, Guangdong Province, where Hong Kong is located, and just north of that, Fujian Province, whose major city is Fuzhou, a large seafaring center and probably the most popular point of embarkation for illegal immigrants beginning their journeys to other lands.

LANGUAGE The written Chinese language is the same throughout the country but as spoken there are great differences from one region to the other. The major dialects are Cantonese in the south, Minnanhua in Fujian and Taiwan, and Mandarin, or Putonghua, in Beijing and the north. The few Chinese words I use in the book are in the Putonghua dialect, which is the official language of the country.

NAMES Chinese names are traditionally given in the reverse order from that used in the United States and Europe. For example, with Li Kangmei, Li is the family name and Kangmei is the given name. Some Chinese in the more urbanized regions of China or with close ties to the United States or other Western cultures may adopt a Western given name, which they use in addition to or instead of a Chinese given name. In such a case the Anglicized name precedes the family name, such as Jerry Tang.

—J.D.

I

The Snakehead

———◆———

Tuesday, the Hour of the Tiger, 4:30 A.M.,
to the Hour of the Dragon, 8 A.M.

The word Wei-Chi consists of two Chinese words—
Wei, which means to "encircle," and Chi, which means
"piece." As the game represents a struggle for life, it
may be called the "war game."

—Danielle Pecorini and Tong Shu,
The Game of Wei-Chi

Chapter One

They were the vanished, they were the unfortunate.

To the human smugglers—the snakeheads—who carted them around the world like pallets of damaged goods, they were *ju-jia*, piglets.

To the American INS agents who interdicted their ships and arrested and deported them they were *undocumenteds*.

They were the hopeful. Who were trading homes and family and a thousand years of ancestry for the hard certainty of risky, laborious years ahead of them.

Who had the slimmest of chances to take root in a place where their families could prosper, where freedom and money and contentment were, the story went, as common as sunlight and rain.

They were his fragile cargo.

And now, legs steady against the raging, five-meter-high seas, Captain Sen Zi-jun made his way from the bridge down two decks into the murky hold to deliver the grim message that their weeks of difficult journeying might have been in vain.

It was just before dawn on a Tuesday in August. The stocky captain, whose head was shaved and who sported an elaborate bushy mustache, slipped past the empty containers lashed to the deck of the seventy-two-meter *Fuzhou Dragon* as camouflage and opened the heavy steel door to the hold. He looked down at the two-dozen people huddled there, in the grim, windowless space. Trash and children's plastic blocks floated in the shallow tide under the cheap cots.

Despite the pitching waves, Captain Sen—a thirty-year veteran of the seas—walked down the steep metal steps without using the handrails and strode into the middle of the hold. He checked the carbon dioxide meter and found the levels acceptable though the air was vile with the smell of diesel fuel and humans who'd lived for two weeks in close proximity.

Unlike many of the captains and crew who operated "buckets"— human smuggling ships—and who at best ignored or sometimes even beat or raped the passengers, Sen didn't mistreat them. Indeed he believed that he was doing a good thing: transporting these families from difficulty to, if not certain wealth, at least the hope of a happy life in America, *Meiguo* in Chinese, which means the "Beautiful Country."

On this particular voyage, however, most of the immigrants distrusted him. And why not? They assumed he was in league with the snakehead who'd chartered the *Dragon:* Kwan Ang, known universally by his nickname, Gui, the Ghost. Tainted by the snakehead's reputation for violence, Captain Sen's efforts to engage the immigrants in conversation had been rebuffed and had yielded only one friend. Chang Jingerzi—who preferred his Western name of Sam Chang—was a forty-five-year-old former college professor from a suburb of the huge port city of Fuzhou in southeastern China. He was bringing his entire family to America: his wife, two sons and Chang's widower father.

A half-dozen times on the trip Chang and Sen had sat in the hold, sipped the potent *mao-tai* that the captain always had in good supply on his ship and talked about life in China and in the United States.

Captain Sen now saw Chang sitting on a cot in a forward corner of the hold. The tall, placid man frowned, a reaction to the look in the captain's eyes. Chang handed his teenage son the book he'd been reading to his family and rose to meet the captain.

Everyone around them fell silent.

"Our radar shows a fast-moving ship on course to intercept us."

Dismay blossomed in the faces of those who'd overheard.

"The Americans?" Chang asked. "Their Coast Guard?"

"I think it must be," the captain answered. "We're in U.S. waters."

Sen looked at the frightened faces of the immigrants around him. Like most shiploads of illegals that Sen had transported, these people— many of them strangers before they'd met—had formed a close bond of friendship. And they now gripped hands or whispered among themselves, some seeking, some offering reassurance. The captain's eyes settled on a woman holding an eighteen-month-old girl in her arms. Her mother—whose face was scarred from a beating at a reeducation camp—lowered her head and began to cry.

"What can we do?" Chang asked, troubled. Captain Sen knew he was a vocal dissident in China and had been desperate to flee the country. If he was deported by U.S. Immigration he'd probably end up in one of the infamous jails in western China as a political prisoner.

"We're not far from the drop-off spot. We're running at full speed. It may be possible to get close enough to put you ashore in rafts."

"No, no," Chang said. "In these waves? We'd all die."

"There's a natural harbor I'm steering for. It should be calm enough for you to board the rafts. At the beach there'll be trucks to take you to New York."

"And what about you?" Chang asked.

"I'll head back into the storm. By the time it's safe for them to board you'll be on highways of gold, heading toward the city of diamonds. . . . Now tell everyone to get their belongings together. But only the most important things. Your money, your pictures. Leave everything else. It will be a race to the shore. Stay below until the Ghost or I tell you to come up top."

Captain Sen hurried up the steep ladder, on his way to the bridge. As he climbed he said a brief prayer for their survival to Tian Hou, the goddess of sailors, then dodged a wall of gray water that vaulted the side of the ship.

On the bridge he found the Ghost standing over the radar unit, staring into the rubber glare shade. The man stood completely still, bracing himself against the rolling of the sea.

Some snakeheads dressed as if they were wealthy Cantonese gangsters from a John Woo film but the Ghost always wore the standard outfit of most Chinese men—simple slacks and short-sleeved shirts. He was muscular but diminutive, clean-shaven, hair longer than a typical businessman's but never styled with cream or spray.

"They will intercept us in fifteen minutes," the snakehead said. Even now, facing interdiction and arrest, he seemed as lethargic as a ticket seller in a rural long-distance bus station.

"Fifteen?" the captain replied. "Impossible. How many knots are they making?"

Sen walked to the chart table, the centerpiece of all ocean-crossing vessels. On it sat a U.S. Defense Mapping Agency nautical chart of the area. He had to judge the two ships' relative positions from this and from the radar; because of the risk of being traced, the *Dragon*'s global positioning system and her EPIRB emergency beacon and Global Maritime Distress and Safety System were disconnected.

"I think it will be at least forty minutes," the captain said.

"No, I timed the distance they've traveled since we spotted them."

Captain Sen glanced at the crewman piloting the *Fuzhou Dragon,* sweating as he gripped the wheel in his struggle to keep the Turk's head knot of twine, tied around a spoke, straight up, indicating that the rudder was aligned with the hull. The throttles were full forward. If the Ghost was right in his assessment of when the cutter would intercept them they would not be able to make the protected harbor in time. At best they could get within a half mile of the nearby rocky shore—close enough to launch the rafts but subjecting them to merciless pounding by the tempestuous seas.

The Ghost asked the captain, "What sort of weapons will they have?"

"Don't you know?"

"I've never been interdicted," the Ghost replied. "Tell me."

Ships under Sen's command had been stopped and boarded twice before—fortunately on legitimate voyages, not when he was running immigrants for snakeheads. But the experience had been harrowing. A dozen armed Coast Guard sailors had streamed onto the vessel while another one, on the deck of the cutter, had trained a two-barreled machine gun on him and his crew. There'd been a small cannon too.

He now told the Ghost what they might expect.

The Ghost nodded. "We need to consider our options."

"What options?" Captain Sen now asked. "You're not thinking of *fighting* them, are you? No. I won't allow it."

But the snakehead didn't answer. He remained braced at the radar stand, staring at the screen.

The man seemed placid but, Sen supposed, he must've been enraged. No snakehead he'd ever worked with had taken so many precautions to avoid capture and detection as the Ghost on this voyage. The two-dozen immigrants had met in an abandoned warehouse outside of Fuzhou and waited there for two days, under the watch of a partner of the Ghost's—a "little snakehead." The man had then loaded the Chinese onto a chartered

Tupolev 154, which had flown to a deserted military airfield near St. Petersburg in Russia. There they'd climbed into a shipping container, been driven 120 kilometers to the town of Vyborg and boarded the *Fuzhou Dragon,* which Sen had sailed into the Russian port just the day before. He himself had meticulously filled out the customs documents and manifests—everything according to the book, so as not to arouse suspicion. The Ghost had joined them at the last minute and the ship had sailed on schedule. Through the Baltic Sea, the North Sea, the English Channel, then the *Dragon* had crossed the famous starting point of transatlantic voyages in the Celtic Sea—49°N 7°W—and had begun steaming southwest toward Long Island, New York.

There was not a single thing about the voyage that would arouse the suspicion of the U.S. authorities. "How did the Coast Guard do it?" the captain asked.

"What?" the Ghost responded absently.

"Find us. No one could have. It's impossible."

The Ghost straightened up and pushed outside into the raging wind, calling back, "Who knows? Maybe it was magic."

Chapter Two

"We're right on top of 'em, Lincoln. The boat's headin' for land but are they gonna make it? Nosir, nohow. Wait, do I hafta call it a 'ship'? I think I do. It's too big for a boat."

"I don't know," Lincoln Rhyme said absently to Fred Dellray. "I don't really do much sailing."

The tall, lanky Dellray was the FBI agent in charge of the federal side of the efforts to find and arrest the Ghost. Neither Dellray's canary yellow shirt nor his black suit, as dark as the man's lustrous skin, had been ironed recently—but then no one in the room looked particularly well rested. These half-dozen people clustered around Rhyme had spent the past twenty-four hours virtually living here, in this improbable headquarters—the living room of Rhyme's Central Park West town house, which resembled not the Victorian drawing room it had once been but a forensics laboratory, chock-full of tables, equipment, computers, chemicals, wires and hundreds of forensics books and magazines.

The team included both federal and state law enforcers. On the state side was Lieutenant Lon Sellitto, homicide detective for the NYPD, far more rumpled than Dellray—stockier too (he'd just moved in with his girlfriend in Brooklyn, who, the cop announced with rueful pride, cooked like Emeril). Young Eddie Deng, a Chinese-American detective from the NYPD's Fifth Precinct, which covered Chinatown, was present too. Deng was trim and athletic and stylish, sporting glasses framed by Arm, and black hair spiked up like a hedgehog's. He was serving as Sellitt, temporary partner; the big detective's usual coworker, Roland Bell, ha, gone down to his native North Carolina for a family reunion with his two sons a week ago and, as it turned out, had struck up a friendship with a local policewoman, Lucy Kerr. He'd extended his vacation another few days.

Assisting on the federal portion of the team was fifty-something Harold Peabody, a pear-shaped, clever middle manager who held a senior spot at the Immigration and Naturalization Service's Manhattan office. Peabody was close-lipped about himself, as are all bureaucrats narrowing in on their retirement pension, but his far-ranging knowledge of immigration issues attested to a lengthy and successful stint in the service. Peabody and Dellray had faced off more than once during this investigation. After the *Golden Venture* incident—in which ten illegal immigrants drowned after a smuggling vessel of that name ran aground off Brooklyn—the president of the United States had ordered that the FBI take over primary jurisdiction from the INS on major human smuggling cases, with backup from the CIA. The Immigration Service had far more experience with snakeheads and their human smuggling activities than the FBI and didn't take kindly to yielding jurisdiction to other agencies—especially one that insisted on working shoulder-to-shoulder with the NYPD and, well, *alternative* consultants like Lincoln Rhyme.

Assisting Peabody was a young INS agent named Alan Coe, a man in his thirties with close-cropped dark red hair. Energetic but sour and moody, Coe too was an enigma, saying not a word about his personal life and little about his career aside from the Ghost case. Rhyme had observed that Coe's suits were outlet-mall chic—flashy but stitched with obvious thread—and his dusty black shoes had the thick rubber soles of security guard footwear: perfect for running down shoplifters. The only time he grew talkative was when he'd give one of his spontaneous—and tedious—lectures on the evils of illegal immigration. Still, Coe worked tirelessly and was zealous about collaring the Ghost.

Several other underlings, federal and state, had appeared and disappeared over the past week on various errands relating to the case.

Goddamn Grand Central Station, Lincoln Rhyme had thought—and said—frequently in the past day or so.

Now, at 4:45 A.M. on this stormy morning, he maneuvered his battery-powered Storm Arrow wheelchair through the cluttered room toward the case status board, on which was taped one of the few existing pictures of the Ghost, a very bad surveillance shot, as well as a picture of Sen Zi-jun, the captain of the *Fuzhou Dragon*, and a map of eastern Long Island and the ocean surrounding it. Unlike during his bedridden days of self-imposed retirement after a crime scene accident turned him into a C4 quadriplegic, Rhyme now spent half of his waking hours in his cherry red Storm Arrow, outfitted with a new state-of-the-art MKIV touchpad drive controller that his aide, Thom, had found at Invacare. The controller, on which his one working finger rested, gave him far more flexibility in driving the chair than the older sip-and-puff controller.

"How far offshore?" he called, staring at the map.

Lon Sellitto, on the phone, glanced up. "I'm finding out."

Rhyme frequently worked as a consultant for the NYPD but most of his efforts were in classic forensic detection—criminalistics, as the jargon-happy law enforcement world now preferred to call it; this assignment was unusual. Four days ago Sellitto, Dellray, Peabody and taciturn young Alan Coe had come to him at his town house. Rhyme had been distracted—the consuming event in his life at the moment was an impending medical procedure—but Dellray had snagged his attention by saying, "You're our last hope, Linc. We got us a big problem and don't have a single idea where else to turn."

"Go on."

Interpol—the international clearinghouse on criminal intelligence—had issued one of its infamous Red Notices about the Ghost. According to informants, the elusive snakehead had surfaced in Fuzhou, China, flown to the south of France then gone to some port in Russia to pick up a load of illegal Chinese immigrants—among whom was the Ghost's *bangshou*, or assistant, a spy masquerading as one of the passengers. Their destination was supposedly New York. But then he'd disappeared. The Taiwanese, French and Russian police and the FBI and INS could find him nowhere.

Dellray had brought with him the only evidence they had—a briefcase containing some of the Ghost's personal effects from his safehouse in France—in hopes that Rhyme could give them ideas where his trail might lead.

"Why all hands on deck?" Rhyme had asked, surveying the group, which represented three major law enforcement organizations.

Coe said, "He's a fucking sociopath."

Peabody gave a more measured response. "The Ghost's probably the most dangerous human smuggler in the world. He's wanted for eleven deaths—immigrants *and* police and agents. But we know he's killed more. Illegals're called 'the vanished'—if they try to cheat a snakehead, they're killed. If they complain, they're killed. They just disappear forever."

Coe added, "And he's raped at least fifteen women immigrants—that we know of. I'm sure there're more."

Dellray said, "Looks like mosta the high-level snakeheads like him don't make the trips themselves. Th' only reason he's bringing these folk over personally is 'cause he's expandin' his operation here."

"If he gets into the country," Coe said, "people're going to die. A lot of people."

"Well, why *me*?" Rhyme asked. "I don't know a thing about human smuggling."

The FBI agent said, "We tried ever-thing else, Lincoln. But we came up with nothin'. We don't have any personal info 'bout him, no good photos, no 'prints. Zee-row. 'Cept that." A nod toward the attaché case containing the Ghost's effects.

Rhyme glanced at it with a skeptical expression. "And where exactly did he *go* in Russia? Do you have a city? A state or province or whatever they have over there? It's a rather big country, so I'm told."

Sellitto replied with a lifted eyebrow, which seemed to mean: We have no idea.

"I'll do what I can. But don't expect miracles."

Two days later Rhyme had summoned them back. Thom handed Agent Coe the attaché case.

"Was there anything helpful in it?" the young man asked.

"Nup," Rhyme replied cheerfully.

"Hell," muttered Dellray. "So we're outta luck."

Which had been a good enough cue for Lincoln Rhyme. He'd leaned his head back into the luxurious pillow Thom had mounted to the wheelchair and spoke rapidly. "The Ghost and approximately twenty to thirty illegal Chinese immigrants are on board a ship called the *Fuzhou Dragon*, out of Fuzhou, Fujian Province, China. It's a seventy-two-meter combination container and break-bulk cargo ship, twin diesels, under the command of Sen Zi-jun—that's *last* name Sen—fifty-six years old, and has a crew of seven. It left Vyborg, Russia, at 0845 hours fourteen days ago and is presently—I'm estimating now—about three hundred miles off the coast of New York. It's making for the Brooklyn docks."

"How the hell'd you figure that out?" Coe blurted in astonishment. Even Sellitto, used to Rhyme's deductive abilities, barked a laugh.

"Simple. I assumed that they'd be sailing east to west—otherwise he would have left from China itself. I've got a friend on the Moscow police—does crime scene work. I've written some papers with him. Expert in soils by the way, best in the world. I asked him to call the harbor masters in ports in western Russia. He pulled some strings and got all the manifests from Chinese ships that left port in the past three weeks. We spent a few hours going over them. By the way, you're getting a very obese bill for the phone calls. Oh, and I told him to charge you for translation services too. *I* would. Now, we found that only one ship took on enough fuel for an 8000-mile trip when the manifest reported it was making a 4400-mile one. Eight thousand would get them from Vyborg to New York and back to Southampton, England, for refueling. They weren't going to dock in Brooklyn at all. They were going to drop off the Ghost and the immigrants then scoot back to Europe."

"Maybe fuel's too expensive in New York," Dellray had offered.

Rhyme had shrugged—one of the few dismissive gestures his body allowed and said sourly, "Everything's too expensive in New York. But there's more: the *Dragon*'s manifest said she was transporting industrial machinery to America. But you need to report your ship's draft—that's how far the hull sinks into the water, if you're interested—to make sure you don't run aground in shallow ports. The *Dragon*'s draft was listed at three meters. But a fully loaded ship her size should draw at least seven and a half meters. So she was empty. Except for the Ghost and the immigrants. Not offended by calling the ship 'she,' anyone? It is customary. Oh, I say twenty to thirty immigrants because the *Dragon* took on enough fresh water and food for that many, when—like I said—the crew was only seven."

"Damn," offered the otherwise stiff Harold Peabody with an admiring grin.

Later that day, spy satellites had picked up the *Dragon* about 280 miles out to sea, just as Rhyme had predicted.

The Coast Guard cutter *Evan Brigant*, with a boarding party of twenty-five sailors backed up by twin fifties and an 80mm cannon, had gone to ready status but kept its distance, waiting until the *Dragon* had sailed closer to shore.

Now—just before dawn on Tuesday—the Chinese ship was in U.S. waters and the *Evan Brigant* was in pursuit. The plan was to take control of the *Dragon*, arrest the Ghost, his assistant and the ship's crew. The Coast Guard would sail the ship to the harbor at Port Jefferson, Long Island, where the immigrants would be transferred to a federal detention center to await deportation or asylum hearings.

A call was patched through from the radio of the Coast Guard cutter closing in on the *Dragon*. Thom put it on the speakerphone.

"Agent Dellray? This is Captain Ransom on the *Evan Brigant*."

"I'm readin' you, Captain."

"We think they've spotted us—they had better radar than we thought. The ship's turned hard for shore. We need some direction on the assault plan. There's some concern that if we board, there'll be a firefight. I mean, considering who this particular individual is. We're worried about casualties. Over."

"Among who?" Coe asked. "The undocumenteds?" The disdain in his voice when he used the word that described the immigrants was clear.

"Right. We were thinking we should just make the ship come about and wait until the Ghost surrenders. Over."

Dellray reached up and squeezed the cigarette he kept behind his ear, a memento from his smoking days. "Negative on that. Follow your original rules of engagement. Stop the ship, board it and arrest the Ghost. The use of deadly force is authorized. You copy that?"

After a moment of hesitation the young man responded, "Five by five, sir. Out."

The line went dead and Thom disconnected the call. Electric tension flowed into the room on the heels of the silence that followed. Sellitto wiped his palms on his forever-wrinkled slacks then adjusted his service pistol on his belt. Dellray paced. Peabody called INS headquarters to tell them he had nothing to tell them.

A moment later Rhyme's private line rang. Thom took the call in the corner of the room. He listened for a moment then looked up.

"It's Dr. Weaver, Lincoln. About the surgery." He glanced at the roomful of tense law enforcers. "I'll tell her you'll call her back."

"No," Rhyme answered firmly. "I'll take it."

Chapter Three

The winds were stronger now, the waves arcing high over the sides of the intrepid *Fuzhou Dragon*.

The Ghost hated water crossings. He was a man used to luxury hotels, to being pampered. Human smuggling voyages were dirty, oily, cold, dangerous. Man has not tamed the sea, he thought, and never will. It is an icy blanket of death.

He scanned the rear of the ship but could not find his *bangshou* anywhere. Turning toward the bow, he squinted into the wind and could see no land either, just more restless mountains of black water. He climbed to the bridge and pounded on the window of the rear door. Captain Sen looked up and the Ghost gestured for him.

Sen pulled a knit cap on his head and dutifully walked outside into the rain.

"The Coast Guard will be here soon," the Ghost shouted over the raging wind.

"No," Sen replied, "I can get close enough to off-load before they intercept us. I'm sure I can."

But the Ghost turned his still eyes on the captain and said, "You will do this. Leave those men on the bridge and you and the rest of the crew go below with the piglets. Hide with them, get everyone out of sight in the hold."

"But why?"

"Because," the Ghost explained, "you're a good man. Too good to lie. I'll pretend to be the captain. I can look a man in the eye and he will believe what I tell him. You cannot do that."

The Ghost grabbed Sen's cap. In reaction the man started to reach for it but then lowered his hand. The Ghost put it on. "There," he said humorlessly. "Do I look like a captain? I think I make a good captain."

"This is my ship."

"No," the Ghost shot back. "On this voyage the *Dragon* is *my* ship. I'm paying you in one-color cash." U.S. dollars were far more valuable and negotiable than Chinese yuan, the currency many low-level snakeheads paid in.

"You are not going to fight with them are you? The Coast Guard?"

The Ghost gave an impatient laugh. "How could I fight them? They have dozens of sailors, right?" A nod toward the crewmen on the bridge. "Tell your men to follow my orders." When Sen hesitated the Ghost leaned forward with the placid, yet chilling gaze that so unsettled everyone who looked into his eyes. "Is there something you want to say?"

Sen looked away then stepped onto the bridge to give the instructions to the crewmen.

The Ghost turned back to the stern of the ship, looking again for his assistant. He then pulled the captain's cap tighter over his head and strode onto the bridge to take command of the rocking ship.

The ten judges of hell . . .

The man crawled along the main deck to the stern of the ship, stuck his head over the side of the *Fuzhou Dragon* and began retching again.

He'd been lying beside a life raft all night long, ever since the storm picked up and he'd fled from the stinking hold to purge his body of the disharmony wrought by the rocking sea.

The ten judges of hell, he thought again. His gut was in agony because of the dry heaving and he was as cold and miserable as he'd ever been in his life. Slumping against the rusty railing, he closed his eyes.

He was called Sonny Li, though the given name ruthlessly bestowed upon him by his father was Kangmei, which meant "Resist America." It was typical of children born under Mao's reign to have such politically correct—and thoroughly shameful—given names. Still, as often happened with youngsters from coastal China—Fujian and Guangdong—

he'd taken a Western name too. His was the one that the boys in his gang gave him: Sonny, after the dangerous, bad-tempered son of Don Corleone in the movie *The Godfather*.

True to the character after whom he was named, Sonny Li had seen—and been the cause of—much violence in his life but nothing had ever brought him to his knees, literally, like this seasickness.

Judges of hell . . .

Li was ready for the infernal beings to take him. He'd own up to everything bad he'd done in life, all the shame he'd brought to his father, all the foolishness, all the harm. Let the god T'ai'shan assign me a place in hell. Just stop this fucking sickness! Light-headed from nearly two weeks of meager food, dizzy from the vertigo, he fantasized that the sea was in turmoil thanks to a dragon gone mad; he wanted to rip his heavy pistol from his pocket and fire bullet after bullet into the beast.

Li glanced behind him—toward the bridge of the ship—and he thought he saw the Ghost but suddenly his stomach lurched and he had to turn back to the railing. Sonny Li forgot about the snakehead, forgot about his dangerous life back in Fujian Province, forgot about anything except the ten judges of hell gleefully urging demons to prod his dying belly with their spears.

He began heaving once again.

The tall woman leaned against her car, the contrasts stark: her red hair tossed by the fierce wind, the yellow of the old Chevy Camaro, the black nylon utility belt securing a black pistol to her hip.

Amelia Sachs, in jeans and a hooded windbreaker on the back of which were the words NYPD CRIME SCENE, looked out over the turbulent water of the harbor near Port Jefferson, on the north shore of Long Island. She surveyed the staging area around her. Immigration and Naturalization, the FBI, the Suffolk County Police and her own shop had cordoned off a parking lot that on an average day in August would normally have been packed with families and teenagers here to catch some rays. The tropical storm, however, had kept vacationers far away from the shore.

Parked nearby were two large Department of Corrections prisoner buses the INS had borrowed, a half-dozen ambulances and four vans filled with tactical officers from the various agencies. In theory, by the time the *Dragon* arrived here, it would be under the control of the crew of the cutter *Evan Brigant* and the Ghost and his assistant would be in custody. But there would be a certain period of time after the Ghost had spotted the Coast Guard cutter and before the actual boarding by the crew—perhaps as much as forty minutes. That would give the Ghost and his *bangshou* plenty of time to masquerade as immigrants and hide weapons, a tactic that snakeheads frequently used. The Coast Guard might not be able to effectively search the immigrants and the ship before it arrived at the harbor here and the snakehead and any assistants might try to shoot their way to freedom.

Sachs herself would be in particular danger. Her job was to "walk the grid," to sweep the ship for crime scene evidence that would bolster the various cases against the Ghost and to find leads to his confederates. If the searcher is running a scene where, say, a body is found or a robbery has occurred long after the perp has fled, there is relatively little danger to the CS officer. But if the scene is the actual takedown site, involving an unknown number of perps whose appearance isn't well known, the risks can be great, particularly in the case of human smugglers, who have ready access to good weaponry.

Her cell phone rang and she dropped into the tight seat of the Chevy to answer it.

The caller was Rhyme.

"We're all in place," she told him.

"We think they're on to us, Sachs," he said. "The *Dragon* turned toward land. The cutter'll get there before they make it to shore but we're thinking now that the Ghost is gearing up for a fight."

She thought of the poor people on board.

When Rhyme paused, Sachs asked him, "Did she call?"

A hesitation. Then he said, "Yes. About ten minutes ago. They have a slot open at Manhattan Hospital next week. She's going to call back with the details."

"Ah," Sachs said.

The "she" was Dr. Cheryl Weaver, a renowned neurosurgeon who'd come up to the New York area from North Carolina to teach for a semester at Manhattan Hospital. And the "slot" referred to an opening for some experimental surgery that Rhyme was having—an operation that might improve his quadriplegic condition.

An operation Sachs was not in favor of.

"I'd get some extra ambulances in the area," Rhyme said. His tone was now curt—he didn't like personal subjects intruding in the midst of business.

"I'll take care of it."

"I'll call you back, Sachs."

The phone went silent.

She ran through the downpour to one of the Suffolk County troopers and arranged for more med techs. She then returned to her Chevy and sat down in the front bucket seat, listening to the rattle of the powerful rain on the windshield and cloth roof. The dampness made the interior smell of plastic, motor oil and old carpeting.

Thinking about Rhyme's operation put her in mind of a recent conversation with another doctor, one who had nothing to do with his spinal cord surgery. She didn't want her thoughts to go back to that meeting—but go there they did.

Two weeks ago Amelia Sachs had been standing by the coffee machine in a hospital waiting room, up the hall from Lincoln Rhyme's examining room. She remembered the July sun falling brutally on the green tile floor. The white-jacketed man had approached and then addressed her with a chilling solemnity. "Ah, Ms. Sachs. Here you are."

"Hello, Doctor."

"I've just been meeting with Lincoln Rhyme's physician."

"Yes?"

"I've got to talk to you about something."

Her heart pounding, she'd said, "You're looking like it's bad news, Doctor."

"Why don't we sit down over there in the corner?" he'd asked, sounding more like a funeral home director than an M.D.

"Here's fine," she'd said firmly. "Tell me. Let me have it straight."

A gust of wind now rocked her and she looked out over the harbor again, at the long pier, where the *Fuzhou Dragon* would dock.

Bad news . . .

Tell me. Let me have it straight. . . .

Sachs flicked her Motorola to the Coast Guard's secure frequency not only to learn what was happening with the *Dragon* but to keep her thoughts from returning to that scaldingly bright waiting room.

.   .   .

"How far from land?" the Ghost asked the two remaining crewmen on the bridge.

"A mile, maybe less." The slim man at the helm glanced quickly at the Ghost. "We'll turn just before the shallows and try for the harbor."

The Ghost gazed forward. From the vantage point of the crest of a wave he could just see the line of light gray land. He said, "Steer straight on course. I'll be back in a moment."

Bracing himself, he stepped outside. The wind and rain lashed his face as the Ghost made his way down to the container deck and then to the one below it. He came to the metal door that opened into the hold. He stepped inside and looked down at the piglets. Their faces turned toward him with fear and distress. The pathetic men, the frumpy women, the filthy children—even some pointless girls. Why had their foolish families bothered to bring *them*?

"What is it?" Captain Sen asked. "Is the cutter in sight?"

The Ghost didn't answer. He was scanning the piglets for his *bangshou*. But there was no sign of him. Angry, he turned away.

"Wait," the captain called.

The snakehead stepped outside and closed the door. *"Bangshou!"* he shouted.

There was no response. The Ghost didn't bother to call a second time. He screwed down the latches so that the door to the hold couldn't be opened from the inside. He hurried back toward his cabin, which was on the bridge deck. As he struggled up the stairs he took from his pocket a battered black plastic box, just like the door opener for the garage of his luxurious house in Xiamen.

He opened the box and pushed one button and then a second. The radio signal zipped through two decks down to the duffel bag he'd placed in the aft hold below the waterline. The signal closed the circuit and sent an electrical charge from a nine-volt battery into a blasting cap embedded in two kilos of composition 4 explosive.

The detonation was huge, much larger than he'd expected, and it sent a tall spume of water shooting into the air, higher than the highest waves.

The Ghost was thrown off the stairs onto the main deck. He lay on his side, stunned.

Too much! he realized. There'd been too much explosive. Already the ship was starting to list as she took on seawater. He'd thought it would take half an hour for the ship to sink. Instead, she would go down in minutes. He looked toward the bridge deck, where his money and guns sat in the small cabin, then once again scanned the other decks for his *bang-shou*. No sign of him. But there was no time to look further. The Ghost rose and scrabbled across the listing deck to the nearest rubber life raft and began undoing the tie-down ropes.

The *Dragon* lurched again, rolling farther onto her side.

Chapter Four

The sound had been deafening. A hundred sledgehammers on a piece of iron.

Nearly all of the immigrants had been thrown to the cold, wet floor. Sam Chang climbed to his feet and picked up his youngest boy, who'd fallen into a puddle of greasy water. He then helped up his wife and his elderly father.

"What happened?" he shouted to Captain Sen, who was struggling through the panicked crowd to the door that led up to the deck. "Did we hit the rocks?"

The captain called back, "No, no rocks. The water's a hundred feet deep here. Either the Ghost has blown up the ship or the Coast Guard is firing on us. I don't know."

"What is happening?" asked a panic-stricken man sitting near Chang. He was the father of the family that had camped out in the hold next to the Changs. Wu Qichen was his name. His wife lay listlessly on the cot nearby. She'd been feverish and lethargic throughout the entire voyage and even now seemed hardly aware of the explosion and chaos. "What's going on?" Wu repeated in a high voice.

"We're sinking!" the captain called and together he and several of his crewmen grabbed the latches of the door and struggled to open them. But they didn't move. "He's jammed them!"

Some of the immigrants, both men and women, began wailing and rocking back and forth; children stood frozen with fear, tears running down their dirty cheeks. Sam Chang and several of the crew joined the captain and tugged on the latches. But the thick metal bars wouldn't give a millimeter.

Chang noticed a suitcase sitting on the floor. Slowly it toppled to its side and hit the floor with a splash; the *Dragon* was listing sharply. Cold seawater was shooting into the hold from seams in the metal plates. The puddle his son had fallen into was now a half meter deep. Several people slid into the deepening pools, filled with trash, luggage, food, Styrofoam cups, papers. They screamed and flailed about in the water.

Desperate men and women and children, futilely slamming luggage into the walls to break through the metal, hugging one another, sobbing, screaming for help, praying. . . . The scar-faced woman clutched her young daughter the way the child herself clung to a filthy yellow Pokémon toy. Both were sobbing.

A powerful groaning from the dying ship filled the stale air, and the brown, vile water grew deeper.

The men at the hatch were making no headway with the latches. Chang wiped his hair out of his eyes. "This won't work," he said to the captain. "We need another way out."

Captain Sen replied, "There's an access panel on the floor, in the back of the hold. It leads to the engine room. But if that's where the hull was breached we won't be able to open it. Too much pressure—"

"Where?" Chang demanded.

The captain pointed it out, a small door secured by four screws. It was only large enough for one person to pass through at a time. He and Chang pushed toward it, struggling to stay upright against the sharp angle of the floor. Scrawny Wu Qichen helped his sick wife to her feet; the woman shivered with chills. Chang bent down to his own wife and said in a firm voice, "Listen to me. You will keep our family together. Stay close to me by that doorway."

"Yes, husband."

Chang joined the captain at the access door and, using Sen's flick-knife, they managed to undo the screws. Chang pushed hard on the door and it fell into the other room without resistance. Water was filling the engine room too but it wasn't as deep as in the hold. Chang could see steep stairs leading to the main deck.

Screams and shouts as the immigrants saw the open passageway. They pushed forward in panic, crushing some people against the metal walls. Chang struck two of the men with his large fist. He cried, "No! One at a time or we'll all die."

Several others, desperation in their eyes, started for Chang. But the captain turned on them, brandishing his knife, and they backed away. Captain Sen and Chang stood side by side, facing the crowd. "One at a time," the captain repeated. "Through the engine room and up the ladder. There're rafts on the deck." He nodded to the immigrants closest to the doorway and they crawled outside. The first was John Sung, a doctor and a dissident, whom Chang had spent some time talking with on the voyage. Sung stopped outside the doorway and crouched down to help the others out. A young husband and wife climbed out next and scurried to the ladder.

The captain caught Chang's eye and he nodded. "Go!"

Chang motioned to Chang Jiechi, his father, and the old man went through the door, John Sung gripping him by his arm. Then Chang's sons: teenage William and eight-year-old Ronald. Next, his wife. Chang went last and pointed his family toward the ladder. He turned back to help Sung get the others out.

The Wu family was next: Qichen, his sick wife, their teenage daughter and young son.

Chang reached into the hold to take the hand of another immigrant but two of the crewmen raced for the doorway. Captain Sen grabbed for them. He raged, "I'm still in charge. The *Dragon* is my ship. The passengers go first."

"Passengers? You idiot, they're cattle!" one of the crew screamed and, knocking aside the scar-faced mother and her little girl, crawled through the opening. The other followed right behind him, pushing Sung to the floor and running for the stairs. Chang helped the doctor to his feet. "I'm all right," Sung shouted and clutched a charm he wore around his neck, muttering an abbreviated prayer. Chang heard the name Chen-wu, the god of the northern sky and protector against criminals.

The ship lurched hard and tilted faster. The wind of escaping air began to shoot out through the doorway as water flooded in, filling the hold. The screams were heartbreaking and were soon mixed with the sound of choking. She's going down, Chang thought. Another few minutes at the most. He heard a hissing, sparking sound behind him. He glanced up and saw water flowing down the stairwell onto the massive, grimy engines.

One of the diesels stopped running and the lights went out. The second engine then went silent.

John Sung lost his handhold and slid across the floor into the wall. "Get out!" Chang called to him. "We can't do anything more here."

The doctor nodded, scrabbled for the stairs and climbed out. But Chang himself turned back to the doorway to try to rescue one or two more. He shivered, sickened at the sight in front of him: water was pouring out of the doorway, from which four desperate arms extended into the engine room, clawing for help. Chang grabbed one man's arm but the immigrant was so jammed among the others that he couldn't be dislodged. The arm shivered once and then Chang felt the fingers go limp. Through the roiling water now bubbling into the engine room Chang could just see Captain Sen's face. Chang motioned for him to try to climb out but the captain disappeared into the blackness of the hold. A few seconds later, though, the bald man swam back to the doorway and shoved something up through the fountain of seawater toward Chang.

What was it?

Gripping a pipe to keep from sliding away, Chang reached into the frothy water to take what the captain offered. He closed his muscular hand around cloth and pulled hard. It was a young child, the daughter of the scarred woman. She rose from the doorway through the stalks of lifeless arms. The toddler was choking but conscious. Chang held her to his chest firmly then let go of the pipe. He slid through the water to the wall then swam to the stairwell, where he climbed through the icy cascade to the deck above.

He gasped at what he saw—the stern of the ship was barely above water, and gray, turbulent waves were already covering half the deck. Wu Qichen and Chang's father and sons were struggling to untie a large orange inflatable launch on the stern of the boat. It was already floating but would soon be underwater. Chang stumbled forward, handed the baby to his wife and began to help the others undo the rope. But soon the knot securing the raft was beneath the waves. Chang dove under the surface and tugged futilely on the hemp knot, his muscles quivering from the effort. Then a hand appeared near his. His son William was holding a long, sharp knife that he must've found on the deck. Chang took it and sawed on the rope until it gave way.

Chang and his son surfaced and, gasping, helped his family, the Wus,

John Sung and the other couple into the raft, which was quickly drawn away from the ship by the massive waves.

He turned to the outboard motor. He pulled the cord to start the engine but it wouldn't engage. They needed to get it going immediately; without the control of a motor, they'd be overturned by the sea in seconds. He began yanking furiously and finally the motor buzzed to life.

Chang braced himself in the back of the raft and quickly turned their small craft into the waves. It bucked furiously but didn't capsize. He accelerated and then steered carefully in a circle, heading back through the fog and rain toward the dying ship.

"Where are you going?" Wu asked.

"The others," Chang shouted. "We have to find the others. Some might have—"

That was when the bullet snapped through the air no more than a meter from them.

The Ghost was furious.

He stood at the bow of the sinking *Fuzhou Dragon,* his hand on the lanyard of the forward life raft, and looked back fifty meters to sea where he'd just spotted some of the fucking piglets who'd escaped.

He fired his pistol once more. Another miss. The pitching seas made accurate shooting from this distance impossible. He scowled in fury as his targets maneuvered behind the *Dragon,* out of his sight. The Ghost surveyed the distance to the bridge deck, on which his cabin was located, where he had his machine gun and his money: more than a hundred thousand in one-color cash. He wondered momentarily if he could make it back to the cabin in time.

As if in answer, a huge spume of venting air broke through the hull of the *Dragon* and she began to sink even more quickly, rolling farther on her side.

Well, the loss hurt but it wasn't worth his life. The Ghost climbed into the raft and pushed away from the ship with an oar. He scanned the nearby water, struggling to see through the fog and rain. Two heads bobbed up and down, their arms waving frantically, fingers splayed in panic.

"Here, here!" the Ghost shouted. "I'll save you!" The men turned to him, kicking hard to rise from the water so he could see them better. They were two of the crew members, the ones who'd been on the bridge. He lifted his Chinese military Model 51 automatic pistol again. He killed the two crewmen with one shot each.

Then the Ghost got the outboard motor going and, riding the waves, looked once more for his *bangshou*. But there was no sign of him. The assistant was a ruthless killer and fearless in shoot-outs but he was a fool when he was out of his element. He'd probably fallen into the water and drowned because he wouldn't throw away his heavy gun and ammunition. Well, the Ghost had other matters to attend to. He turned the raft toward where he'd last seen the piglets and twisted the outboard's throttle up high.

There'd been no time to find a life vest.

No time for anything.

Just after the explosion shattered the *Dragon's* rusty hull, knocking Sonny Li to his belly, the ship began to list, the water rushing over him and tugging him relentlessly toward the ocean. Suddenly he found himself off the side of the ship, alone and helpless in the frantic hills of water.

Ten fuck judges of hell, he thought bitterly in English.

The water was cold, heavy, breathtakingly salty. The waves slammed him onto his back then lifted him high and dunked him. Li managed to kick to the surface and looked around for the Ghost but, in the cloudy air and stinging rain, couldn't see anyone. Li swallowed a mouthful of the sickening water and began gasping and coughing. He smoked three packs of cigarettes a day and drank liters of Tsingtao beer and *mao-tai;* soon he was winded and the little-used muscles in his legs started to cramp painfully.

Reluctantly he reached into his belt and withdrew his automatic pistol. He released it and the gun sank quickly from his fingers. He did the same with the three clips of ammunition in his back pocket. This helped his buoyancy some but it wasn't enough. He needed a vest, anything that floated, anything to share the agonizing burden of staying on the surface.

He thought he heard the sound of an outboard motor and he twisted around as best he could. Thirty meters away was an orange raft. He raised his hand but a wave caught him in the face as he was inhaling and his lungs filled with stinging water.

Searing pain in his chest.

Air . . . I need air.

Another wave slammed into him. He sank below the surface, tugged down by the great muscles of gray water. He glanced at his hands. Why weren't they moving?

Paddle, kick! Don't let the sea suck you down!

He struggled once more to the surface.

Don't let . . .

He inhaled more water.

Don't let it . . .

His vision began to crinkle to black.

Ten judges of hell . . .

Well, Sonny Li thought, it seemed that he was about to meet them.

Chapter Five

They lay at his feet, a dozen or so, in the cold soup at the bottom of the raft, caught between the mountains of water beneath them and the lacerating rain from above. Their hands desperately gripped the rope that circled the orange raft.

Sam Chang, reluctant captain of the fragile craft, looked over his passengers. The two families—his own and the Wus—huddled in the back of the raft around him. In the front were Dr. John Sung and the two others who'd escaped from the hold, whom Chang knew only by their first names, Chao-hua and his wife, Rose.

A wave crashed over them, soaking the hapless occupants even more. Chang's wife, Mei-Mei, pulled off her sweater and wrapped it around the tiny daughter of the scar-faced woman. The girl, Chang recalled with a pang, was named Po-Yee, which meant Treasured Child; she'd been the good-luck mascot of their voyage.

"Go!" Wu cried. "Go for shore."

"We have to look for the others."

"He's shooting at us!"

Chang looked at the boiling sea. But the Ghost was nowhere to be seen. "We'll go soon. But we have to rescue anyone who can be saved. Look for them!"

Seventeen-year-old William struggled to his knees and squinted through the sharp spray. Wu's teenage daughter did the same.

Wu shouted something but his head was turned away and Chang couldn't hear the words.

Chang entwined his arm around the rope and pushed his feet hard against an oar clamp to brace his body as he struggled to nurse the raft in a circle around the *Fuzhou Dragon,* twenty meters away. The ship slipped farther into the water, a blast of foamy water occasionally shooting high as air escaped from a rent in the side or a porthole or hatch. The groaning, like that of an animal in pain, rose and fell.

"There!" William cried. "I think I see somebody."

"No," Wu Qichen called. "We have to leave! What are you waiting for?"

William was pointing. "Yes, Father. There!"

Chang could see a dark lump next to a much smaller white lump, ten meters from them. A head and a hand perhaps.

"Leave them," Wu called. "The Ghost will see us! He'll shoot us!"

Ignoring him, Chang steered closer to the lumps, which indeed turned out to be a man. He was pale and choking, thrashing the air, a look of terror on his face. Sonny Li was his name, Chang recalled. While most of the immigrants had spent time talking and reading to one another, several of the men traveling without families had kept to themselves. Li was among these. There'd been something ominous about him. He'd sat alone for the entire voyage, sullen, occasionally glaring at the children who were noisy around him and often sneaking up on deck, which was strictly forbidden by the Ghost. When he'd talk at all, Li would ask too many questions about what the families planned to do when they got to New York and where they would live—subjects that wise illegal immigrants didn't discuss.

Still, Li was a human being in need and Chang would try to save him.

The man was swallowed up by a wave.

"Leave him!" Wu whispered angrily. "He's gone."

From the front of the raft the young wife, Rose, called, "Please, let's go!"

Chang turned the raft into a large wave to keep from tipping over. By the time they were stable again Chang saw a flash of orange about a fifty meters away, rising and falling. It was the Ghost's raft. The snakehead started toward them. A wave rose between the two crafts and they lost sight of each other momentarily.

Chang gunned the throttle and turned toward the drowning man. "Down, everybody down!"

He reversed the motor quickly just as they reached Li, leaned over the thick rubber and grabbed the immigrant by the shoulder, pulling him into the raft, where he collapsed on the floor, coughing fiercely. Another gunshot. A burst of water flew up near them as Chang sped the raft around the *Dragon*, putting the sinking ship between them and the Ghost once more.

The snakehead's attention turned away from them for a moment when he saw several other people in the water—crew members, bobbing on the surface in orange life vests, about twenty or thirty meters away from the killer. The Ghost sped toward the two, his motor running full.

Understanding now that the man was going to kill them, they waved their arms desperately toward Chang and kicked furiously away from the approaching raft. Chang gauged the distance to the crewmen, wondering if he could reach them before the snakehead was close enough to have a clear shot. The mist and rain—and the rolling waves—would make it hard for the Ghost to shoot accurately. Yes, he thought he could do it. He started to apply the power.

Suddenly a voice was in his ear. "No. It's time to leave."

It was his father, Chang Jiechi, who'd spoken; the old man had pulled himself to his knees and was leaning close to his son. "Take your family to safety."

Chang nodded. "Yes, Baba," using the affectionate Chinese term for "father." He aimed the raft toward shore and turned the motor up full.

A minute later came the crack of a gun firing, then another, as the snakehead murdered the two crew members. Sam Chang's soul cried in dismay at the sounds. Forgive me, he thought to the sailors. Forgive me.

Glancing back, he saw an orange shape through the fog; the Ghost's raft coming after them. He felt the despair in his bones. As a dissident in China, Sam Chang was used to fear. But in the People's Republic fear was an insidious unease that you learned to live with; it was nothing like this, the terror of seeing a mad killer hunting down your beloved family and companions.

"Stay down! Everyone stay down." He concentrated on keeping the raft upright and making as much speed as possible.

Another shot. The bullet struck the water nearby. If the Ghost hit the rubber they'd sink in minutes.

A huge, unearthly groan filled the air. The *Fuzhou Dragon* turned completely on her side and vanished under the surface. The massive wave created by the sinking ship rolled outward like the shock ring from a bomb blast. The immigrants' raft was too far away to be affected but the

Ghost's was much closer to the ship. The snakehead looked back and saw the tall wave heading toward him. He veered away and, after a moment, was lost to sight.

Though he was a professor, an artist, a political activist, Sam Chang was also, like many Chinese, more accepting of spirituality and portents than a Western intellectual might be. He thought for a moment that Guan Yin, the goddess of mercy, might have interceded on their behalf and sent the Ghost to a watery death.

But only a moment later John Sung, who was facing backward, shouted, "He's still there. He's coming. The Ghost is coming after us."

So, Guan Yin is busy elsewhere today, Sam Chang thought bitterly. If we're going to survive we'll have to do it on our own. He adjusted their course toward land. And sped away from the limp corpses and the flotsam that were like floating tombstones marking the graves of Captain Sen and his crew and the many people who'd become Chang's friends over the past weeks.

"He scuttled the ship."

Lon Sellitto's voice was a whisper. "Christ." The phone drooped away from his ear.

"What?" Harold Peabody said, shocked. A fat hand rose to his cumbersome glasses and removed them. "He sank it?"

The detective nodded a grim confirmation.

"Lord, no," Dellray said.

Lincoln Rhyme's head, one of the few parts of his physique that was still mobile, turned toward the heavyset cop. Shocked at this news, he felt a wave of heat pass through his entire body—solely an emotional sensation, of course, when it sped below his neck.

Dellray stopped pacing and Peabody and Coe stared at each other. Sellitto looked down at the yellow parquet as he listened once more into the phone and then looked up. "Jesus, Linc, the ship's gone. With everybody on board."

Oh, no . . .

"The Coast Guard doesn't know exactly what happened but they picked up an underwater explosion and ten minutes later the *Dragon* vanished from the radar."

"Casualties?" Dellray asked.

"No idea. The cutter's still a few miles away. And they don't know the location—nobody on board the *Dragon* hit any emergency distress signals. They send out the exact coordinates."

Rhyme stared at the map of Long Island, its eastern end split like a fishtail. His eye was on a red sticker that marked the *Dragon's* approximate location. "How far offshore?"

"About a mile."

Rhyme's sweeping mind had run through a half-dozen logical scenarios of what might happen when the Coast Guard interdicted the *Fuzhou Dragon,* some optimistic, others involving some injury and the loss of life. Criminal apprehension was a trade-off and you could minimize the risks but never completely eliminate them. But drowning everyone on board? All those families and children? No, *that* thought had never occurred to him.

Christ, he'd lain in his luxurious $3,000 bed and listened to the INS's little problem of the Ghost's whereabouts as if it were a diverting game at a cocktail party. Then he'd drawn his conclusions and snappily given them the solution.

And he'd let it go at that—never thinking one step further, never thinking that the immigrants might be at such terrible risk.

Illegals're called "the vanished"—if they try to cheat a snakehead, they're killed. If they complain, they're killed. They just disappear forever.

Lincoln Rhyme was furious with himself. He knew how dangerous the Ghost was; he should have anticipated this deadly turn. He closed his eyes momentarily and adjusted the burden somewhere in his soul. Give up the dead, he often told himself—and the CS techs who'd worked for him—and he reiterated this command silently now. But he couldn't quite give them up, not these poor people. The sinking of the *Dragon* was different. These dead weren't corpses at a crime scene, whose glassy eyes and rictus grin you learned to ignore in order to do your job. Here were whole families dead *because* of him.

After they'd interdicted the ship, arrested the Ghost and run the crime scene, his involvement in the case would end, Rhyme had thought, and he'd get back to preparing for his surgery. But now he knew he couldn't abandon the case. The hunter within him had to find this man and bring him to justice.

Dellray's phone rang and he answered. After a brief conversation he snapped off the call with a long finger.

"Here'sa deal. The Coast Guard thinks a coupla motorized rafts're heading toward shore." He stalked to the map and pointed. "Prob'ly around here. Easton—little town on the road to Orient Point. They can't get a chopper in the air with the storm being's nasty as it is but they got some cutters on the way to look for survivors and we're going to get our people at Port Jefferson out to where the rafts're headed."

Alan Coe brushed his red hair, only slightly darker than Sachs's, and said to Peabody, "I want to go out there."

The INS supervisor replied pointedly, "I'm not making personnel decisions around here." A none-too-subtle comment about at the fact that Dellray and the FBI were running the show, one of many such barbs that had been exchanged between the two agents over the past few days.

"How 'bout it, Fred?" Coe asked.

"Nup," the preoccupied agent said.

"But I—"

Dellray shook his head emphatically. "There's nothin' you can do, Coe. If they collar him you can go question him in detention. Jabber at him all you want. But this's a tactical apprehension op now and that ain't your specialty."

The young agent had provided good intelligence about the Ghost but Rhyme thought he was difficult to work with. He was still angry and resentful that he hadn't been allowed to actually be on board the cutter interdicting the ship—another battle Dellray had had to fight.

"Well, that's bullshit." Coe dropped moodily into an office chair.

Without a response, Dellray sniffed his unlit cigarette, tucked it behind his ear and took another call. After he hung up he said to the team, "We're trying to set up roadblocks on the smaller highways out of the area—Routes 25, 48 and 84. But it's rush hour and nobody's got the balls to close the Long Island Expressway or Sunrise Highway."

Sellitto said, "We can call the toll takers at the tunnel and the bridges."

Dellray shrugged. "That's somethin', but it's not enough. Hell, China-town's that boy's turf. Once he's there it'll be hell to find him. We *gotta* get him on the beach if there's any way."

"And when," Rhyme asked, "are the life rafts going to land?"

"They're guessin' twenty, twenty-five minutes. And our folk're fifty miles away from Easton."

Peabody asked. "Isn't there *any* way to get somebody out there sooner?"

Rhyme debated for a moment then said into the microphone attached to his wheelchair, "Command, telephone."

The 1969 Indianapolis 500 pace car was a General Motors Camaro Super Sport convertible.

For this honor, GM picked the strongest of their muscle car line—the SS fitted with a 396-cubic-inch TurboJet V-8 engine, which could churn 375 horsepower. And if you were inclined to tinker with the vehicle—by removing sound deadeners, undercoating, sway bars and interior wheel wells and playing around with the pulleys and cylinder heads, for instance—you could goose the effective hp up to 450.

Which made it a boss machine for drag racing.

But a bitch to drive at 130 miles per hour through a gale.

Squeezing the leather-clad wheel, feeling the pain in her arthritic fingers, Amelia Sachs piloted the car eastbound on the Long Island Expressway. She had a blue flasher on the dash—a suction cup doesn't stick well to convertible roofs—and wove perilously in and out of the commuter traffic.

As she and Rhyme had decided when he'd called five minutes before and told her get the hell out to Easton, Sachs was one-half of the advance team, which, if they were lucky, might get to the beach at the same time the Ghost and any surviving immigrants did. The other half of the impromptu team was the young officer from the NYPD Emergency Services Unit sitting next to her. The ESU was the tactical branch of the police department, the SWAT team, and Sachs—well, Rhyme actually—had decided that she should have some backup with firepower of the sort that now sat in the man's lap: a Heckler & Koch MP5 machine gun.

Miles behind them now were the ESU, the crime scene bus, a half-dozen Suffolk County troopers, ambulances and assorted INS and FBI vehicles, making their way through the vicious storm as best they could.

"Okay," said the ESU officer. "Well. Now."

He offered this in response to a brief bit of hydroplaning.

Sachs calmly brought the Camaro back under control, recalling that she'd also removed the steel plates behind the backseat, put in a fuel cell in lieu of the heavy gas tank and replaced the spare with Fix-A-Flat and a plug kit. The SS was about 500 pounds lighter than when her father had bought it in the seventies. Could use a little of that ballast now, she thought, and snipped another skid short.

"Okay, we're okay now," the ESU cop said, apparently far more comfortable in a shoot-out than driving down the wide expanse of the Long Island Expressway.

Her phone rang. She juggled the unit and answered it.

"Say, miss," the ESU cop asked, "you gonna use one of those hands-free things? I'm just thinking it might be better." And this from a man dressed like Robocop.

She laughed, plugged the earpiece in and upshifted.

"How's the progress, Sachs?" Rhyme asked.

"Doing the best I can. But we turn off onto surface roads in a few miles. I may have to slow up for some of the red lights."

"'May'?" the ESU cop muttered.

"Any survivors, Rhyme?" Sachs asked.

"Nothing further," he answered. "The Coast Guard can only confirm two rafts. Looks like most people didn't get off."

Sachs said to the criminalist, "I hear that tone, Rhyme. It's not your fault."

"Appreciate the sentiment, Sachs. That's not an issue. Now, you driving carefully?"

"Oh, yeah," she said, calmly steering into the spin that took the car forty degrees off center, her heart rate rising not a single digit. The Camaro straightened as if it were on guy wires and continued down the expressway, its speed goosed up to 140. The ESU cop closed his eyes.

"It's going to be close, Sachs. Keep your weapon handy."

"It always is." Another brief skid.

"We're getting calls from the Coast Guard cutter, Sachs. I've got to go." He paused for a moment. Then said, "Search well but watch your back."

She laughed. "I like that. We need to print it up on T-shirts for the Crime Scene Unit."

They hung up.

The expressway ended and she skidded off onto a smaller highway. Twenty-five miles to Easton, where the lifeboats would land. She'd never been there; city-girl Sachs wondered what the topography was like. Would it be a beach? Rocky cliffs? Would she have to climb? Her arthritis had been bad lately and this thick humidity doubled the pain and stiffness.

Wondering too: If the Ghost was still at the beach, were there plenty of hiding places for him to snipe from?

She glanced down at the speedometer.

Ease back?

But the treads on her wheels were true and the only moisture on her palms was from the rain that had drenched her back at Port Jefferson. She kept her foot near the floor.

As the launch smashed through the water, closer to the shore, the rocks grew more distinct.

And more jagged.

Sam Chang squinted through the rain and spray. There were some short stretches of beach ahead, covered with pebbles and dirty sand, but much of the shoreline was dark rock and bluffs well over their heads. And to reach a portion of beach where they could land he'd have to maneuver through an obstacle course of jutting stone.

"He's still there, behind us," Wu shouted.

Chang looked back and could see the tiny orange dot of the Ghost's raft. It was heading directly for them but was making slower progress than theirs. The Ghost was hampered by the way he handled the raft. He aimed right toward the shore and fought the waves, which slowed his progress. But Chang, true to his Taoist leanings, piloted his craft differently; he sought the natural flow of the water, not fighting it but steering around the stronger crests in a serpentine pattern and using the shore-bound waves to speed them forward more quickly. The distance between them and the snakehead was increasing.

Before the Ghost landed, there should be enough time to find the trucks that were waiting to take them to Chinatown, Chang estimated. The truck drivers wouldn't know about the sinking but Chang would tell them that the Coast Guard was after them and order the men to leave immediately. If they insisted on waiting, Chang and Wu and the others would overpower them and drive the trucks themselves.

He studied the shoreline and beyond—past the beach were trees and grass. It was hard to see in the windblown rain and mist but he detected what looked like a road. Some lights too, not far away. A cluster of them: a small village, it seemed.

Wiping the stinging seawater from his eyes, Chang watched the people at his feet, falling silent as they gazed at the shore ahead of them, the turbulent currents here, riptides and whirlpools, the approaching rocks, sharp as knives, dark as dried blood.

Then, just ahead of them, under the surface of the water, appeared a bank of rock. Chang throttled back fast and turned hard to the side, just missing the stone shelf. The raft was now sideways, buffeted by the ragged waves, which flooded the vessel. They nearly capsized once, then again. Chang tried to steer through a gap in the bank but the motor suddenly cut out. He grabbed the lanyard and tugged hard. A chug, then silence. Again, a dozen times. But nothing happened. The motor didn't even turn over. His older son scrabbled forward and tipped the gasoline can. "Empty!" William shouted.

Desperate, weak with fear for his family's safety, he looked behind them. The fog was thicker now and obscured them—but it also hid the Ghost. How close was he?

The raft rose on a high wave then dropped into a gully of water with a jarring crash. "Down, everybody down!" Chang shouted. "Stay low." He dropped to his knees in the dark water sloshing on the floor of the raft. He grabbed the oar and tried to use it as a rudder. But the waves and current were too powerful, the raft too heavy. A fist of water struck him and ripped the oar from his hands. Chang fell backward. He glanced in the direction they were headed and he saw a line of rocks just ahead, a few meters away.

The water caught the launch like a surfboard and sped it forward. They struck the rocks with stunning force, bow first. The rubber shell ripped open with a gasping hiss and began to deflate. Sonny Li, John Sung and the young couple in the front—Chao-hua and Rose—were pitched out into the turbulent water just past the rocks and swept away in the surf.

The two families—the Wus and the Changs—were in the rear of the raft, which remained partially inflated and they managed to hold on. The raft struck the rocks again. Wu's wife was thrown hard into a ledge of stone but she didn't go overboard; screaming, she fell back into the raft, blood covering her arm, and lay stunned on the floor. No one else was injured by the impact.

Then the raft was past the rocks and headed toward shore, deflating quickly.

Chang heard a distant cry for help—from one of the four who'd vanished when they struck the rock but he couldn't tell where the shout had come from.

The raft slid over another rock, low in the water, fifteen meters from shore. They were trapped in the surf now, battered and being dragged toward the pebbly beach. Wu Qichen and his daughter struggled to keep his injured and half-conscious wife above the surface—her arm torn open and bleeding badly. In Mei-Mei's arms Po-Yee, the baby, had stopped crying and was staring listlessly around her.

But the motor of the raft was hung up on a rock ledge, trapping them eight or nine meters from shore. The water wasn't deep here—two meters—but the waves were still pounding them hard.

"The shore," he shouted, coughing water. "Now!"

The swim took forever. Even Chang, the strongest among them, was gasping for breath and racked by cramps before he reached land. Finally, under his feet, he felt stones, slippery with kelp and slime, and stumbled forward out of the water. He fell once, hard, but quickly regained his foothold and helped his father out of the water.

Exhausted, they all stumbled to a nearby shelter on the beach, open on the sides, but with a corrugated roof that protected them from the slashing rain. The families collapsed on the dark sand underneath it, coughing water, crying, gasping, praying. Sam Chang finally managed to stand. He gazed out to sea but saw no sign of the Ghost's raft or the immigrants who'd been swept overboard.

Then he sank down to his knees and lay his forehead on the sand. Their companions and friends were dead, and they themselves injured, tired beyond words and pursued by a killer . . . Still, Sam Chang reflected, they were alive and were on firm land. He and his family had at last finished the endless journey that had taken them halfway around the world to their new home, America, the Beautiful Country.

Chapter Six

Half a kilometer out to sea the Ghost hunched over his cell phone, trying to protect it from the rain and waves as his raft plowed through the water toward the piglets.

The reception was bad—the signal was bouncing via satellite through Fuzhou and Singapore after it left his phone—but he managed to get through to Jerry Tang, a *bangshou* he sometimes used in New York's Chinatown and who was now waiting somewhere on the shore nearby to pick him up.

Breathless from the rough ride, the Ghost managed to describe to the driver more or less where he'd be landing—about three or four hundred meters east from what seemed to be a strip of stores and houses.

"What weapons do you have?" the Ghost shouted.

"What?" Tang shouted.

He had to repeat the question several times. "Weapons!"

But Tang was a debt collector—more of a businessman than an enforcer—and it turned out that he had with him only a pistol.

"*Gan,*" the Ghost spat out. Fuck. Armed only with his old Model 51 handgun, he'd hoped for an automatic weapon of some kind.

"The Coast Guard," Tang told him, the transmission lost in static and the sound of the wind, "they're on . . . here. I'm listening . . . scanner . . . have to get away. Where . . . "

The Ghost shouted, "If you see any of the piglets, kill them. Did you hear me? They're on the shore nearby you. Find them! Kill them!"

"Kill them? You want—"

But a wave washed over the side of the raft and drenched him. The phone went silent and the Ghost glanced at the screen. It was dead, shorted out. Disgusted, he flung it to the floor.

A wall of rock loomed and the Ghost steered around it, making for a broad beach far to the left of the small town. It would take some time to get back to where the piglets had landed but he didn't want to risk injuring himself on the outcroppings of stone. Still, beaching the raft proved to be harrowing. As he closed in on the sand the small craft rose on the crest of a wave and nearly tipped over but the Ghost throttled back fast and the raft settled onto the water. A wave, though, caught him in the back and knocked him to the floor of the boat, drenching him and spinning the raft sideways. It slammed into the shore in an explosion of surf and tossed its occupant hard onto the beach. The propeller tipped out of the water and the motor screamed as it raced. The Ghost, afraid the sound would give him away, crawled frantically back to the engine and managed to shut it off.

He saw Jerry Tang, in a silver four-by-four BMW on a sandy asphalt road about twenty meters from the shore. He rose and jogged toward the vehicle. Fat, unshaven Tang caught sight of him and drove forward. The Ghost leaned down to the window of the driver's side. "Did you see the others?"

The nervous man said, "We have to go!" He nodded at a police scanner. "The Coast Guard knows we're here. They're sending the police to search."

"The others?" the Ghost snapped. "The piglets?"

"I didn't see anybody else. But—"

"I can't find my *bangshou* either. I don't know if he got off the ship." The Ghost scanned the shoreline.

"I haven't seen anyone," Tang said, his voice high. "But we can't stay here."

From the corner of his eye the Ghost saw motion near the surf: a man in gray cloth was crawling on the rocks away from the water, like an injured animal. The Ghost stepped away from the truck and pulled his gun from his belt. "Wait here."

"What are you doing?" Tang asked desperately. "We can't stay here anymore! They're coming. They'll be here in ten minutes. Don't you understand me?"

But the Ghost was paying no attention to the thug as he walked back across the road. The piglet looked up and saw the Ghost approaching but the man had apparently broken his leg in the landing and couldn't even stand, much less flee. He began to crawl desperately back to the water. The Ghost was curious why he was even bothering.

Sonny Li opened his eyes and thanked the ten judges of hell—not for surviving the sinking but because for the first time in two weeks, the slippery twist of nausea within his gut was virtually gone.

When the raft had hit the rocks he and John Sung and the young couple had been thrown into the water and swept away by the strong current. Li had immediately lost sight of the other three and had been dragged down the beach for what seemed like a kilometer until he'd been able to kick his way onto the sand. Then, crawling as far away as he could from the ocean, Li collapsed.

He'd lain motionless under the pounding rain as the seasickness dissipated and the throbbing in his head lessened. Now, struggling to his feet, Li started slowly toward the road, his skin irritated from the cloth of his jeans and sweatshirt, which were filled with sand and saturated with the pungent residue of salt water. He could see nothing in either direction. He remembered, though, the lights of a small village to his right and it was in that direction that he now began to walk along the sand-swept road.

Where was the Ghost? Li wondered.

Then, as if in answer, came a brief pop, which Li recognized immediately as a pistol shot. It reverberated through the dark, wet dawn.

But was it the Ghost? Or some local resident? (Everyone knew that all Americans carried guns.) Maybe it was a U.S. public security officer.

Better to be safe. He was eager to find the Ghost quickly but he knew he had to be careful. He stepped off the road into some brush, where he was less visible, and started forward as fast as his cramped and exhausted legs could carry him.

At the sound the families paused.

"It was—" Wu Qichen began.

"Yes," Sam Chang muttered. "A gunshot."

"He's killing us. He's tracking us down and killing us."

"I know," Chang snapped back. His heart cried for them—for Dr.

Sung, for Sonny Li, for the couple—whoever among them had just died. But what could he do?

Chang looked at his father and observed that Chang Jiechi was breathing hard but, despite the battering in the raft and the swim to shore, the old man didn't seem to be in great pain. He nodded to his son, meaning it was all right to continue. The cluster of people started walking once again through the rain and wind.

Their concerns about begging or coercing the drivers to take them to Chinatown were unfounded; there'd been no trucks waiting for them. Chang supposed that the vehicles were at a different location altogether, or perhaps as soon as the Ghost decided to scuttle the ship he'd called and had them return. He and Wu had spent several minutes calling for Sung and Li and the others who'd been washed overboard. But then Chang had seen the orange raft of the snakehead approaching and he'd led the two families off the road into the grass and bushes, where they'd be out of sight, and they made their way toward the lights, where he hoped to find a truck.

The beacons that drew them turned out to be a line of restaurants, a petrol station, several stores selling souvenirs like on the waterfront at Xiamen, ten or twelve houses, a church.

The hour was just around dawn—perhaps 5:30 or 6—but there were signs of life: a dozen cars were parked in front of the two restaurants, including a driverless one with the motor running. But it was a small sedan and Chang needed a vehicle with room for ten. And he needed one whose theft wouldn't be noticed for at least two or three hours—the length of time he'd been told it would take them to get to Chinatown in New York City.

He told the others to wait behind a tall hedge of bushes and motioned his son William and Wu to follow him. Crouching, they moved behind the buildings. There were two large trucks behind the petrol station but they were both well in view of a young attendant in the garage. Rain pelted the glass, making visibility poor, but he would have noticed immediately if they'd started to drive a truck away.

Twenty meters farther on was a darkened house and behind it was a pickup truck. But Chang didn't want to expose his father or the children to the rain and weather. Also, ten shipwrecked Chinese would be easily spotted in a rickety old vehicle of this sort, driving toward New York City like a band of the "floating population"—itinerant laborers who travel from town to town in China looking for work.

"Stay out of the mud," Chang ordered his son and Wu. "Walk only on the grass or branches or stones. I don't want to leave footprints." Caution was instinctive for Chang; with both public security bureau and People's Liberation Army agents constantly following them, dissidents in China learn quickly to obscure their movements.

They moved on, through brush and trees whipped by the ferocious wind, past more houses, some dark, some showing signs of families waking: televisions flickering, breakfasts being prepared. Seeing this poignant evidence of normal life, Chang was stabbed by the hopelessness of their plight. But, as he'd learned to do in China, where the government had taken so much away from him, he pushed these sentimental feelings aside and urged his son and Wu to move more quickly. Finally they came to the last building on this strip of habitation: a small church, dark and apparently unoccupied.

Behind the weathered building they found an old white van. From his hours on the Internet and watching TV, Chang knew a little English but these words he didn't understand. At his urging, though, both of his sons had studied the language, and American culture, for years. William glanced at the van and explained, "It says, 'Pentecostal Baptist Church of Easton.'"

Another soft crack in the distance. Chang froze at the sound. The Ghost had killed another one of them.

"Let's go!" anxious Wu said. "Hurry. See if it's open."

But the van's door was locked.

As Chang looked around for something they could use to break the window William surveyed the lock closely. He called over the noisy wind, "Do you have my knife?"

"Your knife?"

"The one I gave you on the ship—to cut the rope holding the raft."

"That was *yours?*" What on earth had his son been doing with a weapon like that? It was a switchblade.

"Do you have it?" the boy repeated.

"No, I dropped it getting into the raft."

The boy grimaced but Chang ignored the expression—why, it was almost impertinent—and scanned the rain-pelted ground. He found a piece of metal pipe and swung it hard into the window of the van. The glass shattered into a hundred tiny pieces of ice. He climbed into the passenger seat and looked through the map box for keys. He couldn't find any and stepped out onto the muddy ground. Glancing at the building, he wondered if there would be a set inside the church? And if so where? An office? There might be a caretaker inside; what if the man heard and confronted them? Chang believed that he couldn't hurt anyone innocent even if—

He heard a loud snap and spun around in alarm. His son was crouched in the driver's seat and had shattered the plastic housing of the ignition lock with a kick from his boot. As Chang watched, astonished and dismayed, the boy pulled out wires and began brushing them against each other. Suddenly the radio came on with a blare: *"He will always love you, let Our Savior into your heart . . . ."*

William touched a button on the dash and the volume lowered. He touched other wires together. A spark. . . . The engine fired up.

Chang stared in disbelief. "How did you know how to do that?"

The boy shrugged.

"Tell me—"

Wu clutched Chang's arm. "Let's go! We have to get our families and leave. The Ghost is looking for us."

The father pierced his son with a look of shock. He expected the boy to lower his eyes in shame. But William stared back coldly in a way that Chang himself never would have done with his own father, at any age.

"Please," Wu begged. "Let's go back for the rest."

"No," Chang said after a moment. "Have them come here. Follow our path—and make sure they don't leave any footprints."

Wu hurried off to get them.

In the van William found a booklet of maps of the area and studied them carefully. He nodded, as if memorizing directions.

Resisting his desire to interrogate his son about hot-wiring the ignition, Chang asked him, "Do you know where to go?"

"I can figure it out." The boy looked up. "Do you want me to drive?" Then he added bluntly, "You're not very good at it." Like most urban Chinese, Sam Chang's main means of transportation was a bicycle.

Chang blinked at these words of his son's—spoken once again in a tone that approached insolence. Then Wu appeared with the rest of the immigrants and Chang ran forward to help his wife and father into the van, calling back to his son, "Yes, you drive."

Chapter Seven

He'd killed two of the piglets on the beach—the injured man and a woman.

But there'd been about a dozen people in the raft. Where were the rest?

A horn blared. The Ghost whirled around. It was Jerry Tang, drawing his attention. He held up the police scanner, his gestures frantic. "The police will be here any minute! We have to go!"

The Ghost turned away and scanned the beach once more, the road. Where had they gotten to? Maybe they'd—

With a squeal of tires Tang's four-by-four pulled into the road, accelerating fast.

"No! Stop!"

Seized by fury, the Ghost aimed his pistol and fired once. The slug hit the rear door but the vehicle continued, not slowing, to an intersection and then skidded through the turn and disappeared. The Ghost stood frozen, the pistol at his side, staring through the mist at the road where his means of escape had just vanished. He was eighty miles from his safe-houses in Manhattan, his assistant was missing and probably dead, he had no money and no cell phone. Dozens of policemen and troopers were on their way. And Tang had just abandoned him. He could—

He tensed. Not far away a white van suddenly appeared out of a field on the other side of a church and turned onto the road. It was the piglets!

The Ghost lifted his pistol again but the vehicle disappeared into the fog. Lowering the gun, the Ghost took several deep breaths. After a moment he grew serene. He was plagued by troubles at the moment, yes, but he'd experienced much adversity in his life, far worse than this.

You are part of the old.

You will reform your ways.

You will die for your old beliefs. . . .

A reversal, he'd come to learn, was merely a temporary unbalance and even the most horrific events in his life had ultimately been harmonized by good fortune. His abiding philosophy was found in one word: *naixin.* This translated as "patience" in Chinese but meant something more in the Ghost's mind. The English equivalent would be "All in good time." He had survived these forty-some years because he'd outlasted trouble and danger and sorrow.

For the moment the piglets had gotten away. Their deaths would have to wait. Now there was nothing to do but escape from the police and the INS.

He put his old pistol into his pocket and trudged through the rain and wind along the beach toward the lights of the small town. The closest building was a restaurant, in front of which was a car with its engine running.

So, some good fortune already!

And then, glancing out to sea, he saw something that actually made him laugh. Yet more good luck: not far offshore he saw another piglet, a man struggling to stay afloat. At least he could kill one more of them before he escaped to the city.

The Ghost pulled his gun from his pocket and started back toward the shoreline.

The wind was wearing him down.

Making his way toward the small town, Sonny Li slogged through the sand. He was a slight man and in the hard, dangerous world in which he made his way he relied on bluff and surprise and wits (weapons too, of course), not on physical strength. He was now at his limits, exhausted from this morning's ordeal.

The wind . . . Twice it actually knocked him to his knees.

No more, he thought. Despite the risk of being seen, struggling through the soft sand was simply too much for him and he stumbled back onto the rain-swept asphalt road and continued toward the lights of the small village. He pushed forward as best he could, afraid that the snake-head would leave before Li found him.

But a moment later he receive the reassurance that the man was still here: several more gunshots.

Li struggled up a hill and peered into the streaming wind and rain but he could see no one. The sound had apparently been carried some distance on the wind.

Discouraged, he continued forward. For ten endless minutes he battled his way along the road, throwing his head back occasionally and letting the rain soak his parched mouth. After all the seawater he'd swallowed he was desperately thirsty.

Then he saw, on his right, a small orange life raft sitting on the beach. He assumed that it was the Ghost's. He looked up and down the shore for the snakehead but it was impossible to see very far through the mist and the rain.

He started toward the raft, thinking that perhaps he could follow the man's footprints and find him hiding in town. But as he took a step off the road a flashing light appeared. He wiped the rain from his eyes and squinted. The light was blue and moving rapidly toward him along the road.

INS? Security bureau officers?

Li hurried into some dense bushes on the far side of the asphalt. He crouched and watched the light grow brighter as the vehicle in which it was mounted, a sporty yellow convertible, materialized out of the rain and murk and skidded to a stop 100 meters away. In a crouch Li began to move slowly toward the car.

Amelia Sachs stood on the rain-swept beach, staring down at the woman's body, slumped in the grotesque pose of death.

"He's killing them, Rhyme," Amelia Sachs, dismayed, whispered into the headset mike of her Motorola SP-50 handy-talkie. "He's shot two of them, a man and a woman. In the back. They're dead."

"*Shot* them?" The criminalist's voice was hollow and she knew that he was shouldering the responsibility for yet more deaths.

The ESU officer trotted toward her, holding his machine gun ready. "No sign of him," the man shouted over the wind. "People in that restaurant a half click up the road said that somebody stole a car about twenty minutes ago." The officer gave Sachs the description of a Honda and the tag number and she relayed it to Rhyme.

"Lon'll put it on the wire," he said. "Was he alone?"

"Think so. Because of the rain there're no footprints in the sand but I found some in the mud, where he was standing to shoot the woman. He was by himself then."

"So we'll assume his *bangshou*'s still unaccounted for. He could've gotten to shore in another raft. Or he might've been in the wrecked one."

Her hand near her weapon, she scanned the scenery. Fog-bleached forms of rocks and dunes and brush surrounded her. A man with a gun would be invisible.

Then she said, "We're going to look for the immigrants, Rhyme."

She expected him to disagree, to tell her to run the scene first, before the raging elements destroyed *all* the evidence. But he said simply, "Good luck, Sachs. Call me back when you start on the grid." The line went dead.

Search well but watch your back. . . .

The two officers trotted along the beach. They came across a second raft, a smaller one, beached a hundred yards from the first. Sachs's instinctive reaction was to search it for evidence but she stayed true to her immediate mission and, arthritis stabbing her joints, ran with the wind at her back as she scanned the landscape for the immigrants—and signs of an ambush or a hidey-hole where the Ghost might've gone to ground.

They found neither.

Then she heard sirens in the distance, carried on the streaming wind, and saw the carnival of emergency vehicles speed into town. The dozen or so residents who'd been ensconced in the restaurant and gas station now braved the weather to find out exactly what kind of excitement the storm had brought to their miniature town.

The first mission of a crime scene officer is controlling the scene—so that contamination is minimal and evidence doesn't vanish, either accidentally or at the hands of souvenir hunters or the perp himself, masquerading as a bystander. Sachs reluctantly gave up her search for other immigrants and crew—there were plenty of other people to do that now—and ran to the NYPD blue-and-white crime scene bus to direct the operation.

As the CS techs roped off the beach with yellow tape, Sachs pulled the latest in forensic couture over her soaked jeans and T-shirt. The NYPD's new crime scene overalls, a hooded full-body suit made of white Tyvek, prevented the searcher from sloughing off his or her own trace evidence—hair, skin or sweat, for instance—and contaminating the scene.

Lincoln Rhyme approved of the suit—he'd lobbied for something similar when he'd been running the Investigation and Resources Division, which oversaw crime scene. Sachs wasn't so pleased, however. The fact that the overalls made her look like an alien from a bad space movie wasn't the problem; what troubled her was that it was brilliant white—easily spotted by any perps who, for whatever reason, might wish to hang around the crime scene and try out their marksmanship on cops picking up evidence. Hence, Sachs's pet name for the garb: "the bull's-eye suit."

A brief canvass of the patrons in the restaurant, employees of the gas station and residents living in the few houses on the beach yielded nothing except facts they'd already learned about the Honda in which the Ghost had escaped. No other vehicles had been stolen and no one had seen anybody swimming to shore or hiding out on land or even heard the gunshots over the wind and rain.

So it fell exclusively to Amelia Sachs—and Lincoln Rhyme—to wring from the crime scene whatever information about the Ghost, the crew and the immigrants might reside here.

And what a crime scene it was, one of the biggest they'd ever run: a mile of beach, a road and, on the other side of the asphalt strip, a maze of scruffy brush. Millions of places to search. And possibly still populated by an armed perp.

"It's a bad scene, Rhyme. The rain's let up a little but it's still coming down hard and the wind's twenty miles an hour."

"I know. We've got the Weather Channel on." His voice was different now, calmer. The sound spooked her a bit. It reminded her of the eerily placid quality of his voice when he talked about endings, about killing himself, about finality. "All the more reason," he prodded, "to get on with the search, wouldn't you say?"

She looked up and down the beach. "It's just . . . Everything's too big. There's too much here."

"How can it be too big, Sachs? We work every scene one foot at a time. Doesn't matter if it's a square mile or three feet. It just takes longer. Besides, we *love* big scenes. There're so many wonderful places to find clues."

Wonderful, she thought wryly.

And, starting closest to the large deflated raft, she began walking the grid. The phrase described one technique for physically searching a crime scene for clues, in which the CS officer covers the floor or ground in one direction, back and forth, like mowing a lawn, then turns perpendicular and covers the same ground again. The theory behind this method of searching is that you see things from one angle that you might miss when looking at them from a different angle. Although there were dozens of other methods of searching crime scenes, all of them faster, the grid—the most tedious type of search—was also the most likely to yield gold. It was the one that Rhyme insisted that Sachs use—just as he'd done with the officers and techs who worked for him at NYPD forensics. Thanks to Lincoln Rhyme, "walking the grid" had become synonymous with searching a crime scene among cops in the metropolitan area.

Soon she was out of sight of the village of Easton and the only sign that she wasn't alone was the diffuse flashing of the emergency vehicle lights, like blood pulsing through pale skin, unsettling and eerie.

But soon the lights too vanished in the fog. The solitude—and a creepy sense of vulnerability—curled snug around her. Oh, man, I don't like this. The fog was worse here and the sounds of the rain tapping loudly on the hood of her suit, the waves and the wind would mask an attacker's approach.

She slapped the grip of her black Glock pistol for reassurance and kept on the grid.

"I'm going to go quiet for a while, Rhyme. I've got this feeling there's somebody still here. Somebody watching me."

"Call me when you're through," he said. His hesitant tone suggested there was something more he wished to say but after a moment the line clicked off.

Watch your back. . . .

For the next hour, through the wind and rain, she searched the beach and road and the foliage beyond, like a child hunting for seashells. She examined the intact raft, in which she found a cell phone, and the deflated one, which two ESU officers had muscled up onto the beach. Finally she assembled her collection of evidence, shell casings, blood samples, fingerprints and Polaroids of footprints.

Then she paused and looked around. Then she clicked on the radio and was patched through to a cozy town house light years away. "Something's funny, Rhyme."

"That's not helpful, Sachs. 'Funny'? What does that mean?"

"The immigrants . . . ten or so of them, they just vanish. I don't understand it. They leave a shelter on the beach then cross the road and hide in the bushes. I see the prints in the mud on the other side of the road. Then they just disappear. I guess they've gone inland to hide but I can't find any tracks. And nobody's going to give a ride to hitchhikers like them around here and none of the people in town saw any trucks waiting to pick them up. There aren't any tire treads here anyway."

"All right, Sachs, you've just walked in the Ghost's footsteps. You've seen what he's done, you know who he is, you've been where he's been. What's going through your mind?"

"I—"

"You're the Ghost, now," Rhyme reminded in a lulling voice. "You're Kwan Ang, nicknamed Gui, the Ghost. You're a multimillionaire, a human trafficker—a snakehead. A killer. You've just sunk a ship and killed over a dozen people. What's in your mind?"

"Finding the rest of them," she answered immediately. "Finding them and killing them. I don't want to leave. Not yet. I'm not sure why but I have to find them." For an instant an image jolted her mind. She *did* see herself as the snakehead, filled with a salivating lust to find the immigrants and kill them. The sensation was harrowing. "Nothing," she whispered, "is going to stop me."

"Good, Sachs," Rhyme replied softly, as if he was afraid of breaking the thin wire that was connecting a portion of her soul to the snakehead's. "Now, think about the immigrants. They're being pursued by someone like that. What would *they* do?"

It took her a moment to transform herself from a heartless murderer and snakehead into one of the poor people on that ship, appalled that the man she'd paid her life's savings to had betrayed her in this way, had killed people she'd grown close to, perhaps family members too. And was now compelled to kill her.

"I'm not going to hide," she said firmly. "I'm getting the hell out of here as fast as I can. Any way I can, as far away as possible. We can't go back into the ocean. We can't walk. We need a ride."

"And how would you get one?" he asked

"I don't know," she said, feeling the frustration of being close to an answer yet having it evade her.

"Any houses inland?" he asked

"No."

"Any trucks at the gas station?"

"Yes, but the troopers asked the attendants. None of 'em're missing."

"Anything else?"

Sachs scanned the street. "Nothing."

"There can't be *nothing*, Sachs," he scolded. "These people're running for their lives. They escaped *somehow*. The answer's there. What else do you see?"

She sighed and began reciting, "I see a stack of discarded tires, I see a sailboat upside down, I see a carton of empties—Sam Adams beer. In front of the church there's a wheelbarrow—"

"Church?" Rhyme pounced. "You didn't mention a church before."

"It's Tuesday morning, Rhyme. The place is closed and ESU cleared it."

"Get over there, Sachs. Now!"

Stiffly she began to walk toward the place but had no clue what she might find that would be helpful.

Rhyme explained, "Didn't you do vacation Bible school, Sachs? Ritz crackers, Hawaiian Punch and Jesus on summer afternoons? No potluck picnics? No youth group conventions?"

"Once or twice. But I spent most of my Sundays rebuilding carburetors."

"How do you think churches get the younguns to and from their little theological diversions? Minivans, Sachs. Minivans—with room for a dozen people."

"Could be," she added skeptically.

"And maybe not," Rhyme conceded. "But the immigrants didn't sprout wings and fly, did they? So let's check out the more likely possibilities."

And, as so often happened, he was right.

She walked around to the back of the church and examined the muddy ground: footprints, tiny cubes of broken safety glass, the pipe used to shatter the window, the tread marks of a van.

"Got it, Rhyme. A bunch of fresh prints. Damn, that's smart. . . . They walked on rocks, grass and weeds. To avoid the mud so they wouldn't leave prints. And it looks like they got into the van and it drove away through a field before it turned onto the road. So nobody'd see it on the main street."

Rhyme ordered, "Get the scoop on the van from the minister."

Sachs asked a trooper to call the minister of the church. A few minutes later the details came back—it was a white Dodge, five years old, with the name of the church on the side. She took down the tag number then relayed this to Rhyme, who said he would in turn put out another vehicle locator request, in addition to the one on the Honda, and tell the Port Authority police to pass the word to the toll takers at the bridges and tunnels, on the assumption that the immigrants were headed for China-town in Manhattan.

She walked the grid carefully behind the church but found nothing else. "I don't think there's much more we can do here, Rhyme. I'm going to log the evidence in and get back." She disconnected the call.

Returning to the crime scene bus, she packed away the Tyvek suit then logged in what she'd found and attached the chain of custody cards that must accompany every item collected at a crime scene. She told the techs to get everything to Rhyme's town house ASAP. Though it seemed hope-less she wanted to make another sweep for survivors. Her knees were on fire—the chronic arthritis inherited from her grandfather. The disease often bothered her but now, alone, she allowed herself the luxury of moving slowly; whenever she was among fellow officers she tried hard not to show the pain. She was afraid that if the brass got wind of her condition they'd desk her for disability.

After fifteen minutes, though, of not finding any sign of more immi-grants, she started toward her Camaro, which was the only vehicle left on this portion of the beach. She was alone; the ESU officer who'd accompa-nied her here had opted for a safer ride back to the city.

The fog was lighter now. A half mile away, on the other side of the town, Sachs could just make out two Suffolk County rescue trucks and an unmarked Ford sedan parked nearby. She believed it was an INS vehicle.

Sachs dropped stiffly into the front seat of her Camaro, found a piece of paper and began to write out notes of what she'd observed at the scene to present to Rhyme and the team back at his town house. The wind buf-feted the light car and the rain pelted the steel bodywork furiously. Sachs happened to glance up in time to see a dramatic spume of seawater flying ten feet into the air as it hit a jutting black rock.

She squinted hard and wiped the steam off the inside of the windshield with her sleeve.

What is that? An animal? Some wreckage from the *Fuzhou Dragon*?

No, she realized with a start; it was a man. He clung desperately to the rock.

Sachs grabbed her Motorola, clicked to the local ops frequency and radioed, "This is NYPD Crime Scene Five Eight Eight Five to Suffolk County Rescue at Easton Beach. You copy?"

"Roger, Five Eight Eight Five. Go ahead."

"I'm a half click east of the town. I've got a vic in the water. I need some help."

"K," came the reply, "we're on our way. Out."

Sachs stepped out of the car and started down to the shore. She saw a large wave lift the man off the rock and pitch him into the water. He tried to swim but he was injured—there was blood on his shirt—and the best he could do was keep his head above water, but just barely. He went down once and struggled to the surface.

"Oh, brother," Sachs muttered, glancing back at the road. The yellow rescue truck was just then moving forward off the sand.

The immigrant gave a choked cry and slipped under the waves. No time to wait for the pros.

From the police academy she knew the basic lifesaving rule: "Reach, throw, row then go." Meaning, try to rescue a drowning victim from the shore or a boat before you yourself swim out to save him. Well, the first three weren't options at all.

So, she thought: Go.

Ignoring the searing pain in her knees, she ran toward the ocean, stripping off her gun and ammo belt. At the shoreline she unlaced her standard-issue shoes, kicked them off and, eyes focused on the struggling swimmer, waded into the cold, turbulent water.

Chapter Eight

Crawling from the bushes, Sonny Li got a better look at the woman with the red hair as she pulled off her shoes and plowed into the rough water then kicked away from the shore toward somebody struggling in the waves.

Li couldn't make out who it was—either John Sung or the husband of the couple who'd sat next to him in the raft—but, in any case, his attention was drawn back immediately to the woman, whom he'd been studying from his hiding spot in the bush since she'd arrived at the beach over an hour ago.

Now, she wasn't his type of girl. He didn't care for Western women, at least the ones he'd seen around Fuzhou. They were either on the arms of rich businessmen (tall and beautiful, casting disdainful glances at the Chinese men who'd stare at them) or tourists with their husbands and children (badly dressed, casting disdainful glances at men spitting on the sidewalks and the bicyclists who never let them cross the street).

This woman, though, intrigued him. At first he hadn't been able to figure out what she was doing here; she'd arrived in her bright yellow car, accompanied by a soldier with a machine gun. Then she'd turned her back and he'd glimpsed NYPD on her windbreaker. So, she was a public security bureau officer. Safely hidden across the road, he'd watched her search for survivors and clues.

Sexy, he'd thought, despite his vast preference for quiet, elegant Chinese women.

And that hair! What a color! It inspired him to give her a nickname, "Hongse," pronounced hoankseh, Chinese for "red."

Looking up the road, Li saw a yellow emergency truck speeding toward them. As soon as it turned into a shallow parking lot and stopped he crawled to the edge of the road. There was a chance he'd be spotted, of course, but he had to act now, before she returned. He waited until the rescue workers' attention was on Hongse and then scrabbled across the road and up to the yellow car. It was an old one, the sort you saw in American TV shows like *Kojak* and *Hill Street Blues*. He wasn't interested in stealing the car itself (most of the security bureau officers and soldiers had left but there were still enough nearby to pursue and capture him—especially behind the wheel of a car as bright as an egg yolk). No, at the moment he just wanted a gun and some money.

Opening the passenger door of the yellow car, he eased inside and began going through the map box. No weapons. He angrily thought of his Tokarev pistol sitting at the bottom of the ocean. No cigarettes either. Fuck her. . . . He then went through her purse and found about fifty dollars in one-color money. Li pocketed the cash and looked over a paper she'd been writing on. His spoken English was good—thanks to American movies and the *Follow Me* program on Radio Beijing—but his reading skills were terrible (which hardly seemed fair considering that English only had 25 or so letters while the Chinese language had 40,000). After some stumbling, he recognized the Ghost's real name, Kwan Ang, in English, and made out some other writing. He folded this up and slipped it into his pocket then scattered the rest of the sheets on the ground outside the open driver's side door, so it would look as if the wind had blown them away.

Another car was approaching—a black sedan that smelled to Li like a government vehicle. Crouching, he made his way back to the road. Hidden once more in the bushes, he glanced out into the turbulent sea, observing now that Hongse seemed to be struggling in the choppy ocean just as much as the drowning man. He felt a pang that such a beautiful woman was in danger. But that wasn't really his concern; finding the Ghost and simply staying alive were his priorities now.

The effort of swimming against the battering surf to reach the drowning immigrant had nearly exhausted Amelia Sachs and she found she had to kick furiously to keep them both above water. Her knee and hip joints protested in pain. The immigrant himself wasn't any help at all. He was of medium build and trim—without much fat for buoyancy. He kicked his feet lethargically and his left arm was useless—thanks to a gunshot wound in his chest.

Gasping, spitting out the vile salt water that kept spilling into her mouth and nose, she fought her way toward shore. The water stung her eyes and blurred her vision but she could see on the sand near the breaking surf two medics with a stretcher and a large green oxygen tank, motioning broadly for her to swim toward them.

Thanks, boys. . . . I'm *trying*.

She steered toward them as best she could but the undertow was fierce. She glanced back at the rock the immigrant had been clinging to and saw that, despite her massive efforts, they'd swum only about ten feet.

Kick harder. Harder!

Reciting to herself one of her personal mantras: When you move they can't getcha. . . .

Another eight or nine feet. But Sachs finally had to stop and catch her breath, watching in dismay as the undertow tugged them back out to sea.

Come on, get out of here. . . .

The listless immigrant, now nearly unconscious, kept pulling her down. Sachs kicked harder. A cramp seized her calf and she cried out and sank fast. The murky gray water, filled with seaweed and sand, swallowed her up. One hand holding the immigrant's shirt, the other pounding on her own calf to break the cramp, she struggled to hold her breath for as long as she could.

Oh, Lincoln! she thought. Going down . . . Farther into the gray linen water.

Then: Jesus! What's this?

A barracuda, a shark, a black eel . . . shot out of the foggy water and grabbed her around the chest. She instinctively reached for the switchblade she kept in her back pocket but her arm was pinned to her body by the terrible fish. It tugged her upward and a few seconds later she was on the surface, sucking sweet air into her stinging lungs.

She looked down. The fish turned out to be a man's arm encased in a black wetsuit.

The Suffolk County Rescue diver spit a regulator from a pony bottle of compressed air out of his mouth and said, "It's okay, miss, I got you. It's okay."

A second diver was gripping the immigrant, keeping his lolling head out of the water.

"Cramp," Sachs gasped. "Can't move my leg. Hurts."

He reached underwater with one hand, straightened her leg and then pressed her toes toward her body, stretching out the muscles of her calf. After a moment the pain went away. She nodded.

"Don't kick. Just relax. I'll take you in." He began to tow her and she leaned her head back, concentrated on breathing. His powerful legs, aided by the flippers, moved them rapidly toward shore. He said, "That was gutsy, going out. Most people would've just watched him die."

They swam through the chill water for what seemed like forever. Finally Sachs felt pebbles under her feet. She staggered onto the shore and took the blanket one of the medics offered her. After catching her breath she walked over to the immigrant, who was lying on the stretcher, an oxygen mask over his face. His eyes were dazed but he was conscious. His shirt was open and the medic was cleaning a bloody wound with disinfectant and bandages.

Sachs brushed as much sand off her feet and legs as she could then replaced her shoes and hooked her gunbelt around her once more. "How is he?"

"Wound's not bad. The shooter hit him in the chest but from an angle. But we'll have to watch the hypothermia and exhaustion."

"Can I ask him a few questions?"

"Just the minimum for now," the first paramedic said. "He needs oxygen and rest."

"What's your name?" Sachs asked the immigrant.

He lifted away the oxygen mask. "John Sung."

"I'm Amelia Sachs, with the New York City police department." She showed him her shield and ID, as procedure dictated. She asked, "What happened?"

The man lifted away the oxygen mask. "I was thrown out of our raft. The snakehead on the ship—we call him the Ghost—he saw me and came down to the shore. He shot at me and missed. I swam underwater but I had to come back for air. He was waiting. He shot again and hit me. I pretended to be dead and when I looked again I saw him get into a red car and drive off. I tried to swim to the beach but I couldn't. I just held on to those rocks and waited."

Sachs studied the man. He was handsome and appeared to be in good shape. She'd recently seen a TV special on China and had learned that unlike Americans—who exercise temporarily, usually out of vanity— many Chinese work out all their lives.

The man asked, "How are . . . " He coughed again. The spasms turned violent. The medic let him cough out the water for a few moments and, when Sung stopped, knelt down and placed the oxygen mask on his face. "Sorry, Officer, but he really needs to suck air now."

But Sung lifted the mask off. "How are the others? Are they safe?"

It wasn't NYPD procedure to share information with witnesses but she saw the concern in his eyes and she said, "I'm sorry. Two are dead."

He closed his eyes and with his right hand clutched a stone amulet he wore on a leather strap around his neck.

"How many were on the raft?" she asked.

He thought for a moment. "Fourteen altogether." Then he asked, "Did he get away? The Ghost?"

"We're doing everything we can to find him."

Again Sung's face filled with dismay and he again squeezed the amulet.

The medic handed her the immigrant's wallet. She flipped through it. Most of it was turning to mush from the seawater and nearly all of the contents were in Chinese. But one card that was still legible was in English. It identified him as Dr. Sung Kai.

"Kai? Is that your first name?"

He nodded. "But I use John mostly."

"You're a doctor?"

"Yes."

"Medical doctor?"

He nodded again.

Sachs was looking at a picture of two young children, a boy and a girl. She felt a jolt of horror, thinking that they'd been on the ship.

"And your . . ." Her voice faded.

Sung understood. "My children? They're at home in Fujian. They're living with my parents."

The medic was standing near his patient, unhappy that he kept lifting off the mask. But Sachs had her job to do too. "Dr. Sung, do you have any idea where the Ghost might be going? Does he have a house or apartment here in this country? A company? Any friends?"

"No. He never talked to us. He never had anything to do with us. He treated us like animals."

"How about the other immigrants? Do you know where they might've gone?"

Sung shook his head. "No, I'm sorry. We were going to houses somewhere in New York but they never told us where." His eyes strayed back to the water. "We thought maybe the Coast Guard shot us with a cannon. But then we realized he sank the ship himself." His voice was astonished. "He locked the door in our hold and blew the boat up. With everyone on board."

A man in a suit—an INS agent Sachs remembered meeting in Port Jefferson—stepped out of the black car, which had just joined the rescue vehicle on the sand. He pulled on a windbreaker and crunched through the sand toward them. Sachs handed him Sung's wallet. He read through it and crouched down. "Dr. Sung, I'm with the U.S. Immigration and Naturalization Service. Do you have a valid passport and entry visa?"

Sachs thought the question was absurd, if not provocative, but she supposed this was one of the formalities that needed to be performed.

"No, sir," Sung replied.

"Then I'm afraid we're going to have to detain you for illegally entering United States territory."

"I'm seeking political asylum."

"That's fine," the agent said wearily. "But we're still going to have to detain you until the bond hearing."

"I understand, " Sung said.

The agent asked the medic, "How is he?"

"He'll be all right. But we need to get him to a trauma center. Where's he being processed?"

Sachs interrupted to ask the INS agent, "Can he go to your Manhattan detention center? He's a witness in the case and we've got a task force working there."

The INS agent shrugged. "Doesn't matter to me. I'll do the paperwork."

Sachs rocked from one leg to the other and winced as the pain shot through her knee and hip. Still absently clutching the amulet around his neck, Sung studied her and said in a low heartfelt voice, "Thank you, miss."

"For what?"

"You saved my life."

She nodded, holding his dark eyes for a moment. Then the medic replaced the oxygen mask.

A flash of white from nearby caught her eye and Amelia Sachs looked up to see that she'd left the door of the Camaro open and that the wind was blowing her notes on the crime scene out to sea. Wincing, she trotted back to her car.

The
Beautiful
Country

Tuesday, the Hour of the Dragon, 8 A.M.,
to the Hour of the Rooster, 6:30 P.M.

The battle is won by the player who sees the fur-
thest—the one, that is, who can see through his opponent's move, can guess his plan and counter it, and
who, when attacking, anticipates all the defensive
moves of his opponent.

—*The Game of Wei-Chi*

Chapter Nine

The life of a tollbooth operator guarding the portals to New York City is not particularly glamorous.

Occasionally there's a little excitement—like the time a thief stuck up a toll taker and netted a clean $312, the only problem being that the robber struck at the *entrance* to the Triboro Bridge, at the other end of which a dozen bemused cops were waiting for him at the only possible exit he could take.

But the operator sitting in a Queens Midtown Tunnel booth this stormy morning, just after 8 A.M.—a retired NYC transit cop working part-time as a toll taker—hadn't seen any serious trouble in years and he was excited that something had happened to break the monotony: all the tollbooth operators in Manhattan had gotten a priority call from Port Authority headquarters about a ship that'd sunk off the coast of Long Island, one of those illegal immigrant ships. The word was that some of the Chinese on board were now headed into town, as was the smuggler himself. They were in a white van bearing the name of a church and in a red Honda. Some or all of them were reportedly armed.

There were several ways to get into the city from Long Island by surface transportation: bridges or tunnels. Some of these were free—no tolls were charged at the Queensboro or the Brooklyn Bridges, for instance—but the most direct route from the end of Long Island was through the Queens Midtown Tunnel. The police and FBI had gotten permission to shut down all of the express pass and exact change lanes, so that the perps would have to go through a manned booth.

The ex-cop had never thought that he'd be the one to spot the immigrants.

But it looked like that was the way things were going to fall out. He was now wiping his sweaty palms on his slacks and watching a white van, some writing on the side, driven by a Chinese guy, easing toward *his* booth.

Ten cars away, nine . . .

He pulled his old service piece from its holster, a Smith & Wesson .357 with a four-inch barrel and rested the pistol on the far side of the cash register, wondering how to handle the situation. He'd call it in but what if the guys in the van acted funny or evasive? He decided he'd draw down on them and order them out of the van.

But what if one of them reached under the dash or between the seats?

Hell, here he was in an exposed glass booth, no backup, with a vanload of Chinese gangsters heading toward him. They might even be armed with Russia's crowning contribution to small arms: AK-47 machine guns.

Fuck it, he'd shoot.

The operator ignored a woman complaining about the E-ZPass lanes' being closed and looked at the line of traffic. The van was three cars away.

He reached onto his belt and pulled off his Speedloader, a metal ring holding six bullets, with which he could reload his Smittie in seconds. He rested this next to his pistol and wiped his shooting hand on his slacks once again. He debated for a moment, picked up the gun, cocked it and set it back on the counter. This was against regulations but then *he* was the one in the fishbowl, not the brass who wrote the regs.

At first Sam Chang had worried that the long line of cars meant a roadblock but then he saw the booths and decided this was some kind of a border crossing.

Passports, papers, visas . . . They had none of these.

In panic he looked for an exit but there was none—the road was surrounded by high walls.

But William said calmly, "We have to pay."

"Pay why?" Sam Chang asked the boy, their resident expert on American customs.

"It's a toll," he explained as if this were obvious. "I need some U.S. dollars. Three and a half."

In a moneybelt Chang had thousands of yuan—soggy and salty though they were—but hadn't dared change the money into U.S. dollars on the black markets of Fuzhou, which would've tipped off public security that they were about to flee the country. In a well beside the two front seats, though, they'd found a five-dollar bill.

The van crawled slowly forward. Two cars were in front of them.

Chang glanced up at the man in the booth and observed that he seemed very nervous. He kept looking at the van while appearing not to.

One car ahead of them in line now.

The man in the booth now studied them carefully from the corner of his eye. His tongue touched the side of his lip and he rocked from one foot to the other.

"I don't like this," William said. "He suspects something."

"There's nothing we can do," his father told him. "Go forward."

"I'll run it."

"No!" Chang muttered. "He may have a gun. He'll shoot us."

William eased the van to the booth and stopped. Would the boy, in his newfound rebellion, disregard Chang's order and speed through the gate?

The man in the booth swallowed and gripped something next to a large cash register. Was it a signal button of some kind? Chang wondered.

William looked down and pulled the U.S. money from the plastic divider between the front seats.

The officer seemed to flinch. He ducked, moving his arm toward the van.

Then he stared at the bill William was offering him.

What was wrong? Had he offered too much? Too little? Did he expect a bribe?

The man in the booth blinked. He took the bill with an unsteady hand, leaning forward to do so, and glanced at the side of the van, on which were the words:

THE HOME STORE

As the guard counted out change he looked into the back of the van itself. All that the man could see—Chang prayed—were the dozens of saplings and bushes that Chang, William and Wu had dug up in a park on the way here from the beach and packed into the van to make it look like they were delivering plants for a local store. The rest of the families were lying on the floor, hidden beneath the foliage.

The officer gave him the change for the toll. "Good place. The Home Store. I shop there all the time."

"Thank you," William replied.

"Bad day for making deliveries, huh?" he asked Chang, nodding up at the stormy skies.

"Thank you," Chang said.

William eased the van forward. He accelerated and a moment later they plunged into a tunnel.

"Okay, we're safe, we're past the guards," Chang announced and the rest of the passengers sat up, brushing leaves and dirt off their clothing.

Well, his idea had worked.

As they'd sped down the highway from the beach Chang realized that the police here might do what the Chinese PLA and security bureau officers did frequently to search for wanted dissidents—set up roadblocks.

So they'd stopped at a huge shopping center, in the middle of which was The Home Store. It was open twenty-four hours and—with few employees so early in the morning—Chang, Wu and William had no trouble slipping in through the loading dock. From the stockroom they stole some cans of paint, brushes and tools, then slipped outside again. But not before Chang had snuck to the doorway that led to the store itself and looked at the astonishing place. He saw acres of aisles. It was breathtaking—Chang had never seen so many tools and supplies and appliances. Kitchens ready-made, a thousand light fixtures, outdoor furniture and grills, doors, windows, carpets. Whole rows devoted to nuts and bolts and nails. Chang's first reaction was to bring Mei-Mei and his father inside, just to show them the place. Well, there would be time for that later.

Chang told William, "I'm taking these things now because we need to—for our survival. But as soon as I get some one-color I'm going to pay them back. I'll send them the money."

"You're crazy," the boy replied. "They have more than they'll need. They expect things to be stolen. It's built into the price."

"We will pay them back!" Chang snapped. This time the boy didn't even bother to respond. Chang found a colorful newspaper in a large pile on the loading dock. Struggling with the English, he realized that this was a sales flyer and that it had the address of a number of Home Stores on it.

When he got his first pay envelope or converted some yuan he would send them the money.

They'd returned to the van and found a truck parked nearby. William swapped the number plates and then they drove toward the city until they found a deserted factory. They parked in the loading dock, out of the rain, and Chang and Wu painted over the letters spelling the name of the church. After the white paint dried, Chang, a lifelong calligrapher, expertly drew the words "The Home Store" on the side in a typeface similar to that in the flyer he'd taken.

Yes, the trick had worked and, unstopped by security officers and the guard at the tollbooth, they now sailed out of the tunnel into the streets of Manhattan. William had studied the map carefully as they had waited in line at the toll and knew generally where they should go to get to Chinatown. The one-way streets caused a bit of confusion but soon he oriented himself and found the highway he sought.

Through dense rush-hour traffic, further slowed by the intermittent rain and patches of fog, they drove along a river whose shade perfectly matched the ocean they had just survived.

The gray land, Chang reflected. Not highways of gold and a city of diamonds, as the unfortunate Captain Sen had promised.

As Chang looked around at the streets and buildings he wondered what now awaited them.

In theory he still owed the Ghost a great deal of money. The going rate for smuggling someone from China to the United States was about U.S.$50,000. Since Chang was a dissident and desperate to leave he expected that the Ghost's agent in Fuzhou would charge him a premium. Yet he'd been surprised to find that the Ghost's fee was only $80,000 for his entire family, his father included. Chang had raided his meager savings and had borrowed the rest from friends and relatives to make up the ten percent down payment.

In his contract with the Ghost, Chang had agreed that he, Mei-Mei and William—and Chang's youngest son when he was old enough—would give money to the Ghost's debt collectors monthly until the remainder of the fee was paid off. Many immigrants worked directly for the snakehead who'd smuggled them into the country—the men generally in Chinatown restaurants, the women in garment factories—and lived in safehouses provided by them for a stiff fee. But Chang didn't trust snakeheads, especially the Ghost. There were too many rumors of immigrants being beaten and raped and kept prisoner in rat-infested safehouses. So he had made his own arrangements for a job for him and William and had located an apartment in New York through the brother of a friend back in China.

Sam Chang had always intended to pay his obligation. But now, with the sinking of the *Fuzhou Dragon* and the Ghost's attempts to murder them, the contract was void and they were out from under the crushing debt—if, of course, they could stay alive long enough for the Ghost and his *bangshous* to be captured or killed by the police or to flee back to China, and this meant going to ground as soon as possible.

William drove expertly through the traffic. (Where *had* he learned that? The family didn't even own a car.) Sam Chang looked back at the others in the van. They were disheveled and stank of seawater. Wu's wife, Yong-Ping, was in a bad way. Her eyes were closed and she shivered, sweat covering her face. Her arm was shattered from their collision with the rocks and the wound was still bleeding through an impromptu bandage. Wu's pretty teenage daughter, Chin-Mei, seemed unhurt but was clearly frightened. Her brother, Lang, was the same age as Chang's youngest son, and the two boys, with nearly identical bowl-shaped haircuts, sat close to each other, staring out the window and whispering.

Elderly Chang Jiechi sat motionless in the back of the van with his legs crossed and arms at his side, thin white hair slicked back, saying nothing, but observing all through eyes half covered by drooping lids. The old man's skin seemed more jaundiced than when they'd left Fuzhou over two weeks ago but perhaps that was just Chang's imagination. In any case, he'd decided that the first thing he'd do after they were settled in their apartment was get the man to a doctor.

The van slowed to a stop because of the traffic. William pressed the horn impatiently.

"Quiet," his father snapped. "Don't draw attention to us."

The boy hit the horn once more.

Chang glanced toward his son, the boy's lean face, the long hair, which fell well below his ears. He asked in a harsh whisper, "The van . . . how did you learn to start it that way?"

"What does it matter?" the boy asked.

"Tell me."

"I heard somebody talking about it at school."

"No, you're lying. You've done it before."

"I only steal from party undersecretaries and commune bosses. That'd be all right with you, wouldn't it?"

"You do *what*?"

But the boy grinned in a snide way and Chang understood he was joking. The comment, though, was cruelly intended; it was a reference to Chang's anticommunist political writings, which had caused the family so much pain in China—and necessitated the flight to America itself.

"Who do you spend time with, thieves?"

"Oh, Father." The boy shook his head, a condescending gesture, and Chang wanted to slap him.

"And what did you have that knife for?" Chang asked.

"A lot of people have knives. Yeye has one." This was the affectionate term for "grandfather," which many Chinese children used.

"That's a penknife for cleaning pipes," Chang said, "not a weapon." He finally lost his temper. "How can you be so disrespectful?" he shouted.

"If I didn't have the knife," the boy answered angrily, "and if I didn't know how to start the engine we'd probably be dead now."

The traffic sped up and William fell into a moody silence.

Chang turned away, feeling as if he'd been physically assaulted by the boy's words, by this very different side of his son. Oh, certainly there'd been problems with William in the past. As he'd neared his late teens he'd grown sullen and angry and withdrawn. His attendance at school dropped. When he'd brought home a letter from his teacher reprimanding him for bad grades Chang had confronted the boy—whose intelligence had been tested and was far higher than average. William had said that it wasn't his fault. He was persecuted at school and treated unfairly because his father was a dissident who'd flouted the one-child rule, spoke favorably about Taiwanese independence and—the worst sacrilege of all—was critical of the CCP, the Chinese Communist Party, and its hardline views on freedom and human rights. Both he and his younger brother were taunted regularly by "superbrats," youngsters who, as only children in comfortable rich and middle-class Communist families, were spoiled by hordes of doting relatives and tended to bully other students. It didn't help that William was named after the most famous American entrepreneur in recent years, and young Ronald for a U.S. president.

But neither his behavior, nor this explanation for it, had seemed to Chang very serious and he hadn't paid much mind to his son's moods.

Besides, it was Mei-Mei's task to rear the children, not his.

Why was the boy suddenly behaving so differently?

But then Chang realized that between working ten hours a day at a print shop and engaging in his dissident activities for most of the night, he'd spent virtually no time with his son—not until the voyage from Russia to *Meiguo*. Perhaps, he thought with a chill, this is how the boy *always* behaved.

For a moment he felt another burst of anger—though only partially directed toward William himself. Chang couldn't tell exactly *what* he was furious at. He stared at the crowded streets for a few moments then said to his son, "You're right. I wouldn't have been able to start the car myself. Thank you."

William didn't acknowledge that his father had even spoken and hunched over the wheel, lost in his own thoughts.

Twenty minutes later they were in Chinatown, driving down a broad road that was named in both Chinese and English, "Canal Street." The rain was letting up and there were many people on the sidewalks, which were lined with hundreds of grocery and souvenir shops, fish markets, jewelry stores, bakeries.

"Where should we go?" William asked.

"Park there," Chang instructed and William pulled the van to a curb. Chang and Wu climbed out. They walked into a store and asked the clerk about the neighborhood associations—tongs. These organizations were usually made up of people from common geographic areas in China. Chang was seeking a Fujianese tong, since the two families were from the province of Fujian. They would not, Chang assumed, be welcomed in a tong with roots in Canton, where most of the early Chinese immigrants had come from. But he was surprised to learn that much of Manhattan's Chinatown was now heavily populated with people from Fujian and many of the Cantonese had moved away. There was a major Fujianese tong only a few blocks away.

Chang and Wu left the families in the stolen van and walked through the crowded streets until they found the place. Painted red and sporting a classic Chinese bird-wing roof, the dingy three-story building might have been transported here directly from the shabby neighborhood near the North Bus Station in Fuzhou.

The men stepped inside the tong headquarters quickly, with their heads down, as if the people lounging about in the lobby of the building were about to pull out cell phones and call the INS—or the Ghost—to report their arrival.

Jimmy Mah, wearing a gray suit dusted with cigarette ash and about to burst at the seams, greeted them and invited them into his upstairs office.

President of the East Broadway Fujianese Society, Mah was the de facto mayor of this portion of Chinatown.

His office was a large but plain room, containing two desks and a half-dozen mismatched chairs, piles of paper, a fancy computer and a television set. A hundred or so Chinese books sat on a lopsided bookcase. On the wall were faded and flyblown posters of Chinese landscapes. Chang wasn't fooled by the run-down appearance of the place, however; he suspected that Mah was a millionaire several times over.

"Sit, please," Mah said in Chinese. The broad-faced man with black hair slicked straight back offered them cigarettes. Wu took one. Chang shook his head no. He'd stopped smoking after he lost his teaching job and money grew scarce.

Mah looked over their filthy clothes, their mussed hair. "Ha, you two look like you have a story to tell. *Do* you have an interesting story? A compelling story? What would it be? I bet I would like very much to hear it."

Chang indeed did have a story. Whether it was interesting or compelling he couldn't have said but one thing he did know: it was fictional. He had decided not to tell any strangers that they'd been on the *Fuzhou Dragon* and that the Ghost might be searching for them. He said to Mah, "We've just come into the port on a Honduran ship."

"Who was your snakehead?"

"We never learned his name. He called himself Moxige."

"Mexican?" Mah shook his head. "I don't work with Latino snakeheads." Mah's dialect was tainted with an American accent.

"He took our money," Chang said bitterly, "but then he just left us on the dock. He was going to get us papers and transportation. He vanished."

With curiosity Wu watched him spin this tale. Chang had told the man to keep quiet and let him talk to Mah. On the *Dragon* Wu drank too much and grew impulsive. He'd been careless about what he'd told the immigrants and crew in the hold.

"Don't they do that sometimes?" Mah said jovially. "Why do they cheat people? Isn't it bad for business? Fuck Mexicans. Where are you from?"

"Fuzhou," Wu offered. Chang stirred. He was going to mention a different city in Fujian—to minimize any connection between the immigrants and the Ghost.

Chang continued, feigning anger. "I have two children and a baby. My father too. He's old. And my friend here, his wife is sick. We need help."

"Ah, help. Well, that *is* an interesting story, isn't it? But what kind of help do you want? I can do some things. Other things I can't do. Am I one of the Eight Immortals? No, of course I'm not. What do you need?"

"Papers. ID papers. For myself, my wife and my oldest son."

"Sure, sure, I can do some of them. Driver's licenses, social security cards, some old company ID cards—*bankrupt* companies so no one can check on you. Aren't I clever? Only Jimmy Mah thinks of things like this. These cards, they'll make you *look* like citizens but you won't be able get a real job with them. The INS bastards make companies check everything nowadays."

"I've got an arrangement for work," Chang said.

"And I don't do passports," Mah added. "Too dangerous. No green cards either."

"What is that?"

"Resident permits."

"We're going to stay underground and wait for an amnesty," Chang explained.

"Are you? May wait a long time."

Chang shrugged. He then said, "My father needs to see a doctor." A nod toward Wu. "His wife too. Can you get us health cards?"

"I don't do health cards. Too easy to trace. You'll have to go to a private doctor."

"Are they expensive?"

"Yes, very expensive. But if you don't have money go to a city hospital. They will take you."

"Is the care good?"

"What do I know if the care is good? Besides, what choice do you have?"

"All right," Chang said. "For the other documents. How much?"

"Fifteen hundred."

"Yuan?"

Mah laughed. "One-color."

Chang showed no emotion but he thought: Fifteen hundred U.S. dollars! That was insane. In the money belt around his waist he had about five thousand dollars' worth of Chinese yuan. It was all the cash that his family had left in the world. Shaking his head. "No, impossible." After a few minutes of animated haggling they settled on $900 for all the documents.

"You too?" Mah asked Wu.

The gaunt man nodded but added, "Only for myself. That will be less, won't it?"

Mah drew heavily on his cigarette. "Five hundred. I won't go lower than that."

Wu tried to bargain too but Mah held firm. Finally the skinny man grudgingly agreed.

Mah said, "You'll have to get me pictures of everybody for the driver's licenses and employee cards. Go into an amusement arcade. You can have the pictures made there."

Chang remembered poignantly the night he sat with Mei-Mei in such a booth at a large entertainment center in Xiamen years ago, not long after they'd first met. The pictures were presently in a suitcase sitting within the corpse of the *Fuzhou Dragon* at the bottom of the dark ocean.

"We also need a van. I can't afford to buy one. Can I rent one from you?"

The tong leader scoffed. "Don't I have everything? Of course, of course." After more bargaining, they agreed on a rental. Mah calculated the total that the men owed and then figured the exchange rate for paying in yuan. He told the men the astonishing sum and they reluctantly agreed. "Give me the names and address for the documents." He turned to his computer and, as Chang dictated the information, Mah typed with fast keystrokes.

Chang himself spent a lot of time on his old laptop computer. The Internet had become the main means for dissidents in China to communicate with the outside world, though doing so was very difficult. Chang's modem was woefully slow and the public security bureaus, as well as agents from the People's Liberation Army, were constantly looking for emails and postings by dissidents. Chang had a firewall on his computer that would often give a beep, signaling that the government was trying to break into his system. He'd log off immediately and have to establish a new service provider account. His laptop too, he thought sadly, was sleeping forever inside the *Fuzhou Dragon*.

As Chang dictated the address, the tong leader looked up from the keyboard. "So you'll be staying in Queens?"

"Yes. A friend arranged a place for us."

"Is it a big place? Is it comfortable for all of you? Don't you think my broker could do better? I'm thinking he could. I have contacts in Queens."

"He is my best friend's brother. He's already arranged for the lease."

"Ah, friend's brother. Good. Well, we have an affiliated association there. The Flushing Neighborhood and Merchants Association. Very big. Powerful. That's the new Chinatown in the New York area: Flushing. Maybe you won't like your apartment. Maybe the children won't be safe. That's possible, don't you think? Go to the association and mention my name."

"I'll remember that."

Mah nodded toward the computer screen and asked Wu, "You're both at this address?"

Chang started to say that they were but Wu interrupted. "No, no. I want to stay in Manhattan, Chinatown here. Can your broker find us a house?"

"But—" Chang said, frowning.

"You don't mean house, do you?" Mah inquired, amused. "There are no houses." He added, "That you could afford."

"An apartment then?"

Mah said, "Yes, he has temporary rooms. You can get a place today and then stay there until he finds you a permanent home." As Mah typed some more and the hiss of the modem filled the office, Chang put his hand on Wu's arm and whispered, "No, Qichen, you must come with us."

"We're staying in Manhattan."

Leaning closer so that Mah could not hear, Chang whispered, "Don't be a fool. The Ghost will find you."

Wu laughed. "Don't worry about him."

"Don't worry? He just killed a dozen of our friends." Gambling with Wu's own life was one thing but to risk his wife and children was unthinkable.

But Wu was adamant. "No. We are staying here."

Chang fell silent as Mah logged off the computer and then wrote a note, handed it to Wu. "This is the broker. He's only a few blocks from here. You'll pay him a fee." He added, "I won't charge you for this. Am I generous? Everybody says Jimmy Mah is generous. Now, for Mr. Chang's car." Mah made a call and began to speak quickly into the phone. He made arrangements for a van to be brought around. He hung up and turned to the two men. "There. That concludes our business. Isn't it a pleasure to work with reasonable men?"

They rose in unison and shook hands.

"Do you want a cigarette to take with you?" he asked Wu, who took three.

When the immigrants were at the door Mah asked, "One thing. This Mexican snakehead? There's no reason for him to come after you, is there? You're even with him?"

"Yes, we're even."

"Good. Don't we have enough reason to look over our shoulders?" Mah asked jovially. "Aren't there enough demons after us in this life?"

Chapter Ten

In the distance, sirens pierced the early morning air.

The sound grew louder and Lincoln Rhyme hoped it would mark the arrival of Amelia Sachs. The evidence she'd gathered at the beach had already arrived, delivered by a young tech who'd sheepishly entered the den of the legendary Lincoln Rhyme without a word and scurried about to deposit the bags and stacks of pictures as the criminalist gruffly directed.

Sachs herself had been diverted on the way back from the beach, however, to run a secondary crime scene. The church van stolen at Easton had been found in Chinatown—abandoned in an alley next to an uptown subway stop forty-five minutes ago. The van had slipped past the roadblocks because not only did it sport stolen plates but one of the immigrants had painted over the name of the church and replaced it with a good facsimile of the logo for a local home improvement store.

"Smart," Rhyme had said, with some dismay; he didn't like smart perps. He'd then called Sachs—who was speeding back to the city on the Long Island Expressway—and ordered her to meet a crime scene bus downtown and process the van.

The INS's Harold Peabody was gone—summoned to juggle press conferences and calls from Washington about the fiasco.

Alan Coe, Lon Sellitto and Fred Dellray remained, as did the trim, hedgehog-haired detective Eddie Deng. An addition as well: Mel Cooper, slim, balding, reserved. He was one of the NYPD's top forensic lab workers and Rhyme often borrowed him. Walking silently on his crepe-soled Hush Puppies, which he wore during the day because they were comfortable and at night because they gave him good traction for ball-room dancing, Cooper was assembling equipment, organizing examination stations and laying out the evidence from the beach.

At Rhyme's direction Thom taped a map of New York City on the wall, next to the map of Long Island and the surrounding waters, which they'd used in following the *Fuzhou Dragon*'s progress. Rhyme stared at the red dot that represented the ship and he once again felt the pain of guilt that his lack of foresight had resulted in the deaths of the immigrants.

The sirens grew louder then stopped outside his window, which faced Central Park. A moment later the door opened and Amelia Sachs, limp-ing slightly, hurried into the room. Her hair was matted and flecked with bits of seaweed and dirt and her jeans and work shirt were damp and sandy.

Those in the room nodded distracted greetings. Dellray studied her clothes and lifted an eyebrow.

"Had some free time," she said. "Went for a swim. Hi, Mel."

"Amelia," Cooper said, shoving his glasses higher on his nose. He blinked at her appearance.

Rhyme noted with eager anticipation what she carried: a gray milk crate, filled with plastic and paper bags. She handed the evidence to Cooper and started for the stairs, calling, "Back in five."

A moment later Rhyme heard the shower running and, indeed, five minutes after she'd left, she was back, wearing some of the clothes she kept in his bedroom closet: blue jeans and a black t-shirt, running shoes.

Wearing rubber gloves, Cooper was laying the bags out, organizing them according to the scenes—the beach and the van in Chinatown. Rhyme gazed at the evidence and felt—in his temples, not his numb chest—a quickening of his heart, the breathtaking excitement of a hunt that was about to begin. Indifferent toward sports and athletics, Rhyme nonetheless supposed that this edgy exhilaration was what ski racers, for instance, felt when they stood at the top of a run, looking down the moun-tain. Would they win? Would the course defeat them? Would they make a tactical mistake and lose by a fraction of a second? Would they be injured or die?

"Okay," he said. "Let's get to it." He looked around the room. "Thom?

Thom! Where is he? He was here a minute ago. Thom!"

"What, Lincoln?" the harried aide appeared in the doorway, with a pan and dish towel in hand.

"Be our scribe . . . write our pithy insights down"—a nod at the white-board—"in that elegant handwriting of yours."

"Yes, bwana." Thom started back to the kitchen.

"No, no, just leave it," Rhyme groused. "Write!"

Sighing, Thom set down the pan and wiped his hands on the towel. He tucked his purple tie into his shirt to protect it from the marker and walked to the whiteboard. He'd been an unofficial member of several forensic teams here and he knew the drill. He now asked Dellray, "You have a name for the case yet?"

The FBI always named major investigations with acronym-like varia-tions of the key words describing the case—like ABSCAM. Dellray pinched the cigarette that rested behind his ear. He said, "Nup. Nothing yet. But less just do it ourselves and make Washington live with it. How 'bout the name of our boy? GHOSTKILL. That good enough for ever-body? That *spooky* enough?"

"Plenty spooky," Sellitto agreed though with the tone of someone who was rarely spooked.

Thom wrote this at the top of the whiteboard and turned back to the law enforcers.

Rhyme said, "We've got two scenes: the beach in Easton and the van. The beach first."

As Thom was writing the heading Dellray's phone rang and he took the call. After a brief conversation he hung up and told the team what he'd just learned: "No other survivors so far," he said. "And the Coast Guard hasn't found the ship. But they did recover some bodies out to sea. Two shot, one drowned. ID on one of them had merchant papers. Nothing on the other two. They're sending prints and pictures to us and copies to China."

"He even killed the *crew*?" Eddie Deng asked in disbelief.

"What do you expect?" Coe responded. "You know him by now. You think he'd leave a single witness alive?" A grim laugh. "Besides, with the crew dead he won't have to pay the balance due for chartering the boat. And back in China he'll probably claim that the Coast Guard fired on them and sank the *Dragon*."

But Rhyme had no time for anger at the Ghost or for dismay at the cruel potential of the human heart. "Okay, Sachs," he said curtly. "The beach. Tell us what happened."

She leaned against a lab table and consulted her notes. "Fourteen people came ashore in a life raft about a half mile east of Easton, on the road to Orient Point." She walked to the wall and touched a spot on the Long Island map. "Near the Horton Point lighthouse. As they got closer to shore the raft hit some rocks and started to deflate. Four of the immigrants were thrown into the water and were washed down the beach. The other ten stayed together. They stole the church van and got away."

"Photos of the footprints?" Rhyme asked.

"Here you go," Sachs said, handing Thom an envelope. He taped up Polaroids. "I found them under a shelter near the raft. It was too wet to use electrostatic," she explained to the team. "I had to take pictures."

"And fine artwork they are too," Rhyme said, wheeling back and forth in front of them."I'm counting nine," Dellray said. "Why you sayin' ten, Amelia?"

"Because," Rhyme said, "there's a baby, right?"

Sachs nodded. "Right. Under the shelter I found some patterns in the sand I couldn't identify, looked like something had been dragged but there were no footprints in front of it—only behind. I figured it was a crawling child."

"Okay," Rhyme said, studying the sizes of the shoes, "looks like we've got seven adults and/or older teens, two young children and one infant. One of the adults could be elderly—he's shuffling. I say 'he' because of the shoe size. And somebody's injured—probably a woman, to judge from the size of *her* shoes. The man next to her is helping her."

Sachs added, "There were bloodstains on the beach and in the van."

"Samples of the blood?" Cooper asked.

"There wasn't much on the raft or the beach—the rain had washed most of it away. I got three samples from the sand. And plenty in the van, still wet." She found a plastic bag containing some vials. Handed it to him.

The tech prepared samples for typing and filled out a form. He called in an expedited request for typing and gendering into the serology lab at the Medical Examiner's office and arranged for a uniformed officer to take the sample downtown.

Sachs continued her scenario. "Now, the Ghost—in a second launch—landed about two hundred yards east of where the immigrants did."

Her fingers disappeared into her abundant red hair and worried the flesh of her scalp. Sachs would often injure herself in minor ways like this. A beautiful woman, a former fashion model, she often had stubby, sometimes bloody fingernails. Rhyme had given up trying to figure out where this painful compulsion came from but, oddly, he envied her. The same cryptic tensions drove him as well. The difference was that he didn't have her safety valve of fidgety motion to bleed off the stress.

He silently sent out a plea to Dr. Weaver, his neurosurgeon: Do *something* for me. Release me just a little from this terrible confinement. Please . . . Then he slammed the door on these personal thoughts, angry with himself, and turned his attention back to Sachs.

"Then," she continued with a splinter of emotion in her voice, "then he started tracking down the immigrants and killing them. He found two who'd fallen off the raft and killed them. Shot them in the back. He wounded one. The fourth immigrant's still missing."

"Where's the wounded one?" Coe asked.

"They were taking him to a trauma center then to the INS Manhattan detention facility. He said he doesn't know where the Ghost or the immigrants might've been going once they got here."Sachs again consulted her soggy handwritten notes. "Now there was a vehicle on the road near the beach but it left—fast, spun the wheels and skidded to make a turn. I think the Ghost took a shot at it. So we may have a witness, if we can track down the make and model. I got dimensions of the wheelbase and—"

"Wait," Rhyme interrupted. "What was it near? The car?"

"Near?" she asked. "Nothing. It was just parked by the roadside."

The criminalist frowned. "Why would somebody park there on a stormy day before dawn?"

"Drivin' by and saw the rafts?" Dellray suggested.

"No," Rhyme said. "In that case he would've gone for help or called. And there weren't any nine-one-ones reporting anything. No, I think the driver was there to pick up the Ghost but when it turned out the snakehead wasn't in any hurry to leave, he took off."

"So he got abandoned," Sellitto observed.

Rhyme nodded.

Sachs handed a sheet of paper to Mel Cooper. "Dimensions of the wheelbase. And here are pictures of the tread marks."

The tech scanned the marks into the computer and then sent the image, along with the dimensions, to the NYPD's VI—Vehicle Identifier—database. "Shouldn't be long," Cooper's calm voice reported.

Young detective Eddie Deng asked, "What about the other trucks?"

"What other trucks?" Sachs asked.

Coe filled in. "The terms of a smuggling contract include land transport too. There should've been some trucks to take the immigrants back to the city."

Sachs shook her head. "I didn't see any sign of them. But when he sank the ship the Ghost probably called the driver and had them go back to the city." She looked over the evidence bags again. "I found this . . ." She held up a bag containing a cell phone.

"Excellent!" Rhyme said. He'd dubbed clues like this "NASDAQ evidence," after the high-tech-heavy stock market. Computers, cell phones, personal electronic organizers. A whole new breed of evidence, these telltale devices could provide huge amounts of information about perps and the people they'd been in contact with. "Fred, let's get your people to look it over."

"Gotcha."

The bureau had recently added a computer and electronics team to the New York office. Dellray made a call and arranged for an agent to pick up the cell phone and take it to the federal forensics lab downtown for analysis.

Rhyme said, musing, "Okay, he's hunting them down, shooting the immigrants, shooting *at* the driver who abandoned him. He's doing it by himself, right, Sachs? No sign of the mysterious assistant?"

She nodded at the footprint Polaroids. "No, I'm sure the Ghost was the only one in the second raft and the only one shooting."

Rhyme frowned. "I don't like unidentified perps out there someplace when we're running crime scenes. *Nothing* on who this *bangshou* is?"

Sellitto muttered, "Nope. Not a clue. The Ghost's got dozens of them around the world."

"And no sign of the fourth immigrant? The other one who fell out of the raft?"

"No."

The criminalist then asked Sachs, "What about ballistics?"

Sachs held up a plastic bag containing shell casings for Rhyme to examine.

"Seven-point-six-two millimeter," he said, "but the brass's an odd length. And it's uneven. Cheap." Though he had a body that couldn't move, his eyes were as sharp as those of the peregrine falcons that lived on the windowsill outside his bedroom upstairs. "Check out the casings online, Mel."

When Rhyme had been head of NYPD forensics he'd spent months putting together databases of evidence standards—samples of substances and materials along with the sources they came from, like motor oil, thread, fibers, dirt and so on—to facilitate tracing evidence found at crime scenes. One of the largest, and most often-used, databases was the compilation of bullet shell casings and slugs information. The combined FBI and NYPD collection had samples and digitized images of nearly every projectile that had ever been fired from a weapon in the past hundred years.

Cooper opened the plastic bag and then reached in with chopsticks—appropriately, considering the case they were now working on. This was the tool that Rhyme had found was the least damaging to evidence and he'd ordered all his techs to learn to use the sticks, preferring them to tweezers or forceps, which could too easily crush delicate samples.

"Back to your captivating narrative about the beach, Sachs."

She continued. "Things were heating up by now. The Ghost had been on land for a while. He knew the Coast Guard had a rough idea of his location. He found the third immigrant in the water, John Sung, shot him, then stole the Honda and left." She glanced at Rhyme. "Any word about it?"

An emergency vehicle locator notice had gone out to all nearby law enforcement agencies. As soon as the stolen red Honda was spotted anywhere in the New York metropolitan area, Sellitto or Dellray would get a call. But there'd been no word, the homicide detective told her. Then added, "The Ghost's been to New York before, though, plenty of times. He'd know the transit system. I'd guess he stuck to back roads west until he got close to the city then dumped the car and took the subway into town. He's got to be here by now."

Rhyme noticed a frown of concern on the FBI agent's face. "What is it, Fred?"

"I wish we'da found the prick 'fore he got over the city line."

"Why?"

"Reports my people're feeding me're that he's got a nice, tidy network in town. Tongs and street gangs in Chinatown, course. But it's way beyond that—even got people in the government on his 'roll."

"Government?" Sellitto asked, surprised.

"What I hear," Dellray said.

"I believe it," Deng said cynically. "If he's got dozens of officials in China in his pocket, why not here too?"

So, Rhyme reflected, we've got an unidentified, presumably armed assistant and a homicidal snakehead *and* now spies within our own ranks. It's never easy but really. . . .

A glance at Sachs, which meant: keep going. "Friction ridges?" he asked. The technical name for finger-, palm- and footprints.

She explained, "The beach was a mess—the rain and wind. I got a few partials from the outboard motor and the rubber sides of the rafts and the cell phone." She held up the cards of the prints she'd lifted. "The quality's pretty bad."

Rhyme called, "Scan 'em and get them into AFIS."

The Automated Fingerprint Identification System was a huge network of digitized federal and state fingerprint files. AFIS reduced the search time for matching prints from months to hours or even minutes in some cases.

"I also found this." She held up a metal pipe in a plastic bag. "One of them used it to break the window of the van. There were no visibles on this one so I thought we better raise the prints here."

"Go to work, Mel."

The thin man took the bag, pulled on cotton gloves and extracted the pipe, holding it only by the ends. "I'll use VMD."

Vacuum metal deposition is considered the Rolls-Royce of fingerprint-raising systems. It involves binding a microscopic coating of metal to the object to be printed and then radiating it. After a few minutes Cooper had a razor-sharp image of several latent prints. He shot pictures of them and ran the photos through the scanner then sent them off to AFIS. He handed the pictures to Thom, who pinned them up.

"That's about it for the beach, Rhyme," Sachs said.

The criminalist glanced at the chart. The evidence told him little yet. But he wasn't discouraged; this was how criminalistics worked. It was like dumping a thousand jigsaw puzzle pieces out on the table—incomprehensible at first; only after trial and error and much analysis did patterns begin to appear. He said, "The van next."

Sachs pinned up pictures of the van on the whiteboard.

Recognizing the location in Chinatown from the Polaroid, Coe said, "It's crowded around that subway station. There must've been some witnesses."

"Nobody saw a thing," Sachs said wryly.

"Where've I heard *that* before," Sellitto added. It was astonishing, Rhyme knew, what kind of amnesia was induced by the mere act of flashing a gold shield in front of your average citizen.

"What about the plate?" Rhyme asked.

"Stolen off a truck in a parking lot in Suffolk County," the burly homicide cop said. "No wits there either."

"What'd you find in the van?" he asked Sachs.

"They'd dug up a bunch of plants and had them in the back."

"Plants?"

"To hide the others, I'm guessing, and make it look like they were a couple of employees making deliveries for that place, The Home Store. But I didn't get much else. Just the fingerprints, some rags and the blood—the spatter was on the window and door so I'm guessing the injury was above the waist. Arm or hand, probably."

Rhyme asked, "No paint cans? Brushes? From when they painted the logo on the side."

"Nope, they ditched it all." She shrugged. "That's it, aside from the friction ridges." She handed Cooper the cards and Polaroids of the fingerprints she'd lifted from the van and he scanned and ran them: digitized them and then fed them into the AFIS.

Rhyme's eyes were glued to the chart. He studied the items for a moment the way a sculptor sizes up a raw piece of stone before he begins carving. Then he turned away and said to Dellray and Sellitto, "How do you want to handle the case?"

Sellitto deferred to the FBI agent, who said, "We gotta split the effort. Don't see a single other way to handle it. One, we'll be going after the Ghost. Two, we gotta find those families 'fore he does." He glanced at Rhyme. "We'll do the command post thing from here, if that's okay?"

Rhyme nodded. He no longer cared about the intrusion, no longer cared about his town house's conversion to Grand Central Station. Whatever it took, the criminalist was going to find the man who'd ruthlessly taken so many innocent lives.

"Now here's what I'm thinkin'," Dellray said, pacing on his long legs. "We're not fuckin' around with this guy. I'm gettin' a dozen more agents assigned to the case here in the Southern and Eastern Districts and I'll get us a SPEC-TAC team up from Quantico."

SPEC-TAC was short for Special Tactics, though it was pronounced as in "spectacular." This little-known outfit within the FBI was the best tactical unit in the country. It regularly engaged in practice operations with Delta Force and the Navy Seals—and usually won. Rhyme was glad to hear that Dellray was beefing up their side. From what they now knew about the Ghost, their present resources were inadequate. Dellray, for instance, was the only FBI agent assigned full-time to the Ghost case and Peabody was only mid-level INS.

"Gonna be tough to get ever-body on board down at the Federal Building," the agent said, "but I'll make sure it happens."

Coe's phone rang. He listened for a few moments, nodding his head. After he hung up he said, "That was INS Detention in Midtown—about that undocumented, John Sung. He was just released on bond by one of our hearing officers." Coe raised an eyebrow. "Everybody who's caught coming ashore tries for asylum—it's standard procedure. But it looks like Sung may just get it. He's a pretty well-known dissident in China."

"Where is he now?" Sachs asked.

"With the lawyer he was assigned from the Human Rights Law Center downtown. He's going to set Sung up at some apartment off Canal Street. I've got the address. He'll be there in a half hour. I'll go interview him."

"I'd rather go," Sachs said quickly.

"You?" Coe said. "You're Crime Scene."

"He trusts me."

"Trusts you? Why?"

"I saved his life. More or less."

"This is still an INS case," the young agent said adamantly.

"Exactly," Sachs pointed out. "How much do you think he's going to open up with a federal agent."

Dellray intervened. "Let *Aye*-melia do it."

Coe reluctantly handed her the address. She showed it to Sellitto. "We should have an RMP baby-sit outside his place." Meaning a Remote Mobile Patrol—coptalk for squad car. "If the Ghost finds out Sung's still alive he'll be a target too."

The detective jotted the address down. "Sure. I'll do it now."

"Okay, everybody, what's the theme of the investigation?" Rhyme called out.

"Search well but watch your backs," Sachs responded with a laugh.

"Keep that in mind. We don't know where the Ghost is, we don't know where—or who—his *bangshou* is."

Then his attention faded. He was vaguely aware of Sachs's grabbing her purse and starting to the door, just as he was aware of Coe's disgruntled sigh at his limited jurisdiction, Dellray's pacing and fashionable Eddie Deng's amusement at their running the case from this oddball command post. But these impressions were fading from his thoughts as his quick eyes made the circuit of the evidence culled from the crime scenes. He gazed at these items intently, as if imploring the inanimate evidence assembled before him to come to life, give up whatever secrets it might hold and guide them to the killer and the unfortunate prey that the snakehead was hunting.

GHOSTKILL

Easton, Long Island, Crime Scene	Stolen Van, Chinatown
· Two immigrants killed on beach; shot in back.	· Camouflaged by immigrants with "The Home Store" logo.
· One immigrant wounded—Dr. John Sung. One missing.	· Blood spatter suggests injured woman has hand, arm or shoulder injury.
· "Bangshou" (assistant) on board; identity unknown.	· Blood samples sent to lab for typing.
· Ten immigrants escape: seven adults (one elderly, one injured woman), two children, one infant. Steal church van.	· Fingerprints sent to AFIS.
· Blood samples sent to lab for typing.	
· Vehicle awaiting Ghost on beach left without him. One shot believed fired by Ghost at vehicle. Request for vehicle make and model sent out, based on tread marks and wheelbase.	
· No vehicles to pick up immigrants located.	
· Cell phone, presumably Ghost's, sent for analysis to FBI.	
· Ghost's weapon is 7.62mm pistol. Unusual casing.	
· Ghost is reported to have gov't people on payroll.	
· Ghost stole red Honda sedan to escape. Vehicle locator request sent out.	
· Three bodies recovered at sea—two shot, one drowned. Photos and prints to Rhyme and Chinese police.	
· Fingerprints sent to AFIS.	

Chapter Eleven

The Ghost waited for the three men in decadent surroundings.

Showered and dressed in clean, unobtrusive clothes, he sat on the leather couch and looked over New York Harbor from the vantage point of his eighteenth-floor apartment that was his main safehouse in New York. It was in a fancy high-rise near Battery Park City, in the southwest corner of Manhattan, not far from Chinatown but away from its crowded streets, the smells of seafood, the stink of rancid oil from the tourist restaurants. He reflected now on how elegance and comfort like this, which he'd fought hard to achieve, had long been targets of the Communist Party.

Why do you pursue the path of decadence?

You are part of the old! Do you repent your ways?

You must rid yourself of old culture, old customs, old habits, old ideas! You must reject your decadent values.

You are infected with wrong thought and wrong desires!

Wrong desires? he considered, smiling cynically to himself. *Desires?* Feeling the familiar crawling sensation in his groin. An urge he'd been very familiar with—and often ruled by—all his life.

Now that he'd survived the sinking of the ship and had escaped from the beach, his thoughts were returning to his normal priorities: he needed a woman badly.

He'd had none for over two weeks—a Russian prostitute in St. Petersburg, a woman with a broad mouth and breasts that lolled alarmingly toward her armpits when she lay on her back. The event was satisfying— but only barely.

And on the *Fuzhou Dragon*? None. Usually it was a snakehead's pre- rogative to ask one of the prettier women piglets to his stateroom, promis- ing to reduce her transit fee in exchange for a night in his bed. Or, if she was traveling alone or with a weak man, simply to drag her to his cabin and rape her. What was she going to do, after all? Call the police when they arrived in the Beautiful Country?

But his *bangshou*, hiding out in the hold as his spy, had reported that the women piglets on the *Dragon* weren't particularly attractive or young and the men were defiant and smart, perfectly capable of causing trouble. So, it had been a long, celibate voyage.

He now resumed fantasizing about the woman he called Yindao, the Chinese word for female genitals. The nickname was contemptuous, of course, but not particularly so in her case—for the Ghost thought of all women, except a few businesswomen and female snakeheads he respected, solely in terms of their bodies. A number of images came to mind about the liaison he had planned with Yindao: her lying beneath him, the distinctive sound of her voice in his ear, her arching back, his hands gripping her long hair . . . such beautiful silken hair. . . . He found himself painfully aroused. For a moment he thought about forgetting the Changs and the Wus. He could meet Yindao—she was here in New York—and make the fantasies real. But, of course, it wasn't in his nature to do that. First, the piglet families would die. Then he would be able to spend long hours with her.

Naixin.

All in good time.

A glance at his watch. It was nearly 11 A.M. Where were the three Turks? he wondered.

When the Ghost had arrived at the safehouse not long ago he'd used one of the stolen cell phones he kept there to call a community center in Queens with which he'd done business several times in the past. He'd hired three men to help him find and kill the piglets. Ever paranoid and wishing to keep his connections between himself and his crimes as distant as possible, the Ghost hadn't gone to any of the traditional tongs in Chi- natown; he'd hired Uighurs.

Racially the vast majority of mainland China is Han, tracing their ancestry back to the dynasty of that name, which established itself about 200 B.C. The other eight or so percent of the population is made up of minority groups like the Tibetans, Mongolians and Manchus. The Uighurs (pronounced "wee-gur"), whose people are from western China, were one such minority. Predominantly Islamic, their native region is considered central Asia and before being annexed by China was called East Turkestan. Hence, the Ghost's name for them: "Turks."

Like the other minorities in China the Uighurs were often persecuted and under great pressure from Beijing to assimilate into Chinese culture. Separatists were often brutalized and killed and Uighurs were very vocal in their demands for independence; most of the terrorist acts in China could be traced to Uighur freedom fighters.

The Uighur community in New York was quiet, devout and peaceful. But this particular group of men from the Turkestan Community and Islamic Center of Queens, was as ruthless as any triad the Ghost had ever dealt with. And since this assignment involved killing families who were Han Chinese they were the perfect choice to help him; they were motivated by both years of oppression and the generous amounts of cash the Ghost would pay them, part of which would ultimately go to the western Chinese province of Xinjiang to help fund the foundering Uighur independence movement.

Ten minutes later they arrived. Hands were shaken and they gave their names: Hajip, Yusuf, Kashgari. They were dark, quiet, thin—of smaller stature than he, and the Ghost was not particularly big. They wore black suits, gold bracelets or necklaces and fancy cell phones on their hips like badges.

Uighurs spoke Turkic, a language the Ghost didn't understand, and they weren't comfortable with any of the Chinese dialects. They settled on English. The Ghost explained what was needed and asked if they'd have any trouble killing people who were unarmed—women and children too.

Yusuf, a man in his late twenties with eyebrows that met above his nose, was the spokesman; his English was better than the others'. Without consulting them he said, "No problem. We do that. We do what you want." As if he killed women and children regularly.

And perhaps, the Ghost reflected, he did.

The Ghost gave them each $10,000 from a cashbox he kept in the safehouse and then called the head of the Turkestan community center and handed the phone to Yusuf, who told his boss in English how much money the Ghost had distributed, so there would be no dispute about underpayment and where the money had gone. They hung up.

The Ghost now said, "I'm going out for a while. I need to get some information."

"We will wait. May we have coffee?"

The Ghost nodded them into the kitchen. Then he walked to a small shrine. He lit a joss stick of incense, muttered a prayer to Yi, the divine bowman in Chinese mythology, whom the Ghost had adopted as his personal deity. He then put his pistol into an ankle holster and left his decadent apartment.

Sonny Li sat on a Long Island Commuter Services bus, which was nudging its way through the rain-spattered early morning traffic, as the skyline of Manhattan slowly grew larger.

Cynical and hard by nature, Li nonetheless was in awe of what he was examining. Not the massive size of the city they were approaching—Li's world was the Southeast China coast, which was the most populous metropolitan sprawl on earth. Shanghai was twice the size of New York and 50 million people lived in the Pearl Delta between Hong Kong and Guangzhou.

No, what fascinated him was the bus in which he rode.

In China the main means of public transit is buses. They're cramped, filthy vehicles, often broken down, stifling in the warm months, freezing in the fall and winter, windows greasy from smoke residue and hair oil and soot. The bus stations too were old, decrepit places. Li had shot a man behind the infamous North Bus Station in Fuzhou and had himself been knifed not far from the same spot.

So Li had never seen any vehicle like this behemoth—it was huge and luxurious, with thick padded seats, clean floors and spotless windows. Even on this oppressive, dank day in August the air-conditioning worked perfectly. He'd spent two weeks being violently sick every day, was virtually broke, had no idea where the Ghost was. He had no gun, not even a pack of cigarettes. But at least the bus was a blessing from heaven.

After he'd fled from the beach where the survivors of the *Fuzhou Dragon* had landed, Li had begged a ride from a trucker at a rest stop on the highway several kilometers away. The man had looked over his wet,

92 / Jeffery Deaver

disheveled clothes and let him ride in the back of the truck. After a half hour or so the trucker dropped him in a sleek bus station in a massive parking lot. Here, the driver explained, Sonny Li could take a commuter bus to where he wanted to go—Manhattan.

Li wasn't sure what was required to buy a ticket but apparently no passports or documents were necessary. He'd handed one of the twenty-dollar bills he'd stolen from red-headed Hongse's car to the clerk and said, "New York City please." He enunciated in his best accent, mimicking the actor Nicolas Cage. Speaking so clearly, in fact, that the clerk, perhaps expecting unintelligible words, blinked in surprise and handed him a computer-printed chit along with six dollars in change. He counted the money twice and decided that either the clerk had robbed him or, as he muttered under his breath in English, he was now in "one fuck expensive country."

He'd gone to a newsstand connected to the station and bought a razor and comb. In the men's room, he'd shaved and washed the salt water out of his hair and dried it with paper towels. Then he combed the thinning strands back and brushed as much sand off himself as he could. He joined the well-dressed commuters on the platform.

Now, approaching the city, the bus slowed for a tollbooth and then continued through a long tunnel. Finally it emerged into the city itself. Ten minutes later the vehicle parked on a busy commercial street.

Li climbed out like everyone else and stood on the sidewalk.

His first thought: Where're all the bicycles and motorbikes? They were the main means of private transport in China and Li couldn't imagine a city this big without millions of Seagull bicycles coursing through the streets.

His second thought: Where can I buy some cigarettes?

He found a kiosk selling newspapers and bought a pack.

When he looked at his change this time he thought: Ten judges of hell! Nearly three dollars for a single pack! He smoked at least two packs a day, three when he was doing something dangerous and needed to calm his nerves. He'd go broke in a month living here, he estimated. He lit a cigarette and inhaled deeply as he walked through the crowds. He asked a pretty Asian woman how to get to Chinatown and was directed to the subway.

Jostling his way through the mass of commuters, Li bought a token from the clerk. This too was expensive but he'd given up comparing costs between the two countries. He dropped the token in the turnstile, walked through the device and waited on the platform. He had a bad moment when a man began shouting at him. Li thought the man might be deranged, even though he was wearing an expensive suit. In a moment he realized what the man was saying. Apparently, it was illegal to smoke on the subway.

Li thought this was madness. He couldn't believe it. But he didn't want to make a scene so he stubbed out his cigarette and put it in his pocket, muttering under his breath another assessment: "One crazy fuck country."

A few minutes later the train roared into the station and Sonny Li got on board as if he'd been doing it all his life, looking around attentively—though not for security officers but simply to see if anyone else was smoking so that he could light up again. To his dismay, no one was.

At Canal Street Li stepped out of the car and climbed up the stairs into the bustling, early morning city. The rain had stopped and he lit the snuffed cigarette then slipped into the crowd. Many of the people around him were speaking Cantonese, the dialect of the south, but aside from the language, this neighborhood was just like portions of his town, Liu Guoyuan—or any small city in China: movie theaters showing Chinese action and love films, the young men with long slicked-back hair or pompadours and challenging sneers, the young girls walking with their arms around their mothers or grandmothers, businessmen in suits buttoned snugly, the ice-filled boxes of fresh fish, the bakeries selling tea buns and rice pastries, the smoked ducks hanging by their necks in the greasy windows of restaurants, herbalists and acupuncturists, Chinese doctors, shop windows filled with ginseng roots twisted like deformed human bodies.

And somewhere near here, he was hoping, would be something else he was very familiar with.

It took Li ten minutes to find what he sought. He noticed the telltale sign—the guard, a young man with a cell phone, smoking and examining passersby as he lounged in front of a basement apartment whose windows were painted black. It was a twenty-four-hour gambling hall.

He walked up and asked in English, "What they play here? Fan tai? Poker? Maybe thirteen points?"

The man looked at Li's clothes and ignored him.

"I want play," Li said.

"Fuck off," the young man spat out.

"I have money," Li shouted angrily. "Let me inside!"

"You Fujianese. I hear your accent. You not welcome here. Get outta here or you get hurt."

Li raged, "My dollar good as fuck Cantonese dollar. You boss, he want you turn away customers?"

"Get outta here, little man. I'm not going to tell you again."

And he pulled aside his nice black jacket, revealing the butt of an automatic pistol.

Excellent! This is what Li had been hoping for.

Appearing frightened, he started to turn away then spun back with his arm outstretched. He caught the young man in the chest with his fist, knocking the wind out of him. The boy staggered back and Li struck him in the nose with his open palm. He cried out and fell hard to the pavement. The guard lay there, gasping frantically for breath, blood pouring from his nose, while Li delivered a kick to his side.

Taking the gun, an extra clip of ammunition and the man's cigarettes, Li looked up and down the street. Two young women, walking arm in arm, pretended that they hadn't seen. Aside from them the street was empty. He bent down to the miserable man again and took his wristwatch too and about three hundred dollars in cash.

"If you tell anyone I did this," Li said to the guard, speaking in Putonghua. "I'll find you and kill you."

The man nodded and sopped up the blood with his sleeve.

Li started to walk away then he glanced back and returned. The man cringed. "Take your shoes off," Li snapped.

"I—"

"Shoes. Take them off."

He undid the black lace-up Kenneth Coles and pushed them toward Li. "Socks too."

The expensive black silk socks joined the shoes.

Li took off his own shoes and socks, gritty with sand and still wet, and flung them away. He put on the new ones.

Heaven, he thought happily.

Li hurried back to one of the crowded commercial streets. There he found a cheap clothing store and bought a pair of jeans, a T-shirt and a thin Nike windbreaker. He changed in the back of the store, paid for his purchases and tossed his old clothes into a trash bin. Li then went into a Chinese restaurant and ordered tea and a bowl of noodles. As he ate he pulled a folded piece of paper out of his wallet, the sheet that he'd stolen from Hongse's car at the beach.

August 8

From: Harold C. Peabody, Assistant Director of Enforcement,
*   U.S. Immigration and Naturalization Service*
To: Det. Capt. Lincoln Rhyme (Ret.)
Re: Joint INS/FBI/NYPD Task Force in the matter of Kwan Ang,
*   AKA Gui, AKA The Ghost*

This confirms our meeting at ten a.m. tomorrow to discuss the
plans for the apprehension of the above-referenced suspect. Please
see attached material for background.

Stapled to the memo was a business card, which read:

Lincoln Rhyme
345 Central Park West
New York, NY 10022

He flagged down the waitress and asked her a question.

Something about Li seemed to scare her and warn that she shouldn't help this man. But a second glance at his face must've told her that it would be worse to say no to him. She nodded and, eyes down, gave him what Li thought were excellent directions to the street known as Central Park West.

Chapter Twelve

"You look better," Amelia Sachs said. "How are you feeling?"

John Sung motioned her into the apartment. "Very sore," he said, and closed the door, joined her in the living room. He walked slowly and winced occasionally. An understandable consequence of having been shot, she supposed.

The apartment that his immigration lawyer had arranged for him to stay in was a dingy place on the Bowery, two dark rooms, containing mismatched, damaged furniture. Directly below, on the first floor, was a Chinese restaurant. The smell of sour oil and garlic permeated the place.

A compact man, with a few stray gray hairs, Sung walked hunched over from the wound. Watching his unsteady gait, she felt a poignant sympathy for him. In his life in China, as a doctor, presumably he would have enjoyed some respect from his patients and—even though he was a dissident—may have had some prestige. But here Sung had nothing. She wondered what he was going to do for a living—drive a taxi, work in a restaurant?

"I'll make tea," he said.

"No, that's all right," she said. "I can't stay long."

"I'm making some for myself anyway." There was no separate kitchen but a stove, half-size refrigerator and a rust-stained sink lined one wall of the living room. He put a cheap kettle on the sputtering flame and took a box of Lipton from the cabinet over the sink. He smelled it and gave a curious smile.

"Not what you're used to?" she asked.

"I'll go shopping later," he said ruefully.

Sachs asked, "The INS let you out on bond?"

Sung nodded. "I've formally petitioned for asylum. My lawyer tells me that most people try for it but don't qualify. But I spent two years in a reeducation camp. And I've published articles attacking Beijing for human rights violations. We downloaded some as evidence. The examining officer wouldn't guarantee anything but he said there's a good case for asylum."

"When's the hearing?" she asked.

"Next month."

Sachs watched his hands as he took two cups from the cupboard and carefully washed, dried and arranged them on a tray. There was something ceremonial about the way he did this. He tore open the bags of tea and put them in a ceramic pot and poured the hot water over them then whisked the brew with a spoon.

All for a cup of mass-market Lipton . . .

He carried the pot and cups into the living room, sat stiffly. He poured two cups and offered one to her. She rose to help him. She took the cup from his hands, which she found to be soft but very strong.

"Is there any word on the others?" he asked.

"They're in Manhattan somewhere, we think. We found a truck they stole abandoned not far from here. I'd like to ask you about them."

"Of course. What can I tell you?"

"Anything that you know. Names, descriptions . . . anything."

Sung brought the tea to his lips and took a very small sip. "There were two families—the Changs and the Wus—and a few other people who escaped. I don't remember their names. Some crewmen got off the ship too. Chang tried to save them—he was steering our raft—but the Ghost shot them."

Sachs tried her tea. It seemed to taste very different from the grocery-store beverage she was used to. My imagination, she told herself.

Sung continued. "The crew was decent to us. Before we left I heard bad rumors about the crews on the smuggling ships. But on the *Dragon* they treated us okay, gave us fresh water and food."

"Have you remembered anything about where the Changs or the Wus might've gone?"

"Nothing other than what I told you on the beach. All we heard was that we were going to be dropped at a beach on Long Island. And then trucks were going to take us to someplace in New York."

"And the Ghost? Can you tell me *anything* that might help us find him?"

He shook his head. "The little snakeheads in China—they were the Ghost's representatives—said that once we landed, we'd never see him again. And they warned us not to try to contact him."

"We think he had an assistant on board, pretending to be one of the immigrants," Sachs said. "The Ghost generally does that. Do you know who that might've been?"

"No," Sung replied. "There were several men in the hold who stayed by themselves. They didn't say much to anyone. It might've been one of them. But I never paid any attention. I don't know their names."

"Did the *crew* say anything about what the Ghost would do when he got to the country?"

Sung grew grave and seemed to be considering something. He said, "Nothing specific—they were afraid of him too, I think. But one thing . . . I don't know if it will help you but it's something I heard. The captain of the ship was talking about the Ghost and used the expression, '*Po fu chen zhou,*' about him. It translates literally 'break the caldrons and sink the boats.' You'd say, I suppose, 'There is no turning back.' It refers to a warrior from the Qin dynasty. After his troops had crossed a river to attack some enemy, that's what he ordered his men to do—break the cauldrons and sink the boats. So there'd be no possibility of either encamping or retreating. If they wanted to survive, they had to push forward and destroy the other side. The Ghost is that kind of enemy."

So he won't stop until he finds and kills the families, Sachs reflected uneasily.

Silence fell between them, interrupted by the grating sounds of traffic on Canal Street. On impulse Sachs asked, "Your wife is in China?"

Sung looked into her eyes and said evenly, "She died last year."

"I'm sorry."

"In a reeducation camp. The officials said that she got sick. But they never told me what her illness was. And there was no autopsy. I hope that she did get sick, though. Rather that, than to think she was tortured to death."

Sachs felt a chill surge through her at these words. "She was a dissident too?"

He nodded. "That's how we met. At a protest in Beijing ten years ago. On the anniversary of Tiananmen Square. Over the years she became more outspoken than me. Before she was arrested we were going to come here together, with the children." Sung's voice faded and he let the ellipses following his words explain the essential sorrow of his present life.

Finally he said, "I decided I couldn't stay in the country any longer. Politically it was dangerous, of course. But more than that, there were too many associations with my wife. I decided to come here, apply for asylum and then send for my children." A faint smile. "After my mourning is over I'll find a woman here to be the mother to my children." He shrugged and sipped tea. "But that will be in the future."

His hand went to the amulet he wore. Her eyes followed it. He noticed and took it off his neck and handed it to her.

"My good-luck charm. Maybe it works," he laughed. "It brought you to me when I was drowning."

"What is it?" she asked, holding the carving close.

"It's a carving from Qingtian, south of Fuzhou. The soapstone there is very famous. It was a present from my wife."

"It's broken," she observed, rubbing the fracture with her nail. Some of the soft stone flaked off.

"It got chipped on the rock I was holding on to when you saved me."

The design was of a monkey, sitting on his haunches. The creature seemed humanlike. Wily and shrewd. Sung explained, "He is a famous character in Chinese mythology. The Monkey King."

She handed the amulet back to him. He replaced it and the charm dropped back against his muscular, hairless chest. The bandages from the Ghost's gunshot wound were just visible under the blue work shirt. Suddenly she was keenly aware of Sung's presence, inches away from her. She could smell disinfectant soap and harsh laundry detergent from his clothes. She felt an inexplicable comfort coming from him—this man who was virtually a stranger.

She told him, "We're leaving a patrol car outside your apartment."

"To protect *me?*"

"Yes."

This amused Sung. "The public security bureau officers in China wouldn't do that—they'd only park outside your door to spy or intimidate you."

"You're not in Kansas anymore, John."

"Kansas?"

"An expression. I have to get back to Lincoln."

"To—?"

"The man I work with. Lincoln Rhyme."

She rose, felt a stab of pain in her knee.

"Wait," Sung said. He took her hand. She felt a serene power radiating from his touch. He said, "Open your mouth."

"What?" She laughed.

"Lean forward. Open your mouth."

"Why?"

"I'm a doctor. I want to look at your tongue."

Amused, she did and he examined her mouth quickly. "You have arthritis," he said, releasing her hand and sitting back.

"Chronic," she said. "How did you know that?"

"As I said, I'm a doctor. Come back and I will treat you."

She laughed. "I've been to dozens of doctors."

"Western medicine, Western doctors, they have their place. Chinese medicine is best for curing chronic pains and discomfort—problems that seem to arise for no apparent reason. There always is a reason, though. There are things I can do that will help. I'm indebted to you. You saved my life. I would be shamed if I didn't repay that."

"That was two big guys in black rubber suits."

"No, no, if not for you I would have drowned. I know that. So, please, you will come back and let me help you?"

She hesitated for a moment.

But then, as if prodding her to act, a bolt of pain shot through her knee. She gave no outward reaction to the twinge but kept a placid face as she took out her pen and gave Sung her cell phone number.

Standing on Central Park West, Sonny Li was confused.

What was with the public security bureau here? Hongse drove that fast yellow car, bang, bang, like a TV cop, and now, it seemed, the officers were hunting the Ghost from a building as luxurious as *this*? No PSB officer in China could afford such an apartment, even the most corrupt (and there were some pretty damn corrupt public security officers).

Li tossed his cigarette away, spat on the grass and then, with his head down, walked quickly across the street into the alley that led to the back of the building. Even the alley was spotless! In Li's home of Liu Guoyuan—which was richer than most towns in China—an alley like this would have been piled high with trash and discarded appliances. He paused, looked around the corner and found the back door of the building open. A young man, with perfectly trimmed blond hair, wearing dark slacks, a light shirt and a flowery tie, stepped out. He carted two green plastic trash bags with him, which he carried to a large blue metal container and tossed inside. The man glanced around the alley, picked up a few stray pieces of paper and threw those out too. He brushed his hands together then returned inside, pulling the door closed. It didn't, however, latch.

Thank you, sir.

Sonny Li slipped into the basement, smelling the powerful musty scent of the place, listening for sounds. The young man's footsteps ascended the stairs. Li waited behind a stack of large cartons for him to return but the man had apparently gone on to other chores. There were creaks from upstairs and the sound of running water. Li glanced into cardboard boxes on the floor. Some were filled with clothes, others seemed to be memorabilia. Plaques, awards, degrees from schools. University of Illy-noise, Li pronounced the English to himself. The American Institute of Forensic Science Achievement Award, a Federal Bureau of Investigation Letter of Commendation signed by the director himself. Dozens of others.

The recipient of all of these commendations was Lincoln Rhyme.

The blond man was apparently not bringing any more trash downstairs and Li left his hiding place. Up a flight of stairs, walking slowly. The wood was old and he stepped carefully to avoid creaks. He paused behind the door at the top and pushed it open slightly.

Then loud footsteps came toward him, several people, it seemed like. Li pressed himself back against the wall, beside some mops and brooms.

Voices calling: "We'll be back in a couple of hours, Linc. We'll have forensics call . . ." Some other things that Li couldn't understand.

The footsteps stopped and Li heard another man ask, "Hey, Lincoln, you want one of us to stay?"

Another voice, irritated, responded. "Stay? Why would I want some-body to *stay*? I want to get some *work* done. And I don't want any inter-ruptions!"

"I'm just saying it might be better to have somebody with a weapon. The Ghost's fucking vanished. His assistant too. You said yourself to watch our backs."

"But how's he going to find *me*? How's he going to know where on God's green earth I live? I don't need anyone to baby-sit me. I need you to get me that goddamn information I wanted."

"Okay, okay."

From above: the sounds of people walking, a door opening and clos-ing. Then silence. Sonny Li listened for a moment. He pushed the door open fully and glanced out. In front of him was a long corridor that led to the front door, the one through which the men—presumably other secu-rity bureau officers—had just left.

To Li's right was an entryway to what must have been a living room. Staying close to the baseboards to keep his footsteps quiet, Li moved through this hallway. He paused outside the living room then looked in quickly. An odd sight: the room was filled with scientific equipment, com-puters, tables, charts and books of all kinds. Which was the last thing one would expect to find in this fine old building.

But what was more curious was the dark-haired man sitting in a com-plicated red wheelchair in the middle of the room, leaning forward, look-ing at a computer screen, talking to himself, it seemed. Then Li realized that, no, the man was talking into a microphone near his mouth. The mike must have been sending signals to the computer, telling it what to do. The screen responded to his commands.

So, was this creature Lincoln Rhyme?

Well, it hardly mattered who he was and, besides, Li had no time to speculate. He didn't know when the other officers would return.

Lifting the gun, Sonny Li stepped into the room.

Chapter Thirteen

One meter forward. Another. Sonny Li was a slight man and he moved silently.

Sneaking closer to the back of the wheelchair, looking on the tabletops for any evidence or information about the Ghost. He would—

Li had no idea where the men came from.

One of them—far taller than Li—was black as coal and was wearing a suit and bright yellow shirt. He'd been hiding against the wall inside the room. In a seamless motion he swept the gun from Li's hand and pressed a pistol against his temple.

Another man, short and fat, flung Li to the ground and knelt on his back, pushing the air from his lungs as sharp pain coursed through his belly and sides. Handcuffs were ratcheted on fast as an eel.

"English?" the black man asked.

Li was too shocked to answer.

"I'ma ask you once more, skel. Do. You. Speak. English?"

A Chinese man, who'd also been hiding in the room, stepped forward. He wore a stylish dark suit and had a badge dangling from a chain around his neck. He asked the same question in Chinese. It was the Cantonese dialect but Li was able to understand.

"Yes," Li responded breathlessly. "I talk English."

The man in the wheelchair spun around. "Let's see what we've caught."

The black man hauled him to his feet, nearly off the ground, ignoring Li's moans and gasps of pain. Holding him with one hand he began patting his pockets with the other. "Listen here, you little skel, I find any needles in your pockets? I find anything that's gonna poke me unpleasantly?"

"I—"

"Answer the question now and tell the truth. 'Cause if I get poked, you gonna get poked too." He shook Li by the collar and shouted, "Needles?"

"You saying, drug stuff? No, no."

The man pulled the cash out of his pockets, his cigarettes, ammunition, the sheet of paper he'd stolen from the beach. "Ah, looks like this boy here borrowed something he shoudn'ta from Aye-melia. An' while she was busy savin' lives, no less. Shame on him."

"That's how he found us," Lincoln Rhyme said, eyeing the sheet of paper with his card attached. "I *was* wondering."

The trim blond man appeared in the doorway. "So you got him," he said without surprise. And Li understood then that this young man had spotted him in the alley when he'd taken out the bags, and had left the door open on purpose. To draw him upstairs. And the other men had made a noisy show of departing, pretending to leave Lincoln alone.

So you got him. . . .

The man in the wheelchair noticed the disgust in Li's eyes. He said, "That's right—my observant Thom here spotted you when he took the trash out. And then . . . " He nodded at the computer screen and said, "Command, security. Back door."

On the computer screen a video image of the back door of the building and the alley popped up.

Li suddenly understood how the Coast Guard had located the *Fuzhou Dragon* floating in the endless ocean: this man. Lincoln Rhyme.

"Judges of hell," he muttered.

The fat officer laughed. "Don'tcha just hate days like this?"

Then the black man pulled Li's wallet out of his pocket. He squeezed the damp leather. "Our li'l skel here been swimming, I *de*-duce." He opened the wallet and handed it to the Chinese officer.

The fat man pulled out a radio and spoke into it. "Mel, Alan, come on back in. We got him."

Two men, probably the ones Li had heard leaving a few moments ago, returned. A balding, slight man ignored Li and walked to a computer, began to type frantically on it. The other was a man in a suit with striking red hair. He blinked in surprise and said, "Wait, that's not the Ghost."

"His missing assistant then," Rhyme said. "His *bangshou.*"

"No," the red-haired man said. "I know him. I've seen him before."

Li realized that there was something familiar about this man too.

"Seen him?" the black officer asked.

"Some of us from INS were at a meeting last year in the Fuzhou public security bureau—about human smuggling. He was there. He was one of them."

"One of who?" the fat officer grumbled.

The Chinese officer gave a laugh and held up an ID card from Li's wallet, comparing Li's picture with his face. "One of *us*," he said. "He's a cop."

Rhyme too examined the card and the driver's license, both of which had pictures of the man. They gave his name as Li Kangmei, a detective with the Liu Guoyuan Public Security Bureau.

The criminalist said to Dellray, "See if any of our people in China can confirm it." A tiny cell phone appeared in the agent's large hand. And he started punching keys.

Looking over the diminutive man, Rhyme asked, "'Li' is your first or last name?"

"Last. And I not like 'Kangmei,'" he explained. "I use Sonny. Western name."

"What're you doing here?" Rhyme asked.

"Ghost, he kill three people in my town last year. He had meeting, I'm saying. Had meeting with little snakehead in restaurant. You know what is little snakehead?"

Rhyme nodded. "Go on."

"The little snakehead cheating him. Big fight. Ghost kill him but woman and her daughter also killed and old man sitting on bench. Got in way and Ghost just kill them to escape, I'm saying."

"Bystanders?"

Li nodded. "We try to arrest him but he has very powerful . . ." He sought for a word. Finally he turned to Eddie Deng and said, "*Guanxi.*"

"That means connections," Deng explained. "You pay off the right people and you get good *guanxi.*"

Li nodded. "No one willing testify against him. Then evidence in shooting disappear from headquarters office. My boss lose interest. Case got collectivized."

"Collectivized?" Sellitto asked.

Li smiled grimly. "When something ruined, we say it got collectivized. In old days, Mao's day, when government turn business or farm into commune or collective, it fail pretty fuck fast."

"But," Rhyme offered, "the case wasn't collectivized to you."

"No," Li said, his eyes hard ebony disks. "He kill people in my town. I want make sure he come to trial."

Dellray asked, "How'dja get on the ship?"

"I have lots informants in Fuzhou. Last month I find out Ghost kill two people in Taiwan, big guys, important guys, and was leaving from China for month until Taiwan NSB stop looking for him. He going to south of France then taking immigrants from Vyborg in Russia to New York on *Fuzhou Dragon.*"

Rhyme laughed. This small, scruffy man's information had been better than the FBI's and Interpol's combined.

"So," Li continued, "I go undercover. Become piglet—immigrant."

Sellitto asked, "You find out anything about the Ghost? Where he stays here? Associates of his?"

"No, nobody talk to me much. Got on deck when crew not looking—mostly for puking." He shook his head, apparently at the unpleasant memory of the voyage. "But not get close to Ghost."

Coe said, "But what were you going to do? We wouldn't extradite him to China."

Perplexed, Li said, "Why I want him extradited? You not listen. *Guanxi*, I'm saying. In China they let him go. I going to arrest him when we land. Then give him *your* public security bureau."

Coe laughed. "You're serious, aren't you."

"Yes. I was going to do."

"He had his *bangshou* with him, the crew of the ship. Little snake-heads to meet and greet here. They would've killed you."

"Risky, you saying? Sure, sure. But that our *job,* right? Always risk." He reached for the cigarettes Dellray had relieved him of.

Thom said, "No smoking here."

"What you mean?"

"No smoking."

"Why not?"

"Because you can't," the aide said firmly.

"That craziest thing. You not make joke?"

"No."

"Subway stupid enough. But this is *house*, I'm saying."

"Yes, a house where you can't smoke."

"Very fuck," Li said. He grudgingly put the pack away.

A faint beeping from across the room. Mel Cooper turned to his computer. He read for a moment and then spun the screen around so that everybody could look. The FBI's Singapore office had sent an email confirmation that Li Kangmei was indeed a detective in the Liu Guoyuan Public Security Bureau of the People's Republic of China. He was presently listed as being on undercover assignment but his office would say no more about it. A picture of Li in a navy-blue uniform accompanied the message. It was clearly the man in the room before them.

Li then explained how the Ghost had scuttled the *Dragon*. Sam Chang and Wu Qichen and their families, along with Dr. Sung, several other immigrants and the baby of a woman on board the ship got away in a life raft. Everyone else drowned. "Sam Chang—he become leader on raft. Good man, smart. Save my life. Pick me up when Ghost shooting people. Wu was father of second family. Wu smart too but not balanced. Liver-spleen disharmony."

Deng saw Rhyme's frown and said, "Chinese medicine. Hard to explain."

Li continued, "Wu too emotion, I'm saying. Does impulse things."

Even the FBI's crack behavioral profiling was out of Rhyme's comfort zone, being the physical scientist that he was; he had no time whatsoever for disharmonious spleens. "Let's stick with facts," he said.

Li then told them how the raft hit the rocks and he, Sung and the others were washed overboard. They were swept down the shoreline. By the time Li made it back to where the raft had beached the Ghost had killed two of the immigrants. "I hurry to arrest him but by time I get there, he gone. I hide in bushes on other side of road. I saw woman with red hair rescue one man."

"John Sung," Rhyme said.

"Dr. Sung." Li nodded. "Sat next to me on raft. He okay?"

"The Ghost shot him but he'll be all right. Amelia—the woman you saw—is interviewing him now."

"Hongse, I call her. Hey, pretty girl. Sexy, I'm saying."

Sellitto and Rhyme shared a humorous glance. Rhyme was picturing the consequences if Li had said that to Sachs's face.

Li pointed around the town house. "I get address from her car and come here, thinking maybe I get stuff that lead me to Ghost. Information, I'm saying. Evidence."

"Steal it?" Coe asked.

"Yes, sure," he said unabashedly.

"Why'd you do that, you little skel?" Dellray asked menacingly, using a popular cop word, short for "skeleton," meaning basically: worthless little snitch.

"*Have* to get it for myself. Because, hey, you not let me help you, right? You just send me back. And I going to arrest him. 'Collar,' right? You say 'collar.'"

Coe said, "Well, you're right—you're *not* helping us. You may be a cop in China. But here you're just one more fucking undocumented. You *are* going back."

Eyes flashing angrily, Sonny Li stepped close to Coe, who towered over the small man.

Sellitto sighed and tugged Li back by the shirt. "Naw, none of that shit."

Amused at the man's bravado, Coe reached for his cuffs. "Li, you're under arrest for entering the United States—"

But Lincoln Rhyme said, "No, I want him."

"What?" the agent asked in shock.

"He'll be a consultant. Like me."

"Impossible."

"Anybody who goes to this much trouble to nail a perp—I want him working on our side."

"You bet I help, Loaban. Do lots, I'm saying."

"What'd you call me?"

Li explained to Rhyme, "'Loaban.' It mean 'boss.' You got keep me. I can help. I know how Ghost think. We from same world, him and me. I in gang when I boy, like him. And spent lots time as undercover officer, working docks in Fuzhou."

"No way," Coe blurted. "For Christ's sake, he's an undocumented. As soon as we turn our back he'll just run off, get drunk and go to a gambling parlor."

Rhyme wondered if a kung fu match was about to break out. But this time Li ignored Coe and spoke in a reasonable voice. "In my country we got four classes people. Not like rich and poor, stuff like you got here. In China what you *do* more important than money you got. And know what highest honor is? Working for country, working for people. That what I do and I one fuck good cop, I'm saying."

"They're all on the take over there," Coe muttered.

"I not on take, okay?" He then grinned. "Not on important case like this."

Coe said, "And how do we know he's not really on the Ghost's payroll?"

Li laughed. "Hey, how we know *you* not working for him?"

"Fuck you," Coe said. He was furious.

The young INS agent's problem, Rhyme assessed, was that he was too emotional to be an effective law enforcer. The criminalist often heard contempt in his voice when he spoke about the "undocumenteds." He seemed affronted that they would break federal law to sneak into this country and had suggested several times that immigrants were motivated essentially by greed to come here, not by a love of freedom or democracy.

Apart from his derisive attitude toward the aliens, however, he had a troubling personal stake in collaring the Ghost. Several years ago Coe had been stationed in Taipei, the capital of Taiwan, running undercover agents in mainland China, trying to identify major snakeheads. During an investigation of the Ghost, one of his informants, a woman, had disappeared and presumably been killed. Later it was learned that the woman had two young children but had so desperately needed money that she was willing to snitch on the Ghost—the INS never would have used her as an informant if they'd known that she had children. Coe was reprimanded—suspended for six months. He'd become obsessed with collaring the Ghost.

But to be a good cop you've got to tuck those personal feelings away. Detachment is absolutely necessary. This was a variation on Rhyme's rule about giving up the dead.

Dellray said, "Listen up. Ain't in the mood t'put you kiddies in a time-out corner so juss settle down. Li stays with us for's long as Lincoln wants him. Make it happen, Coe. Call somebody at the State Department and get him a temporary visa. We all together on that?"

Coe muttered, "No, I'm not all together on that. You can't have one of them on a task force."

"'Them'?" Dellray asked, pivoting on a very long foot. "Who exactly might 'them' be?"

"Undocumenteds."

The tall agent clicked his tongue. "Now, you know, Coe, that word's kinda like marbles in a blender to me. Doesn't sound *respectful*. Doesn't sound *nice*. Specially the way you say it."

"Well, as you folks from the bureau've made clear all along, this isn't really an INS case. Keep him if you want. But I'm not taking any heat for it."

"You make good decision," Sonny Li said to Rhyme. "I help lots, Loaban." Li walked over to the table and picked up the gun he'd been carrying.

"Nup, nup, nup," Dellray said. "Get your hands offa that."

"Hey, I a cop. Like you."

"No, you *ain't* a cop like me or any-single-solitary soul else here. No guns."

"Okay, okay. Keep gun for now, Heise."

"What's that?" Dellray snapped. "Heise?"

"Means black. Hey, hey, don't get offense. Nothing bad, nothing bad."

"Well, can it."

"Sure, I can it. Sure."

"Welcome on board, Sonny," Rhyme said. Then glanced at the clock. It was just noon. Six hours had passed since the Ghost began his relentless pursuit of the immigrants. He could be closing in on the poor families even now. "Okay, let's start on the evidence."

"Sure, sure," Li said, suddenly distracted. "But I need cigarette first. Come on, Loaban. You let me?"

"All right," Rhyme snapped. "But outside. And for Christ's sake, somebody go with him."

Chapter Fourteen

Wu Qichen wiped the sweat off his wife's forehead.

Shivering, burning with fever, soaking with sweat, she lay on a mattress in the bedroom of their tiny apartment.

The basement rooms were down an alley off Canal Street in the heart of Chinatown. They'd been provided by the broker that Jimmy Mah had sent them to—a robber, Wu had thought angrily. The rent was ridiculous, as was the fee the slimy man had demanded. The apartment stank, the place was virtually unfurnished and roaches roamed the floor boldly— even now, in the diffuse noon light bleeding in through the greasy windows.

He studied his wife with concern. The raging headache Yong-Ping had suffered on board the *Dragon*, the lethargy, the chills and sweats, which he'd believed were seasickness, had persisted even after they'd landed. She was afflicted with something else.

His wife opened her fever-glazed eyes. "If I die . . ." she whispered.

"You won't die," her husband said.

But Wu wasn't sure that he believed his own words. He remembered Dr. John Sung in the hold of the *Dragon* and wished he'd asked the man's opinion on his wife's condition; the doctor had treated several of the immigrants for various maladies but Wu had been afraid that he'd charge him money to examine Yong-Ping.

"Sleep," Wu said sternly. "You need rest. You'll be fine if you rest. Why won't you do that?"

"If I die you must find a woman. Someone to take care of the children."

"You won't die."

"Where is my son?" Yong-Ping asked.

"Lang is in the living room."

He glanced through the doorway and saw the boy on the couch and teenage Chin-Mei hanging laundry on a line strung through the room. After they'd arrived the family had taken turns showering then dressing in the clean clothes that Wu had bought at a discount store on Canal Street. After some food—which Yong-Ping had not taken a single bite of—Chin-Mei had directed her brother to the TV set and washed their saltwater-encrusted clothing in the kitchen sink. This is what she was now hanging up to dry.

Wu's wife looked around the room, squinting, as if trying to remember where she was. She gave up and rested her head on the pillow. "Where . . . where are we?"

"We're in Chinatown, in Manhattan of New York."

"But . . ." She frowned as his words belatedly registered in her feverish brain. "The Ghost, husband. We can't stay here. It's not safe. Sam Chang said we should not stay."

"Ah, the Ghost . . ." He gestured dismissively. "He has gone back to China."

"No," Yong-Ping said, "I don't think so. I'm scared for our children. We have to leave. We have to get as far away from here as we can."

Wu pointed out: "No snakehead would risk being captured or shot just to find a few immigrants who'd escaped. Are you foolish enough to think that?"

"Please, husband. Sam Chang said—"

"Forget Chang. He's a coward." He snapped, "We're staying." His anger at her disobedience was tempered by the sight of the poor woman and the pain she must be suffering. He added softly, "I'm going out. I'm going to get you some medicine."

She didn't respond and he rose and walked into the living room.

He glanced at the children, who looked uneasily toward the room where their mother lay.

"Is she all right?" the teenage girl asked.

"Yes. She'll be fine. I'll be back in a half hour," he said. "I'll get some medicine."

"Wait, Father," Chin-Mei said uncertainly, looking down.

"What?"

"May I come with you?" the girl asked.

"No, you will stay with your mother and brother."

"But . . ."

"What?"

"There is something I need."

A fashion magazine? he thought cynically. Makeup? Hair spray? She wants me to spend our survival money on her pretty face. "What?"

"Please let me come with you. I'll buy it myself." She was blushing fiercely.

"What do you want?" he demanded.

"I need some things for . . ." she whispered, head down.

"For what?" he asked harshly. "Answer me."

She swallowed. "For my time. You know. Pads."

With a shock Wu suddenly understood. He looked away from the girl and gestured angrily toward the bathroom. "Use something in there."

"I can't. It's uncomfortable."

Wu was furious. It was his *wife's* job to take care of matters like this. No man he ever knew bought those . . . things. "All right!" he snapped. "All right. I'll buy you what you need." He refused to ask her what kind she wanted. He'd get the first box of whatever was in the closest store. She'd have to use that. He stepped outside and locked the door behind him.

Wu Qichen walked down the busy streets of Chinatown, hearing a cacophony of languages—Minnanhua, Cantonese, Putonghua, Vietnamese and Korean. English too, laced with more accents and dialects than he'd ever known existed.

He gazed at the stores and shops, the piles of merchandise, the huge high-rises ringing the city. New York seemed ten times bigger than Hong Kong and a hundred times the size of Fuzhou.

I'm scared for our children. We have to leave. We have to get as far away from here as we can. . . .

But Wu Qichen had no intention of leaving Manhattan. The forty-year-old man had nurtured a dream all his life and he wouldn't let his wife's sickness or the faint threat from a bully of a snakehead deter him from it. Wu Qichen was going to become a wealthy man, the richest ever in his family.

In his twenties he'd been a bellboy then a junior assistant manager at the Paradise Hotel on Hundong Road, near Hot Springs Park, in the heart of Fuzhou, waiting on rich Chinese and Europeans. Wu had decided then that he would be a successful businessman. He worked hard at the hotel and, even though he gave his parents a quarter of his income, he managed to save enough to buy a sundries and souvenir shop near the famous statue of Mao Zedong on Gutian Road with his two bothers. With the money they made from that store they bought one grocery then two more. They intended to run the businesses for several years and save as much money as they could then buy a building and make their fortune at real estate.

But Wu Qichen made one mistake.

The economic face of China was changing drastically. Economic free zones were prospering and even the top politicos had been speaking favorably of private business—the Chinese leader Deng Xiaoping himself had said, "To be wealthy is glorious." But Wu neglected to remember the first rule of Chinese life: that the CCP—the Chinese Communist Party— runs the show. Wu was bluntly vocal in his call for closer economic ties with Taiwan, ending the iron rice bowl system of guaranteed employment regardless of productivity, and cracking down on party and government officials' taking bribes and levying arbitrary taxes on businesses. Ironically Wu didn't even care about what he advocated; his point was merely to attract the attention of Western trading partners—in Europe and America—who, he dreamed, would come to *him* with money to invest because he was the voice of the new Chinese economy.

But it wasn't the West who listened to the skinny man; it was the cadres and secretaries of the Communist Party. Suddenly governmental inspectors began appearing at the Wus' stores, finding dozens of violations of health and safety codes—many of which they simply made up on the spot. Unable to pay the crushing fines, the brothers were soon broke.

As shamed as he was by his lowered station, though, Wu refused to give up on his goal of becoming rich. And so, seduced by the fat opportunities in the Beautiful Country, Wu Qichen had bundled up his family and risked immigrating illegally. He would become a landlord in Chinatown. He would ride to work in a limousine and—when, finally, he was able to travel back to China—he would walk into the Paradise Hotel and stay in the grandest suite, the penthouse, the very room to which as a young man he had carried hundreds of bags.

No, his dreams had been delayed too long; the Ghost would not drive him from the city of money.

Wu now found a Chinese medicine store. He stepped inside and talked to the herbalist about his wife's condition. The doctor listened carefully and diagnosed deficient *qi*—the life spirit—and obstructed blood, both of which were aggravated by excessive cold. He put together a bundle of herbs for Wu, who reluctantly paid the huge bill of eighteen dollars, furious once again that he'd been taken advantage of.

Leaving the herbalist, he continued down the street to a Chinese grocery store. He stepped inside quickly, before his courage broke, found a basket and grabbed some groceries he didn't need. He swooped past the drug section, picking up a box of women's pads for his daughter. He walked quickly to the counter and kept his eyes on a glass container of ginseng root throughout the entire transaction. The gray-haired woman rang up the purchase and, though she didn't smile or call attention to his purchase, Wu knew she was laughing at him. He left the store with his head down and his face as red as the Chinese flag.

Wu turned in the direction of his apartment but after five minutes of fast walking he slowed and began meandering through the side streets. He was concerned about his wife, of course, and about leaving his children but, gods of heaven, this day had been a nightmare. He'd nearly been killed in a shipwreck, he'd lost all his possessions, had been cheated by Jimmy Mah and the real estate broker. And, worst of all, he'd endured the shame and humiliation of buying what was in the bag in his hand right now. He decided that he needed some diversion, some male companionship.

It took only a few minute to find what he'd sought: a Fujianese gambling den. After showing his money to the guard in front he was admitted.

He sat silently for a time, playing thirteen points, smoking and drinking some *baijiu*. He won a little money and began to feel better. Another cup of the powerful, clear spirits, then another and finally he relaxed—making sure, though, that the grocery bag was completely hidden beneath his chair.

Eventually he struck up a conversation with the men around him and, from the thirty dollars he won—a huge sum to him—he bought them drinks. Drunk and in good humor, he told a joke and a number of the men laughed hard. With the conspiratorial tone of men alone they all shared stories of disobedient wives and disrespectful children, the places they now lived and what jobs they had—or were seeking.

Wu lifted his cup. "Here is to Zai Chen," he announced drunkenly. This was the god of wealth and one of the most revered throughout China. Wu believed that he had a special connection with this folk deity.

The men all tossed back their drinks.

"You're new here," an old man said. "When did you come over?"

Pleased that he had the spotlight among his equals, Wu bragged in a whisper, "Just this morning. On the ship that sank."

"The *Fuzhou Dragon*?" one man asked, his eyebrow raised. "It was on the news. They said the seas were terrible."

"Ah," Wu said, "the waves were fifteen meters high! The snakehead tried to kill us all but I got a dozen people out of the hold. And then I had to swim underwater to cut a life raft off the deck. I nearly drowned. But I managed to get us to shore."

"You did that yourself?"

He looked down sadly. "I couldn't save them all. But I tried."

Another asked him, "Is your family all right?"

"Yes," Wu answered drunkenly.

"Are you in the neighborhood?"

"Up the street."

"What is the Ghost like?" one man asked.

"He's all bluff. And a coward. He's never without a gun. If he'd put it aside and fought like a man—with a knife—I could have killed him easily."

Then Wu fell silent as Sam Chang's words began to echo in his mind. He realized he probably should not be saying these things. He changed the subject. "Can someone tell me? There's a statue I want to see. Maybe you can tell me where it is."

The man nearest Wu asked, "Statue? Which one? There are statues everywhere here."

"It's very famous. It's of a woman and she's holding her accounts."

"Accounts?" another man asked.

"Yes," Wu explained. "You see her in movies about the Beautiful Country. She's on an island somewhere, holding a lantern in one hand and a book of her business accounts in the other. She's holding the torch so she can read her register at any time of the night or day and see how much money she has. Is that here in New York?"

"Yes, she's here," one man said but he began laughing. Several of the others did too. Wu joined in though he had no idea what was so funny.

"You go down to a place called Battery Park and take a boat out to see the statue."

"I will do that."

Another man laughed. "To the lady of accounts." They all emptied their glasses and resumed the game.

Chapter Fifteen

Amelia Sachs returned from the witness's apartment in Chinatown and Rhyme was amused to see the harsh look with which she studied Sonny Li when he announced with consummate pride that he was a "detective with public security bureau in People's Republic of China."

"You don't say," she responded coolly.

Sellitto explained to her about the Chinese cop's presence.

"You check him out?" she asked, closely studying the man, who was nearly a foot shorter than she.

Li spoke before the detective could. "They checked me out good, Hongse. I'm clean."

"Hoankseh? What the hell's that?" she barked.

He held up his hands defensively. "Means 'red.' Only that. Nothing bad. Your hair, I'm saying. I saw you on beach, saw your hair." Rhyme believed that there was the dabbling of a flirt in his crooked-tooth smile.

Eddie Deng confirmed that the word meant only the color; there was no secondary, derogatory meaning to it.

"He's okay, Amelia," Dellray confirmed.

"Though he oughta be in a holding cell," Coe muttered.

Sachs shrugged and turned to the Chinese cop. "What'd you mean about the beach? You were spying on me?"

"Not say anything then. Afraid you send me back. Wanted chance to get Ghost too."

Sachs rolled her eyes.

"Wait, Hongse, here." He held out some crumpled dollars.

She frowned. "What's that?"

"On beach, your bag, I'm saying. I need money. I borrow it."

Sachs looked into her purse, snapped it shut loudly. "Jesus Christ." A glance at Sellitto. "Can I collar him now?"

"No, no, I am paying back. Not thief. Here. Look, all there. Ten dollar extra even."

"Ten *extra*?"

"Interest, I'm saying."

"Where'd you get it?" she asked cynically. "I mean, who'd you steal *this* from?"

"No, no, it okay."

"Well, there's a defense for you. 'It's okay.'" Sachs sighed, took the money and handed back the questionable ten.

She then told the team what the witness—John Sung—had said. Rhyme relaxed a bit more about his decision to keep Sonny Li when he heard that Sung confirmed the information Li had given them, bolstering the Chinese cop's credibility. He was troubled, though, when Sachs mentioned John Sung's story about the captain's assessment of the Ghost.

"'Break the cauldrons and sink the boats,'" she said, explaining the meaning of the expression.

"'*Po fu chen zhou*,'" Li said, nodding grimly. "That describe Ghost good. Never relax or retreat until you win."

Sachs then began helping Mel Cooper log in the evidence from the van, cataloging it and carefully filling out chain of custody cards to show at trial that the evidence was accounted for and hadn't been tampered with. She was bagging the bloody rag she'd found in the van when Cooper looked at the sheet of newsprint on the table underneath the bag she was holding. He frowned. The tech pulled on latex gloves and extracted the bloody rag from the plastic. Using a magnifying glass, he looked it over carefully.

"This's odd, Lincoln," Cooper said.

"'Odd'? What does *odd* mean? Give me details, give me anomalies. Give me specifics!"

"I missed these fragments. Look." He held the cloth over a large sheet of newsprint and caressed it carefully with a brush.

Rhyme couldn't see anything.

"Some kind of porous stone," Cooper said, leaning over the sheet with a magnifying glass. "How could I miss it?" The tech seemed disheartened.

Where had the fragments come from? Had they been embedded in a fold? What were they?

"Oh, hell," Sachs muttered, looking at her hands.

"What?" Rhyme asked.

Blushing, she held up her fingers. "That was from me. I picked it up without gloves."

"Without gloves?" Rhyme asked, an edge in his voice. This was a serious error by a crime scene tech. Apart from the fact that the rag contained blood, which might be tainted with HIV or hepatitis, she'd contaminated the evidence. As head of the forensic unit at the NYPD, Lincoln Rhyme had fired people for this type of lapse.

"I'm sorry," Sachs said. "I know what it's from. John . . . Dr. Sung was showing me this amulet he wore. It was chipped and I guess I picked at it with my nail."

"Are you sure that's it?" Rhyme demanded.

Li nodded and said, "I remember . . . Sung let children on *Fuzhou Dragon* play with it. Qingtian soapstone. Worth some money, I'm saying. Good luck." He added, "It was of Monkey. Very famous in China."

Eddie Deng nodded. "Sure, the Monkey King . . . He was a mythological figure. My father'd read me stories about him."

But Rhyme wasn't interested in any myths. He was trying to catch a killer and save some lives.

And trying to figure out why Sachs had made a mistake of this magnitude.

A rookie's mistake.

The mistake of someone who's distracted. And what *exactly* is on her mind? he wondered.

"Throw out the—" he began.

"I'm sorry," she repeated.

"Throw out that top sheet of newsprint," Rhyme said evenly. "Let's move on."

As the tech tore off the sheet of paper his computer beeped. "Incoming." He read the screen. "Okay, we've got the blood types back. All samples're from the same person—presumably from the injured woman. It's type AB negative and the Barr Body test confirms that it's a woman's blood."

"Up on the wall, Thom," Rhyme called. And the aide wrote.

Before he was finished Mel Cooper's computer summoned them again. "It's the AFIS search results."

They were discouraged to find that the search of the fingerprints Sachs had collected came back negative. But as he examined the prints, which were digitized and sitting on the screen in front of them, Rhyme observed something unusual about the clearest prints they'd lifted—from the pipe used to break into the van. They knew these were the prints of Sam Chang because they matched a few lifted from the outboard motor and Li had confirmed that Chang had piloted the raft to shore. "Look at those lines," he said.

"Whatcha see, Lincoln?" Dellray asked.

Rhyme said nothing to the agent but, wheeling close to the screen, ordered, "Command, cursor down . . . stop. Cursor left . . . stop." The arrow of the cursor on the screen stopped on a line—an indentation on the pad of the index finger of Chang's right hand. There were similar ones on his middle finger and his thumb—as if Chang had been tightly gripping a thin cord.

"What is that?" Rhyme wondered aloud.

"Callus? A scar?" Eddie Deng offered.

Mel Cooper offered, "Never seen that before."

"Maybe it's a cut or wound of some kind."

"Maybe a rope burn," Sachs suggested.

"No, that'd be a blister. It must be a wound of some kind. Did you see any scars on Chang's hands?" Rhyme asked Li.

"No. I not see."

Indentations, calluses and scars on fingers and palms can be revealing about the professions or hobbies of the people who leave the prints—or on the actual fingers themselves in the case of suspects or victims. These are less useful nowadays where the only physical skill required by so many professions is keyboarding or jotting notes. Still, people who are in the manual trades, for instance, or who play certain sports frequently develop distinctive markings on their hands.

Rhyme had no idea what this pattern meant but some additional information might reveal that. He instructed Thom to write the observation down on the board. He then took a call from special agent Tobe Geller, one of the FBI's computer and electronics gurus, presently assigned to the Manhattan office. He'd completed his analysis of the Ghost's cell phone, which Sachs had found in the second raft at Easton Beach. The criminalist transferred the call to the speakerphone and a moment later Geller's animated voice said, "Now, let me tell you, this is an *excessively* interesting phone."

Rhyme didn't know the young man well but he remembered curly hair, an easy disposition and a consuming passion for anything containing microchips.

"Howsat?" Dellray asked.

"First of all, don't get your hopes up. It's virtually untraceable. We call 'em 'hot phones.' The memory chip's been deactivated so that the phone doesn't record the last call dialed or incoming calls—the log features are out completely. And it's a satellite phone—you can call anywhere in the world and you don't need to go through local service providers. The signals are relayed through a government network in Fuzhou. The Ghost or somebody working for him hacked into the system to activate it."

Dellray snapped, "Well, let's juss call somebody in the People's fuckin' Republic and tell 'em this bad guy's using their system."

"We tried that. But the Chinese position is that nobody can hack their phone system so we must be mistaken. Thank you for your interest."

"Even if it means helpin' collar the Ghost?"

Geller said, "I mentioned Kwan Ang by name. They still weren't interested. Meaning they were probably paid off."

Guanxi . . .

Rhyme thanked the young agent and they hung up. Score one for the Ghost, the criminalist thought angrily.

They were somewhat more successful with the firearms database. Mel Cooper found that the shell casings matched one of two weapons, both of them dating back nearly fifty years: a Russian Tokarev 7.62mm automatic was one type. "But," Cooper continued, "I'm betting he was using the Model 51, a Chinese version of the Tokarev. Virtually the same gun."

"Yeah, yeah," Sonny Li said. "Gotta be 51, I'm saying. I had Tokarev but lost it in ocean. More peoples in China got 51's."

"Ammunition?" Rhyme asked. "He might need to replenish it here somewhere." He was thinking that if the ammo was rare they might stake out the most likely places the Ghost would go to purchase more.

But Cooper shook his head. "You can buy the shells in any good-sized gun shop."

Damn.

A messenger arrived with an envelope. Sellitto took it and tore the end off. He extracted a handful of photographs. He glanced at Rhyme with a raised eyebrow. "The three bodies the Coast Guard recovered from the water. About a mile offshore. Two shot. One drowned."

The photos were facial shots of the dead men, eyes partially open but glazed. One had a hole in his temple. The other two showed no sign of visible injuries. There were fingerprint cards too.

"Those two," Li said, "they crew members. Other guy, one of immigrants. Down in hold with us. Don't know name."

"Pin them up," Rhyme said, "and run the prints through AFIS."

Sellitto taped them to the board under the GHOSTKILL heading and Rhyme realized that the room had gone silent as the members of the team stared at the macabre additions to the evidence charts. He supposed that Coe and Deng had little experience with corpses. That was one thing about crime scene detail, he recalled: how fast one becomes immune to the countenance of death.

Sonny Li continued to gaze at the photos silently for a moment. He muttered something in Chinese.

"What was that?" Rhyme asked.

He glanced at the criminalist. "I said, 'judges of hell.' Just expression. We have myth in China—ten judges of hell decide where your name go in *Register of Living and Dead.* Judges decide when you born and when you die. Everybody in world, name is in register."

Rhyme thought momentarily of recent doctors' appointments and of his upcoming operation. He wondered exactly where his own name was entered in *The Register of the Living and the Dead.* . . .

The silence was then broken by another beep from the computer. Mel Cooper glanced at the screen. "Got the make of the driver's car at the beach. BMW X5. It's one of those fancy four-by-fours." He added, "I myself drive a ten-year-old Dodge. Good mileage, though."

"Put it on the chart."

As Thom wrote, Li looked at the board and asked, "Whose car that?"

Sellitto said, "We think somebody was at the beach to pick up the Ghost. That's what he was driving." A nod at the board.

"What happen him?"

"Looks like he panicked and took off," Deng said. "The Ghost shot at him but he got away."

"He leave Ghost behind?" Li asked, frowning.

"Yep," Dellray confirmed.

Rhyme ordered, "Run the make through Motor Vehicles. New York, Jersey and Connecticut too. Can you break the search down to, let's say, a hundred fifty miles outside of Manhattan?"

"Yup." Cooper logged online, heading for the secure DMV sites. "Remember when this took weeks?" he mused. With a faint hum Rhyme's wheelchair drove up to the screen in front of the tech. Only a moment later he could see the screen fill with the names and addresses of all the registered owners of X5's.

"Shit," Dellray muttered, walking close. "How many we got?"

"More popular car than I'd hoped," Cooper said. "Hundreds."

"What're the names?" Sellitto asked. "Any Chinese?"

Cooper scrolled through the list. "Sounds like two. Ling and Zhao." He looked at Eddie Deng, who nodded his confirmation. "Yep, they're Chinese."

Cooper continued, "But neither of them're close to downtown. One's in White Plains and the other's in New Jersey, Paramus."

"Have New York and Jersey troopers check 'em out," Dellray ordered.

The tech continued to scroll through the list. "Here's a possibility— there're about forty X5's registered to corporations and another fifty or so registered to leasing agents."

"Any of the *corporations* sound Chinese?" Rhyme asked, wishing he himself could pound on the keys and scroll quickly through the list.

"Nope," Cooper replied. "But they're all pretty generic—holding companies. You know, it'd be a bear but we *could* contact all of them. And the leasing companies too. Find out who's actually driving the cars."

"Too much of a long shot," Rhyme said. "Waste of resources. It'll take days. Have a couple of officers from downtown check the ones closest to Chinatown but—"

"No, no, Loaban," Sonny Li interrupted. "You got to find that car. Number one thing you do. Fast."

Rhyme lifted a querying eyebrow.

The Chinese cop continued, "Find it *now*. Beemer, right? You call them Beemers. Put lots people on it. All your cops, I'm saying. Whole bunch."

"It'll take too much time," Rhyme muttered, irritated at the distraction. "We don't have the manpower. We'd have to find somebody in the corporation who was in charge of buying cars and, if it was leased, talk to the dealer's leasing agent, get the records and half of them wouldn't do it without a court order. I want to concentrate on finding the Changs and the Wus."

"No, Loaban," Li insisted. "The Ghost, he going to kill that driver. That what he doing now, looking for him."

"Nup, I'ma thinking you're wrong," Dellray said. "His *pri*-ority's killing the wits from the boat."

"What you mean 'wit'?"

"Witnesses," Sellitto explained.

Sachs agreed. "My take is that, sure, he's pissed about the driver leaving him and maybe he'll go after him if he has time later. But not now."

"No, no," Li said, shaking his head emphatically. "Important, I'm saying. Find man in Beemer."

"Why?" Sachs asked.

"Very clear. Very obvious. Get that driver. He lead you to snakehead. Maybe use him as bait to find Ghost."

"And what, Sonny," a testy Lincoln Rhyme muttered darkly, "is your *basis* for that conclusion. Where're the *data* to support it?"

"Lots data, I'm saying."

"What?"

The small man shrugged. "When I on bus coming to city this morning I saw sign."

"A road sign?" Rhyme asked. "What do you mean?"

"No, no, what you say it? I don't know. . . ." He spoke in Chinese to Eddie Deng.

The young detective said, "He means an omen."

"An omen?" Rhyme barked, as if he were tasting spoiled fish.

Li reached absently for his cigarettes then left them untouched when he saw Thom's sharp glance. He continued, "I am coming into town on bus, I'm saying. I saw crow on road picking at food. Another crow tried steal it and first crow not just scare other away—he chase and try to peck eyes out. Not leave thief alone." Li raised his palms. This was, apparently, his entire argument.

"And?"

"Not clear, Loaban? What I say?"

"No, what you're saying isn't the least fucking bit clear."

"Okay, okay. I remember that crow now and I start thinking about Ghost and who he is and thinking about driver—man in fancy *Beemer*— and who he is. Well, he is *enemy* to Ghost. Like crow stealing food. The families—the Wus, the Changs—they not *do* anything bad to him personal, I'm saying. The driver . . ." Li frowned, looked frustrated and spoke again to Deng, who offered, "'Betray'?"

"Yes, *betray* him. He now Ghost's enemy."

Lincoln Rhyme tried not to laugh. "Noted, Sonny." He turned back to Dellray and Sellitto. "Now—"

"I see your face, Loaban," Li said. "I not saying gods come down and give me sign of crows. But remembering birds make me think different way, open up my mind. Get wind flowing through it. That good, you not think?"

"No, I think it's superstitious," Rhyme said. "It's woo woo and we don't have any time for— What the hell are you laughing at?"

"Woo woo. You say woo woo. You speaking Chinese. 'Woo' mean fog. So you say something woo woo, it foggy, unclear."

"Well, to us it means supernatural bullshit."

Even facing Rhyme's considerable bluster, Li wouldn't back down. "No, this not bullshit. Find that driver. You got to, Loaban."

Sachs's eyes were studying the small, persistent man. "I don't know, Rhyme."

"No way."

"Fuck good idea, I'm saying," Li assured the criminalist.

There was thick silence for a moment.

Sellitto intervened. "How 'bout if we put Bedding and Saul on it, give 'em a half-dozen guys from Patrol, Linc? They can check corporate and lease X5 registrations in Manhattan and Queens, only those—Chinatown here and the one in Flushing. And if there're any other breaks and we need bodies, we'll pull 'em off."

"All right, all right," Rhyme said angrily. "Just get moving on it."

"Half dozen just six, right?" Li complained. "Need more than that." But Rhyme's glare silenced him. "Okay, okay, Loaban."

Pecking crows, stone monkeys and *The Register of the Living and the Dead* . . . Rhyme sighed then looked over the team. "Now, if it's not too much to ask, can we get back to some *real* police work?"

GHOSTKILL

Easton, Long Island, Crime Scene

· Two immigrants killed on beach; shot in back.

· One immigrant wounded—Dr. John Sung.

· "Bangshou" (assistant) on board; identity unknown.

· Ten immigrants escape: seven adults (one elderly, one injured woman), two children, one infant. Steal church van.

· Blood samples sent to lab for typing.

  · Injured woman is AB negative.

· Vehicle awaiting Ghost on beach left without him. One shot believed fired by Ghost at vehicle. Request for vehicle make and model sent out, based on tread marks and wheelbase.

  · Vehicle is a BMW X5. Checking registered owners.

· No vehicles to pick up immigrants located.

· Cell phone, presumably Ghost's, sent for analysis to FBI.

  · Untraceable satellite secure phone. Hacked Chinese gov't system to use it.

· Ghost's weapon is 7.62 mm pistol. Unusual casing.

  · Model 51 Chinese automatic pistol.

· Ghost is reported to have gov't people on payroll.

· Ghost stole red Honda sedan to escape. Vehicle locator request sent out.

· Three bodies recovered at sea—two shot, one drowned. Photos and prints to Rhyme and Chinese police.

· Fingerprints sent to AFIS.

  · No matches on any prints but unusual markings on Sam Chang's fingers and thumbs (injury, rope burn?)

· Profile of Immigrants: Sam Chang and Wu Qichen and their families, John Sung, baby of woman who drowned, unidentified man and woman (killed on beach).

Stolen Van, Chinatown

· Camouflaged by immigrants with "The Home Store" logo.

· Blood spatter suggests injured woman has hand, arm or shoulder injury.

· Blood samples sent to lab for typing.

  · Injured woman is AB negative.

· Fingerprints sent to AFIS.

  · No matches.

Chapter Sixteen

The family name Chang means archer.

His father, wife and children sitting around him, Sam Chang, with a calligrapher's magic touch, drew the Chinese characters for this name on a slat of broken wood he'd found in the backyard of their new apartment. The silk case holding his prized wolf-, goat- and rabbit-hair brushes, ink stick and stone well, had gone down with the *Fuzhou Dragon* and he was forced to use a dreadful American plastic pen.

Still, Chang had learned calligraphy from his father when he was young and had practiced the art all his life, so, although the line width of the ink didn't vary, the strokes were perfectly formed—they were, he decided, like the studies by sixteenth-century artist Wan Li, who would do a simple rendering to record a scene he would later paint on ceramic—the sketch was half-formed but beautiful in its own right. Chang took the piece of wood representing the family name and rested it on the impromptu cardboard altar sitting on the fireplace mantel in the living room.

China is a theological shopping mall, a country in which the Buddha is the most recognized traditional deity but where the philosophers Confucius and Lao-tzu stand as demigods, where Christianity and Islam have large pockets of devotees and where the vast majority of people hedge their bets by regularly praying and sacrificing to folk gods so numerous no one knows exactly how many there are.

But highest in the pantheon of gods for most Chinese are their ancestors.

And it was to the Chang progenitors that this red altar was devoted, decorated with the only ancestral likenesses that had survived the sinking of the ship: seawater-stained snapshots from Chang's wallet of his parents and grandparents.

"There," he announced. "Our home."

Chang Jiechi shook his son's hand and then gestured for tea, which Mei-Mei poured for him. The old man cupped the hot brew and looked around the dark rooms. "Better than some."

Despite the man's words, though, Sam Chang felt another wave of shame, like hot fever, that he was subjecting his father to such a mean place as this. The strongest duty after that owed to the ruler of the government, according to Confucius, is that which a son owes to his father. Ever since Chang had planned their escape from China he'd worried about how the trip would affect the elderly man. Ever quiet and unemotional, Chang Jiechi had taken the news of their impending flight silently, leaving Chang to wonder if he was doing the right thing in the old man's eyes.

And now, after the sinking of the *Dragon*, their life wasn't going to get better any time soon. This apartment would have to be their prison until the Ghost was captured or went back to China, which might be months from now.

He thought again about that place they'd stopped at to steal the paint and brushes—The Home Store. The rows of glistening bathtubs and mirrors and lights and marble slabs. He wished he could have moved his father and family into a home outfitted with the wonderful things he'd seen there. This was squalor. This was—

A firm knock on the door.

For a moment no one in the family moved. Then Chang looked out through the curtain and relaxed. He opened the door and broke into a smile at the sight of the middle-aged man wearing jeans and a sweatshirt. Joseph Tan walked inside and the men shook hands. Chang glanced outside into the quiet residential street and saw no one who looked like enforcers for the snakehead. In the humid, overcast air was a foul smell; the apartment, it turned out, was not far from a sewage treatment plant. He stepped inside, locked the door.

Tan, the brother of a good friend of Chang's in Fujian, had come over here some years ago. He was a U.S. citizen and, since he had no history of dissident activity, traveled freely between China and New York. Chang had spent several evenings with him and his brother in Fuzhou last spring and had finally grown comfortable enough to share with Tan the news that he intended to bring his family to the Beautiful Country. Tan had volunteered to help. He had arranged for this apartment and for Chang and his oldest son to work in one of Tan's businesses—a quick printing shop not far from the apartment.

The easygoing man now paid respects to elderly Chang Jiechi and then to Mei-Mei and they sat down to tea. Tan offered cigarettes. Sam Chang declined but his father took one and the two men smoked.

"We heard about the ship on the news," Tan said. "I thanked Guan Yin you were safe."

"Many died. It was terrible. We nearly drowned, all of us."

"The TV said the snakehead was the Ghost."

Chang replied that it was and that he'd tried to kill them even after they came ashore.

"Then we will have to be very careful. I will not mention your name to anyone. But I have people around the shop who will be curious about you. I had thought you should start work right away but now, with the Ghost . . . It would be better to wait. Maybe next week. Or the week after. I'll train you then. Do you know about American printing equipment?"

Chang shook his head no. In China he'd been a professor of art and culture—until his dissident status had gotten him fired. Just like the displaced, and despised, artists who'd lost their jobs during the Cultural Revolution of the 1960s, Chang had been forced to do "right-thinking" work—labor. And like many of the calligraphers and artists from that earlier era he'd gotten a job as a printer. But he'd operated only outdated Chinese or Russian presses.

They spoke for a time about life in China and life here. Then Tan wrote out directions to the shop and the hours Chang and his son would be working. He asked to meet William.

Chang opened the door to the boy's bedroom. He stared—first in surprise, then in dismay—at the empty room. William was not there.

He turned to Mei-Mei. "Where is our son?"

"He was in the bedroom. I didn't see him leave."

Chang strode to the back door and found it was unlocked. William had left it unlatched when he'd snuck out.

No!

The backyard was empty. The alleyway behind it too. He returned to the living room. He asked Tan, "Where would a teenage boy go around here?"

"He speaks English?"

"Better than we do."

"At the corner there's a Starbucks, do you know them?"

"Yes, the coffee place."

"A lot of Chinese teenagers go there. He won't say anything about the *Dragon*, will he?"

Chang said, "No, I'm sure. He knows the danger."

Tan, who had children himself, said, "He'll be your biggest problem. He'll watch that"—gesturing at the television set—"and want everything he sees on it. Video games and cars and clothes. And he'll want them without working for them. Because in the television you see people *have* things, you don't see them *earning* them. You came all this way, you survived the Atlantic Ocean, you survived the Ghost. Don't get deported because the police arrest your son for shoplifting and turn him over to the INS."

Chang understood what the man was saying but was panicking at the moment, not able to concentrate on the advice. The Ghost might have *bangshous* all over the streets here. Or men who would sell their whereabouts to him. "I must go find my boy now."

He and Tan walked outside, to the sidewalk. Tan pointed him toward the corner, where the coffee shop was located. "I'll leave you now. Be strong with your son. Now that he's here it will be far more difficult. But you must control him."

Chang kept his head down as he walked past the cheap apartments, laundromats, delicatessens, restaurants and stores. This neighborhood was less congested than Manhattan's Chinatown, sidewalks wider, fewer people on the streets. More than half the people here were Asian but the population was mixed: Chinese, Vietnamese and Korean. There were many Hispanics too and a number of Indians and Pakistanis. Hardly any whites.

He glanced into the shops as he walked past and didn't see his son in any of them.

He prayed to Chen-wu that the boy had merely gone for a walk by himself and that he hadn't met someone and told them how they'd come here—perhaps trying to impress a girl.

A small park—no sign of him.

A restaurant. Nothing.

He walked into the Starbucks coffee shop and a number of cautious teenagers and complacent old men glanced at the immigrant's troubled face. William was not here. Chang ducked out quickly.

Then, happening to glance down a dim alley he saw his son. The boy was talking with two young Chinese men, both wearing black leather jackets. Their hair was long and high, swept back with spray or oil. William handed one of them something Chang couldn't see. The man nodded to his friend and slipped a small bag into William's hand. Then the two turned quickly and walked back down the alley. William looked into the bag, examining what he'd just received, then stuffed it into his pocket. No! Chang thought in shock. What was this? Drugs. *His* son was buying drugs?

Chang ducked back out of the alley and, when his son stepped out, grabbed the shocked boy by his arm and pressed him against the wall.

"How could you do this?" Chang demanded.

"Leave me alone."

"Answer me!"

William glanced at the nearby coffee shop, where three or four people sat outside, enjoying the momentary absence of rain. They'd heard Chang's raised voice and glanced toward the boy and his father. Chang noticed them and released his son, nodding with his head for the boy to follow.

"Don't you know that the Ghost is looking for us? He wants to kill us!"

"I wanted to go outside. It's like a prison here! That fucking little room, with my brother."

Chang grabbed his son's arm again. "Don't use that language with me. You can't disobey me like this."

"It's a shitty little place. I want a room of my own," the boy replied, pulling away.

"Later. We all have to make sacrifices."

"It was your choice to come here. *You* can make the sacrifices."

"Don't speak to me that way!" Chang said. "I'm your father."

"I want a room. I want some privacy."

"You should be grateful we have someplace to stay at all. None of us have rooms of our own. Your grandfather sleeps with your mother and me."

The boy said nothing.

He'd learned many things about his son today. That he was insolent, that he was a car thief, that the iron cables of obligation to family that had so absolutely guided Sam Chang's life meant little to the boy. Chang wondered superstitiously if he had made a mistake in giving the boy his Western name when he started school, calling him after the American computer genius Gates. Perhaps this had somehow caused the boy to veer onto a path of rebellion.

As they approached the apartment Chang asked, "Who were they?"

"Who?" the boy answered evasively.

"Those men you were with."

"Nobody."

"What did they sell you? Was it drugs?"

Irritated silence was the response.

They were at the front door to the apartment. William started to walk past his father but Chang stopped him. He reached into the boy's pocket. William's arms rose hostilely and for a shocked moment Chang thought his son would shove him away or even hit him. But after an interminable moment he lowered his hands.

Chang pulled out the bag and looked inside, stunned at the sight of the small silver pistol.

"What are you doing with this?" he whispered viciously. "So you can rob people?"

Silence.

"Tell me, son." His strong calligrapher's hand closed firmly on the boy's arm. "Tell me!"

"I got it so I can protect us!" the boy shouted.

"I will protect us. And not with this."

"You?" William laughed with a sneer. "*You* wrote your articles about Taiwan and democracy and made our life miserable. *You* decided to come here and the fucking snakehead tries to kill us all. You call that taking care of us?"

"What did you pay for this with?" He held up the bag containing the pistol. "Where did you get the money? You have no job."

The boy ignored the question. "The Ghost killed the others. What if he tries to kill us? What will we do?"

"We'll hide from him until the police find him."

"And if they don't?"

"Why do you dishonor me like this?" Chang asked angrily.

Pushing inside the apartment, William shook his head, a look of exasperation on his face, and walked brusquely into the bedroom. He slammed the door.

Chang took the tea his wife offered him.

Chang Jiechi asked, "Where did he go?"

"Up the street. He got this." He showed him the gun and the elder Chang took it in his gnarled hands.

Chang asked, "Is it loaded?"

His father had been a soldier, resisting Mao Zedong on the Long March that swept Chiang Kai-shek and the Nationalists into the sea, and was familiar with weapons. He examined it closely. "Yes. Be careful. Keep the safety lever in this position." He handed the gun back to his son.

"Why does he disrespect me?" Chang asked angrily. He hid the weapon on the top shelf of the front closet and led the old man to the musty couch.

His father said nothing for a moment. The pause was so long that Chang looked at the old man expectantly. Finally, with a wry look in his eyes, his father responded, "Where did you learn all your wisdom, son? What formed your mind, your heart?"

"My professors, books, colleagues. You mostly, Baba."

"Ah, *me*? You learned from your *father*?" Chang Jiechi asked in mock surprise.

"Yes, of course." Chang frowned, unsure what the man was getting at.

The old man said nothing but a faint smile crossed his gray face.

A moment passed. Then Chang said, "And you are saying that William learned from me? I've never been insolent to you, Baba."

"Not to me. But you certainly have been to the Communists. To Beijing. To the Fujianese government. Son, you're a *dissident*. Your whole life has been rebellion."

"But . . ."

"If Beijing said to you, 'Why does Sam Chang dishonor us?' what would your response be?"

"I'd say, 'What have you done to earn my respect?'"

"William might say the same to you." Chang Jiechi lifted his hands, his argument complete.

"But *my* enemies have been oppression, violence, corruption." Sam Chang loved China with his complete heart. He loved the people. The culture. The history. His life for the past twelve years had been a consuming, passionate struggle to help his country step into a more enlightened era.

Chang Jiechi said, "But all William sees is you hunched over your computer at night, attacking authority and being unconcerned about the consequences."

Words of protest formed in Chang's mind but he fell silent. Then he realized with a shock that his father perhaps was right. He laughed faintly. He thought about going to speak to his son but something was holding him back. Anger, confusion—maybe even fear of what his son might say to him. No, he'd speak to the boy later. When—

Suddenly the old man winced in pain.

"Baba!" Chang said, alarmed.

One of their few possessions that had survived the sinking of the *Dragon* was the nearly full bottle of Chang Jiechi's morphine. Chang had given his father a tablet just before the ship sank and he'd had the bottle in his pocket. It was tightly sealed and no seawater had gotten inside.

He now gave his father two more pills and placed a blanket over him. The man lay back on the couch and closed his eyes.

Sam Chang sat heavily in a musty chair.

Their possessions gone, his father desperately needing treatment, a ruthless killer their enemy, his own son a renegade and criminal . . .

So much difficulty around them.

He wanted to blame someone: Mao, the Chinese Communist Party, the People's Liberation Army soldiers. . . .

But the reason for their present hardship and danger seemed to lie in only one place, where William had assigned it: at Chang's own feet.

Regret would serve no purpose, though. All he could now do was pray that the stories about life here were true, and not myths—that the Beautiful Country was indeed a land of miracles, where evil was brought to light and purged, where the most pernicious flaws within our bodies could quickly be made right, and where generous liberty fulfilled its promise that troubled hearts would be troubled no more.

Chapter Seventeen

At 1:30 that afternoon the Ghost was walking quickly through Chinatown, head down, worried as always about being recognized.

To most Westerners, of course, he was invisible, his features blending together into one generic Asian man. White Americans could rarely tell the difference between a Chinese, Japanese, Vietnamese or Korean. Among the Chinese, though, his features would be distinct and he was determined to remain anonymous. He'd once bribed a traffic magistrate in Hong Kong $10,000 one-color cash to avoid being arrested in a minor brawl some years ago so there would be no picture of him in criminal records. Even Interpol's Automated Search and Archives section and the Analytical Criminal Intelligence Unit didn't have any reliable surveillance photos of him (he knew this because he'd used a hacker in Fuzhou to break into Interpol's database through its supposedly secure X400 email system).

So he now strode quickly, keeping his head down—most of the time.

But not always.

He would lift his eyes to study women, the pretty and young ones, the voluptuous ones, the svelte ones, the coy and flirtatious and the timid. The clerks, the teenage girls, the wives, the businesswomen, the tourists. Eastern or Western made no difference to him. He wanted a body lying beneath him, whimpering—in pleasure or pain (that made no difference either), as he pulsed up and down on top of her, gripping her head tightly between his palms.

A woman with light brown hair passed by, a Western woman. He slowed and let himself be touched by the veil of her perfume. He hungered—though he realized too that his lust wasn't for *her* but for his Yindao.

He had no time for his fantasies, though, he'd come to the merchants association, where the Turks awaited him. He spat on the sidewalk, found the back entrance, which they'd left open, and stepped inside. He made his way up to the top floor. It was time to conduct some important business.

Inside the large office, he found Yusuf and the two other Turks. It hadn't taken much—a few phone calls, a threat and a bribe—to find the name of the man who was sitting, nervous to the point of tears, in a chair in front of his own desk.

Jimmy Mah's eyes fell to the floor when the Ghost walked into the room. The snakehead pulled up a chair and sat beside him. The Ghost took Mah's hand casually—a gesture not unusual among Chinese men—and he felt the trembling of muscles and the pulsing of a frightened heart.

"I didn't know they came in on the *Dragon*. They didn't tell me! I swear that. They lied to me. When they were here I hadn't even *heard* about the ship. I didn't watch the news this morning."

The Ghost continued to hold the man's hand, adding slight pressure to his grip but saying nothing.

"Are you going to kill me?" Mah asked the question in such a whisper that he repeated it though the Ghost had heard perfectly.

"The Changs and the Wus. Where are they?" The Ghost squeezed the man's hand slightly harder and received a pleasant whimper for his effort. "Where are they?"

Mah's eyes glanced at the Turks. He'd be wondering what kind of terrible weapons they'd have on them, knives or garrotes or guns.

But in the end it was simply the faint pressure of the Ghost's palm against poor Jimmy Mah's that loosened his tongue.

"Two different places, sir. Wu Qichen is in an apartment in Chinatown. A broker I use set him up with a place."

"The address?"

"I don't know. I swear! But the broker knows. He'll tell you."

"Where is this broker?"

Mah quickly recited the name and address. The Ghost memorized it.

"And the others?"

"Sam Chang took his family to Queens."

"Queens?" the Ghost asked. "Where?" A particularly delicate squeeze of the hand. He imagined momentarily that he was touching Yindao's breast.

Mah nodded toward the desk. "There! It's on that piece of paper."

The Ghost picked it up, glanced at the address and then pocketed the note. He released the tong leader's hand and slowly rubbed his thumb in the sweat that had poured from Mah's palm. "You won't tell anyone I asked about this," the Ghost murmured.

"No, no, of course not."

The Ghost smiled. "You did me a favor, for which I am thankful. I am indebted to you. Now, I will do you a favor in return."

Mah fell silent. Then cautiously he asked in a shaky voice, "A favor?"

"What other business arrangements do you have, Mr. Mah? What other activities are you involved in? You help piglets, you help snakeheads. But do you run massage parlors?"

"Some." The man was looking calmer. He wiped his hand on his slacks. "Mostly gambling."

"Ah gambling, sure. Much gambling here in Chinatown. I like to gamble. Do you?"

Mah swallowed and wiped his face with a white handkerchief. "Don't we all love to gamble? Yes, yes."

"Tell me then: Who interferes with your gambling operation? Another tong? A triad? Some *Meiguo* gang? The police? I can talk to people. I have connections throughout the government. My connections go very high. I can make sure nobody bothers your gambling parlors."

"Yes, sir, yes. Aren't there always problems? It's not the Chinese, though, or the police. It's the Italians. Why do they cause us such trouble? I don't know. The young men, they firebomb us, beat up our customers, rob the gambling halls."

"The Italians," the Ghost mused. "What are they called? There's a derogatory term . . . . I can't think of it."

"Wops," Mah said in English.

"Wops."

Mah smiled. "It's a reference to those in your line of work."

"Mine?"

"Immigration. Wop means 'without passport.' When Italian immigrants came here years ago without documentation they were labeled WOP. It's very insulting."

The Ghost looked around the room, frowning.

"Is there something you need, sir?" Mah asked.

"Do you have a thick marker? Some paint perhaps?"

"Paint?" Mah's eyes followed the Ghost's. "No. But I can call my assistant downstairs. I can have her get some. Whatever you like, I can get. Anything."

"Wait," the Ghost said, "that won't be necessary. I have another thought."

Lon Sellitto looked up from his Nokia and announced to the GHOSTKILL team, "We've got a body in Chinatown. Detective from the Fifth Precinct's on the line." He turned back to his phone.

Alarmed, Rhyme looked up at him. Had the Ghost tracked down and killed another of the immigrants?

Who? Rhyme wondered. Chang, Wu? The baby?

But Sellitto hung up and said, "Doesn't look related to the Ghost. Vic's name's Jimmy Mah."

"Know him," Eddie Deng said. "Heads a tong."

Coe nodded. "I've heard of him too. Smuggling's not his speciality but he does a little meeting and greeting."

"What's that mean?" Rhyme asked acerbically when Coe explained no further.

The agent answered, "When undocumenteds get to Chinatown there's an official who helps them out—gets them into a safehouse, gives them a little money. Called 'meeting and greeting' the illegals. Most of the meeters work for snakeheads but some do it freelance. Like Mah. It's just that there's not a lot of profit there. If you're corrupt and you want big bucks you'll go with drugs or gambling or massage parlors. That's what Mah's into. Well, *was*, apparently."

Rhyme asked, "Why don't you think it's related?"

Sellitto said, "There was a message painted on the wall behind his desk, where they found the body. It said, 'You call us wops, you take our homes.' It was written in Mah's blood, by the way."

Nodding, Deng said, "Major rivalry between the third-generation Mafiosi—you know the *Sopranos* crowd—and the tongs. Chinese gambling and massage parlors—some drugs too—they've just about kicked the Italians out of Manhattan O.C."

The demographics of organized crime, Rhyme knew, were as fluid as those of the city itself.

"Anyway," Coe said, "those people off the *Dragon*, they're going to dig underground as fast as they can. They'd avoid somebody public like Mah. I would."

"Unless they were desperate," Sachs said. "Which they are." She looked at Rhyme. "Maybe the Ghost killed Mah and made it look like an O.C. hit. Should I run the scene?"

Rhyme debated for a moment. Yes, the families *were* desperate but Rhyme had already seen the immigrants' resourcefulness, presumably the work of Sam Chang. It would leave too many trails to go to somebody like Mah for help, he assessed. "No, I need you here. But send a special team from Crime Scene and tell them to copy us on the crime scene report stat."

To Eddie Deng, Rhyme said, "Call Dellray and Peabody at the Federal Building. Let them know about the killing."

"Yessir," Deng said.

Dellray had gone downtown to arrange for the extra agents from the two relevant federal jurisdictions in New York—the Southern and Eastern, which covered Manhattan and Long Island. He was also wielding his influence to get the SPEC-TAC team on site, which Washington was reluctant to do; the special unit was generally reserved for major hostage standoffs and embassy takeovers, not for manhunts. Still, Rhyme knew, Dellray was a tough man to say no to and if anybody could get the much-needed tactical force up here it'd be the lanky agent.

Rhyme maneuvered the chair back to the evidence and the whiteboards.

Nothing, nothing, nothing . . .

What else can we do? he wondered. What haven't we exhausted? Scanning the board . . . Finally he said, "Let's look at the blood some more." He looked over the samples that Sachs had found: that from the injured immigrant, the woman with the broken or gashed arm, hand or shoulder.

Lincoln Rhyme loved blood as a forensic tool. It was easy to spot, it stuck like glue to all kinds of surfaces, it retained its important forensic information for years.

The history of blood in criminal investigation, in fact, largely reflects the history of forensic science itself.

The earliest effort—in the mid-1800s—to use blood as evidence focused simply on *classifying* it, that is, determining if an unknown substance was indeed blood and not, say, dried brown paint. Fifty years later the focus was on *identifying* blood as human, as opposed to animal. Not long after that detectives began looking for a way to *differentiate* blood—break it down into a limited number of categories—and scientists responded by creating the process of blood typing (the A, B, O system as well as the MN and the Rh systems), which narrows down the number of sources. In the sixties and seventies forensic scientists sought to go one step further—to *individuate* the blood, that is, trace it back to a single individual, like a fingerprint. Early efforts at doing this biochemically—identifying enzymes and proteins—could eliminate many individuals as the source, but not all. It wasn't until DNA typing that true individuation was achieved.

Classification, identification, differentiation, individuation . . . that's criminalistics in a nutshell.

But there was more to blood than linking it to an individual. The way it fell on surfaces at crime scenes—spatter, it was called—provided great information about the nature of the attack. And Lincoln Rhyme often examined the *content* of blood to determine what it could tell about the individual who'd shed it.

"Let's see if our injured woman's got a drug habit or's taking some rare medicine. Call the M.E.'s office and have them do a complete workup. I want to know everything that's in her bloodstream."

As Cooper was talking to the office Sellitto's phone rang and he took the call.

Rhyme could see in the detective's face that he was receiving some bad news.

"Oh, Jesus . . . oh, no . . ."

The criminalist sensed an odd fibrillation in the core of his body—an area where he could by rights feel nothing at all. People who are paralyzed often feel phantom pain from limbs and parts of their body that cannot have any sensation. Rhyme not only had experienced *this* feeling but he'd felt shock and adrenaline rushes too, when his logical mind knew that this was impossible.

"What, Lon?" Sachs asked.

"Fifth Precinct again. Chinatown," he said, wincing. "Another killing. This time it's *definitely* the Ghost." He glanced at Rhyme and shook his head. "Man, it's not good."

"What do you mean?"

"I mean, they're saying it's fucking unpleasant, Linc."

Unpleasant was not a word that one heard often from an NYPD homicide detective, especially Lon Sellitto, as hardened a cop as you'd ever find.

He wrote down some information then hung up the phone and glanced at Sachs. "Suit up, Officer, you've got a scene to run."

GHOSTKILL

Easton, Long Island, Crime Scene	Stolen Van, Chinatown
· Two immigrants killed on beach; shot in back.	· Camouflaged by immigrants with "The Home Store" logo.
· One immigrant wounded—Dr. John Sung.	· Blood spatter suggests injured woman has hand, arm or shoulder injury.
· "Bangshou" (assistant) on board; identity unknown.	· Blood samples sent to lab for typing.
· Ten immigrants escape: seven adults (one elderly, one injured woman), two children, one infant. Steal church van.	· Injured woman is AB negative. Requesting more information about her blood.
· Blood samples sent to lab for typing.	· Fingerprints sent to AFIS.
· Injured woman is AB negative. Requesting more information about her blood.	· No matches.
· Vehicle awaiting Ghost on beach left without him. One shot believed fired by Ghost at vehicle. Request for vehicle make and model sent out, based on tread marks and wheelbase.	
· Vehicle is a BMW X5. Checking registered owners.	
· No vehicles to pick up immigrants located.	
· Cell phone, presumably Ghost's, sent for analysis to FBI.	
· Untraceable satellite secure phone. Hacked Chinese gov't system to use it.	
· Ghost's weapon is 7.62 mm pistol. Unusual casing.	
· Model 51 Chinese automatic pistol.	
· Ghost is reported to have gov't people on payroll.	
· Ghost stole red Honda sedan to escape. Vehicle locator request sent out.	
· Three bodies recovered at sea—two shot, one drowned. Photos and prints to Rhyme and Chinese police.	
· Fingerprints sent to AFIS.	
· No matches on any prints but unusual markings on Sam Chang's fingers and thumbs (injury, rope burn?)	
· Profile of Immigrants: Sam Chang and Wu Qichen and their families, John Sung, baby of woman who drowned, unidentified man and woman (killed on beach).	

Chapter Eighteen

Amelia Sachs had left the Camaro on the street near Rhyme's town house and was driving a crime scene bus downtown on the FDR Drive.

The vehicle was functional city property—a Ford station wagon—but she drove it pretty much the same as if she'd been behind the wheel of her gaudy yellow sports car. The time was 2:45 P.M., before rush hour, but the roads were still crowded and maneuvering through traffic took all her skill.

"Hey, Hongse," Sonny Li began nervously as she skidded around a taxi at 70 m.p.h. But he apparently preferred she keep her attention on the road and fell silent.

In the backseat were Eddie Deng, who wasn't concerned about her driving, and agent Alan Coe, who like the Chinese cop, clearly was. He gripped the chest strap of his seat belt as if he were holding the ripcord of a parachute during a skydive.

"Did you see that?" Sachs asked casually as a cab ignored the siren and light on the CS bus and pulled out directly in front of her to make the exit at Houston Street.

"We moving real fast," Li said then seemed to remember that he didn't want to distract her and stopped talking again.

"Which way, Eddie?" Sachs asked.

"The Bowery, turn left, two more blocks then a right."

She pulled off onto a rain-slick Canal Street at fifty, controlled the skid before they went into a garbage truck and accelerated into Chinatown, the tires, goosed by the big, cop engine, steaming up the wheel wells.

Li muttered something in Chinese.

"What?"

"Ten judges of hell," he translated his own words.

Sachs recalled—the ten judges of hell, who kept the book called *The Register of the Living and the Dead*, containing the name of everybody in the world. The balance sheet of life and death.

My father Herman, she thought, is already inscribed on the dead side.

Where does my name fall in the register? she wondered.

And the names of people I'm now close to? The people yet to be?

Thinking of life and death . . .

"*Ah, Ms. Sachs. Here you are.*"

"*Hello, Doctor.*"

"*I've just been meeting with Lincoln Rhyme's physician.*"

"*Yes?*"

"*I've got to talk to you about something.*"

"*You're looking like it's bad news, Doctor.*"

"Uhm, Officer," Deng interrupted her thoughts. "I think that's a red light ahead of us."

"Got it," she said and slowed to thirty to sweep through the intersection.

"*Gan,*" Li whispered. Then offered what Sachs had guessed was the translation: "Fuck."

Three minutes later the crime scene bus skidded to a stop in front of an alley surrounded by a small crowd of onlookers, kept back by a spider strand of yellow police tape and a half-dozen uniformed officers from the Patrol division. The front door to what seemed to be a small warehouse was open. Sachs climbed out, followed by Deng, who called, "Hey, Detective," to a blond man in a suit. He nodded and Deng introduced her to a homicide detective from the Fifth Precinct.

"You're running the scene?" he asked.

Sachs nodded. "What is this place?"

"Warehouse. Owner's clean, looks like. We've contacted him and he doesn't know anything except that the victim—name was Jerry Tang—worked here. Eight arrests, two convictions. Mostly he boosts wheels and drives getaway. Does—*did*—some muscle work."

He nodded at the silver BMW four-by-four in the alley. An X5. This was the SUV that Tang had driven out to Long Island to pick up the Ghost this morning. There was a bullet hole in the back door from the Ghost's gunshot as Tang had fled, abandoning him.

A patrol officer responding to some screams had noticed a late-model BMW four-by-four next to the building where the commotion had come from. Then he'd seen the bullet hole in the back and, with his partner, they'd entered the warehouse.

And found what was left of Jerry Tang. He'd been tortured with a knife or razor—skin was missing, including his eyelids—then killed.

Rhyme, she knew, hated to be one-upped by other law enforcers almost as much as he hated being one-upped by perpetrators and when it turned out that Sonny Li, the crow detective, had been right—that the Ghost's first mission was to kill the man who'd abandoned him—the criminalist's mood darkened even more. It hadn't helped, of course, that Li'd said, "Hey, should have listen to me, Loaban. Should have listen."

The detective from the Fifth now continued, "We've got two canvassers from downtown, checking out wits. Oh, there they are now."

Sachs nodded to two detectives she'd worked with before. Bedding and Saul were no longer needed to track down registered owners of BMW X5's and were back at their usual assignment: post-crime canvassing, "spadework," as it was called. They were known for their consummate skill in double-teaming witnesses. Despite their different heights, builds and complexions (one had freckles), their identical sandy hair and their demeanor resulted in their nickname: the Twins. They were also known as the Hardy Boys.

"Got here twenty minutes after the first sighting," said either Bedding or Saul. The tall one.

"Was a teenage girl on her way home from drama club at school. Heard a scream in the building. But didn't report it till she got home. She was—"

"—afraid, you know. Can't blame her, considering what the respondings found at the scene inside. I'd be too."

"Afraid, he means. Blood everywhere. And body parts."

Sachs winced, but not from the gore; it was only because she was lifting her knees to pull on the white Tyvek crime scene suit and her arthritic joints protested painfully.

"We've talked to about eight people in the building—" Bedding or Saul said.

"—and around it. This is even more a case of the deaf and dumbs than usual."

"Yeah, most people here got the blinds too."

"We think they heard it was the Ghost who worked on Tang and that scared everybody off. Nobody'll help. The most anybody'll tell us is that two or—"

"—three or four—"

"—people, presumably men, kicked in the door to the warehouse there."

"And there was major screaming for ten minutes. Then two gunshots. Then it got quiet."

"The girl's mother called nine-one-one."

"But everybody was gone by the time Patrol got here."

Sachs looked up and down the alleyway and the street in front of the warehouse. As she'd feared, the rain had destroyed any hope of finding tread marks of whatever kind of car the Ghost and his assistants had been driving.

"Who's been inside?" she asked the blond detective from the Fifth Precinct.

"Only one uniform—to see if the vic was alive. We heard from upstairs you wanted it virgin so we didn't even let the tour doc from the Medical Examiner's office go in."

"Good," she said. "I want the patrol officer who was inside."

"I'll track 'em down."

A moment later he returned with a uniformed patrolwoman. "I was first officer. You wanted to see me?"

"Just your shoe."

"Well, okay." The woman slipped it off and handed it to Sachs, who shot a picture of the tread and noted the size of the sole so that she could differentiate it from the prints of the Ghost and his accomplices.

She then put rubber bands around her own shoes to distinguish her footprints. Looking up, she noticed Sonny Li standing in the doorway of the warehouse. "Excuse me," she said testily, "you mind standing back?"

"Sure, sure, Hongse. That big room. Man, lot to look at. But you know Confucius, right?"

"Not really," she said, concentrating on the scene.

"He write, 'Longest journey must begin with first step.' I *think* he write that. Maybe somebody else. I read Mickey Spillane more than Confucius."

"Could you wait over there, Officer Li?"

"Call me Sonny, I'm saying."

He stepped aside and Sachs walked into the warehouse. The headset went on and she clicked the Motorola handy-talkie to life.

"Crime Scene Five Eight Eight Five to Central. Need a patch to a landline, K?"

"Roger, Five Eight Eight Five. What's the number, K?"

She gave them Lincoln Rhyme's phone number and a moment later she heard his voice. "Sachs, where are you? At the scene yet? We've got to *move* on this."

As always—and inexplicably—his feisty impatience reassured her. She scanned the carnage. "Jesus, Rhyme, this's a mess."

"Tell me," he said. "Give me the blueprint first."

"Warehouse and office combined. Thirty by fifty feet, more or less, office area about ten by twenty. A few desks and—"

"Few? Two or eighteen?"

Rhyme was hell on anyone guilty of sloppy observation.

"Sorry," she said. "Four metal desks, eight chairs, no nine—one's overturned."

The one that Tang had been tied to when the Ghost had tortured and killed him.

"Rows of metal shelves, stacked with cardboard boxes, food inside. Canned goods and cellophane packages. Restaurant supplies."

"Okay, Thom's ready to start writing. You *are* ready aren't you, Thom? Write big, so I can see it. Those words over there, I can't make them out. Redo them . . . All right, all right . . . *Please* redo them." He then said, "Start on the grid, Sachs."

She began to search the scene, thinking: A first step . . . the longest journey.

But twenty minutes of one-step-at-a-time searching revealed virtually nothing useful. She found two shell casings, which appeared to be the same as those from the Ghost's gun at the beach. But there was nothing that would lead them directly to where he might be hiding out in New York. No cigarettes, no matchbooks, no fingerprints—the assailants had worn leather gloves.

She studied the ceiling and smelled the scene—two of Rhyme's important directives to crime scene searchers—but detected nothing that would help. Sachs jumped when Rhyme's voice popped into her ear. "Talk to me, Sachs. I don't like it when you're quiet."

"The place is a mess," she repeated.

"You said that. A. Mess. That doesn't really tell us very much, now, does it? Give me details."

"It's been ransacked, drawers opened, posters torn off the walls, desks swept clean, statues, figurines, fishbowl, cups and glasses smashed."

"In a struggle?"

"I don't think so."

"Theft of anything in particular?"

"Maybe but it's mostly vandalism, I'd say."

"What're their shoe treads like?" Rhyme asked.

"All smooth."

"Stylish bastards," he muttered.

He was, she knew, hoping for some dirt or fibers that might lead them to the Ghost's safehouse but, while the gullies in deep-tread-soled shoes can retain such evidence for months, smooth-soled shoes lose trace far more quickly.

"Okay, Sachs, keep going. What do the footprints tell you?"

"I'm thinking that—"

"Don't *think*, Sachs. That's not the way to understand a crime scene. You know that. You have to *feel* it."

His seductive, low voice was hypnotizing and with each word he spoke she felt herself uneasily being transported back to the crime itself, as if she were a participant. Her palms began to sweat copiously in the latex gloves.

"He's there. Jerry Tang is at his desk and they—"

"'*We*,'"Rhyme corrected sternly. "You're the Ghost, remember."

"—we kick the door in. He gets up and runs toward the back door but we get him and drag him back to his chair."

"Let's narrow it down, Sachs. You're the snakehead. You've found the man who's betrayed you. What are you going to do?"

"I'm going to kill him."

I saw crow on road picking at food. Another crow tried steal it and first crow not just scare other away—he chase and try to peck eyes out.

Suddenly she was filled with a burst of unfocused anger. It nearly took her breath away. "No, wait, Rhyme. It's like his death is secondary. What I really want is to hurt him. I've been betrayed and I want to hurt him bad."

"What do you do? Exactly."

She hesitated, sweating hard in the hot suit. Several places on her body itched at once. She felt like ripping a hole in the suit to scratch her skin.

"I can't—"

"'I,' Sachs. Who's 'I'? You're the Ghost, remember?"

Solidly in her own persona, though, she said, "I'm having trouble with this one, Rhyme. There's something about him, about the Ghost. He's way on the other side." She hesitated. "It feels really bad there."

A place where families die, where children are trapped in the holds of sinking ships, where men and women are shot in the back scrabbling for the only sanctuary they can find: a heartless, cold ocean. A place where they die for no reason other than that they are irritations and stumbling blocks.

Sachs stared at the ever-open eyes of Jerry Tang.

"Go there, Sachs," he murmured. "Go on. I'll get you back. Don't worry."

She wished she could believe him.

The criminalist continued. "You've found your betrayer. You're furious with him. What do you do?"

"The other three men with me tie Tang to a chair and we use knives or razors on him. He's terrified, screaming. . . . We're taking our time. All around me—there're bits of flesh. What looks like part of an ear, strips of skin. We cut his eyelids off. . . ." She hesitated. "But I don't see any clues, Rhyme. Nothing that'll help us."

"But there *are* clues there, Sachs. You *know* there are. Remember Locard."

Edmond Locard was an early French criminalist, who stated that at every crime scene there's an evidence exchange between the victim and the perpetrator, or between the scene itself and the perp. It might be difficult to identify the evidence that's been exchanged and harder yet to trace it to its source but, as Rhyme had said dozens of times, a criminalist must ignore the apparent impossibilities of the job.

"Keep going—further, further . . .You're the Ghost. You're holding your knife or razor."

Then, suddenly, the phantom anger she felt vanished, replaced by an eerie serenity. This shocking, yet oddly magnetic, sensation filled her. Breathing hard, sweating, she stared at Jerry Tang and was possessed fully by the foul spirit of Kwan Ang, Gui, the Ghost. She *did* feel what he had experienced—a visceral satisfaction at the sight of his betrayer's pain and slow death.

Gasping, she realized she felt a deep lust to see more, to hear Tang's screams, watch his blood spiral down his shaking limbs . . .

And with that thought came another: "I'm . . ."

"What, Sachs?"

"*I'm* not the one torturing Tang."

"You're not?"

"No. I want the others to do it. So that I can watch. It's more satisfying that way. It's like a porno tape. I want to see everything, hear everything. I don't want to miss a single detail. And I have them cut his eyelids off first so Tang has to watch *me* watch him." She whispered, "I want it to keep going on and on."

A whisper. "Ah, good, Sachs. And that means there's a place you're watching *from*?"

"Yes. There's a chair here, facing Tang, about ten feet away from the body." Her voice cracked. "I'm watching," she whispered. "I'm enjoying it." She swallowed and felt sweat pouring from her scalp. "The screams lasted for five, ten minutes. I'm sitting in front of him all that time, enjoying every scream, every drop of blood, every slice." Her breathing was fast now.

"How you doing, Sachs?"

"Okay," she said.

But she wasn't okay at all. She was trapped—in that very place where she didn't want to be. Suddenly everything good in her life was negated and she slipped further into the core of the Ghost's world.

You're looking like it's bad news . . .

Her hands shook. She was desperate and alone.

You're looking like it's bad—

Stop it! she told herself.

"Sachs?" Rhyme asked.

"I'm fine."

Stop thinking about it, stop thinking about the bits of curled flesh, the smears of blood . . . Stop thinking about how much you're enjoying his pain.

Then she realized that the criminalist wasn't saying anything.

"Rhyme?"

No answer.

"You okay?" she asked.

"Not really," he finally answered.

"What is it?"

"I don't know. . . . What good does knowing where he sat do us? He was wearing those fucking smooth-soled shoes. It's the only place we know the Ghost himself spent any time but what kind of evidence is there?"

Still feeling nauseous, tainted by the Ghost's spirit within her, she glanced at the chair. But she looked away, unable to concentrate.

Discouraged, angry, he continued, "I can't think."

"I . . ."

"There's got to be *something*," he continued. She heard frustration in his voice and she supposed he was wishing he could come down and walk the grid himself.

"I don't know," she said, her voice weak.

She stared at the chair but she saw in her mind the knife working its way up and down Jerry Tang's flesh.

"Hell," Rhyme said, "I don't know either. Is the chair upright?"

"The one the Ghost sat in to watch from? Yes?"

"But what do we *do* with that fact?" His voice was frustrated.

Well, this wasn't like him. Lincoln Rhyme had opinions about everything. And why was he sounding as if he'd failed? His tone alarmed her. Was he still brooding over his role in the deaths of the immigrants and crew on the *Fuzhou Dragon*?

Sachs focused again on the chair, which was covered with debris from the vandalism. She studied it carefully. "I've got an idea. Hold on." She walked closer to the chair and looked beneath it. Her heart thudded with excitement. "There're scuff marks here, Rhyme. The Ghost sat down and leaned forward—to see better. He crossed his feet under the chair."

"And?" Rhyme asked.

"That means that any trace in the seam between the uppers and his sole might've fallen out. I'll vacuum underneath it. If we're lucky we might find something that'll lead us to his front door."

"Excellent, Sachs," Rhyme said. "Get the Dustbuster."

Excited at this find she started for the CS kit near the door to retrieve the vacuum. But then she stopped. She gave a faint laugh. "You got me, Rhyme."

"I did what?"

"Don't sound so innocent." She realized now that he'd known there was trace beneath the chair from the moment she'd deduced that the Ghost had sat watching the carnage. But he'd recognized that she was still lost in the Ghost's terrible world and that he needed to get her to a better place—the haven of the job they did together. He'd pretended to be frustrated to draw her attention back to him and ease her out of the darkness.

A misrepresentation, she supposed, but it is in such feints as this that love is found.

"Thanks."

"I promised I'd get you back. Now, go do some vacuuming."

Sachs swept the floor under and around the chair and then removed the filter from the portable vacuum and placed it in a plastic evidence bag.

"What happens next?" Rhyme asked.

She judged the angle of the blood spatter from the bullets that killed Tang. "Looks like when Tang finally passed out from the pain the Ghost stood up and shot him. Then he leaves and the assistants trash the place."

"How do you know things happened in that order?"

"Because there was debris covering one of the shell casings. And there was broken glass and some torn poster paper on the chair the Ghost'd been sitting in."

"Good."

Sachs said, "I'm going to do electrostatic prints of the shoes."

"Don't tell me, Sachs," Rhyme muttered, being Rhyme once again. "Just do it."

She stepped outside and returned with the equipment. In this process, a plastic sheet is placed over a shoeprint and an electric charge is sent through the sheet. The result is an image, like a plastic Xerox copy, of a foot- or shoeprint.

It was as she was crouching down, her back to the dark warehouse, that she smelled the cigarette smoke. Oh, Jesus, she thought suddenly—one of the killers was back, maybe aiming his weapon on the radiant white suit.

Maybe the Ghost himself . . .

No, she realized, it was the missing *bangshou!*

Sachs dropped the electrostatic equipment with a crash and spun around, falling hard to the floor on her back, her Glock .40 in her hand. The notch and blade sight rested squarely on the intruder's chest.

"What the fuck're you doing here?" she raged, in agony from the jarring fall.

Sonny Li, smoking a cigarette, was wandering through the office, looking around.

"What I doing? I investigate too."

"What's going on, Sachs!" Rhyme asked.

"Li's in the perimeter. He's smoking."

"What? Get him the hell out."

"I'm trying to." She rose painfully and stormed up to the Chinese cop. "You're contaminating the scene."

"A little smoke. You Americans are worry too much—"

"And the trace on your shoes, on your clothes, your footprints . . . You're ruining the scene!"

"No, no, I investigate."

"Get him out of there, Sachs!" Rhyme called.

She took him by the arm and walked him to the door. She called to Deng and Coe. "Keep him out."

"Sorry, Officer," Eddie Deng said. "He said he was going to help you run the scene."

"I am doing," Li said, perplexed. "What is problem?"

"Keep him here. Cuff him if you have to."

"Hey, Hongse, you got temper. You know that?"

She stormed back to the scene and finished the printing.

Rhyme said, "Is Eddie Deng there?"

"He's outside," Sachs replied.

"I know the company's supposedly clean but have him go through the files anyway—I assume they're in Chinese. See if he can find anything about the Ghost or smuggling, other snakeheads. Anything helpful."

Outside, she waved to Eddie Deng. He plucked a telephone earbud out of his ear and joined her. She relayed Rhyme's request and, as the Photo and Identification Units took over for Sachs, Deng dug through the desks and file cabinets. After a half hour of diligent work he told her, "Nothing helpful. It's all about restaurant supplies."

She told this to Rhyme and added, "I've got everything here. I'll be back in twenty minutes."

They disconnected the radio.

Massaging her sore spine, she reflected, And what *about* the Ghost's *bangshou*? Was he in the city? Was he really a threat to them?

Watch your backs . . .

She was just at the doorway when her cell phone rang. She answered it and was surprised, and pleased, to hear John Sung identify himself.

"How are you?" she asked.

"Fine. The wound itches some." He then added, "I wanted to tell you—I got some herbs for your arthritis. There's a restaurant downstairs in my building. Could you meet me there?"

Sachs looked at her watch. What could it hurt? She wouldn't be long. Handing off the evidence to Deng and Coe, she told them she had a stop to make and would be at Rhyme's in a half hour. They and Sonny Li got a ride back to Rhyme's from another officer. Li looked relieved he wouldn't be riding with her.

Sachs slipped out of the Tyvek suit and packed it away in the CS bus.

As she dropped into the driver's seat she glanced into the warehouse in which she could clearly see the body of Jerry Tang, his ever-open eyes staring at the ceiling.

Another corpse at the hand of the Ghost. Another name transferred from one balance sheet column to the other in *The Register of the Living and the Dead.*

No more, she thought to the ten judges of hell. Please no more.

Chapter Nineteen

Amelia Sachs, nursing the crime scene bus through the narrow streets of Chinatown, pulled into an alley near John Sung's apartment.

Climbing out, she glanced at a hand-painted sign in the florist shop on the ground floor of his building, next to the restaurant. "Need luck in you're life—buy our lucky bamboo!"

She then noticed Sung through the window of the restaurant. He waved, smiling.

Inside, he winced as he rose to greet her.

"No, no," Sachs said. "Don't get up."

She sat opposite him in a large booth.

"Would you like some food?"

"No. I can't stay long."

"Tea, then." He poured it and pushed the small cup toward her.

The restaurant was dark but clean. Several men sat hunched together in various booths, speaking in Chinese.

Sung asked, "Have you found him yet? The Ghost?"

Disinclined to talk about an investigation, she demurred and said only that they had some leads.

"I don't like this uncertainty," Sung said. "I hear footsteps in the hall and I freeze. It's like being in Fuzhou. Someone slows down outside your home and you don't know if they're neighbors or security officers the local party boss sent to your house to arrest you."

An image of what had happened to Jerry Tang came to her and she glanced out the window for a reassuring look at the squad car parked across the street in front of his building, guarding him.

"After all the press about the *Fuzhou Dragon*," she said, "you'd think the Ghost'd go back to China. Doesn't he know how many people're looking for him?"

Sung reminded, "'Break the cauldrons—'"

"'—and sink the boats.'" She nodded. Then she added, "Well, he's not the only one who's got that motto."

Sung assessed her for a moment. "You're a strong woman. Have you always been a security officer?"

"We call them police. Or cops. Security officers are private."

"Oh."

"Naw, I went to the police academy after I'd been working for a few years." She told him about her stint as a model for a Madison Avenue agency.

"You were a fashion model?" His eyes were amused.

"I was young. Interesting to try for a while. Was mostly my mother's idea. I remember once I was working on a car with my dad. He was a cop too but his hobby was cars. We were rebuilding an engine in this old Thunderbird. A Ford? A sports car. You know it?"

"No."

"And I was, I don't know, nineteen or something, I'd been doing freelance work for a modeling agency in the city. I was under the car and he dropped a crescent wrench. Caught me on the cheek."

"Ouch."

A nod. "But the big ouch was when my mother saw the cut. I don't know who she was madder at—me, my father or Ford Motor Company."

Sung asked, "And your mother? Is she who watches your children when you work?"

A sip of tea, a steady gaze. "I don't have any."

He frowned. "You . . . I'm sorry." Sympathy flooded his voice.

"It's not the end of the world," she said stoically.

Sung shook his head. "Of course not. I reacted badly. . . . East and West have different ideas about families."

Not necessarily, she thought, but wouldn't let her mind go any further than that.

Sung continued. "In China children are very important to us. Sure, we have the overpopulation problem but one of the most hated parts of the central government is the one-child rule. That only applies to the Han—the majority race in China—so we actually have people in borderline areas claiming to be racial minorities to have more than one child. I will have more some day. I will bring my children over here and then, when I meet someone, have two or three more."

He watched her when he said this and she felt that comfort radiating from his eyes again. From his smile too. She knew nothing of his competence as a practitioner of Chinese medicine but his face alone would go a long way in calming a patient and helping the healing process.

"You know our language is based on pictograms. The Chinese character for the word 'love' is brushstrokes that represent a mother holding a child."

She felt an urge to tell him more, to tell him that, yes, she wanted children very badly. But suddenly she felt like crying. Then controlled it fast. None of that. No bawling when you're wearing one of Austria's finest pistols on one hip and a can of pepper spray on the other. She realized that they'd been gazing at each other silently for a moment. She looked down, sipped more tea.

"Are you married?" Sung asked.

"No. I have someone in my life, though."

"That's good," he said, continuing to study her. "I sense he's in the same line of work. Is he by any chance that man you were telling me about? Lincoln . . ."

"Rhyme." She laughed. "You're pretty observant."

"In China, doctors are detectives of the soul." Then Sung leaned forward and said, "Hold your arm out."

"What?"

"Your arm. Please."

She did and he rested two fingers on her wrist.

"What?"

"Shhh. I'm taking your pulse."

After a moment he sat back. "My diagnosis is correct."

"About the arthritis, you mean?"

"Arthritis is merely a symptom. We think it's misguided to merely cure symptoms. The goal of medicine should be to rebalance harmonies."

"So what's unbalanced?"

"In China we like our numbers. The five blessings, the five beasts for sacrifice."

"The ten judges of hell," she said.

He laughed. "Exactly. Well, in medicine we have *liu-yin*: the six pernicious influences. They are dampness, wind, fire, cold, dryness and summer heat. They affect the organs of the body and the *qi*—the spirit—as well as the blood and essence. When they are excessive or lacking they create disharmony and that causes problems. Too much dampness must be dried out. Too much cold must be warmed."

The six pernicious influences, she reflected. Try putting *that* on a Blue Cross/Blue Shield form.

"I see from your tongue and pulse that you have excessive dampness on the spleen. That results in arthritis, among other problems."

"Spleen?"

"It is not just your actual spleen, according to Western medicine," he said, noting her skepticism. "Spleen is more of an organ system."

"So what does my spleen need?" Sachs asked.

"To be less damp," Sung answered as if it were obvious. "I got you these." He pushed a bag toward her. She opened it and found herbs and dried plants inside."Make them into tea and drink it slowly over the course of two days." Then he handed her a small box as well. "These are Qi Ye Lien tablets. Herbal aspirin. There're instructions in English on the box." Sung added, "Acupuncture will also help a great deal. I'm not licensed for acupuncture here and I don't want to risk any trouble before my INS hearing."

"I wouldn't want you to."

"But I can do massage. I think you call it acupressure. It's very effective. I'll show you. Lean toward me. Put your hands in your lap."

Sung leaned forward over the table, the stone monkey swinging away from his strong chest. Beneath his shirt she could see the fresh bandages over the wound from the Ghost's gunshot. His hands found spots on her shoulders and pressed into her skin hard for five seconds or so, then found new places and did the same.

After a minute of this he sat back.

"Now lift your arms."

She did and, though there was still some pain in her joints, she believed it much less than she'd been feeling lately. She said a surprised, "It worked."

"It's only temporary. Acupuncture lasts much longer."

"I'll think about it. Thank you." She glanced at her watch. "I should be getting back."

"Wait," Sung said, an urgency in his voice. "I'm not through with my diagnosis." He took her hand, examining the torn nails and worried skin. Normally she was very self-conscious about these bad habits of hers. But she didn't feel the least embarrassed by this man's perusal.

"In China doctors look and touch and talk to determine what is ailing a patient. It's vital to know their frame of mind—happy, sad, worried, ambitious, frustrated." He looked carefully into her eyes. "There's more disharmony within you. You want something you can't have. Or you *think* you can't have it. It's creating these problems." He nodded at her nails.

"What harmony do I want?"

"I'm not sure. Perhaps a family. Love. Your parents are dead, I sense."

"My father."

"And that was difficult for you."

"Yes."

"And lovers? You've had trouble with lovers."

"I scared 'em off in school—I could drive faster than most of them." This was meant as a joke, though it was true, but Sung didn't laugh.

"Go on," he encouraged.

"When I was a model the worthwhile men were too scared to ask me out."

"Why would a man be scared of a woman?" Sung asked, genuinely bewildered. "It's like yin being scared by yang. Night and day. They should not compete; they should complement and fulfill each other."

"Then the ones who had the guts to ask me out wanted pretty much only one thing."

"Ah, that."

"Yeah, that."

"Sexual energy," Sung said, "is very important, one of the most important parts of *qi*, spiritual power. But it's only healthy when it comes out of a harmonized relationship."

She laughed to herself. Now there's a phrase to try out on the first date: You interested in a harmonized relationship?

After a sip of tea she continued, "Then I lived with a man for a while. On the force."

"The what?" Sung asked.

"He was a cop too, I mean. It was good. Intense, challenging, I guess I'd say. We'd have dates at the small arms range and try to out-shoot each other. Only he got arrested. Taking kickbacks. You know what I mean?"

Sung laughed. "I've lived in China all my life—of course I know what kickbacks are. And now," he added, "you're with that man you work with."

"Yes."

"Maybe this is the source of the problem," Sung said quietly, studying her even more closely.

"Why d'you say that?" she asked uneasily.

"I would say you are yang—that word means the side of a mountain with the sun on it. Yang is brightness, movement, increase, arousal, beginnings, soft, spring and summer, birth. This is clearly you. But you seem to inhabit the world of the yin. That means the shadowy side of the mountain. It is inwardness, darkness, introspection, hardness and death. It is the end of things, autumn and winter." He paused. "I think perhaps the disharmony is that you aren't being true to your yang nature. You have let the yin too far into your life. Could that be the trouble?"

"I . . . I'm not sure."

"I've just been meeting with Lincoln Rhyme's physician."

"Yes?"

"I've got to talk to you about something."

Her cell phone rang and Sachs jumped at the sound. As she reached for the phone she realized that Sung's hand was still resting on her arm.

Sung eased back into the booth bench and she answered, "Hello?"

"Officer, where the hell are you?" It was Lon Sellitto.

She was reluctant to say but she glanced at the patrol car across the street and had a feeling that they might have told the detective where she was. She said, "With that witness, John Sung."

"Why?"

"Just needed to follow up on a few things."

Not a lie, she thought. Not exactly.

"Well, finish following up," the man said gruffly. "We need you here, at Rhyme's. There's evidence to look at."

Jesus, she thought. What's eating him?

"I'll be right there."

"Make sure you are," the detective snapped.

Perplexed at his attitude, she disconnected the line and said to Sung, "I have to go."

A hopeful expression on his face, the doctor asked, "Have you found Sam Chang and the others from the ship?"

"Not yet."

As she rose he startled her by asking quickly, "I'd be honored if you would come back to see me. I could continue my treatment." Sung pushed the bag of herbs and pills toward her.

She hesitated only a moment before saying, "Sure. I'd like that."

Chapter Twenty

"Hope we didn't interrupt anything important, Officer," Lon Sellitto said gruffly when she walked into Rhyme's living room.

She began to ask the detective what he meant but the criminalist himself began sniffing the air. Sachs responded with a querying glance.

"Recall my book, Sachs? 'Perfumes should not be worn by crime scene personnel because—'"

"'—odors not native to the scene may help identify individuals who have been present there.'"

"Good."

"But it's not perfume, Rhyme."

"Incense maybe?" he suggested.

"I met John Sung at a restaurant in his building. There was some incense burning."

"It stinks," Rhyme concluded.

"No, no," Sonny Li said. "Peaceful. Very peaceful."

No, it stank, petulant Rhyme thought. He glanced at the bag she carried and wrinkled his nose. "And what is *that*?"

"Medicine. For my arthritis."

"That stinks even more than the incense. What do you do with it?"

"Make it into tea."

"Probably tastes so vile that you forget about the pain in your joints.

Hope you enjoy it. *I'll* stick to scotch." He examined her closely for a moment. "Enjoy your visit with Dr. Sung, Sachs?"

"I—" she began uneasily, troubled by his edgy tone.

"How's he doing?" Rhyme asked blithely.

"Better," she answered.

"Talk much about his home in China? Where he travels? Whom he spends time with?"

"What're you getting at?" she asked cautiously.

"I'm just curious if what occurred to *me* occurred to *you*?"

"And that would be?"

"That *Sung* was the Ghost's *bangshou*. His assistant. His *co*-conspirator."

"What?" she gasped.

"Apparently it didn't," Rhyme observed.

"But there's no way. I've spent some time talking to him. He *can't* have any connection with the Ghost. I mean—"

"As a matter of fact," Rhyme interrupted, "he *doesn't*. We just got a report from the FBI office in Singapore. The Ghost's *bangshou* on the *Dragon* was Victor Au. The prints and picture match one of the three bodies the Coast Guard found this morning at the site of the sinking." He nodded toward the computer.

Sachs looked at the picture on Rhyme's screen and then glanced at the whiteboard on which were taped the Coast Guard's pictures of the bodies. Au was the one who'd drowned, not been shot.

Rhyme said sternly, "Sung's clean. But we didn't *know* that until ten minutes ago. I told you to be careful, Sachs. And you just dropped by Sung's to socialize. Don't go getting careless on me." His voice rose, saying, "And that goes for everybody!"

Search well but watch your back. . . .

"Sorry," she muttered.

What *was* distracting her? Rhyme wondered again. But he said only, "Back to work, boys and girls." Then nodded at the electrostatic shoeprints from the Tang crime scene that Thom had mounted on the evidence board. There was not much they could tell except that the Ghost's shoeprints, though an average size shoe, about an 8 in America, were larger than the three prints of his accomplices.

"Now, what about the trace that was in the Ghost's shoes, Mel?"

"Okay, Lincoln," the tech said slowly, looking over the screen of the chromatograph. "We've got something here. Very old oxidized iron flakes, old wood fibers and ash and silicon—looks like glass dust. And then the main act is a dark, low-luster mineral in large concentrations—montmorillonite. Alkaline oxide, too."

Okay, Rhyme mused. Where the hell did it come from? He nodded slowly then closed his eyes and began, figuratively, to pace.

When he'd been head of IRD—the Investigation and Resources Division of the NYPD, the forensic unit—Rhyme had walked everywhere in New York City. He carried small bags and jars in his pockets for the samples of soil and concrete and dust and vegetation he'd collect to add to his knowledge of the city. A criminalist must know his territory in a thousand different ways: as sociologist, cartographer, geologist, engineer, botanist, zoologist, historian.

He realized that there was something familiar about the trace that Cooper was describing. But what?

Wait, there's a thought. Hold on to it.

Damn, it slipped away.

"Hey, Loaban?" a voice called, but from a distance. Rhyme ignored Li and continued to walk intently through, then fly over, the various neighborhoods of the city.

"Is he—?"

"Shhhhh," Sachs said firmly.

Freeing him to continue on his journey.

He sailed over the Columbia University tower, over Central Park with its loam and limestone and wildlife excrement, through the streets of Midtown coated with the residue of the tons of soot that fall upon them daily, the boat basins with their peculiar mix of gasoline, propane and diesel fuel, the decaying parts of the Bronx with their lead paint and old plaster mixed with sawdust as filler. . . .

Soaring, soaring . . .

Until he came to one place.

His eyes opened.

"Downtown," he said. "The Ghost's downtown."

"Sure." Alan Coe shrugged. "Chinatown."

"No, not Chinatown," Rhyme replied. "Battery Park City or one of the developments around there."

"How'd you figure that out?" Sellitto asked.

"That montmorillonite? It's bentonite. That's a clay used as slurry to keep groundwater out of foundations when construction crews dig deep foundations. When they built the World Trade Center they sunk the foundation sixty-five feet down to the bedrock. The builder used millions of tons of bentonite. It's all over the place down there."

"But they use bentonite in a lot of places," Cooper pointed out.

"Sure, but the other trace materials Sachs found are from there too. That whole area is landfill and it's full of rusted metal and glass trace. And the ash? To clear the old piers down there the builders burned them."

"And it's only twenty minutes from Chinatown," Deng pointed out.

Thom wrote this on the evidence chart.

Still, it was a huge area and contained many high-density buildings: hotels, apartments and office buildings. They would need more information in order to narrow down exactly where the Ghost might be staying.

Sonny Li was pacing, walking in front of the board.

"Hey, Loaban, I got some ideas too."

"About what?" Rhyme grumbled. The man reeked of cigarette smoke. Rhyme had never smoked but he felt a huge burst of crip envy—that this man could partake in his vices all by himself, without having to track down a conspirator to help him.

Fucking surgery better do something, he thought.

"Hey, Loaban, you listening?"

"Go ahead, Sonny," Rhyme said, distracted.

"I was at crime scene too."

"Yeah," Sachs said, giving him an exasperated look. "Walking around, smoking."

"See," Rhyme explained, trying against his nature to be patient, "anything that comes into the crime scene after the perpetrator can contaminate it. That makes it harder to find the evidence that would lead to the suspect."

"Hey, Loaban, you think I don't know that? Sure, sure, you pick up dust and dirt and put in gas chromatograph and then spectrometer and use scanning electron microscope." The complicated English words fell awkwardly from his tongue. "Match against data bases."

"You know about forensic equipment?" Rhyme asked, blinking in surprise.

"*Know* about it? Sure, we use that stuff. Hey, I study at Beijing Institute of Forensics. Got nice medal. Second in class. I know *all* that, I'm saying." He added testily, "We not back in Ming dynasty, Loaban. I got own computer—Windows XP. All kinds databases too. And cell phone and pager."

"Okay, Sonny, got the point. What'd you see at the scene?"

"Disharmony. *That* what I saw."

"Explain," Rhyme said.

"Harmony very important in China. Even crime has harmony. At that place back there, that warehouse, no harmony at all."

"What's a harmonious killing?" Coe asked wryly.

"The Ghost find man who betray him. He torture him, kill him and leave. But, hey, Hongse, remember? Place all destroyed. Posters of China torn up, statues of Buddha and dragons broken. . . . Han Chinese not do that."

"That's the racial majority in China—the Han," Eddie Deng explained. "But the Ghost's Han, isn't he?"

"Sure but *he* not do it. Office got messed up *after* Tang killed. I hear her say that."

Sachs confirmed this.

"Probably Ghost left and then those men work for him, they vandal the office. I'm thinking he hire ethnic minority for his *ba-tu*."

"Muscle, thugs," Deng translated.

"Yeah, yeah, thugs. Hire them from minorities. Mongols, Manchus, Tibetans, Uighurs."

"That's crazy, Sonny," Rhyme said. "Harmony?"

"Crazy?" Li replied, shrugging broadly. "Sure, you right, Loaban. I crazy. Like when I say you find Jerry Tang first, I crazy. But, hey, you listen me then, we maybe found Tang when he alive, strap him down and use ox prod till he tell us where is Ghost." The entire team turned to him in shock. Li hesitated a moment then laughed. "Hey, Loaban, joke."

Though Rhyme wasn't completely sure he was kidding.

Li continued, pointing at the board, "You want evidence? Okay, here evidence. Shoeprints. Smaller than Ghost's. Han—Chinese—not big people. Like me. Not big like you. But people from west and north minorities, lot of them even smaller than us. There, you like that *forensic* stuff, Loaban? Thought you would. So go find some minorities. You get lead to Ghost, I'm saying."

Rhyme glanced at Sachs and he could tell she was thinking the same thing. What can it hurt? Rhyme asked Eddie Deng, "What *about* it? You know these minorities?"

"I don't have a clue," he replied. "Most of the people we deal with in the Fifth Precinct are Han—Fujianese, Cantonese, Mandarin, Taiwanese. . . ."

Coe agreed, adding, "The minorities would keep to themselves."

Impatient now that there was a lead to be pursued, Rhyme snapped, "Well, who *would* know? I want to follow up on it. How?"

"Tongs," Li said. "Tongs know everything. Han, non-Han, everything."

"And what exactly *is* a tong?" Rhyme asked, having only a vague memory from some bad movie he'd watched when recovering from his accident.

Eddie Deng explained that tongs were societies of Chinese who had common interests: people who came from a particular area in China or who practiced the same trade or profession. They were shrouded in secrecy and, in the old days, met only in private—"tong" means "chamber." In the United States they arose for protection from whites and for self-governance; traditionally Chinese resolved disputes among themselves, and the head of one's tong had more power over his members than did the president of the United States.

Though they had a long tradition in crime and violence, he continued, in recent years tongs had cleaned themselves up. The word "tong" was out and they began calling themselves "public associations," "benevolent societies," or "merchant guilds." Many were still just as involved in gambling, massage parlors, extortion and money laundering as ever but they distanced themselves from violence. They hired young men with no connection to the tongs to act as enforcers.

"Outsourcing," Deng joked.

"Were you in one, Eddie?" Rhyme asked.

The detective polished his stylish glasses as he responded defensively, "For a while. It was a kid thing."

"Is there anybody at one we can talk to?" Sachs asked.

Deng thought for a moment. "I'd give Tony Cai a call. He helps us some—up to a point—and he's one of the best connected *loaban*s in the area. Lot of *guanxi*. He runs the Eastern Chinese Public Association. They're on the Bowery."

"Call him," Rhyme ordered.

Coe shook his head. "Won't talk on the phone."

"Bugged?"

Deng said, "No, no, it's a cultural thing. For some matters you have to meet face-to-face. But there's a catch—Cai won't want to be seen around police, not with the Ghost involved."

A thought occurred to Rhyme. "Get a limo and bring him here."

"What?" Sellitto asked.

"The heads of tongs . . . they have egos, right?"

"You bet," Coe said.

"Tell him we need his help and that the mayor's sending a limo to pick him up."

While Sellitto called about the car Eddie Deng rang up Cai's community association. The conversation was in the clipped and singsongy cadence of rapidly spoken Chinese. Eddie put his hand over the mouthpiece. "Let me get this straight—I'm telling him this is at the mayor's request."

"No," Rhyme said. "Tell him it's the *governor's* office."

"We oughta be a little careful here, Linc," Sellitto said delicately.

"We'll be careful after we collar the Ghost."

Deng nodded, returned to the phone and they spoke some more. He hung up. "Okay. He'll do it."

Sonny Li was patting the pockets of his trousers absently, looking for cigarettes undoubtedly. He seemed uneasy.

"Hey, Loaban, I ask you something. Maybe you do me favor?"

"What?"

"I make phone call? Back to China. Cost some money I not have. But I pay you back."

"That's all right," Rhyme said.

"Who're you calling?" Coe asked bluntly.

"Private. My business."

"No. You don't *have* a private life around here, Li. Tell us, or no call."

The cop offered a cold glance at the INS agent and said, "Call is to my father."

Coe muttered, "I know Chinese—Putonghua and Minnanhua. I understand *hao*. I'll be listening."

Rhyme nodded at Thom, who got an international operator on the line and placed the call to the town of Liu Guoyuan in Fujian. He handed the receiver to Li, who took it uncertainly. He glanced at the plastic hand piece for a moment then turned away from Rhyme and the others and slowly brought it to his ear.

Rhyme suddenly saw a different Sonny Li. One of the first words he heard was "Kangmei"—Sonny's formal name. The man was obsequious, slumped, nervous, nodding like a young student as he spoke. Finally he hung the phone up and stood looking down at the floor for a moment.

Sachs asked, "Something wrong?"

The Chinese cop was suddenly aware that someone had spoken to him. He shook his head in reply to the question and turned back to Rhyme. "Okay, Loaban, what we going do now?"

"We're going to look at some harmonious evidence," Rhyme responded.

Chapter Twenty-one

A half hour later the doorbell sounded and Thom vanished into the hall. He returned with a heavyset Chinese man in a gray, fully buttoned suit, white shirt and striped tie. His face revealed no surprise or shock at seeing Rhyme in the Storm Arrow chair or at the collection of forensic equipment in the quaint Victorian town house. The only bit of emotion was when he glanced at Sachs and saw her sipping tea, redolent of herbs the man seemed to recognize by smell.

"I am Mr. Cai."

Rhyme introduced himself. "You're comfortable with English?"

"Yes."

"We have a problem, Mr. Cai, and I hope you can help us."

"You work for governor?"

"That's right."

In a distant sort of way we do, Rhyme thought, raising an ironic eyebrow toward the still-uneasy Lon Sellitto.

As Cai sat down, Rhyme explained about the *Fuzhou Dragon* and the immigrants hiding in town. Another flash of emotion when the name the Ghost was mentioned but then the face went blank again. Rhyme nodded to Deng, who told him about the killers and their suspicion that the men were from a Chinese ethnic minority group.

Cai nodded, considering this. Beneath large, wire-rimmed bifocals, his eyes were quick. "The Ghost, we know about him. He does much harm to all of us here. I will help you. . . . Ethnic minorities? In Chinatown there are none but I'll make some inquiries into other areas around the city. I have many connections."

"It's very important," Sachs said to him. "Those ten people, the witnesses . . . the Ghost is going to kill them if we don't find them first."

"Of course," Cai said sympathetically. "I'll do whatever I can. If your driver can take me back now I'll begin."

"Thank you," Sachs said. Sellitto and Rhyme nodded their gratitude too.

Cai rose and shook hands though unlike most visitors there was not even a vestigial gesture of his arm toward Rhyme but merely a nod, which told the criminalist that he was very much in control of himself and far more perceptive and intelligent than his distracted demeanor suggested.

He was glad this man would be helping them.

But as Cai walked toward the door Sonny Li said abruptly, *"Ting!"*

"He said, 'Wait,'" Eddie Deng explained to Rhyme in a whisper.

Cai turned around, a frown on his face. Li strode up to him and, gesturing broadly, began speaking harshly. The tong leader leaned closer to Li and the two began an explosive conversation.

Rhyme thought they were going to come to blows.

"Hey!" Sellitto said to Li. "What the hell're you doing?"

Li ignored him and, red-faced, continued to pummel Cai with words. The tong leader finally grew quiet. His head finally dipped and his eyes scanned the floor.

Rhyme looked at Deng, who shrugged. "Too fast for me. I couldn't follow it."

As Li continued to speak, more calmly now, Cai began to nod and respond. Finally Li asked a question and the tong leader extended his hand and they shook.

Cai gave another brief nod to Rhyme, his face completely emotionless, and then left.

"What on earth was that?" Sachs asked.

"Why you just let him leave before?" Li said gruffly to Rhyme. "He not going to help you."

"Yes, he was."

"No, no, no. Not matter what he said. Dangerous for him help us. He has family, not want them hurt. He not getting nothing from you. Limo not fool him." He waved around the room. "He know governor not involved."

"But he *said* he'd help us," Sellitto said.

"Chinese not like say no," Li explained. "Easier for us to find excuse or just say yes and then forget it. Cai was going back to office and forget you, I'm saying. He say he help but he was really saying, '*Mei-you.*' You know what is *mei-you*? Means, I not help you; go away."

"What'd you say? What were you fighting about?"

"No, no, not fight. We negotiation. You know, business. *Now* he going to look for your minorities. He really do it."

"Why?" Rhyme asked.

"You pay him money."

"What?" Sellitto asked.

"Not so much. Only cost you ten thousand. Dollar, not yuan."

"No way," Alan Coe said.

"Jesus Christ," Sellitto said. "We haven't got that in the budget."

Rhyme and Sachs looked at each other and laughed.

Li scoffed, "You a big city, you rich. You got strong dollar, Wall Street, you run World Trade Organization. Hey, Cai want lot more at first."

"We can't pay—" Sellitto began.

"Come on, Lon," Rhyme said, "you've got your snitch fund. Anyway, technically this's a federal operation. The INS'll cough up half of it."

"I don't know about that," Coe said uneasily, running his hand over his red hair.

"It's okay—I'll sign the chit myself," Rhyme said and the agent blinked, not sure whether it was appropriate to laugh at this. "Call Peabody. And we'll get Dellray to contribute too." He glanced at Li. "What're the terms?"

"I did good bargain. He give us names first and then he get paid. Course, he wants pay in cash."

"Of course."

"Okay, I need a cigarette. I take break for while, Loaban? I need good cigarettes. You got fuck worst ones in this country. Not taste like nothing. Get some food too."

"Go ahead, Sonny. You earned it."

As the Chinese cop left the room Thom asked, "What do I put down on the chart?" Nodding at the evidence whiteboard. "About Cai and the tongs."

"I don't know," Sachs said. "I think I'd say, 'Checking out the woo-woo evidence.'"

Lincoln Rhyme, however, opted for something somewhat more help-ful. "How 'bout: 'Suspected accomplices from Chinese ethnic minority,'" he dictated. "'Presently pursuing whereabouts.'"

The Ghost, accompanied by the three Turks, was driving a stolen Chevro-let Blazer into Queens en route to the Changs' apartment.

As he drove through the streets, carefully as always, so that he wouldn't get stopped, he reflected on Jerry Tang's death. He hadn't for a moment considered letting the man go unpunished for his betrayal. Nor had he con-sidered delaying the retribution. Disloyalty to your superiors was the worst crime in Confucian philosophy. Tang had abandoned him on Long Island—a situation from which he'd escaped only because of the luck of finding that car with the engine running at the restaurant on the beach. So the man'd had to die and to die painfully. The Ghost thought of the Shang emperor Zhou Xin. Once, sensing disloyalty from one of his vassals, the emperor butchered the man's son and, had him cooked and served to the unsuspecting traitor for dinner, after which he cheerfully revealed the main ingredient of the main course. The Ghost thought such justice was perfectly reasonable, not to mention satisfying.

A block from the Changs' apartment he pulled the Blazer to the curb.

"Masks," he ordered.

Yusuf dug into a bag and handed out ski masks.

The Ghost considered how best to attack the family. Sam Chang had a wife and an elderly father or mother with him, he'd been told. The main risk, though, would be any older children, like teenage boys. Life was for them just a video game and when the Ghost and the others broke in, a teenager might charge them with a knife.

"Kill any sons first," he instructed them. "Then their father and the old people." Then he had a thought. "Don't kill the wife yet. Bring her with us."

The Turks apparently understood the reason for this and nodded.

The Ghost surveyed the quiet street, across which were two long warehouses. Halfway along the block was an alley between the buildings. According to the map, the Changs' address was just on the other side of the warehouses. It was possible that Chang and his sons or father would be watching the front of the house so the Ghost would speed down the alley to the rear and they would rush in through the back door, while one of the Turks ran to the front door in case the family tried to escape that way.

He said in English, "Wear the masks on top of your heads like hats until we're at the house."

They nodded and did so. With their dark complexions and the stocking caps they looked like black gangstas in a bizarre rap video.

The Ghost donned his own mask.

He felt a moment's fear, as he often did at times like this, just before going into battle. There was always a chance that Chang had a gun or that the police had found the family first, had taken them to detention and were themselves waiting for the Ghost at the apartment.

But he reminded himself that fear was part of humility and it was the humble who succeeded in this world. He thought of one of his favorite passages from the *Tao*.

Yield and you need not break.

Bent, you can straighten.

Emptied, you can hold.

Torn, you can mend.

The Ghost now added his own line: Afraid, you can be brave.

He glanced at Yusuf, sitting next to him in the passenger seat. The Uighur nodded firmly in reply. And with the skill of seasoned craftsmen they began checking their weapons.

Chapter Twenty-two

Sonny Li had found some very good cigarettes indeed.

Camels, without filters on the end, which tasted pretty close to the brand he regularly bought in China. He inhaled deeply and said, "Bet five." Li pushed the chips forward and watched the other poker players consider how to respond as the bet went around the cheap fiberboard table, stained from years of sweaty hands and spilled liquor.

The gambling parlor was on Mott Street, in the heart of Chinatown, the neighborhood to which he'd come to buy his cigarettes. Such a long trip probably wasn't what Loaban had in mind when he gave Li permission to buy some smokes. But no matter. He'd return soon enough. There was no hurry.

The parlor was a large one, populated mostly with Fujianese (he wanted to avoid running into the Cantonese guard he'd mugged that morning) and featured a full bar and three cigarette machines. The room was dark, except for dim lights over the tables, but with his sharp security bureau officer's eye he had spotted five armed guards.

This was not a problem, though. No stealing guns now or beating up pretty boys. He was here only to gamble, drink and chat.

He won the hand and laughed then poured *mao-tai* into the glasses of everyone at the table, except the dealer, who was not allowed to drink. The men lifted the glasses and quickly tossed back the clear, potent liquor. *Mao-tai* was China's version of moonshine and you didn't sip it; you poured it into your gullet as fast as you could.

Li struck up conversations with the men hunched over the table around him. A bottle of liquor and a dozen Camels later Sonny Li estimated his net loss to be merely seven dollars.

He decided against another glass and rose to go.

Several of the men asked him to stay. They were enjoying his company.

But Li told them that his mistress awaited and the men nodded enthusiastically.

"She fuck you every way," an old, drunk man said. It wasn't clear to Li if this was a question or a statement.

Sonny Li walked to the door, giving them a smile that confirmed the high quality of his love life. The truth, however, was that this particular gambling parlor had turned out to have little for him and he wanted to try another.

The Blazer, speeding down the alleyway that led to the rear of the Changs' apartment.

The Ghost, gripping his Model 51 pistol in one hand, the leather-clad steering wheel in the other.

The Turks, poised to leap from the SUV.

They burst from the alley into a large parking lot—and found a huge semitruck bearing down on them, head-on.

With a deep groan of brakes the truck began to skid.

The Ghost shoved his foot down on the brake pedal—instinctively striking the floor with his left foot as well, hitting the spot where the clutch in his BMW sports car was. The Blazer swerved and skidded to a stop door-to-door with the truck. He gasped and felt his heart stutter from the near-miss.

"What the fuck're you doing?" the truck driver shouted. He leaned down toward the Blazer's driver's side window. "It's one-way, you fucking Jap! You come to this country, learn the fucking rules."

The Ghost was too shaken to answer.

The driver put the truck in gear and pulled past the Chevy.

The Ghost thanked his god, Yi the archer, for saving him from death. Ten seconds later and they would have collided head-on with the truck.

Starting forward slowly, the Ghost glanced at the Turks, who were looking around with frowns. They were confused, troubled.

"Where it is?" asked Yusuf, who was gazing at the large parking lot in which they found themselves. "The Changs' apartment? I cannot see it."

There were no residences anywhere around here.

The Ghost checked the address. The number was correct; this was the place. Except . . . except that it was a large retail shopping center. The alleyway that the Ghost had turned onto was one of the exits from the parking lot.

"*Gan,*" the Ghost spat out.

"What happened?" one of the Turks in the back asked him.

What had happened was that Chang hadn't trusted Jimmy Mah, the Ghost realized. He'd given the tong leader a fake address. He'd probably seen an advertisement for this place. He glanced up at the big sign over their heads.

THE HOME STORE
YOUR SOURCE FOR EVERY HOUSE AND LAWN NEED

The Ghost considered what to do. The other immigrant, Wu, probably hadn't been so clever. He had used Mah's broker to get an apartment. The Ghost had the name of the broker and they could find out the location of that family quickly.

"We'll get the Wus now," the Ghost said. "Then we'll find the Changs."

Naixin.

All in good time.

Sam Chang hung up the phone.

Numb, he stood for a moment, staring at a TV show, which depicted a living room very different from the one he was now in and a content and silly family very different from his own. He glanced at Mei-Mei, who was looking at him with a querying glance. He shook his head and she dutifully returned to Po-Yee, the baby. Chang then crouched down beside his father and whispered to him, "Mah is dead."

"Mah?"

"The *loaban* in Chinatown, the one who helped us. I called to ask about our papers. His girl said that he was dead."

"The Ghost? That was who killed him?"

"Who else?"

His father asked, "Did Mah know where we are?"

"No." Chang hadn't trusted Mah. So he'd given the address of one of the Home Stores in the flyer he'd found at the shopping center where they'd stolen the paint and brushes.

The Changs were, in fact, not in Queens at all but in Brooklyn, a neighborhood called Owls Head, near the harbor. That this had been their destination was a secret he'd kept from everyone except his father.

The old man nodded and winced as some pain shot through him.

"Morphine?"

His father shook his head and breathed deeply for a moment. "This news about Mah—it confirms that the Ghost is looking for us."

"Yes." Then Chang had a troubling thought. "The Wus! The Ghost can find them. They got their apartment through Mah's broker. I have to warn him." He stepped toward the door.

"No," his father said. "You can't save a man from his own foolishness."

"He has a family too. Children, his wife. We can't let them die."

Chang Jiechi thought for some moments. Finally the old man said, "All right but don't go yourself. Use the phone. Call that woman back. Tell her to get a message to Wu, warn him."

Chang picked up the phone and dialed. He spoke to the woman from Mah's office again and asked her to get a message to Wu. "Tell him he must move at once. He and his family are in great danger. You will tell him that?"

"Yes, yes," she said but she was clearly distraught and Chang had no idea if she actually would do as he'd asked.

His father closed his eyes and lay back on the couch. Chang wrapped the blanket around his feet. The old man would need to see a doctor very soon.

So many things to do, precautions to take. For a moment he was overwhelmed by the hopelessness of it all. He thought of the amulet that Dr. John Sung wore—the Monkey King. In the hold of the ship he'd let young Ronald play with the charm and had told him stories about Monkey. One of them was how the gods punished Monkey for his effrontery by burying him under a huge mountain. This is how Sam Chang now felt—covered by a million kilos of fear and uncertainty.

But his eyes then fell on his family and the burden lessened somewhat.

William laughed at something on the television; Chang believed this was the first time that his oldest son had been free from the anger and sour spirit that he'd radiated all day. He was laughing in genuine good spirits at the frivolous show. Ronald too.

Chang then looked at his wife, completely absorbed in the child, Po-Yee. How comfortable she is with children. Chang himself didn't have this easiness with them. He was forever weighing what he said—should he be stern about this matter, lenient about that?

Mei-Mei perched the baby on her own knees and made the child giggle as she rocked her.

In China families pray for a son to carry on the family name (traditionally, not bearing a male heir was grounds for divorce). Chang of course had been delighted when William had been born, and Ronald after him, proud that he could assure his own father that the Chang line would continue. But Mei-Mei's sadness at not having a daughter had been a source of sorrow for him too. And so Chang had found himself in a curious position for a Chinese man of a certain age—hoping for a girl, should Mei-Mei have gotten pregnant again. As a persecuted dissident and flouter of the one-child rule, the party could not have punished him more for having yet another child so he was fully prepared to try to give his wife a daughter.

But she had been very ill during her pregnancy with Ronald and it had taken her months to recover from the delivery. She was a slight woman, no longer young, and the doctors urged, for her health, that she not have any more children. She had accepted this stoically, as she had accepted Chang's decision to come to the Beautiful Country—which virtually precluded the chance that they could adopt a daughter, because of their illegal status.

Out of this terrible plight, though, had apparently come some good to balance the hardship. The gods or fate or the spirit of some ancestor had bestowed Po-Yee on them, the daughter that they could never have, and restored the harmony within his wife.

Yin-yang, light and dark, male and female, sorrow and joy.

Deprivation and gift . . .

Chang rose and walked to his sons and sat down to watch the television with them. He moved very slowly, very quietly, as if any abrupt motion would shatter this fragile familial peace like a rock dropping into a still morning pond.

III

The Register
of the Living
and the Dead

Tuesday, the Hour of the Rooster, 6:30 P.M.,
to Wednesday, the Hour of the Rat, 1 A.M.

In Wei-Chi . . . the two players facing the empty [board] begin by seizing the points they believe to be advantageous. Little by little the deserted areas disappear. Then comes the clash between the conflicting masses; struggles of defense and offense develop, just as happens in the world.

—*The Game of Wei-Chi*

Chapter Twenty-three

His wife was getting worse.

It was now early evening and Wu Qichen had sat for the past hour on the floor next to the mattress and bathed his wife's forehead. His daughter had painstakingly brewed the herbal tea he'd bought and together he and the girl had fed the hot liquid to the feverish woman. She'd taken the pills too but there seemed to be no improvement.

He leaned forward again and wiped her skin. Why wasn't she getting better? he raged. Had the herbalist cheated him? And why was his wife so thin to start with? She wouldn't have gotten sick on the voyage if she'd eaten right, gotten more sleep before they left. Yong-Ping, a fragile, pale woman, should have forced herself to take better care of herself. She had responsibilities. . . .

"I'm frightened," she said. "I don't know what's real. It's all a dream to me. My head, the pain . . ." The woman began muttering and finally fell silent.

And suddenly Wu realized that he was frightened too. For the first time since they'd left Fuzhou, a lifetime ago, Wu Qichen began to think about losing her. Oh, there were many things about Yong-Ping that he didn't understand. They had married impulsively, without knowing much of each other. She was moody, she was sometimes less respectful than his father, say, would have tolerated. But she was a good mother to the children, she was dependable in the kitchen, she deferred to his parents, she was clever in bed. And she was always ready to sit quietly and listen to him—to take him seriously. Not many people did.

The thin man glanced up and saw their son standing in the doorway. Lang's eyes were wide and he had been crying.

"Go back and watch television," Wu told him.

But the boy didn't move. He stared at his mother.

The man stood. "Chin-Mei," he snapped. "Come here."

The girl appeared in the doorway a moment later. "Yes, Baba?"

"Bring me some of the new clothes for your mother."

The girl disappeared and returned a moment later with a pair of blue stretch pants and a T-shirt. Together they dressed the woman. Chin-Mei got a clean cloth and wiped her mother's forehead.

Wu then went to the electronics store next door to the apartment. He asked the clerk where the closest hospital was. The man told him that there was a big clinic not far away. He wrote down the address in English, as Wu asked; he'd decided to spend the money on a taxi to take his wife there and needed the written note to show the driver; his English was very bad. When he returned to the apartment he said to his daughter, "We'll be back soon. Listen to me carefully. You are not to open the door for anyone. Do you understand that?"

"Yes, Father."

"You and your brother will stay in the apartment. Do not go outside for any reason."

She nodded.

"Lock the door and put that chain on it after we leave."

Wu opened the door, held his arm out for his wife to cling to and then stepped outside. He paused, heard the door latch and the rattle of the chain. Then they started down Canal Street, filled with so many people, so many opportunities, so much money—none of which meant much of anything to the small, frightened man at the moment.

"There!" the Ghost said urgently, as he turned the corner and eased the Blazer to the curb on Canal Street near Mulberry in Chinatown. "It's the Wus."

Before he and the Turks could find their masks and climb out of the vehicle, though, Wu helped his wife into a taxi. He climbed in after her and the cab drove away. The yellow cab was soon lost in the busy traffic of rush-hour Canal Street.

The Ghost eased back into traffic and parked in a space directly across from the apartment whose address, and front-door key, Mah's real estate broker had given him a half hour ago—just before they'd shot him to death.

"Where do you think they've gone?" one of the Turks asked the Ghost.

"I don't know. She looked sick, his wife. You saw how she was walking. Maybe to a doctor."

The Ghost surveyed the street. He measured distances and noted particularly the number of jewelry stores here at the intersection of Mulberry and Canal. It was a smaller version of the Midtown diamond district. This troubled the Ghost. It meant that there would be dozens of armed security guards on the street—if they killed the Wus before the stores closed they might expect one of them to hear the gunshots and come running to the sound. Even after-hours, though, there would be risks: he could see the square boxes of dozens of security cameras covering the sidewalks. They were out of sight of the cameras here but to approach the Wus, they would be well within range of the lenses. They'd have to move fast and wear the ski masks.

"I think here is how we should handle it," the Ghost said in slow English. "Are you listening?"

Each of the Turks turned his attention to him.

After her father and mother had left, Wu Chin-Mei made some tea for her brother and gave him a tea bun and rice. She reflected how badly her father had embarrassed her in front of a handsome young man in the grocery store by actually bargaining for the food they'd bought this morning when they'd arrived in Chinatown.

Saving a few yuan on tea buns and noodles!

She sat eight-year-old Lang down in front of the television with his food and then walked into the bedroom to change the sweat-stained sheets of their mother's bed.

Glancing at the mirror, she studied herself. She was pleased with what she saw: her long black hair, wide lips, deep eyes.

Several people had remarked that she looked like Lucy Liu, the actress, and Chin-Mei could see that was true. Well, she would look more like her after she lost a few pounds—and fixed her nose, of course. And these *ridiculous* clothes! A pale green workout suit . . . how disgusting. Clothes were important to Wu Chin-Mei. She and her girlfriends would raptly study the broadcasts of the fashion shows from Beijing, Hong Kong and Singapore, the tall models swiveling their hips as they walked down the runway. Then the girls, thirteen and fourteen, would stage their own fashion shows, traipsing down a homemade runway then ducking behind screens to change.

One time, before the party cracked down on her father for opening his loud mouth, the family had gone with him to Xiamen, south of Fuzhou. This was a delightful town, a tourist draw, catering to many Taiwanese and Western travelers. At a tobacco shop where her father had gone to buy cigarettes Chin-Mei had been stunned to see more than thirty fashion magazines in the racks. She'd remained in the store for a half hour while her father did some business nearby and their mother took Lang to a park. She worked her way through all of them. Most were from the West but many were published in Beijing or in other cities in the Free Zones along the coast and showed the latest creations of Chinese designers, which were as stylish as anything produced in Milan or Paris.

The teenager had planned to study fashion in Beijing and become a famous designer herself—possibly after a year or two of modeling.

But now her father had ruined that.

She dropped onto the bed, grabbed the phony cloth of her cheap running suit and tugged at it in a fury, wanted to rip it to pieces.

What would she do with her life now?

Work in a factory, stitching together crappy clothes like this. Making two hundred yuan a month and giving it to her pathetic parents. Maybe that would be how she'd spend the rest of her life.

That would be her career in the fashion business. Slavery . . . She was—

A sharp knock on the door interrupted her thoughts.

Gasping in fright, she sat up fast, picturing the snakehead in the raft, a gun in his hand. The pop of the shots as he killed the drowning victims. She walked into the living room and turned the volume on the TV down. Lang looked up with a frown but she touched his lips to keep him silent.

A woman's voice called, "Mr. Wu? Are you there, Mr. Wu? I have a message from Mr. Chang."

Chang, she recalled, the man who had saved them from the hold of the ship and sailed the raft to shore. She liked him. She liked his son too, the one with the Western name, William. He was sullen and lean and handsome. Cute but a risk: he was clearly triad bait.

"It's important," the woman said. "If you're there, open the door. Please. Mr. Chang said you're in danger. I worked with Mr. Mah. He's dead. You're in danger too. You need a new place to stay. I can help you find one. Can you hear me?"

Chin-Mei couldn't get the sound of the gun out of her mind. The terrible man, the Ghost, shooting at them. The explosion in the ship, the water.

Should she go with this woman? Chin-Mei debated.

"Please . . ." More pounding.

But then she heard her father's words ordering her to stay, not to open the door for anyone. And as angry as she was, as wrong as she thought her father was in so many ways, she couldn't disobey him.

She'd wait here silently and not let anyone in. When her parents returned she would give them the message.

The woman in the alleyway must've gone—there was no more knocking. Chin-Mei turned up the volume on the TV again and fixed a cup of tea for herself.

She sat for a few minutes, studying the outfits of the American actresses on a sitcom.

Then she heard the click of a key in the latch.

Her father was back already? She leapt up, wondering what had been wrong with their mother. Was she all right now? Did she have to stay in hospital?

Just as she got to the door and said, "Father—" it opened fast and a small swarthy man pushed inside, slammed the door behind him and pointed a pistol at her.

Chin-Mei screamed and tried to run to Lang but the man leapt forward and grabbed her around the waist. He flung her to the floor. He took her sobbing brother by the collar and dragged him across the room to the bathroom, pushed him inside. "Stay there, be quiet, brat," he snarled in bad English. He pulled the door shut.

The girl wrapped her arms around her chest and scrabbled away from him. She stared at the key. "How . . . where did you get that." Afraid that he'd killed her parents and taken it from them.

He didn't understand her Chinese, though, and she repeated it in English.

"Shut your mouth. If you scream again I'll kill you." He took a cell phone from his pocket and made a call. "I'm inside. The children are here."

The man—dark and Arab-looking, probably from western China—nodded as he listened, looking Chin-Mei up and down. Then he gave a sour sneer. "I don't know, seventeen, eighteen . . . Pretty enough. . . . All right."

He disconnected the call.

"First," he said in English, "some food." He seized her hair and dragged the sobbing girl into the kitchen. "What do you have to eat here?"

But all she could hear were those three words looping over and over through her mind.

First, some food . . . first, some food . . .

And *then?*

Wu Chin-Mei began to cry.

In Lincoln Rhyme's town house, gray and gloomy thanks to the storm's early dusk, the case wasn't moving at all.

Sachs sat nearby, calmly sipping that disgusting-smelling tea of hers, which irritated the hell out of Rhyme for no particular reason.

Fred Dellray was back, pacing and squeezing his unlit cigarette, not in any better mood than anyone else. "I wasn't happy then and I ain't happy now. Not. A. Happy. Person."

He was referring to what he'd been told were "resource allocation issues" within the bureau, which were delaying their getting more agents on the GHOSTKILL team. The tall man contemptuously spat out, "They *ac*-tually said, 'RAI,' if you kin believe it. Yep, yep. 'It's an RAI situation.'" He rolled his eyes and muttered, "Jesus loves his mother."

Dellray's take was that nobody in the Justice Department thought human smuggling was particularly sexy and therefore worth much time. In fact, despite the executive order in the nineties shifting the jurisdiction, the bureau *didn't* have as much experience as the INS. Dellray had tried explaining to the assistant special agent in charge that there was also the little matter that the snakehead in question was a mass murderer. The response to that was also tepid. It fell into the category of LSFH, he'd explained.

"Which is?" Rhyme asked.

"'Let somebody else fuckin' handle it.'" I made that up, butcha get the picture." The SPEC-TAC team too was still cooling their heels down in Quantico, the agent glumly added.

And they were having no better luck with the evidence from any of the crime scenes.

"Okay, what about the Honda he stole at the beach?" Rhyme barked. "It's in the system. Isn't anybody in the hinterland looking for it? I mean, it *is* on an emergency vehicle locator."

"Sorry, Linc," Sellitto said, after he checked with downtown. "Nothing." *SorryLincnothing* . . .

It was a hell of a lot easier to find a ship in a port in Russia than it was to find ten people in his own backyard.

Then the preliminary crime scene report from the Mah killing came back. Thom held the notes up for Rhyme and turned the pages for him. There was nothing to suggest that the Ghost was behind the killing; no evidence "associated" the Ghost with the scene, the forensics term for "connected." No ballistics were involved—Mah's throat had been cut—and the carpet in his office and the hallways hadn't yielded up any footprints. The techs had lifted hundreds of latents and three dozen samples of trace evidence but it would take hours to analyze them all.

All the remaining AFIS requests from the fingerprints that Sachs had lifted at the prior scenes had come back negative, with the exception of Jerry Tang's—but his identity was hardly an issue any longer, of course.

"I want a drink," Rhyme said, discouraged. "It's cocktail hour. Hell, it's *after* cocktail hour."

"Dr. Weaver said no alcohol before the operation," Thom pointed out.

"She said *avoid* it, Thom. I'm sure she said avoid. Avoidance is not abstention."

"I'm not going to argue Webster's here, Lincoln. No booze."

"The operation isn't until next week. Give me a goddamn drink."

The aide was adamant. "You've been working way too hard on this case. Your blood pressure's up and your schedule's shot to hell."

Rhyme said, "We'll compromise. A small glass."

"That's not a compromise. That would be a win for you and loss for me. You can drink after the surgery." He disappeared into the kitchen.

Rhyme closed his eyes, pushed his head back into the chair angrily. Imagining—a moment of absurd fantasy—that the operation would actually fix the nerves that operated his entire arm. He told no one this—not even Amelia Sachs—but, though walking was out of the question, he often fantasized that the surgery would actually let him lift things. He now pictured grabbing the Macallan and taking a hit directly from the bottle. Rhyme could almost feel his hands around the cool, round glass.

A clink on the table beside him made him blink. The astringent smoky smell of whisky rose up and engulfed his head. He opened his eyes. Sachs had placed a small glass of scotch on the wheelchair armrest.

"It's not very full," the criminalist muttered to her. But the subtext of the comment, both Lincoln and she understood, was: thank you.

She winked in reply.

He drank deeply through the straw and felt the warm burn of the liquor in his mouth and throat.

Another sip.

He enjoyed the liquor but found that it did little to dull the urgency and frustration he felt at the slow pace of the case. His eyes fell on the whiteboard. One entry caught his eye.

"Sachs," he called. "Sachs!"

"What?"

"I need a phone number. Fast."

The Ghost held his Model 51 pistol against his cheek.

The hot metal, redolent of oil and sweet grease, gave him reassurance. Yes, he wanted a new weapon, something bigger and more dependable—like the Uzi and the Beretta he'd lost on the *Dragon*. But this was a good-fortune gun, one he'd had for years. He believed it was lucky because he'd come by the pistol in this way: near Taipei once, he'd gone to a temple to pray. Someone had tipped the police that he was inside and two officers stopped him as he came down the stairs. One of them, though, had hesitated to pull a gun at a Buddhist temple and, flustered, he'd dropped this very weapon on the grass. The Ghost had scooped it up, shot both of the young policemen to death then escaped.

From that day on this gun had been his good-luck charm, a present from his bowman god, Yi.

It had been nearly an hour since Kashgari had gone inside to make sure the Wus' children stayed put. The shops had closed along this part of Canal—the armed guards were gone, he was sure, and the sidewalks were largely deserted. Let's get on with it, the Ghost thought and stretched. He

Easton, Long Island, Crime Scene	Stolen Van, Chinatown	Jerry Tang Murder Crime Scene
· Two immigrants killed on beach; shot in back.	· Camouflaged by immigrants with "The Home Store" logo.	· Four men kicked door in and tortured him and shot him.
· One immigrant wounded—Dr. John Sung.	· Blood spatter suggests injured woman has hand, arm or shoulder injury.	· Two shell casings—match Model 51. Tang shot twice in head.
· "Bangshou" (assistant) on board; identity unknown.	· Blood samples sent to lab for typing.	· Extensive vandalism.
· Assistant confirmed as drowned body found near site where *Dragon* sank.	· Injured woman is AB negative. Requesting more information about her blood.	· Some fingerprints.
· Ten immigrants escape: seven adults (one elderly, one injured woman), two children, one infant. Steal church van.	· Fingerprints sent to AFIS.	· No matches except Tang's.
· Blood samples sent to lab for typing.	· No matches.	· Three accomplices have smaller shoe size than Ghost, presumably smaller stature.
· Injured woman is AB negative. Requesting more information about her blood.		· Trace suggests Ghost's safehouse is probably downtown, Battery Park City area.
· Vehicle awaiting Ghost on beach left without him. One shot believed fired by Ghost at vehicle. Request for vehicle make and model sent out, based on tread marks and wheelbase.		· Suspected accomplices from Chinese ethnic minority. Presently pursuing whereabouts.
· Vehicle is a BMW X5.		
· Driver—Jerry Tang.		
· No vehicles to pick up immigrants located.		
· Cell phone, presumably Ghost's, sent for analysis to FBI.		
· Untraceable satellite secure phone. Hacked Chinese gov't system to use it.		
· Ghost's weapon is 7.62mm pistol. Unusual casing.		
· Model 51 Chinese automatic pistol.		
· Ghost is reported to have gov't people on payroll.		
· Ghost stole red Honda sedan to escape. Vehicle locator request sent out.		
· No trace of Honda found.		
· Three bodies recovered at sea—two shot, one drowned. Photos and prints to Rhyme and Chinese police.		
· Drowned individual identified as Victor Au, the Ghost's *bangshou*.		
· Fingerprints sent to AFIS.		
· No matches on any prints but unusual markings on Sam Chang's fingers and thumbs (injury, rope burn?)		
· Profile of Immigrants: Sam Chang and Wu Qichen and their families, John Sung, baby of woman who drowned, unidentified man and woman (killed on beach).		

was tired of waiting. Yusuf and the other Turk were too. They'd been complaining about hunger but he guessed that even some of the restaurants and delis here had security cameras and the Ghost was not going to let himself or any associate be recorded on tape for something as frivolous as food. They'd have to—

"Look," he whispered, glancing up the street.

At the end of the block, he saw two people climb from a cab, nervously keeping their heads down. The Wus. The Ghost recognized them clearly from the cheap running suits they wore. They paid the driver and walked into a drugstore on the corner, the husband clutching his wife around the waist. Her arm was in a cast or was wrapped with thick bandages. He carried a shopping bag.

"Get the masks ready. Check your weapons."

The two Turks complied.

Five minutes later the Wus left the drugstore. They were walking as quickly as they could, considering the wife's condition.

He said to Hajip, "You stay with the car. Keep the engine running. He and I"—a nod toward Yusuf—"will follow the Wus inside. We push them into their apartment and close the door. We'll use pillows for silencers. I want to bring the daughter with us. We'll keep her for a while."

Yindao would, he knew, forgive this infidelity.

The Wus were now five meters from their doorway, shuffling fast, heads down, oblivious to the gods of death who fluttered nearby.

The Ghost found his cell phone and called the Turk in the Wus' apartment.

"Yes?" Kashgari answered.

"The Wus're close to the building. Where are the children?"

"The boy's in the bathroom. The girl's with me."

"As soon as they walk into the alley we'll come in right behind them."

He shut the power off to the phone—so there'd be no distracting ring at inopportune moments. The Ghost and Yusuf pulled their masks down over their faces, and climbed out. The other Turk slipped behind the wheel of the Blazer.

The Wus were moving closer to the door.

The Ghost stepped off the curb and walked straight toward his victims.

Afraid, you can be brave. . . .

Chapter Twenty-four

The Wus in the doorway.

The children in the apartment.

The Ghost and Yusuf, masks over their faces and guns at their sides, were sprinting across Canal Street. He felt the rush of excitement he always did before a kill. His hands vibrated slightly but would grow still when he lifted the gun to shoot.

He thought again about Wu's daughter. *Seventeen, eighteen . . . pretty enough*. He would—

It was at this moment that a loud crack echoed through the street and a bullet slammed into a parked car just behind the Ghost. The alarm began braying.

"Jesus," a man's voice called from somewhere. "Who fired?"

The Ghost and Yusuf stopped and crouched. They lifted their weapons, scanning the street for their attacker.

"Hell," came another voice. "Cease-fire!"

And another: "Who the fuck—"

The Wus too stopped, crouching down on the pavement.

The Ghost's head was swiveling. He gripped Yusuf's arm.

A man's voice cried through a loudspeaker, "Kwan Ang! Stop. This is the United States Immigration Service!" Followed immediately by a second gunshot—from the man who'd called out, it seemed—and a side window of a nearby parked car exploded in a cloudburst of glass.

His heart vibrating from the shock, the snakehead scrabbled backward, his lucky gun up, as he looked for a target. The INS was here? How?

"It's a trap," he raged to Yusuf. "Back to the car!"

Chaos now filled Canal Street. More shouting, passersby and store clerks diving for cover. Up the block the doors of two white vans opened and men and women in black uniforms, carrying guns, leapt out.

And what was *this*? The Wus themselves were drawing weapons! The husband pulled a machine pistol from the plastic bag he'd held. The wife was lifting a weapon from her running suit pocket . . . . And then the Ghost realized that they weren't the Wus at all. They were decoys—Chinese-American police officers or agents wearing the Wus' clothing. Somehow the police had found the couple and sent these people back in their place to lure him out of cover. "Drop your weapons!" the man masquerading as Wu shouted.

The Ghost fired five or six shots at random, to keep people down and stoke the panic. He shot out a window in a jewelry store, adding another siren to the tumult of sounds on the street and bolstering the chaos.

The Turk in the driver's seat opened the door and began firing at the white vans. Running, looking for cover and looking for targets, the police scattered on the far side of Canal.

As he crouched beside their four-by-four, the Ghost heard: "Who fired? . . . Backups aren't in position . . . What the fuck happened? . . . Watch the bystanders, for Christ's sake!"

A panicked driver in a car in front of the Wus' apartment started to speed up to get out of the line of fire. The Ghost fired two shots into the front seat. The window glass vanished and the car skidded into a row of parked vehicles with a huge bang.

"Kwan Ang," came an electronic shout from a bullhorn or vehicle loudspeaker, a different voice this time. "This is the FBI. Put down—"

He shut up the agent by firing twice more in his direction and climbed into the Blazer. The Uighurs climbed into the back. "Kashgari! He is inside," Yusuf cried and nodded toward the Wus' apartment, where the third Turk waited.

"He's dead or captured, " the Ghost snapped. "Understand? We're not waiting."

Yusuf nodded. But just as the Ghost turned the key and started the engine he noticed a police officer step from a line of cars, motioning bystanders to get back and take cover. He lifted his pistol, aimed toward the front of the four-by-four.

"Get down!" the Ghost cried as the officer fired repeatedly. The three men ducked, expecting the windshield to shatter.

But instead they heard loud ring after loud ring as the bullets struck the front of the vehicle. Eight or nine of them. Finally there was a huge clanging as fan blades were knocked out of alignment and jammed into other parts of the engine, which gave a huge squeal, steam pouring from the pierced radiator. Finally it went silent.

"Out!" the Ghost ordered, jumped out and fired several shots at the officer to drive him under cover behind a row of cars.

The three men crouched on the sidewalk. For a moment there was a lull. The police and agents were holding their fire, probably waiting for the arrival of the backup officers—more emergency cars, sirens howling, were racing down Canal Street toward them right now.

"Drop your weapons and stand up," the staticky voice called through the loudspeaker again. "Kwan, drop your weapons!"

"We give up?" asked Hajip, his eyes huge with fear.

The Ghost ignored him and wiped his sweating hand on his slacks, then slipped another clip of ammunition into his Model 51. He looked behind him. "This way!" He rose and fired several times toward the officers then ran into the fish market behind them. Several patrons and clerks were cowering behind bins of fish and eels, racks of food, freezer cases. The Ghost and the two Turks ran to the back alleyway, where they found an old man standing beside a delivery truck. Seeing the guns and the masks, the man dropped to his knees and lifted his arms. He began wailing, "Don't harm me! Please! I have a family. . . ." His voice trailed off into sobbing.

"Inside," the Ghost shouted to the Turks. They leapt in the truck. The snakehead looked behind them through the doorway and could see several officers cautiously approaching the store. He turned and fired several shots in their direction. They scattered for cover.

The Ghost then spun back and froze. The old man had grabbed a long filleting knife and had taken a step forward. He stopped and blinked in terror. The Ghost lowered his pistol to the old man's age-spotted forehead. The knife fell to the wet cobblestones at his feet. He closed his eyes.

Five minutes later Amelia Sachs arrived at the scene. She ran toward the Wus' apartment, her pistol in her hand.

"What happened?" she called to an officer standing beside a shot-up car. "What the hell happened?"

But the young cop was badly shaken and just glanced at her, numb.

She continued down the street and found Fred Dellray crouched over an officer who'd been shot in the arm, holding an improvised bandage on the man's wound. Medics ran up and took over.

Dellray was furious. "This is bad, Amelia. We were an inch away from him. A *half* inch."

"Where is he?" she asked, holstering the Glock.

"Stole a delivery van from that fish market 'cross the street. We got ever-body in town with a badge looking for it."

Sachs closed her eyes in dismay. All of Rhyme's brilliant deductions—and the superhuman efforts to put together a takedown team in time had been wasted.

What Rhyme, frustrated by the lack of leads, had noticed on the evidence chart was the reference to the injured immigrant's blood. The number Sachs had found for him was that of the Medical Examiner's office. He realized the lab had never called back with the results of the tests. Rhyme had bullied a forensic pathologist into quickly completing the analysis.

The doctor had found several helpful things: the presence of bone marrow in the blood, indicating a severe bone fracture; sepsis, suggesting a deep cut or abrasion, and the presence of *Coxiella burnetii,* a bacteria responsible for Q fever, a zoonotic disease—one transmitted from animals to people. The bacteria were often picked up in places where animals were kept for long periods of time, like pens at seaports and the holds of ships.

Which meant that the immigrant was one very sick woman.

And that in turn was something that Rhyme believed might be useful.

"Tell me about this Q fever," Rhyme had asked the pathologist.

Though it wasn't contagious or life-threatening, the symptoms of the disease could be severe, he'd learned. Headache, chills, fever, possibly even liver malfunction.

"Is it rare?" Rhyme had asked.

"Very, around here."

"Excellent," Rhyme had announced, buoyed by this news, and had Sellitto and Deng put together a team of canvassers from the Big Building—One Police Plaza downtown—and the Fifth Precinct. They began calling all the hospitals and emergency clinics in Chinatown in Manhattan and the one in Flushing, Queens, to see if any female Chinese patients had been admitted with Q fever and a badly broken, infected arm.

After only ten minutes they'd received a call from one of the officers manning the phones downtown. It turned out that a Chinese man had just brought his wife into the emergency room of a clinic in Chinatown; she fit the profile perfectly—advanced Q fever and multiple fractures. Her name was Wu Yong-Ping. She'd been admitted and her husband was there too.

Officers from the Fifth Precinct had sped to the hospital—along with Sachs and Deng—to interview them. The Wus, shaken badly over their arrest, had told the police where they were living and that their children were still in the apartment. Then Rhyme had called to tell her that he'd just gotten the AFIS results from the Jimmy Mah killing: some of the prints matched those found at prior GHOSTKILL scenes; the snakehead *had* committed the crime. When Wu explained that Mah's broker had gotten them the apartment Rhyme and Sachs realized that the Ghost knew where the Wus were staying and was probably on his way to kill them at that moment.

Since the bureau's crack SPEC-TAC team was still not on hand to assist on the case, Dellray, Sellitto and Peabody put together a joint take-down team of their own and would have some Chinese-American officers from the Fifth Precinct masquerade as the Wus.

But, because of one premature gunshot, the whole effort was wasted.

Dellray snapped at another agent, "Anything more on the fish-store van? How come nobody's seen it? It's got the fuckin' name of the store on the side in big ugly letters."

The agent made a call on his radio and a moment later reported, "Nothing, sir. No reports of it on the road or abandoned."

Dellray played with the knot of his purple-black tie, just visible above his body armor. "Somethin'. Ain't. Right."

"What do you mean, Fred?" Sachs asked.

But the agent didn't answer. He glanced back at the fish store and strode toward it. Sachs accompanied him. Standing near the large ice bin in the front were three Chinese—store clerks, Sachs assumed—and two NYPD police officers interviewing them.

Dellray looked over the clerks one by one and his gaze settled on an old man, whose eyes dropped immediately to the dozen gray-pink flounders resting on the bed of ice.

He pointed a finger at the man. "He told you the Ghost stole the van, right?"

"That's right, Agent Dellray," one of the cops said.

"Well, he was goddamn lying!"

Dellray and Sachs ran to the back of the shop and into the alleyway behind it. Hidden behind a large Dumpster thirty feet away, they found the fish market's van.

Returning to the front of the store Dellray said to the old man, "Listen, skel, tell me what happen and don't fuck with me. We all together on that?"

"He going kill me," the man said, sobbing. "Make me say they stole van, three men. Had gun at my head. They drove down alley, hid van then got out and run. Don't know where go."

Dellray and the policewoman returned to the impromptu command post. "Can't hardly blame him. But still . . . shit and a half."

"So," she speculated, "they got onto a side street and 'jacked some wheels."

"Prob'ly. And killed the driver."

A moment later an officer indeed called in, saying that there'd been a report of a carjacking. Three armed men in ski masks had run up to a Lexus at a stoplight, ordered the couple out and sped off. Contrary to Dellray's prediction, though, the driver and passenger were unhurt.

"Why didn't he kill 'em?" Dellray wondered.

"Probably didn't want to fire his gun," Sachs said. "Draw too much attention." She added bitterly, "It would've been inconvenient."

As more emergency vehicles pulled up she asked Dellray, "Who was it? Who fired the shot that spooked him?"

"Dunno yet. But I'ma look this one over with a fuckin' magnifyin' glass."

But he didn't need to look too far, as it turned out. Two uniformed officers walked up to the FBI agent and conferred with him. The agent's face compressed into a frown. Dellray looked up and strode over to the guilty party.

It was Alan Coe.

"What in th'living hell happened?" Dellray barked.

Defensive but defiant, the red-haired agent looked back into the FBI agent's eye. "I *had* to fire. The Ghost was going to shoot the decoys, didn't you see?"

"No, I did not. His weapon was at his side."

"Not from my angle."

"Crap on your angle," Dellray snapped. "It was at. His. Side."

"I'm getting sick of you lecturing me, Dellray. It was a fucking judgment call. If you had everybody in position we still could've collared him."

"We set it up to take him down on the sidewalk, without innocents around, not in the middle of a crowded street." Dellray shook his head. "Thirty li'l tiny seconds and he woulda been tied up like a Christmas package." Then the tall agent nodded at the big .45 Glock on Coe's hip. "An' even if he *was* moving on somebody, how the hell couldja miss with a piece like that from fifty feet? Even I coulda hit him and I don't fire *my* pissy weapon but once a year. Fuck."

Coe's defiance slipped and he said contritely, "I thought it was the right thing to do under the circumstances. I was worried about saving some lives."

Dellray plucked the unsmoked cigarette from behind his ear, looking like he was about to light it up. "This's gone way far enough. From now on INS is advisory only. No enforcement, no tactical."

"You can't do that," Coe said, an ominous look in his eyes.

"'Cording to the Executive Order I can, son. I'm going downtown and doing what I gotta to put that in place." He stormed off. Coe muttered something Sachs didn't catch.

She watched Dellray climb into his car, slam the door and speed off. She turned back to Coe. "Did anybody get the children?"

"Children?" the agent asked, absently. "You mean, the Wus' kids? I don't know."

Their parents were frantic that the children be brought to them in the hospital as soon as possible.

"I told downtown about 'em," Coe said dismissively, meaning, she supposed, the INS. "I guess they're sending somebody to take custody. That's procedure."

"Well, I'm not thinking about *procedure*," she snapped. "There're two children alone in there and they just heard a shoot-out in front of their apartment. Wouldn't you think they'd be a little scared?"

Coe had had enough reprimands for one day. Silently he turned and walked back to his car without a word, pulling out his cell phone as he left. He too drove off angrily, his phone pressed against his ear.

Sachs then called Rhyme and gave him the bad news.

"What happened?" Rhyme asked, even angrier than Dellray.

"One of our people fired before we were in position. The street wasn't sealed and the Ghost shot his way out. . . . Rhyme, it was Alan who fired the shot."

"Coe?"

"Right."

"Oh, no."

"Dellray's bumping the INS down a notch."

"Peabody won't like that."

"At this point Fred's in no mood to care about what people like and don't."

"Good," Rhyme said. "We need somebody to take charge. We're groping around in the dark on this one. I don't like it." Then he asked, "Casualties?"

"A few officers and civies wounded. Nothing serious." She noticed Eddie Deng. "I've got to get the Wus' children, Rhyme. I'll call you back after I run the scene."

She disconnected the call and said to Deng, "Need some translation help, Eddie. With the Wus' kids."

"Sure."

Pointing to the bullet-pocked four-by-four, Sachs said to another officer, "Keep it sealed. I'll run the scene in a minute." The cop nodded in response.

Deng and Sachs walked to the apartment. She said, "I don't want the kids to go downtown to the INS alone, Eddie. Can you sneak 'em out of here and get 'em to their parents at the clinic?"

"Sure."

They walked down the few stairs that led to the basement apartments. Garbage littered the alleyway and Sachs knew the rooms here would be dark, probably infested with roaches and would undoubtedly stink. Imagine, she thought: the Wus had risked death and imprisonment and endured the physical pain of their terrible journey just for the privilege of calling this filthy place their home.

"What's the number?" Deng asked, walking ahead of Sachs.

"One B," she answered.

He started toward the door.

It was then that Sachs noticed a key in the front-door lock of the Wus' apartment.

A key? she wondered.

Deng reached for the knob.

"No," Sachs cried, unholstering her weapon. "Wait!"

But it was too late. Deng was pushing the door open anyway. He leapt back—away from the slight, dark man with his arm around a sobbing teenage girl's waist, holding her in front of him as a shield, a pistol pressed against her neck.

Chapter Twenty-five

"Ting, ting!" Eddie Deng shouted in panic.

The young detective's weaponless hands rose above his spiny hair.

No one moved. Sachs heard a multitude of sounds: the girl's whimpering, the low hiss of traffic, horns from the street. The gunman's desperate orders in a language she didn't understand. Her own heartbeats.

She turned sideways, to present a smaller target, and centered the blade sights of her Glock on as much of his head as presented. The rule was this: as difficult as it was, you never sacrificed yourself. You never gave up your weapon, you never turned it aside in a standoff, you never let a perp draw a target anywhere on your body. You had to make them understand that the hostage wasn't going to save them.

The man started forward very slowly, motioning them back, still muttering in his unintelligible language.

Neither Sachs nor the young detective moved.

"You in armor, Deng?" she whispered.

"Yeah," came the shaky reply.

She was too—an American Body Armor vest with a Super Shok heart plate—but at this range a shot could easily do major damage to an unprotected part of their bodies. A nick in the femoral artery could kill you faster than some chest shots would.

"Back out," she whispered. "I need better light for shooting."

"You going to shoot?" Deng asked uncertainly.

"Just back out."

She took a step behind her. Another. The young cop, sweat gleaming between the thorns of his hair, didn't move. Sachs stopped. He was muttering something, maybe a prayer.

"Eddie, you with me?" she whispered. After a pause: "Eddie, goddamn it!"

He shook his head. "Sorry. Sure."

"Come on, slow." To the man gripping the teenage girl Sachs spoke in a cooing voice and very slowly: "Put the gun down. Let's not anybody get hurt. Do you speak English?"

They backed away. The man followed.

"English?" she tried again.

Nothing.

"Eddie, tell him we'll work something out."

"He's not Han," Deng said. "He won't speak Chinese."

"Try it anyway."

A burst of sounds from Deng's mouth. The staccato words were startling.

The man didn't respond.

The two officers backed toward the front of the alleyway. Not a single goddamn cop or agent noticed them. Sachs thought, Where the hell are all of our people?

The assailant and the terrified girl, the gun tucked against her neck, moved forward and stepped outside too.

"You," the man barked to Sachs in crude English, "on ground. Both on ground."

"No," Sachs said, "we're not lying down. I'm asking you to put your gun down. You can't get away. Hundreds of police. You understand?" As she spoke she adjusted her target—his cheek—in the slightly better light here. But it was a very narrow bull's-eye. And the girl's temple was a scant inch to the right of it. He was of very slim build and Sachs had no body shot at all.

The man glanced behind him, up the dark alley.

"He's going to fire and then make a run for it," Deng said in a quavering voice.

"Listen," Sachs called calmly. "We're not going to hurt you. We—"

"No!" The man shoved the gun harder against the girl's neck. She screamed.

Then Deng reached for his sidearm.

"Eddie, don't!" Sachs cried.

"Bu!" the assailant called and thrust his gun forward, firing into Deng's chest. The detective grunted violently from the impact and fell backward, against Sachs, knocking her to the ground. Deng rolled onto his belly, retching—or coughing blood; she couldn't tell. The round might've pierced the body armor at this range. Stunned, Sachs struggled to her knees. The gunman aimed at her before she could raise her weapon.

But he hesitated. There was some distraction behind him. The shooter looked back. In the darkness of the alleyway Sachs could make out a man speeding forward, a small figure, holding something in his hand.

The perp released the girl and spun around, lifting the gun, but before he could shoot, the running figure clocked him in the side of the head with what he was carrying—a brick.

"Hongse!" Sonny Li called to Sachs, dropping the brick and pulling the girl away from the stunned assailant. Li pushed her to the ground and turned back to the dark man, who clutched his bleeding head. But suddenly he jumped back and lifted his pistol toward Li, who stumbled back against the wall.

Three fast shots from Sachs's gun dropped the attacker like a doll onto the cobblestones and he lay motionless.

"Judges of hell," Sonny Li gasped, staring at the body. He stepped forward, checked the man's pulse then lifted the gun out of his lifeless hand. "Dead, Hongse," he called. Then Li turned back to the girl, helping her up. Sobbing, she ran down the alley, past Sachs, and into the arms of a Chinese officer from the Fifth Precinct, who began comforting her in their common language.

Med techs ran to Deng to check him out. The vest had indeed stopped the slug but the impact might have cracked a rib or two. "I'm sorry," he gasped to Sachs. "I just reacted."

"Your first firefight?"

He nodded.

She smiled. "Welcome to the club." The medic helped him up and they took him out to be examined more thoroughly in an EMS bus.

Sachs and two ESU officers cleared the apartment and found a young, panicked boy, about eight, in the bathroom. With the help of a Chinese-American cop from the Fifth Precinct to translate, the medics checked the siblings out and found that neither of them had been hurt or molested by the Ghost's partner.

Sachs glanced back into the alley, where another medic and two uniformed officers stood over the corpse of the assailant. "I have to process the body," she reminded them. "I don't want it disturbed more than necessary."

"Sure, Officer," came the reply.

Nearby, Sonny Li patted his pockets and finally located his pack of cigarettes. If he hadn't found any she wouldn't've been surprised to see him rifle the dead man's pockets.

Putting on her Tyvek suit to search the crime scenes, Amelia Sachs glanced up to see Li walking toward her.

She laughed to see the cheery grin on the little man. "How?" she asked.

"How what?"

"How the hell d'you figure out the Wus were here?"

"I ask you same thing."

"You tell me first." She sensed he was eager to brag—and she was happy to let him.

"Okay." He finished the cigarette and lit another. "Way I work in China. I go places, talk to people. Tonight I go to gambling halls, three of them. Lose some money, win some money, drink. And talk and talk. Finally meet guy at poker table, carpenter. Fuzhounese. He tell me about man come in earlier, nobody know him. Complaining to everybody about women, about what he had to do for family 'cause wife sick and broke arm. Bragging about money he going make. Then he say he on *Dragon* this morning and rescue everybody when it sink. Had to be Wu. Liver-spleen disharmony, I'm saying. He say he living nearby. I ask around and find about this block. Lots meet-and-greet snakeheads put people here who just arrive. I come over and look around, ask people, see if anybody know anything and find out family—just like Wus—move in today. I check out building and look through back window and see guy with gun. Hey, you look in back window first, Hongse?"

"No, I didn't."

"Maybe you should done that. That good rule. Always look in back window first."

"I should have, Sonny." She nodded in the direction of the dead shooter.

"Too bad he not alive," Li said glumly. "Could been helpful."

"You don't *really* torture people to get them to talk, do you?" she asked.

But the Chinese cop just gave a cryptic smile. He asked, "Hongse, how *you* find Wus?"

Sachs explained to Li how they'd found the Wus through the wife's injury.

Li nodded, impressed with Rhyme's deductions. "But what happen to Ghost?"

Sachs explained about the premature gunshot and the snakehead's escape.

"Coe?"

"That's right," she agreed.

"Big fuck. . . . I not like that man, I'm saying. When he over in China at meeting in Fuzhou we not trust him much. Walk into room and not like us, nobody there. Talk like we children, want to do case against Ghost by himself. Talk bad about immigrants. Disappear at times when we need him." Li looked over the Tyvek overalls. He frowned. "Why you wear that suit, Hongse?"

"So I don't contaminate the evidence."

"Bad color. Shouldn't wear white. Color of death in my country, color of funerals, I'm saying. Throw it out. You get red suit. Red is good-luck color in China. Not blue either. Get red suit."

"It's enough of a target in white."

"Not good," he said. "Bad feelings." He remembered a word that Deng had taught him earlier. "Bad *omen*, I'm saying."

"I'm not superstitious," Sachs said.

"I am," Li said. "Lots people in China are. Always saying prayers, sacrificing, cutting demon's tail—"

"Cutting what?" she interrupted.

"Called cutting demon's tail. See, demons follow you always so when you cross traffic you run fast in front of car. That cut off demon's tail and take his power away."

"Don't people ever get hit?"

"Sometimes."

"Then don't they know it doesn't work?"

"No, only know that sometimes you cut his tail, sometimes demon get *you*."

Cutting the demon's tail . . .

Sachs got Li to promise he'd stay out of the crime scene—at least until she was finished—and then processed the dead gunman's body, walked the grid inside the apartment and finally searched the Ghost's bullet-riddled SUV. She bagged and tagged all the evidence and finally stripped off the space suit.

Then she and Li drove back to the clinic, where she found the Wu family reunited in a room guarded by two uniformed cops and a stony-faced woman INS agent. With Li and the agent translating, Sachs got as much information as she could. Though Wu Qichen knew nothing about the Ghost's whereabouts in the city, the scrawny, embittered man gave her some information about the Changs, including the name of the infant with them, Po-Yee, which meant Treasured Child.

What a lovely name, thought Amelia Sachs.

She said to the INS agent, "They're going to detention?"

"Right. Until the hearing."

"Do you have a problem putting them in one of our safehouses?" The NYPD had several nondescript, high-security town houses in the city, used for witness protection. INS detention centers for illegal immigrants were notoriously lax. Besides, the Ghost would be expecting them to go to an Immigration facility and, with his *guanxi*, might pay someone in the detention center to let him or a *bangshou* inside to try to kill the family again.

"Fine with us."

The town house in Murray Hill was free, Sachs knew. She gave the agent the address and the name of the NYPD officer who oversaw the houses.

The INS agent then looked at Wu and, like a bad-tempered schoolteacher, said, "Why don't you people just stay at home? Fix your problems there. You almost got your wife and family killed."

Wu's English wasn't good but apparently he understood her. He rose from his wife's bedside and gestured broadly. "Not our fault!" he snapped, leaning toward the sour woman. "Coming here not our fault!"

Amused, the INS agent asked, "Not your fault? Who do you want to blame?"

"You country!"

"How do you figure that?"

"You not see? Look around! All you money and richnesses, you advertising, you computers, you Nikes and Levis, cars, hair spray . . . You Leonardo DiCaprio, you beautiful women. You pills for everything, you makeup, you televison! You tell whole world you got fuck everything here! *Meiguo* is all money, all freedom, all safe. You tell us everybody how good is here. You take our money, but you say to us *mei-you,* go away! You tell us our human rights terrible, but when we try come here you say *mei-you!*"

The thin man lapsed into Chinese then calmed. He looked the woman up and down, nodded at her blond hair. "What your ancestor? Italians, Englishes, Germans? *They* in this country first? Huh, tell me." He waved angrily and sat down on the bed, put his hand on his wife's uninjured arm.

The agent shook her head, smiling in a condescending way, as if astonished that the immigrant couldn't figure out the obvious.

Sachs left the somber family behind and motioned Li after her to the clinic exit. They paused at the curb then jogged between two fast-moving taxis. Sachs wondered if she'd been close enough to the second one to cut the tail off any demons pursuing her.

The building and the garage beneath it were virtually impregnable but the parking garage annex in an underground structure across the street was far less so.

Concern about terrorist bombs had prompted the Government Services Administration to limit access to the garage under Manhattan Federal Plaza. There were so many federal employees that it would create huge bottlenecks to check every vehicle that entered the garage under the building itself, so that facility was closed to all but the most senior government officials and the one next door constructed for other employees. There was still security in the annex, of course, but since the garage sat beneath a small park, even the worst bomb damage would be limited.

In fact, tonight at 9 P.M. the security was not at its best because the one guard on duty at the entrance booth was watching some excitement: a car fire on Broadway. An old van was burning down to its tires—a conflagration observed by hundreds of happy passersby.

The chunky guard had stepped out of his booth, watching the black smoke and orange flames dancing through the windows of the van.

So he didn't notice the slight man dressed in a suit and carrying an attaché case step quickly into the "autos only" entrance and hurry down the ramp into the half-deserted garage.

The man had memorized the license plate number of the car he sought and it took him only five minutes to find it. The navy blue government-issue vehicle was very close to the main exit door; the driver had this choice spot because he'd arrived only a half hour ago—long after the offices had closed and most of the federal employees had left for the day.

Like nearly all federal cars—the man had been assured—there was no alarm. After a fast glance around the garage he pulled on cloth gloves, quickly drove a wedge between the window and the side of the door, slipped a slim-jim tool inside the space and popped the lock. He opened his attaché case and took out a heavy paper bag, glanced inside for one final check. He saw the cluster of foot-long yellow sticks on whose side were the words: EXPLOSIVE. DANGER. SEE INSTRUCTIONS BEFORE USE. Wires ran from a detonator in one of the sticks to a battery box and from there to a simple pressure switch. He placed the bag under the driver's seat, unwound a length of wire, then slipped the pressure switch between the springs of the seat. Anyone who weighed more than ninety pounds would complete the circuit and set off the detonator simply by sitting down.

The man clicked the power switch on the battery box from OFF to ON and locked the door of the car, closed it as quietly as he could and left the garage, walking matter-of-factly past the still-oblivious security guard, raptly watching the NYFD douse the flames of the burning van though with a little disappointment in his face—as if he was sorry that the gas tank hadn't blown up spectacularly, as they always did in action flicks and TV shows.

Chapter Twenty-six

They sat in silence, watching the small television set, William translating those words that his parents didn't understand.

The special news report didn't give the names of the people who'd nearly been killed on Canal Street but there was no doubt that it was Wu Qichen and his family; the story said they'd been passengers on the *Fuzhou Dragon* that morning. One of the Ghost's confederates had been killed but the snakehead himself had escaped with one or two others.

The story ended and commercials came on the television screen. William rose and walked to the window, looked out at the dark street.

"Get back," Chang snapped to his son. But the boy remained where he was for a defiant moment.

Children . . . Chang thought.

"William!"

The boy finally stepped away and walked into the bedroom. Ronald flipped through channels on the television.

"No," Sam Chang told his younger son. "Read. Get a book and practice your English."

The boy dutifully stood. He went to the shelf and found a volume and returned to the couch to read.

Mei-Mei finished stitching together a small stuffed animal for Po-Yee—a cat, it seemed. The woman made the toy pounce onto the arm of her chair and the girl took it in both hands, studying it with happy eyes. Together they played with the cat, laughing.

Chang heard a moan on the couch, where his own father rested, curled in a blanket that was virtually the same gray shade as his skin.

"Baba," Chang whispered and rose immediately. He found the man's medicine, opened it and gave him a tablet of morphine. He held the cup of cold tea so that the man could take the pill. When he'd first gotten sick—the heat and dampness spreading quickly through the yang organs of his body, the stomach and intestines—they'd gone to their local doctor who'd given them herbs and tonics. Soon, though, that hadn't been enough for the pain and another doctor had diagnosed cancer. But Chang's dissident status had kept his father waiting on the bottom of the list at the hospitals' huge queues for treatment. Medical care in China was changing. The state hospitals were giving way to private clinics but they were extremely expensive—a single visit could cost two months' salary and treating cancer would have been out of the question for a family struggling to survive. The best Chang had been able to find was a "barefoot doctor" in the countryside north of Fuzhou, one of those individuals simply proclaimed by the government to be paramedics and practicing with minimal training. The man had prescribed morphine to ease the man's pain but there was little else he could do.

The bottle of the drug was large but it wouldn't last more than a month and his father was quickly worsening. On the Internet Chang had done a lot of research on the United States. There was a famous hospital in New York that did nothing but treat cancer patients. He knew that his father's condition was advanced but the man wasn't old—not by American standards, only sixty-nine, and he was strong from daily walks and exercise. Surgeons could operate and remove those portions of his body destroyed by the cancerous dampness and give him radiation and medicine to keep the disease at bay. He could live for many more years.

As he gazed at his father the old man suddenly opened his eyes. "The Ghost is angry now that they've killed one of his own people. And that he's failed to kill the Wus. He'll come after us. I know his sort. He won't stop until he finds us."

This was his father's way. To sit and to absorb then give his assessments, which were invariably right. For instance, he'd always considered Mao Zedong a psychopath and had predicted some cataclysm would descend upon the country under his reign. And he'd been right: the near annihilation of the Chinese economy in the fifties thanks to Mao's Great Leap Forward and the Cultural Revolution a decade later, of which his father—like all open-minded artists and thinkers—was a victim.

But Chang Jiechi had survived the disasters. He'd said to his family in the 1960s, "This will pass. The madness cannot be sustained. We have only to stay alive and wait. That is our goal."

Within ten years, Mao was dead, the Gang of Four was imprisoned, and Chang Jiechi had been proven right.

And he was right now too, Sam Chang thought in despair. The Ghost would come after them.

The very name "snakehead" comes from the image of the smugglers crawling furtively through borders to deliver their human cargo to their final destination. Chang sensed the Ghost was doing this now—prowling, calling in favors, wielding his *guanxi*, threatening, perhaps even torturing people to find the Changs' whereabouts. He might—

Outside, a screech of brakes.

Chang, his wife and father all froze.

Footsteps.

"Shut the lights out. Quickly," Chang ordered. Mei-Mei scurried through the apartment, dowsing them.

Chang walked quickly to the closet, pulled William's pistol out from its hiding place and walked to the curtained front window. Hands trembling, he looked outside.

Across the street was a delivery truck—with a large sign for pizza hanging from the window. The driver was carrying a cardboard carton up to an apartment.

"It's all right," he said. "A delivery across the street."

But then he looked through the dim apartment, detecting the vague forms of his father, his wife and the infant, illuminated only by the blue light of the television screen. His smile of relief faded and, like the black cloud from an ink stick in a calligraphy well, he was consumed with intense regret for what his decisions had done to these people he loved so much. In America, Chang had learned, guilt for transgressions tortures one's psyche; in China, though, shame at letting down family and friends is the essential torment. And that is what he now felt: searing shame.

So this is to be the life I've brought to my father and my family: fear and darkness. Nothing but fear and darkness . . .

The madness cannot be sustained.

Perhaps not, Chang thought. But that doesn't mean that it's not any less deadly while it persists.

Sitting on a bench in Battery Park City, the Ghost was watching the lights of the ships in the Hudson River, far more peaceful but less picturesque than the waterfront in Hong Kong. There was a break in the rain but the wind was still rowdy, pushing low purple clouds quickly overhead, their bellies lit by the vast spectrum of city lights.

How had the police found the Wus? the Ghost wondered.

He considered this question but could come to no answer. Probably through the broker they'd killed and through Mah—the investigators hadn't believed that the Italians had killed the tong leader, despite the message he'd written in Mah's blood. The news had reported that the one Uighur they'd left behind was dead and that would mean a big reparation payment to the head of the cultural center.

How had they found the family?

Maybe it was magic . . .

No, not magic at all. He had yet more proof that his adversary and those working with him were relentless and talented. There was something very different about the people who were after him this time. Better than the Taiwanese, better than the French, better than your typical INS agent. If not for the first gunshot on Canal Street he would now be in custody or dead.

And who exactly was this Lincoln Rhyme that his intelligence source had reported to him about?

Well, he believed he was safe now. He and the Turks had taken great care to hide the Lexus, which they'd carjacked to escape in, hidden it better than the Honda he'd stolen at the beach, in fact. They'd split up immediately. He'd worn the mask at the Wus, no one had followed them from the shooting and Kashgari had had no identification on him to link him to either the Ghost or the cultural center in Queens.

Tomorrow, he would find the Changs.

Two young American women slowly walked past, enjoying the view and chatting in a way he found irritating, but the Ghost tuned out their words and stared at their bodies.

Resist? he wondered.

No, the Ghost thought decisively. He pulled out his phone and, before his will stopped him, called Yindao and they arranged to meet later. She was, he noted, pleased to hear from him. Who was she with at the moment? he wondered. What was she doing and saying? He wouldn't have much time tonight to see her—he was exhausted from this endless day and needed sleep. But how badly he wanted to be close to her, to feel her firm body beneath his hands, watch her lying underneath him . . . Touching her, eradicating the shock and anger of the near-disaster from earlier on Canal Street.

After he hung up he held the memory of the woman's sultry voice in his mind, as he continued to watch the fast clouds, the choppy waves . . .

Disappointed, you can be fulfilled.

Hungry, you can be satiated.

Defeated, you can be victorious.

At 9:30 P.M. Fred Dellray stood and stretched, then plucked four empty coffee containers off his desk in the FBI's Manhattan office. He pitched them into his brimming trash can.

Time to call it a night.

He flipped through the report about the shoot-out on Canal Street. It was mostly finished but he knew he'd have to revise it tomorrow. Dellray enjoyed writing and he was good at it (under a pseudonym he'd contributed to various historical and philosophical magazines on many different topics over the years) but this particular opus was going to require some serious massaging.

Hunched over the desk, he glanced at the pages, compulsively jotting changes here and there and all the while wondering why exactly he was working on GHOSTKILL.

Frederick Dellray, with degrees in criminology, psychology and philosophy tucked under his belt, eschewed brainy law enforcement. He was to undercover work what Rhyme was to criminalistics. Known as the Chameleon, he could portray anybody from any culture, provided, of course, that the role could be played by someone well over six feet with skin dark as an Ethiopian's. Which still left an amazing range of parts for the agent—crime being perhaps the only aspect of society where one is judged solely on skill and not on race.

Dellray's talent, and lifelong passion for law enforcement, however, had proved his undoing. He'd been *too* good. In addition to working undercover jobs for his own outfit, the FBI, he'd been borrowed regularly by the Drug Enforcement Administration, Alcohol, Tobacco and Firearms and the police departments in New York, L.A., Washington, D.C. Bad guys have computers, cell phones and email too, of course, and little by little Dellray's reputation spread within the underworld. It became too dangerous to put him into the field.

He was promoted and put in charge of running undercover agents and CIs, confidential informants, in New York.

For his part, Dellray would've preferred a different assignment. His partner, Special Agent Toby Dolittle, had been killed in the Oklahoma City federal building bombing and the death sent Dellray on a perennial quest to be reassigned to the bureau's antiterrorist unit. But he reluctantly recognized that a passion to collar a perp wasn't enough to excel at that area of law enforcement—look at Alan Coe, for instance—and so he was content to remain where his talents lay.

Being assigned to what would become GHOSTKILL had confused Dellray at first; he'd never run any human smuggling cases before. He'd assumed that he was recruited because of his extensive undercover network in Manhattan, Queens and Brooklyn—where the Chinese-American communities in this area were located. But Dellray soon learned that his traditional techniques for running snitches and undercover agents didn't work. A viewer of thoughtful movies, Dellray had seen the famous film *Chinatown,* which made the point that the namesake neighborhood in old-time Los Angeles operated outside of Western laws. This, he found, wasn't a scriptwriter's device. And it was true about New York's Chinatowns as well. Justice was administered through the tongs, and the number of calls to 911 and to the local police stations in Chinese communities of New York was much lower than in other neighborhoods. Nobody snitched to outsiders, and undercover agents were sniffed out almost immediately.

So, with GHOSTKILL, he found himself running a complicated operation dealing with a type of crime he had little experience with. But after his efforts tonight at the office he felt much better. Tomorrow he was going to meet with the special agents in charge of the Southern and Eastern Districts and one of the assistant directors from Washington. He'd get himself named supervising special agent, which would open up a lot of the bureau's resources to him and the GHOSTKILL team. As SSA, he'd bully and connive his way into getting what they needed

for the case: the FBI's—i.e., *his*—complete jurisdiction, the SPEC-
TAC team in town and the INS relegated to an exclusively advisory role,
which meant virtually cutting them out of the case altogether. Peabody
and Coe would be pissed but that was just too bad. He'd already framed
his argument. Yes, the INS was vital in gathering intelligence about
snakeheads and smuggling operations and interdicting their ships. But
now GHOSTKILL was a full-out manhunt for a killer. That was the
bureau's expertise.

He was confident the brass would buy his pitch; undercover agents
like himself, Dellray had learned, are among the best persuaders—and
extorters—in the world.

Dellray snagged his office phone and called his own number, his apartment in Brooklyn.

"Hello?" a woman's voice answered.

"I'll be home in thirty," he said softly. With Serena he never used the
unique patois he'd developed working on the streets of New York and
slung about as his trademark on the job.

"See you then, love."

He hung up. No one in the bureau or the NYPD knew a single thing
about Dellray's personal life—nothing about Serena, a choreographer
with the Brooklyn Academy of Music he'd been seeing off and on for
years. She worked long hours and traveled. He worked long hours and
traveled.

The arrangement suited them.

Walking through the halls of the bureau's headquarters, which resembled the digs of a big, moderately unsuccessful corporation, he nodded at
two agents in shirtsleeves, ties loose in a way that the Boss, J. Edgar Hoover,
would not have tolerated (just as, Dellray reflected, he *himself* wouldn't
have been tolerated by the old G-man, now that he thought about it).

"So much crime," Dellray intoned as he stalked past them on his long
legs, "so little time." They waved good night.

Then down the elevator and out the front door. He crossed the street,
heading for the federal parking annex.

He noticed the scorched frame of a van that had burned earlier in the
evening, still smoldering. He remembered hearing the sirens, wondered
what had happened.

Past the guard, down the ramp into the dim garage, which smelled of
wet concrete and car exhaust.

Dellray found his government-issue Ford and unlocked the door. He opened it and tossed in his battered briefcase, which contained a box of 9mm ammunition, a yellow pad filled with his jottings, various memos on the Kwan Ang case and a well-read book of Goethe's poems.

As Dellray started to climb inside the Ford he noticed on the driver's side of the car the window weather stripping was unseated, which told him immediately somebody had wedged the window to open the door. Shit! He glanced down and saw the wires protruding from under his seat. He lunged for the top of the door with his right hand to keep from putting all his weight on the seat and compressing what he knew was the bomb's pressure switch.

But it was too late.

The tips of his long fingers flapped against the open door frame and slipped off. He began to fall sideways onto the seat beneath him.

Save your eyes! he thought instinctively, lifting his long hands toward his face.

Chapter Twenty-seven

"The Changs're somewhere in Queens," Sachs said, writing this bit of information on the whiteboard. "Driving a blue van, no tag, no make."

"Do we have *anything* specific about it?" Rhyme muttered. "Cerulean, navy, sky, *baby* blue?"

"Wu couldn't remember."

"Oh, my, now, *that's* helpful."

As Sachs paced, Thom took over as the scribe.

The information about the Ghost's four-by-four, which the snakehead had abandoned at the site of the Wu shoot-out, wasn't any better. The Blazer had been stolen and had current but fake dealer tags. Tracing the vehicle identification number revealed only that it had been stolen in Ohio months ago.

Sonny Li sat nearby but wasn't offering his Asian detective insights at the moment; he was rummaging through a large shopping bag he'd brought back from Chinatown a short while before. Lon Sellitto was on his phone, apparently learning that the Ghost had successfully vanished after the shoot-out, to judge from his scowl.

Sachs, Mel Cooper and the criminalist turned to the trace evidence she'd found in the Blazer. She'd located a few small grayish carpet fibers under the brake and accelerator pedals and two matching fibers in the cuff of the dead shooter outside the Wus' apartment. The fibers didn't match the carpet in the Blazer or any of the prior scenes and therefore might've come from the Ghost's safehouse.

"Burn 'em and let's check the database."

Cooper ran two of the fibers through the gas chromatograph/mass spectrometer, which produced a record of the exact substances that went into this type of carpet.

As they waited for the results there was a knock on the door outside and a moment later Thom ushered in the visitor.

It was Harold Peabody.

Rhyme assumed that he'd come here to talk to them about Coe's carelessness at the Wus' apartment. But there was a grimness on his face that suggested something more. Then behind him another man appeared. Rhyme recognized him as the assistant special agent in charge—the ASAC—of the Manhattan office of the FBI, a too-handsome man with a perfect chin and smug manners. Rhyme had worked with him several times and found him efficient and unimaginative—and given, as Dellray had complained, to bureauspeak thick as honey. He too was grim-faced.

Then a third man appeared. His crisp navy-blue suit and white shirt suggested to Rhyme that he was bureau as well, but he identified himself tersely as Webley from State.

So, the State Department was now involved, Rhyme thought. That was a good sign. Dellray must've indeed used his *guanxi* in high places to get them reinforcements.

"Sorry to intrude, Lincoln," Peabody said.

The ASAC: "We need to talk to you. Something happened downtown tonight."

"What?"

"About the case?" Sachs asked.

"We don't think it's related. But it's going to have some implications, I'm afraid. "

Well, get on with it, Rhyme thought and hoped his impatient glare conveyed this message.

"Someone planted a bomb in the garage across from the federal building tonight."

"My God," Mel Cooper whispered.

"It was in Fred Dellray's car."

Oh, Lord, no, thought Rhyme.

"No!" Sachs cried.

"A bomb?" Sellitto blurted, snapping closed his cell phone.

"He's okay," the ASAC said quickly. "The main charge didn't go off."

Rhyme closed his eyes. Both he and Dellray had lost people close to them thanks to explosive devices. It was, even unemotional Rhyme believed, the most insidious and cowardly way to kill someone.

"Not hurt?" Li asked, concerned.

"No."

The Chinese cop muttered something, a prayer perhaps.

"What happened?" the criminalist asked.

"Dynamite with a pressure switch. Dellray triggered it but only the detonator fired. Maybe the cap wasn't seated right. They don't know yet."

The ASAC said, "Our bomb unit rendered safe and handed the parts over to PERT."

Rhyme knew most of the agents and the techs in the bureau's Physical Evidence Response Team and respected them. If there was anything to find he had confidence that they would. "Why don't you think it's related?"

"Anonymous nine-one-one call about twenty minutes before the blast. Male voice, undetermined accent, said the Cherenko family was planning some retaliation for the bust last week. It said more would follow."

Dellray, Rhyme recalled, had just finished running a huge covert operation in Brooklyn, the home of the Russian mob. They'd nailed three international money launderers, their staffs and several supposed hitmen and had confiscated millions of dollars and rubles.

"Origin of the call?"

"Pay phone in Brighton Beach."

The largest Russian community in the area.

"I don't believe in coincidences," Rhyme said. "The Ghost spent some time in Russia, remember? To pick up the immigrants."

He glanced at Sachs, an inquiring eyebrow raised. She answered, "The Ghost and his buddies were pretty hot to get the hell away from the scene of the Wu shooting. I can't see them detouring down to the federal building to set up a bombing. Not to say they couldn't have hired somebody."

Rhyme observed that Webley from State had said not a word since the three men had arrived. He was standing, silent, arms crossed, in front of the evidence charts, staring at them.

"How'd they plant the device?" Sellitto asked the ASAC.

"Team of two, we think. Somebody set a van on fire in front of the parking garage. Distracted the guard. The other guy got into the garage and set it."

Dismayed, Rhyme suddenly understood what "implications" the

ASAC had been referring to. "And Fred wants off the Ghost case, right?"

The ASAC nodded. "The thing with his partner, you know."

Toby Doolittle, Rhyme recalled, the partner killed in the Oklahoma City bombing.

"He's already cleared the decks and's calling in markers from his snitches in Brighton Beach."

Rhyme could hardly blame the agent. But he said, "We need some help, Harold. Fred was getting a SPEC-TAC team together and some more agents." He knew too that Dellray had been arranging to have the INS's role cut down to intelligence gathering and advising, a fact which even Rhyme—never a practitioner of diplomacy—decided it was best not to mention at the moment. "The Ghost's network is too good. He's too far underground. We need more people, better support."

The ASAC said reassuringly, "Oh, we're downcourt with that one, Lincoln. We'll have a new field ops agent for you in the morning and some more news about SPEC-TAC."

Peabody unbuttoned his suit jacket, revealing a badly sweat-stained shirt. He said, "I heard what happened with Alan Coe—at the Wus' apartment, I mean. I'm sorry."

"We would've catch the Ghost," Li said, "if Coe not fire shot."

"I know. Look, he's a good man. I don't have many agents as dedicated as he is. He works twice as hard as most of my people. He's just impulsive. I try to cut him some slack. Had a tough time after that informant of his disappeared. I guess he blamed himself. After his suspension he took a leave of absence. He won't talk about it but I heard he went overseas to find out what happened to her. On his own nickel. Finally came back to work and's been going like a greyhound ever since. One of my best agents."

Except for minor flaws like letting suspects escape, Rhyme thought wryly.

Peabody and the ASAC left, reassuring Rhyme and Sellitto once again that they'd have a new FBI liaison agent in the morning and the SPEC-TAC team en route. "It's definitely agendaed," the ASAC called.

"Goodnight," said Webley from State formally and followed the men out the door.

"Okay, back to work," the criminalist said to Sellitto, Sachs, Cooper and Li. Eddie Deng was at home, nursing his badly bruised chest. "What else did the Wus tell you, Sachs?"

She gave them the details she'd learned in the clinic. The Wus included Qichen, his wife, Yong-Ping, a teenage daughter named Chin-Mei and a young son, Lang. The Changs were Sam, Mei-Mei, William and Ronald, as well as Chang's father, who was known by his full Chinese name, Chang Jiechi. In China, Sam had arranged for jobs for himself and William but Wu didn't know where or even in what line of work. Then she said that the family also had a baby whose mother had drowned on the *Dragon*. "Po-Yee. It means 'Treasured Child.'"

Rhyme noticed a certain look in Sachs's eyes when she mentioned the infant. He knew how much Sachs wanted a child—and wanted a child with him. As bizarre as this idea would have seemed to him several years ago he now secretly liked it. Part of his motive wasn't completely paternal, though. Amelia Sachs was one of the best crime scene searchers he'd ever seen. Most important was her empathy. She, more than any other CS profes- sional he'd known, except himself, had the ability to transport herself into the mind of the perpetrator at the scene and, in that persona, find evidence that most other officers would have missed. Sachs, however, had another aspect to her psyche. What drove her to perfection at crime scenes drove her into danger. A champion pistol shot, an expert driver, she was often first on the scene at takedowns, ready to pull her weapon and engage a perp. Just like tonight, in the alleyway beside the Wus' apartment.

Rhyme would never ask her to give that up. But with a child at home he hoped she'd restrict herself to the crime scene work, where her true talent as a cop lay.

Then Mel Cooper interrupted his thoughts. "Chromatograph results from the carpet." He explained that it was a wool-nylon blend. He deter- mined the color temperature of the gray shade and then went online, log- ging into the FBI's carpet-fiber database.

A few minutes later the results popped onto the screen. "It's Lustre- Rite brand and the manufacturer's Arnold Textile and Carpeting in Wallingham, Mass. I've got phone numbers," the slim man said.

"Get somebody calling them," Rhyme said. "We want to know about installations in Lower Manhattan. Recent, you think, Mel?"

"Probably. With this many fibers."

"Why that?" Li asked.

The tech explained, "Most fiber loss from carpets happens within six months of installation, give or take."

"I'll do it," Sellitto said. "Only don't hope for miracles, considering the company's probably been closed for hours." He nodded at the clock. It was nearly 11 P.M.

Rhyme said, "It's a manufacturing company. And what does that mean?"

"I don't know, Linc. Why don't you tell me?" Sellitto grumbled. Nobody was in the mood for object lessons.

"That there's probably a night shift. And a night shift means a foreman, and a foreman'll have the boss's number at home. In case of fire or some such."

"I'll see what I can do."

Cooper was testing the trace Sachs had found in the Blazer. "More of the bentonite," he said. "On both the Ghost's shoes and on his partners'." The slim man turned to the microscope and examined another bit of material. "What do you think, Lincoln. Is this mulch?" He looked up from the 'scope. "Came from the SUV's carpet, driver's side."

"Command, input, microscope," Rhyme ordered. The image that Cooper was looking at in the microscope came up on Rhyme's computer screen. The criminalist saw what he recognized immediately as traces of fresh cedar mulch, the sort used in decorative gardens. "Good."

"Lot of landscaping around Battery Park City," Sellitto pointed out, referring to the large residential development in downtown Manhattan, where the trace evidence they'd found earlier had suggested the Ghost might maintain his safehouse.

Too *much* landscaping, though, thought Rhyme. "Trace it to a particular manufacturer?"

"Nup," Cooper said. "Generic."

Well, this sample alone wouldn't pin down a particular location. The fact that the mulch was still damp, however, might help. "If we find a number of possible locations we can eliminate the ones that didn't have mulching done in the past few days. Long shot, but it's something." Then Rhyme asked, "How about the body?"

"Not much," she said. She explained that the man had had no identification on him—only some cash, about $900, extra ammo for his weapon, cigarettes and a lighter. "Oh, and a knife, which had traces of blood on it."

Cooper had already ordered the typing test on the blood. But Rhyme knew it would match Jerry Tang's or Jimmy Mah's.

AFIS results came back on the prints from the Blazer and from the dead man. All negative.

Sonny Li pointed to a Polaroid of the face of the corpse. "Hey, I got it right, Loaban. His face—check it out. He's Kazakh, Kyrgyz, Tajik, Uighur. A minority, like I telling you, remember?"

"I remember, Sonny," Rhyme said to him. "Call our friend from the tong—Cai. Tell him that we think the gang is of those minorities you mentioned, Sonny. Might help him narrow things down." Then he asked, "Ballistics?"

"The Ghost was still using his Model 51," Sachs said.

Li offered, "I'm saying, very solid-rock gun."

"I found some nine-millimeter casings too." She held the evidence bag up. "But no distinctive ejection marks. Probably a new Beretta, SIG Sauer, Smittie or Colt."

"And the dead guy's weapon?"

"I processed it," she explained. "His prints only. It was an old Walther PPK. Seven-point-six-five."

"Where is it?" Rhyme studied the evidence bag and saw no sign of the weapon.

A look passed between Sachs and Sonny Li—a look decidedly not for Detective Lon Sellitto. She said, "I think the feds have it."

"Ah."

Li looked away from Rhyme and he knew immediately that Sachs had slipped the Chinese cop the weapon after she was through processing it.

Well, good for him, the criminalist thought. If not for the Chinese detective, then Deng, Sachs and the Wus' daughter might've been killed tonight. Let him have some protection.

Sachs gave Cooper the serial number of the Walther and he ran it through the firearms database. "Zip," he said. "Made in the 1960s. Probably's been stolen a dozen times since then."

Sellitto called, "Just got through to a senior VP at Arnold Textile. Woke him up but he was pretty cooperative, considering. That particular carpeting is for commercial sale only—original developers and installers—and it's the top of their line. He gave me a list of twelve big developers in the area who buy directly from the manufacturer and twenty-six distributors who market to installers and subcontractors."

"Hell," Rhyme said. It would be a marathon of canvassing to find the addresses of buildings where Lustre-Rite had been installed. He said, "Get somebody on it."

Sellitto said, "I'll have 'em start waking people up. Fuck—I'm awake; why the hell shouldn't the rest of the world be?" He made a call to the Big Building to line up some detectives to help and faxed the list downtown to them.

Then Rhyme's private line rang and he answered it.

"Lincoln?" a woman's voice asked through the speakerphone.

He was thrilled to hear the caller's voice. "Doctor Weaver."

Rhyme's neurosurgeon, who'd be performing the operation next week.

"I know it's late. Am I interrupting anything? You busy?"

"Not a thing," Rhyme said and ignored Thom's exaggerated glance at the whiteboard, which attested to the fact that he was somewhat occupied at the moment.

"I've got the details for the surgery. Manhattan Hospital. Week from Friday at 10 A.M. Neurosurgery pre-op. Third floor."

"Excellent," he replied.

Thom jotted the information down and Rhyme and the doctor said good night.

"You going to doctor, Loaban?"

"Yes," he said.

"About . . ." The Chinese cop couldn't seem to think of a way to summarize Rhyme's condition and he waved toward his body.

"That's right."

Sachs said nothing, just stared at the sheet of instructions that Dr. Weaver had dictated to Thom. Rhyme knew that she would prefer he not have the operation. Most of the successes with the technique had occurred with patients whose injuries were far less severe than Rhyme's, those with the damage much lower on the spinal cord, at the lumbar or thoracic level. The surgery, as she'd told him, would probably produce no discernible benefit and was risky—it might even make him worse. And, given his lung impairment, it was possible that he could die on the table. But Sachs understood how important it was to him and was going to support him.

"So," she finally said, a stoic smile on her face, "we'll make sure we nail the Ghost before next Friday."

Rhyme noticed that Thom had been studying him closely.

"What?" the criminalist snapped.

The aide took Rhyme's blood pressure. "Too high. And you don't look good."

"Well, thank you very much," he snapped back, "but I don't think my appearance has anything to do—"

"It's quitting time," the aide said firmly. And he wasn't speaking to his boss.

Sellitto and Cooper also voted to call it a night.

"Mutiny," Rhyme muttered.

"No," Thom retorted. "Common sense."

Sellitto made a call to check on the Wus and John Sung. The family was now in the NYPD safehouse in the Murray Hill section of New York. John Sung had declined Sachs's invitation to join them, afraid that it would remind him too much of the many Chinese security bureau facilities he'd been detained in as a dissident. Instead, Sellitto added another cop to the team guarding him. All of the protective officers reported that the immigrants were safe.

Rhyme said to Sachs, "You taking those herbs with you? I hope you are. They stink."

"I was going to leave them as air freshener but if you don't like them . . ." She leaned close. "How *are* you feeling? You look pale."

"Just tired," he said. Which was the truth. Oddly tired. He supposed he should be concerned about it but he believed his exhaustion was nothing more than the demands of the case, which had been consuming him for days. But the fatigue was something that he knew he should pay attention to—did it indicate anything more serious? One of the major problems plaguing SCI patients, of course, isn't just paralysis. There are related problems because the nerves aren't responding—lung impairment and resulting infections—but perhaps the worst problem is the absence of pain. You have no early warning system of pain from cancer, say, which Rhyme's own father had died of—as had Sachs's. He remembered that his dad had first learned of the disease after he'd gone to the doctor complaining about stomach pain.

"Good night," Mel Cooper called.

"*Wan an,*" Li called.

"Whatever," Sellitto grumbled and walked into the corridor.

"Sonny," Rhyme said. "You'll stay here tonight."

"Not got other place to go, Loaban. Sure."

"Thom'll make up a room. I'll be upstairs, taking care of a few things. Come up and visit if you feel like it. Give me a twenty minutes."

Li nodded then turned back to the whiteboard.

"I'll take you up," Sachs said. Rhyme wheeled into the tiny elevator that ran between the first and second floor, formerly a closet. She joined him and closed the door. Rhyme glanced at her face. It was thoughtful but in a way that didn't have to do with the case, he sensed.

"Anything you want to talk about, Sachs?"

Without answering, she closed the elevator door and pressed the UP button.

GHOSTKILL

Easton, Long Island, Crime Scene	Stolen Van, Chinatown	Jerry Tang Murder Crime Scene
· Two immigrants killed on beach; shot in back.	· Camouflaged by immigrants with "The Home Store" logo.	· Four men kicked door in and tortured him and shot him.
· One immigrant wounded—Dr. John Sung.	· Blood spatter suggests injured woman has hand, arm or shoulder injury.	· Two shell casings—match Model 51. Tang shot twice in head.
· "Bangshou" (assistant) on board; identity unknown.	· Blood samples sent to lab for typing.	· Extensive vandalism.
· Assistant confirmed as drowned body found near site where *Dragon* sank.	· Injured woman is AB negative. Requesting more information about her blood.	· Some fingerprints.
· Ten immigrants escape: seven adults (one elderly, one injured woman), two children, one infant. Steal church van.	· Fingerprints sent to AFIS.	· No matches except Tang's.
· Blood samples sent to lab for typing.	· No matches.	· Three accomplices have smaller shoe size than Ghost, presumably smaller stature.
· Injured woman is AB negative. Requesting more information about her blood.		· Trace suggests Ghost's safehouse is probably downtown, in Battery Park City area.
· Vehicle awaiting Ghost on beach left without him. One shot believed fired by Ghost at vehicle. Request for vehicle make and model sent out, based on tread marks and wheelbase.		· Suspected accomplices from Chinese ethnic minority. Presently pursuing whereabouts.
· Vehicle is a BMW X5.		
· Driver—Jerry Tang.		
· No vehicles to pick up immigrants located.		
· Cell phone, presumably Ghost's, sent for analysis to FBI.		
· Untraceable satellite secure phone. Hacked Chinese gov't system to use it.		
· Ghost's weapon is 7.62mm pistol. Unusual casing.		
· Model 51 Chinese automatic pistol.		
· Ghost is reported to have gov't people on payroll.		
· Ghost stole red Honda sedan to escape. Vehicle locator request sent out.		
· No trace of Honda found.		
· Three bodies recovered at sea—two shot, one drowned. Photos and prints to Rhyme and Chinese police.		
· Drowned individual identified as Victor Au, the Ghost's *bangshou*.		
· Fingerprints sent to AFIS.		
· No matches on any prints but unusual markings on Sam Chang's fingers and thumbs (injury, rope burn?)		
· Profile of Immigrants: Sam Chang and Wu Qichen and their families, John Sung, baby of woman who drowned, unidentified man and woman (killed on beach).		

**Canal Street Shooting
Crime Scene**

· Additional trace suggesting safehouse is in Battery Park City area.

· Stolen Chevrolet Blazer, untraceable.

· No match on prints.

· Safehouse carpet: Arnold company's Lustre-Rite, installed in past six months; calling contractors to get list of installations.

· Fresh gardening mulch found.

· Body of Ghost's accomplice: ethnic minority from west or northwest China. Negative on prints. Weapon was Walther PPK.

· Details on immigrants:

  · The Changs: Sam, Mei-Mei, William and Ronald; Sam's father, Chang Jiechi, and infant, Po-Yee. Sam has job arranged but employer and location unknown. Driving blue van, no make, no tag number. Changs' apartment is in Queens.

  · The Wus: Qichen, Yong-Ping, Chin-Mei and Lang.

Chapter Twenty-eight

In Chinese many words are combinations of their opposites. For instance, "advance-retreat" means "to move."

One of these is the word for "doing business," which is literally translated "buy-sell."

And this was what the four men sitting in the smoky storefront office of the East Broadway Workers' Association were now engaged in, late on this stormy August night: buying and selling.

That the object of the negotiations was human life—selling the Ghost the location of Sam Chang's family—didn't appear to give these men any pause at all.

There were, of course, many legitimate tongs in Chinatown and they provided important services for their members—resolving conflicts among competing businesses, protecting schoolchildren from gangs, running centers for senior citizen and child daycare, discouraging inroads by the restaurant and garment workers unions and serving as a liaison to the "Other Government," that is, city hall and the NYPD.

But this particular tong did none of these. It had one specialty only and that was to serve as a base of snakehead operations in the New York area.

Now, nearly midnight, the three leaders of the Workers' Association—all in their forties or fifties—sat on one side of the table, across from a man whom none of them knew. But he was a man who could be very valuable—since he knew where the Changs were hiding.

"How do you know these people?" the director of the association asked the man, who'd given only his family name, Tan, presumably so that the Ghost couldn't track him down and torture him to find the Changs' location.

"Chang is a friend of my brother in China. I got them an apartment and Chang and his boy a job."

"Where is the apartment?" the director of the tong asked casually.

Tan, gesturing abruptly, said, "That's what I'm here to sell. If the Ghost wants it he has to pay for it."

"You can tell us," an associate said, smiling. "We'll keep it to ourselves."

"I deal only with the Ghost."

Of course the tong bosses knew this. But it was always worth a try. There were many stupid people in this world.

"You have to understand," one of the associates offered, "the Ghost is hard to find."

"Ah," Tan scoffed, "You're not the only ones I can deal with, you know."

"Then why are you here?" the other associate asked quickly.

Tan paused. "Because I'm told you are the most informed."

"It's dangerous," the director said to Tan. "The police are after the Ghost. If they find out that we've contacted him . . . well, they could disrupt our organization."

Tan shrugged. "You have ways to get in touch with him that are secure, don't you?"

"Let's get to the money. What will you pay us to put you in touch with the Ghost?"

"Ten percent of whatever he pays me."

The director waved his arm. "This meeting is over. Go find your other sources."

Laughing in ridicule at the director's comment, Tan said, "And how much did *you* want?"

"Half."

"You are making a poor joke."

The battle lines being drawn, they got down to business. The buy-sell continued for nearly a half hour. Finally, they agreed on thirty percent, provided it was U.S. dollars.

The director pulled out a cell phone and placed a call. The Ghost came on the line and the director identified himself.

"Yes?" the snakehead asked.

"I have someone here who rented an apartment to some of the survivors of the *Dragon,* the Changs. He wants to sell you that information."

The Ghost was silent for a moment. He asked, "Tell him to prove it."

The director relayed this request to Tan, who replied, "The father's western name is Sam. There is an old man too, Chang's father. And two boys. Oh, a wife. Mei-Mei. And they have a baby. She isn't theirs. She was on the ship. Her mother drowned."

"How does he know them?"

The director explained, "He's the brother of a friend of Chang's in China."

The Ghost considered. "Tell him I'll pay one hundred thousand one-color for the information."

The director asked Tan if this was acceptable. He said immediately that it was. Some people you do not buy-sell with.

Keeping a straight face, despite his pleasure at this sum, the director added delicately to the Ghost, "He's agreed to pay us a fee. Perhaps, sir, if it wouldn't be too much trouble . . ."

"Yes, I'll pay you your portion directly. If the information's accurate. What is your cut?"

"Thirty percent."

"You're a fool," the Ghost scoffed. "You were robbed. I would've taken sixty-five percent if I'd been you."

The director flushed and began to defend himself but the Ghost cut him off. "Send him to see me tomorrow morning at eight-thirty. You know where." He hung up.

The director told Tan the arrangement and they shook hands.

In the Confucian order of duty to others, friendships were on the lowest rung—after ruler-subject, father-son, husband-wife and older brother–younger brother. Still, there was something abhorrent, the director thought, about this kind of betrayal.

But no matter. Whenever he arrived in hell, Tan would be judged for his acts. And as for the director and his associates—well, $30,000 was not bad for an hour's work.

His hands shaking, his breath fast, Sam Chang left the storefront of the East Broadway Workers' Association and had to walk three blocks before he found a bar, which are rare in Chinatown. He sat on an uneven stool and ordered a Tsingtao beer. He drank it fast and ordered another.

He was still surprised—no, astonished—that the three men at the tong had believed that he was Joseph Tan and had actually told him where he could meet the Ghost in the morning.

He laughed to himself. What an appalling idea—he was actually bargaining with these men over the price of his family's life.

Sitting in their dark apartment in Brooklyn several hours before, Chang had been thinking: So this is to be our life. Darkness and fear . . .

And his father's keen eyes had narrowed. "What are you thinking of doing?" he'd asked his son.

"The Ghost is looking for us."

"Yes."

"He won't expect me to be looking for *him.*"

Chang Jiechi's eyes remained on his son for a long moment then slid to the name plaque on the improvised altar. *Chang* . . . archer. "And what would you do if you found him?"

He said to the old man, "Kill him."

"Why not go to the police?"

Chang laughed sourly. "Do you trust the police here any more than in China?"

"No," his father answered.

"I will kill him," Chang repeated. He had never in his life disobeyed his father and he wondered if the man would now forbid him to do what he'd decided must be done.

But, to his surprise, his father asked only, "You would be able to do that?"

"Yes, for my family. Yes." Chang then pulled his windbreaker on. "I'll go to Chinatown. I'll see what I can do to find him."

"Listen to me," his father said, whispering. "Do you know how to find a man?"

"How, Baba?"

"You find a man through his weaknesses."

"What's the Ghost's weakness?"

"He cannot accept failure," Chang Jiechi said. "He must kill us or his life will suffer from great disharmony."

And so Sam Chang had done just what his father had suggested—offered the Ghost the chance to find his prey. And it had worked.

Holding the cold beer bottle to his face, Chang now reflected that he himself would probably die. He'd shoot the Ghost immediately—as soon as he opened the door. But the man would have associates and body-guards, who would in turn kill him.

And thinking this, the first image in his mind was William, his firstborn son, the young man who would, sooner than anyone thought, inherit the mantle of the Changs.

The father now heard the son's insolence, saw the contempt in his eyes . . .

Oh, William, he thought. Yes, I neglected you. But if only you under-stood that I did so solely in the hopes of making a better homeland for you and your children. And when it grew too dangerous in China I brought you here, leaving my beloved country behind, to give you what I couldn't back home.

Love, son, is not manifest in the gift of gadgets or coddling foods or rooms of one's own. Love shows itself in discipline and example and sacri-fice—even giving up one's life.

Oh, my son . . .

Sam Chang paid for the beer and left the bar.

Though the hour was late some stores were still open to tempt the last of the tourists. Chang went into a variety and gift shop and bought a small shrine box, a brass plate, electric candles with red bulbs, some incense. He spent some time trying to find the right Buddha statue. He picked a smiling one because—even though he would kill a man tomorrow and would himself die—a cheerful Buddha would bring comfort and solace and ultimately good fortune to the family he was leaving behind.

"The thing is, Amie . . ."

Amelia Sachs was driving downtown, uncharacteristically close to the posted speed limit.

"The thing is, honey," her father had said to her in his dissipated state, ravaged by the greedy cells that were dismantling his body, "you got to look out for yourself."

"Sure, Pop."

"Naw, naw, you say, 'Sure,' but you don't really mean 'sure.' You mean I'm agreeing with the old man 'cause he looks like you know what."

Even lying in West Brooklyn Hospice on Fort Hamilton Parkway, near death, the man hadn't let her get away with a single thing.

"I don't think I mean that at all.".

"Ah, listen, Amie, listen."

"I'm listening."

"I hear your stories about walking the beat."

Sachs, like her father, had been a "portable" at the time, a beat patrolman. In fact her nickname was "PD," for the Portable's Daughter.

"I make up a lot of stuff, Pop."

"Be serious."

Her smile faded and she indeed grew serious, feeling the dusty summer breeze flow though the half-open window, tousling her unencumbered red hair and her father's overwashed sheets as they sat, and lay, in that difficult place.

"Go on," she said.

"Thank you. . . . I hear your stories about your beat. You don't look out for yourself enough. But you've got to, Amie."

"Where's all this coming from, Pop?"

They both knew it was coming from the cancer that would soon kill him and from the urgency to pass along to his only child something more substantive than an NYPD shield, a nickel-plated Colt pistol and an old Dodge Charger in need of a transmission and cylinder heads. But his role as father required him to say, "Humor an old man."

"So let's tell jokes."

"Remember the first time you flew?"

"We went to see Grandma Sachs in Florida. It was a hundred and eighty degrees by the pool and a chameleon attacked me."

Unfazed, Herman Sachs continued. "And the stewardess, or whatever you call them nowadays, said, 'In case of emergency put *your* oxygen mask on and then assist anyone who needs help.' That's the rule."

"They say that," she conceded, buffeted by the emotions she felt.

The old cop, with stains of axle grease permanently seated in the lattice of his hands, continued. "That's gotta be a patrolman's philosophy on the street. You first, then the vic. And it's gotta be your personal philosophy too. Whatever it takes, look out for yourself first. If you're not whole, you'll never be able to take care of anybody else."

Driving now through the faint rain, she heard her father's voice fade and another replace it. The doctor from several weeks ago.

"*Ah, Ms. Sachs. Here you are.*"

"*Hello, Doctor.*"

"*I've just been meeting with Lincoln Rhyme's physician.*"

"*Yes?*"

"*I've got to talk to you about something.*"

"*You're looking like it's bad news, Doctor.*"

"*Why don't we sit down over there in the corner?*"

"*Here's fine. Tell me. Let me have it straight.*"

Her whole world in turmoil, everything she'd planned for the future altered completely.

What could she do about it?

Well, she reflected, pulling to a stop at the curb, here's one thing . . .

Amelia Sachs sat for a long moment. This is crazy, she thought. But then, impulsively, she climbed out of the Camaro and, head down, walked quickly around the corner and into an apartment building. She climbed the stairs. And knocked on the door.

When it opened she smiled at John Sung. He smiled back and nodded her inside.

Whatever it takes, look out for yourself first. If you're not whole, you'll never be able to take care of anybody else. . . .

Suddenly she felt a huge weight lifted off her shoulders.

Chapter Twenty-nine

Midnight.

But, despite the exhausting day, which had led him from a sinking ship to a Central Park West apartment half the globe away from his home, Sonny Li didn't seem tired.

He walked into Lincoln Rhyme's bedroom, carrying a shopping bag. "When I down in Chinatown with Hongse, Loaban, I buy some things. Got present for you."

"Present?" Rhyme asked from his throne, the new Hill-Rom Flexicair bed, which—he'd been told—was exceedingly comfortable.

Li took an object from the bag and began unwrapping a small wad of paper. "Look what I got here." In his hands was a jade figurine of a man with a bow and arrow and looking fierce. Li looked around the room. "Which way north?"

"That's north." Rhyme nodded.

Li put the figurine on top of a table against the wall. Then returned to the bag and took out some sticks of incense.

"You're not going to burn that in here."

"Have to, Loaban. Not kill you."

Despite Li's assertion that Chinese have a difficult time saying no, this was not a trait the cop apparently shared.

He set the incense into a holder and lit it. He then found a Dixie cup in the bathroom and filled it with some liquor from a light green bottle, which had also appeared from the shopping bag.

"What're you doing, making a temple?"

"Shrine, Loaban. Not a temple." Li was amused by Rhyme's failure to miss the obvious distinction.

"Who is that? Buddha? Confucius?"

"With a bow and arrow?" Li scoffed. "Loaban, you know so much about so little, and so little about so much."

Rhyme laughed, thinking that when he'd been married his wife had often said much the same, though at a higher volume and less articulately.

Li continued. "This is Guan Di—god of war. We make sacrifice to him. He like sweet wine and that what I bought for him."

Rhyme wondered how Sellitto and Dellray, not to mention Sachs, would react when they saw the transformation of his room into a shrine to the god of war.

Li bowed toward the icon and whispered some words in Chinese. He extracted a white bottle from the shopping bag and sat in the rattan chair by Rhyme's bed. He filled a Dixie cup for himself and then fiddled with one of Rhyme's tumblers, taking off the lid, filling it halfway up and then replacing the lid and fitting a straw inside.

"And that?" Rhyme asked.

"Good stuff, Loaban. *Chu yeh ching chiew.* We make sacrifice to *us* now. This stuff good. Like whisky."

No, it wasn't like whisky at all, definitely not delicately peat-smoked eighteen-year-old scotch. But, although the taste was pretty bad, it had one hell of a kick to it.

Li nodded toward the impromptu sacristy. "I find Guan Di at store in Chinatown. He very popular god. Thousands shrines all over China devoted to him. But I not buy him because of war. He is god of detectives too, I'm saying."

"You're making that up."

"Joke? No, I'm saying, is true. Every security bureau I ever been in has Guan Di there. Case don't go so good, detectives burn offerings, just like we do." Another shot of the liquor. Li sniffed. "That strong stuff, I'm saying. The *baijiu.*"

"The what?"

He nodded at the bottle of *chu yeh ching chiew.*

"What was your prayer?" Rhyme asked.

"I translate: 'Guan Di, please let us find the Changs and catch the fuck Ghost.'"

"That's a good prayer, Sonny." Rhyme drank more of the liquor. It grew better with every sip—or maybe it was that you tended to forget how bad it was.

The Chinese cop continued, "That surgery you talk about. That make you better?"

"It might. A little. I won't be able to walk but I could regain a little movement."

"How it work?"

He explained to Li about Dr. Cheryl Weaver, whose neurology unit at a branch of the University of North Carolina was performing experimental surgery on spinal cord injury patients. He could still remember almost verbatim the doctor's explanation of how the technique worked.

The nervous system is made up of axons, which carry nerve impulses. In a spinal cord injury those axons're cut or crushed and they die. So they stop carrying impulses and the message doesn't get from the brain to the rest of the body. Now, you hear that nerves don't regenerate. That's not completely true. In the peripheral nervous system—like our arms or legs—damaged axons can grow back. But in the central nervous system— the brain and the spinal cord—they don't. At least they don't on their own. So, when you cut your finger, your skin grows back and you regain your sense of touch. In the spinal cord that doesn't happen. But there are things that we're learning to do that can help regrowth.

Our approach at the Institute here is an all-out assault on the site of the injury. We attack SCI on all fronts. We use traditional decompression surgery to reconstruct the bony structure of the vertebrae themselves and to protect the site where your injury occurred. Then we graft two things into the site of the injury: one is some of the patient's own peripheral nervous system tissue and the other substance we graft is some embryonic central nervous system cells.

"From a shark," Rhyme added to Sonny Li.

The cop laughed. "Fish?"

"Exactly. Sharks are more compatible with humans than other animals are. Then," the criminalist continued, "I'll take drugs to help the spinal cord regenerate."

"Hey, Loaban," Li said, looking him over carefully, "this operation, it dangerous?"

Again, Rhyme heard Dr. Weaver's voice.

Of course there are risks. The drugs themselves aren't particularly dangerous. But there're risks associated with the treatment. Any C4 quad is going to have lung impairment. You're off a ventilator but with the anesthetic there's a chance of respiratory failure. Then the stress of the procedure could lead to autonomic dysreflexia and the resulting severe blood pressure elevation—I'm sure you're familiar with that—which in turn could lead to a stroke or a cerebral event. There's a risk of surgical trauma to the site of your initial injury—you don't have any cysts now and no shunts—but the operation and resulting fluid buildup could increase that pressure and cause additional damage.

"Yes, it's dangerous," Rhyme told him.

"Sound to me like *'yi luan tou shi.'*"

"Which means?"

Li considered then said, "Words translate: 'throwing eggs against rocks.' Means doing something bound to fail, I'm saying. So why you do this operation?"

It seemed obvious to Rhyme. To move a step closer to independence. Perhaps to be able to close his hand around the tumbler, for instance, and lift it to his lips. To scratch his head. To become more *normal*—using the term that was very politically incorrect within the disabled community. To be closer to Amelia Sachs. To be a better father to the child that Sachs wanted so badly.

He said, "It's just something I have to do, Sonny." Then he nodded at the nearby bottle of Macallan scotch. "Let's try *my baifu* now."

Li barked a laugh. *"Baijiu,* Loaban. What you just say was 'Let's try my department store.'"

"Baijiu," Rhyme corrected himself.

Li filled the cup and the tumbler with the aged Scotch.

Rhyme sipped from the straw. Ah, yes, much better.

Li tossed down a whole Dixie cup of scotch. He shook his head. "I'm saying, you should not do this operation."

"I've weighed the risks and—"

"No, no. Embrace who you are! Embrace your limitations."

"But why? When I don't have to?"

"I see all this science shit you have here in *Meiguo*. We not have science everywhere in China like you do. Oh, Beijing, Hong Kong, Guangdong, Fuzhou, sure, sure—we got mostly everything you got, a little behind, thank you, Chairman Mao, but we got computers, we got Internet, we got missiles—yeah, sometime they blow up but usually they go in space okay. But doctors, they not use so much science. They put us back in *harmony*. In China, doctors not gods."

"We have a different view here."

"Yeah, yeah," Li scoffed. "Doctors make you look younger. Give you hair. Give women bigger *xiong,* you know—" He pointed to his chest. "We not understand that. That not in harmony."

"You think I'm in *harmony* like this?" Rhyme asked with an exasperated laugh.

"Fate make you this way, Loaban. And make you this way for purpose. Maybe you best detective you can be because of what happen. Your life balanced now, I'm saying."

Rhyme had to laugh. "I can't walk, I can't pick up evidence . . . How the hell is that better?"

"Maybe your *brain,* it work better now, I'm saying. Maybe you have stronger will. Your *jizhong,* your focus, maybe is better."

"Sorry, Sonny, I don't buy it."

But, as he'd learned, once Sonny Li took a position on an issue, he didn't let go. "Let me explain you, Loaban. You remembering John Sung? Has that good luck stone of Monkey King?"

"I remember."

"You are Monkey."

"I'm what?"

"You are like Monkey, I'm saying. Monkey do miracle things, magic, smart, tough—had temper too, I'm saying. Like you. But he ignore nature—look for ways to cheat gods and stay alive forever. He steal peaches of immortality, got names erased from *Register of Living and Dead.* That when he got in trouble. Got burned and beat up and buried under mountain. Finally Monkey give up wanting to live forever. Found some friends and they all make pilgrimage to holy land in the west. He was happy. In harmony, I'm saying."

"I want to walk again," Rhyme whispered adamantly, wondering why he was baring his soul to this strange little man. "That's not too much to ask."

"But maybe *is* too much ask," Li responded. "Listen, Loaban, look at me. I could wish to be tall and look like Chow Yun-Fat, have all girls chase me. Could wish to run big commune and have hundreds productivity awards so everybody respect me. Could wish to be Hong Kong banker. But not my nature. My nature is being fuck good cop. Maybe you start walking again, you lose some other else—something more important. Why you drink this crap?" He nodded at the scotch.

"It's my favorite *baijiu.*"

"Yeah? How much it cost?"

"About seventy dollars a bottle."

Li made a sour face. Still he downed the glass and poured another. "Listen, Loaban, you know the *Tao*?"

"Me? That New Age crap? You're talking to the wrong person."

"Okay, I am telling you something. In China we got two big philosophs. Confucius and Lao-tzu. Confucius think what is best is for people to obey superiors, follow orders, *kow tow* to betters, keep quiet. But Lao-tzu, he say opposite. What is best is for each person follow the way of life on his own. Find harmony and nature. English name of *Tao* is *Way of Life.* He write something I try to say. It all about you, Loaban."

"About me?" Rhyme asked, reminding himself that his interest in the man's words must've had its source in the well of alcohol within him at the moment.

Li squinted as he translated, "In *Tao*, Lao-tzu say, 'There no need to leave house for better seeing. No need to peer from window. Instead, live in the center of your being. The way to do is to be.'"

"Does everybody in China have a goddamn saying for everything?" Rhyme snapped.

"We got lots sayings, true. You should have Thom write that down and put up on wall, next to altar to Guan Di."

The men fell silent for a minute. *There is no need to leave house for better seeing. No need to peer from window. . . .*

Finally the conversation resumed and Li talked at length about life in China.

Rhyme asked, "And what's your house like?"

"Apartment. Whole place small, size this room."

"Where is it?"

"My town, Liu Guoyuan. Means 'six orchards,' but they all gone now, all cut down. Maybe fifty thousands people. Outside Fuzhou. *Many* people *there.* Over million, I'm saying."

"I don't know the area."

"In Fujian Province, southeast China. Taiwan is just off coast. Many mountains. Min River, big one, run through it. We independent place. Beijing worried about us lots. Fujian was home of first triad—organized gang, I'm saying. The San Lian Hui. Very powerful. Lots smuggling: salt, opium, silk. Lots sailors in Fujian. Merchants, importers. Not so many farmers. Communist Party is powerful in my town but that because the party secretary is private capitalist. Has Internet company like AOL. Real success. Ha, running dog lackey capitalist! His collective make good, good money. His stock not fall like NASDAQ."

"What kind of crime is there in Liu Guoyuan?" Rhyme asked.

Li nodded. "Lots bribes, protection money. In China, you cheat business and people, that okay. But cheat the party or the government, then you fuck die. Convict you, shoot in back of head. We got lots other crime too. Same stuff happen here. Murder and robbery and rape." Li sipped more liquor. "I find man killing women. Kill four of them, going to kill more. I got him." He laughed. "One drop blood. I find one drop on his bicycle tire, small as grain of sand. That what place him at scene. He confess. See, Loaban, not all woo-woo."

"I'm sure it isn't, Sonny."

"Kidnapping women big problem in China—have more men than women. For every hundred women, we got a hundred *twenty* men. People not want baby girls, I'm saying, only boys. But then where brides come from? So lots kidnappers take girls and women, sell them. Sad, families come to us and ask us find their wives or daughters been kidnap. Lot security officers don't bother—hard cases. Sometimes they take women thousands miles away. I find six last year. Record in our office. Good feeling to find kidnapper, arrest him."

Rhyme said, "That's what it's all about."

Li lifted his cup at this and then they drank in silence for a moment. Rhyme, thinking that he was feeling content. Most of the people who came to visit treated him like a freak. Oh, they meant no unkindness. But either they struggled to ignore his "condition," as most of them referred to it. Or they celebrated his disability, making jokes and comments about it to show how closely they connected with him. When in fact they didn't connect at all and as soon as they caught a glimpse of the catheter or the box of adult diapers in the corner of the bedroom they started counting down the minutes until they could escape. These people would never disagree with him, they'd never fight back. They never got below the appearance of a relationship.

But in Sonny Li's face Rhyme could see complete indifference to Rhyme's state. As if it were, well, indeed *natural*.

He realized then that nearly all the people he'd met over the past few years, with the exception of Amelia Sachs, had been merely acquaintances. He'd known the man for less than a day but Sonny Li already seemed more than that.

"You mentioned your father," Rhyme said. "When you called him before, it didn't sound like a good conversation. What's his story?"

"Ah, my father . . ." He drank more scotch, which was apparently growing on the cop the way Rhyme had gotten used to the *baijiu*. Globalization through liquor, Rhyme reflected wryly.

Li poured another shot.

"You might want to sip it," Rhyme suggested.

"Time to sip is after you dead," the cop said and emptied the pink Dixie cup emblazoned with flowers. "My father . . . He not like me much. I am, what is meaning . . . Not live up to what he wants."

"Disappointment?"

"Yes, I am disappointment."

"Why?"

"Ah, lots things. Give you our history in acorn."

"Nutshell."

"Doctor Sun Yat-sen in the 1920s, he unify China but civil war happened. Kuomintangs—the National Party—were under Chiang Kai-shek. But Gongchantang—the communists—they fight against them. Then Japan invade, bad time for everybody. After Japan lose, we have more civil war in China and finally Mao Zedong and communists win, drive the nationalists to Taiwan. My father, he fought with Mao. October 1949, he standing with Chairman Mao at the Gate of Heavenly Peace in Beijing. Oh, Loaban, I hear that story a million times. How he stood there and bands was playing 'The March of the Volunteers.' Big fuck patriotic time.

"So my father, he got *guanxi*. Connections high up. He become big guy in Communist Party down in Fujian. Want me to be too. But I see what communists do in sixty-six—Historically Unprecedented Great Proletarian Cultural Revolution—destroy everything, hurt people, kill people. Government and party not doing right things."

"It wasn't *natural*," Rhyme said. "Wasn't in *harmony*."

"Exact right, Loaban." Li laughed. "My father want me to join party. Order me to. Threaten me. But I not care about party. Not care about collectives." He waved his arms. "Not care about great ideas. What I like is police work. I like catch criminals. . . . Always puzzles, always challenge, I'm saying. My sister, she big and high in the party. Our father proud of her even though she a woman. He say *she* not bring disgrace on him like me. Say that all the time." His face grew dark. "Other bad thing too is I not have a son—no children—when I married."

"You're divorced?" Rhyme asked.

"My wife, she die. Got sick and die. Some fever, bad thing. Only married few years but no children. My father say it my fault. We try, just not have child. Then she die." He rose and paced to the window, stared at the lights of the city. "My father, he lot strict. Hit me all time growing up. Never what I did was good enough for him. Good grades . . . I good student. Got medals in army. Marry nice, respectful girl, get job at security bureau, become detective, not just traffic, I'm saying. Come visit my father every week, give him money, pay respect at mother's grave. But never anything I do is enough. Your parents, Loaban?"

"Both dead."

"My mother, she not so strict as father but she never say much. He not let her. . . . Here, in Beautiful Country, you not so much, what you say, under gravity of your parents?"

Good way to put it, thought Rhyme. "Maybe not so much. Some people are."

"Respect for parents, that number one for us." He nodded toward Guan Di's statue. "Of all gods, most important are our ancestors."

"Maybe your father thinks more of you than he's letting on. A façade, you know. Because he thinks it's good for you."

"No, he just not like me. Nobody to carry on family name, I'm saying. That very bad thing."

"You'll meet somebody and have a family."

"A man like me?" Li scoffed. "No, no. I just cop, got no money. Most men my age in Fuzhou, they work business, got lots money. Money all over place. Remember, I tell you many more men than women? Why a woman pick poor old man when they can have rich young one?"

"You're my age," Rhyme said. "You're not old."

Li looked out the window again. "Maybe I stay here. I speak English good. I be security officer here. Work in Chinatown. Undercover."

He seemed serious. But then Sonny Li laughed and said what they were both thinking. "No, no, too late for that. Lots too late . . . No, we get the Ghost, I go home and keep being fuck good detective. Guan Di and I solve big crime and get my picture in paper in Fuzhou. Maybe chairman give me medal. Maybe my father watch news and see and he think I not be such bad son." He drained the glass of scotch. "Okay, I drunk enough now—you and me, we play game, Loaban."

"I don't play games."

"But what that game on your computer?" Li said quickly. "Chess. I saw it."

"I don't play very *often*," Rhyme qualified.

"Games improve you. I am show you how to play best game." He returned to the magic shopping bag.

"I can't play most games, Sonny. Can't exactly hold the cards, you know."

"Ah, card games?" Li said, sneering. "They games of chance. Only good for make money. See, those, you keep secrets by turning cards away from opponents. Best games are games where you keep secrets in head, I'm saying. *Wei-chi?* You ever hear it? Also called *Go.*"

Rhyme believed he had. "Like checkers or something?"

Li laughed. "Checkers, no, no."

Rhyme surveyed the board that Li took from the shopping bag and set up on the table beside the bed. It was a grid with a number of perpendicular lines on it. He then took out two bags, one containing hundreds of tiny white pebbles, the other black ones.

Suddenly Rhyme had a huge desire to play and he forced himself to pay careful attention to Sonny Li's animated voice as he explained the rules and object of *wei-chi.*

"Seems simple enough," Rhyme said. Players alternated putting their stones on the board in an attempt to surround the opponent's and eliminate them from play.

"*Wei-chi* like all great games: rules simple but winning hard." Li separated the stones into two piles. As he did he said, "Game go back many years. I am study best player of all time. Name was Fan Si-pin. Lived in 1700s—your dates. There nobody better than him ever live. He have match after match with Su Ting-an, who was almost as good. The games were usually draws but Fan had few points more so he was overall better player. Know why he better?"

"Why?"

"Su was defense player—but Fan . . . he play always offense. He charge forward always, was impulsive, crazy."

Rhyme felt the man's enthusiasm. "Do you play much?"

"I am in club at home. I play much, yes." His voice faded for a moment and a wistfulness came over him. Rhyme wondered why. Then Li swept his oily hair back and said, "Okay, we play. You see how you like. Can last long time."

"I'm not tired," Rhyme said.

"Not either," Li said. "Now, you never play before so I give advantage. Give you three piece extra. Seem like not much but big, big advantage in *wei-chi*."

"No," Rhyme said. "I don't want any advantages."

Li glanced at him and must have thought this had to do with his disability and added gravely, "Only give you advantage because you not play before. That only reason. Experience players do that always. Is customary."

Rhyme understood and appreciated Li's reassurance. Still, he said adamantly, "No. You make the first move. Go ahead." And watched Li's eyes lower and focus on the wooden grid between them.

IV

Cutting the
Demon's Tail

—◦•◦—

Wednesday, the Hour of the Dragon, 7 A.M.,
to the Hour of the Rooster, 6:30 P.M.

In Wei-Chi the more equally matched two players are,
the more interesting the game.

—*The Game of Wei-Chi*

Chapter Thirty

On the morning of the day he was to die, Sam Chang awoke to find his father in the back courtyard of their Brooklyn apartment going through the slow movements of tai-chi.

He watched the elderly man for a few moments and a thought occurred to him: Chang Jiechi's seventieth birthday was in three weeks. In China they'd been so poor and so persecuted the family had not been able to have the man's sixtieth birthday celebration, traditionally a huge party that signified the move into old age, the time for veneration. But his family would do so for the seventieth.

Sam Chang's animate body would not make it to the party but his spirit perhaps would.

He gazed at the old man, who moved like a leisurely dancer in the small backyard.

Tai-chi was beneficial to the body and to the soul but it always saddened Chang to watch the exercise. It reminded him of a humid night in June years ago. Chang and a cluster of students and fellow teachers had been sitting together in Beijing, watching a group of people nearby engaged in the balletic movements. It was after midnight and they were all enjoying the pleasant weather and the exhilaration of being among like-minded friends in the center of what was becoming the greatest nation on earth, the new China, the enlightened China.

Chang had turned to a young student next to him to point out a spry elderly woman lost under the spell of tai-chi, when the boy's chest exploded and he dropped to the ground. The People's Liberation Army soldiers had begun firing on the crowd in Tiananmen Square. The tanks came through a moment later, driving the people in front of them, crushing many beneath the treads (the famous televised image of the student stopping the tank with a flower was the rare exception that terrible night).

Chang could never watch tai-chi without thinking of that moment, which solidified his stance as an outspoken dissident and changed his life—and that of his father and family—forever.

He now looked down at his wife and, next to her, the little girl, who slept with her arm around the white stuffed cat Mei-Mei had sewn for her. He gazed at them for a moment. Then walking into the bathroom, he turned the water on full. He stripped off his clothes and stepped in the shower, resting his head against the tiles that Mei-Mei had somehow found the time to scrub last night.

He showered, shut off the scalding water and dried himself with a towel. He cocked his head, hearing the sounds of clanking metal in the kitchen.

Mei-Mei was still asleep and the boys knew nothing of cooking. Alarmed, he climbed out of bed and pulled the pistol from beneath the mattress and walked cautiously into the main room of the apartment. He laughed. His father was making tea.

"Baba," he said, "I'll wake Mei-Mei. She can do that."

"No, no, let her sleep," the old man said. "When your mother died I learned to make tea. I can cook rice too. And vegetables. Though not very well. Let us take tea together." Chang Jiechi lifted the iron pot, the handle wrapped with a rag, and took cups and hobbled into the living room. They sat and he poured the tea.

Last night, when Chang had returned, he and his father had taken a map and located the Ghost's apartment building, which was not, to their surprise, in Chinatown but farther to the west, near the Hudson River.

"When you get to the Ghost's apartment," his father now asked, "how will you get inside? Won't he recognize you?"

Chang sipped the tea. "I don't think he will, no. He only came to the hold of the ship once. It was dark too."

"How will you get in?"

"If there is a doorman I'll tell him I'm there on business and give the name Tan. I practiced my English all night. Then I'll just take the elevator up to his door and knock on it."

"And if he has bodyguards?" Chang Jiechi said. "They'll search you."

"I'll hide the gun in my sock. They won't search carefully. They won't be expecting me to be armed." Chang tried to picture what would happen. He knew they would have guns too. Even if they shot him as soon as they saw the gun he would still be able to shoot one or two bullets into the Ghost. He realized that his father was gazing at him and he looked down. "I will come back," he said firmly. "I will be here to take care of you, Baba."

"You are a good son. I could not have asked for a better one."

"I have not brought you all the honor I should have."

"Yes, you have," the old man said and poured more tea. "I named you well." Chang's given name, Jingerzi, meant "shrewd son."

They lifted their cups and Chang drained his.

Mei-Mei came to the door, glanced at the teacups. "Have you taken rice yet?" she asked, the expression meaning simply, "Good morning." It wasn't a reference to food.

"Wake William," Chang told Mei-Mei. "There are some things I want to say to him."

But his father waved for her to stop. "No." She did.

"Why not?" Chang asked.

"He will want to come with you."

"I'll tell him no."

Chang Jiechi laughed. "And that will stop him? That impetuous son of yours?"

Chang fell silent for a moment then said, "I can't go off like this without talking to him. It's important."

But his father asked, "What is the only reason that a man would do something like you are about to do—something foolhardy and dangerous?"

Chang replied, "For the sake of his children."

His father smiled. "Yes, son, yes. Keep that in mind, always. You do something like this for the sake of your children." Then he grew stern. How well Sam Chang knew this look of his father's. Imperial, unyielding. He had not seen it for some time—ever since the man had grown sick with the cancer. "I know exactly what you intend to say to your son. I will do it. It's my wish that you don't wake William."

Chang nodded. "As you say, Baba." He looked at his wristwatch. The time was seven-thirty. He had to be at the Ghost's apartment in an hour. His father poured him more tea, which Chang drank down quickly. Then he said to Mei-Mei, "I have to leave soon. But I wish that you come sit by me."

She sat beside her husband, lowering her head to his shoulder.

They said nothing but after five minutes Po-Yee began to cry and Mei-Mei rose to take care of the girl. Sam Chang was content to sit in silence and watch his wife and their new daughter. And then it was time to leave and go to his death.

Rhyme smelled cigarette smoke.

"That's disgusting," he called.

"What?" asked Sonny Li, the only other person in the room. The Chinese cop was groggy and his hair stuck out comically. The hour was 7:30.

"The cigarettes," Rhyme explained.

"You should smoke," Li barked. "Relaxes you. Good for you."

Mel Cooper arrived with Lon Sellitto and Eddie Deng not far behind him. The young Chinese-American cop walked very slowly. Even his hair was wilted, no stylish spikes today.

"How are you, Eddie?" Rhyme asked.

"You should see the bruise," Deng said, referring to his run-in with a lead slug yesterday during the shoot-out on Canal Street. "I wouldn't let my wife see it. Put on my pajamas in the bathroom."

Red-eyed Sellitto carried a handful of pages from the overnight team of officers who'd been canvassing recent contractors that had installed gray Arnold Lustre-Rite carpet in the past six months. The canvassing wasn't even finished and the number of construction locations was discouragingly large: thirty-two separate installations in and around Battery Park City.

"Hell," Rhyme muttered, "thirty-two." And each one could have multiple floors that had been carpeted. Thirty-two? He'd hoped there'd be no more than five or six.

INS agent Alan Coe arrived, walking brightly into the lab. He didn't seem the least contrite and began asking questions about how the investigation was going—as if the shoot-out yesterday had never happened and the Ghost hadn't escaped thanks to him.

More footsteps on the corridor outside.

"Hey," Sachs said in greeting, entering the room. She kissed Rhyme. He started to tell her about the list of recently carpeted buildings but Sellitto interrupted. "Get some rest last night?" he asked her. The detective's voice had a definite edge to it.

"What?" she asked.

"Rest? Sleep? You get plenty of rest?"

"Not exactly," she replied cautiously. "Why?"

"I tried you at home about one. Had some questions for you."

Rhyme wondered what the reason for the interrogation was.

"Well, I got home at two," she answered, a flare in her eyes. "I went to see a friend."

"Did you?"

"Yeah, I did."

"Well, I couldn't get in touch with you."

"You know, Detective," she said, "I can let you have my mother's phone number. She can give you some pointers on checking up on me. Even though she hasn't done it for about fifteen years."

"Ho, boy, that was good," said Sonny Li.

"Watch yourself, patrolman," Sellitto said to Sachs.

"Watch *what?*" she snapped. "You got a point to make, make it."

The homicide cop backed down. He muttered, "I couldn't get in touch with you, that's all. Your cell phone was off."

"Was it? Well, I had my pager. Did you try to page me?"

"No."

"Then?" she asked.

The argument mystified Rhyme. True, when she was working, Rhyme insisted that she be instantly available. But after hours it was different. Amelia Sachs was independent. She liked to go for fast drives, she had interests and friends other than him.

Whatever drove her to scratch her skin, to mourn her father, to mourn her former lover, a cop busted for being one of the most crooked in recent history, whatever drove her at the crime scenes—the same force drove her off by herself at times.

Just as there were times when he booted her out, sometimes asking nicely, sometimes ordering her away. A crip needs time alone. To gather strength, to let the aide take care of the piss 'n' shit stuff and to consider little questions like, Do I want to kill myself today?

Rhyme called the Federal Building and asked for Dellray but he was in Brooklyn checking out leads to the attempted bombing last night. Then he spoke to the assistant special agent in charge and was told that they were meeting that morning about assigning another FBI agent to GHOSTKILL to replace Dellray. Rhyme was angry; he'd assumed the bureau had already picked an SSA for the team.

"What about SPEC-TAC?"

The ASAC replied, "That's on the scroll for the powwow this morning too."

The scroll for the powwow?

"Well, we need people and we need them now," Rhyme snapped.

The slick man said, "We're prioritized."

"Oh, that's fucking reassuring."

"I'm sorry, Mr. Rhyme? I missed that."

"I said, call us as soon as you know something. We need more people."

Just after he disconnected, the phone rang again. Rhyme snapped, "Command, answer phone."

There was a click and a Chinese-accented voice asked, "Mr. Li, please."

Li sat down, absently pulled out a cigarette, which Thom swooped by and lifted from his hand. Li leaned toward the speaker and began to talk rapidly in Chinese. There was an explosive exchange between him and the caller. Rhyme thought they were arguing but Li finally sat back, jotting notes in Chinese. Then he hung up and smiled. "Okay, okay," Li said, "here I got something. That was Cai, from the tong. He ask around about minorities. There this group of Chinese called Uighurs. They Muslims, Turks. Tough guys. They got take over by China—like Tibet—and don't like it so good. Treated bad. Cai find that Ghost hire people from Turkestan Community and Islamic Center of Queens. The guy Hongse shot, he one of them. Here address and phone number. Hey, was I right, Loaban? I say he from minority."

"You sure were, Sonny."

Eddie Deng translated the information into English on a second slip of paper.

"Should we raid it?" Sellitto asked.

"Not yet. Might tip off the Ghost," Rhyme said. "I've got a better idea."

Deng was right with him. "Pen register."

"Yep."

These were phone company records of incoming and outgoing calls for a particular number. Since they didn't record the content of a conversation, it was far easier for law enforcers to access these records than to monitor the actual transmissions under a Title 3 or state wiretap.

"What's that going to do?" Coe asked.

"The Ghost got to town yesterday morning and called the center at some point presumably—to arrange for his muscle. We'll check out all incoming and outgoing calls to the number of the place after, say, 9 A.M. yesterday."

In a half hour the phone company had provided a list of about thirty numbers into and out of the Uighur center in Queens in the past two days. Most of those numbers they could eliminate immediately—like those called before the Ghost arrived, as Rhyme had pointed out—but four were cell phones with local exchanges; a total of eighteen calls had gone to and come from those mobiles in the past two days."

"And they're hot phones, right? The mobiles?"

"Stolen as bad as the Mets' second base," Sellitto said.

Because the phones were stolen, this meant there was no billing address where the Ghost might be. But the cell phone providers were able to give the team information about where the callers were located when each call had been made or received. One phone had been in the Battery Park City area and, as the security chief from the company dictated intersections to delineate the cell zone, Thom drew them on the map. The result was a wedge about a half mile square downtown near the Hudson River.

"Now," Rhyme shouted to Sachs, feeling the excitement of narrowing in on his prey, "did any of the buildings in that area have Arnold Lustre-Rite carpet installed?"

"Crossing my fingers," Eddie Deng said.

Finally Sachs looked up from the list and shouted, "Yes! Got one."

"That's the Ghost's safehouse," Rhyme announced.

She said, "A new building. Eight-oh-five Patrick Henry Street. Not far from the river." She circled it on the map. Then she sighed, looking over the information from the Arnold company. "Hell," she muttered. "They installed carpet on nineteen floors. Lots of apartments to check."

"Then," Rhyme said impatiently, "you better get going."

Easton, Long Island, Crime Scene

· Two immigrants killed on beach; shot in back.

· One immigrant wounded—Dr. John Sung.

· "Bangshou" (assistant) on board; identity unknown.

　· Assistant confirmed as drowned body found near site where *Dragon* sank.

· Ten immigrants escape: seven adults (one elderly, one injured woman), two children, one infant. Steal church van.

· Blood samples sent to lab for typing.

　· Injured woman is AB negative. Requesting more information about her blood.

· Vehicle awaiting Ghost on beach left without him. One shot believed fired by Ghost at vehicle. Request for vehicle make and model sent out, based on tread marks and wheelbase.

　· Vehicle is a BMW X5.

　· Driver—Jerry Tang.

· No vehicles to pick up immigrants located.

· Cell phone, presumably Ghost's, sent for analysis to FBI.

　· Untraceable satellite secure phone. Hacked Chinese gov't system to use it.

· Ghost's weapon is 7.62mm pistol. Unusual casing.

　· Model 51 Chinese automatic pistol.

· Ghost is reported to have gov't people on payroll.

· Ghost stole red Honda sedan to escape. Vehicle locator request sent out.

　· No trace of Honda found.

· Three bodies recovered at sea—two shot, one drowned. Photos and prints to Rhyme and Chinese police.

　· Drowned individual identified as Victor Au, the Ghost's *bangshou*.

· Fingerprints sent to AFIS.

　· No matches on any prints but unusual markings on Sam Chang's fingers and thumbs (injury, rope burn?)

· Profile of Immigrants: Sam Chang and Wu Qichen and their families, John Sung, baby of woman who drowned, unidentified man and woman (killed on beach).

Stolen Van, Chinatown

· Camouflaged by immigrants with "The Home Store" logo.

· Blood spatter suggests injured woman has hand, arm or shoulder injury.

· Blood samples sent to lab for typing.

　· Injured woman is AB negative. Requesting more information about her blood.

· Fingerprints sent to AFIS.

　· No matches.

Jerry Tang Murder Crime Scene

· Four men kicked door in and tortured him and shot him.

· Two shell casings—match Model 51. Tang shot twice in head.

· Extensive vandalism.

· Some fingerprints.

　· No matches except Tang's.

· Three accomplices have smaller shoe size than Ghost, presumably smaller stature.

· Trace suggests Ghost's safehouse is probably downtown, Battery Park City area.

· Suspected accomplices from Chinese ethnic minority. Presently pursuing whereabouts.

　· Uighurs from Turkestan Community and Islamic Center of Queens.

　· Cell phone calls lead to 805 Patrick Henry Street, downtown.

Canal Street Shooting
Crime Scene

· Additional trace suggesting safehouse is in Battery Park City area.

· Stolen Chevrolet Blazer, untraceable.

· No match on prints.

· Safehouse carpet: Arnold company's Lustre-Rite, installed in past six months; calling contractors to get list of installations.

  · Location of installations determined: 32 near Battery Park City.

· Fresh gardening mulch found.

· Body of Ghost's accomplice: ethnic minority from west or northwest China. Negative on prints. Weapon was Walther PPK.

· Details on immigrants:

  · The Changs: Sam, Mei-Mei, William and Ronald; Sam's father, Chang Jiechi and infant, Po-Yee. Sam has job arranged but employer and location unknown. Driving blue van, no make, no tag number. Changs' apartment is in Queens.

  · The Wus: Qichen, Yong-Ping, Chin-Mei and Lang.

Chapter Thirty-one

You are part of the old. Do you repent?

The Ghost stood at the window of his high-rise apartment on Patrick Henry Street in Lower Manhattan and watched the boats sailing through the harbor, fifty meters below him, a mile away.

Some streaking fast, some bobbing awkwardly

Some pristine, some rusty like the *Fuzhou Dragon*.

. . . part of the old. Your decadent way of life is disgusting. . . .

He greatly enjoyed watching the panorama below him. He rarely had such views in China, once away from Beijing and the big cities in Fujian and Guangdong there were few towering buildings. Because there were few elevators.

Which was a condition that the Ghost's father came close to rectifying in the 1960s.

His father was a man blessed with the rare combination of careening ambition backed up by sensible schemes. The stocky businessman had his hands in many ventures: selling military products to the Vietnamese, who were gearing up to defeat the Americans in their appendix of a country to the south, operating junkyards, lending money, building private housing and importing Russian machinery—the most lucrative of which were Lemarov elevators, which were cheap, functional and rarely killed anyone.

Under the auspices of a Fuzhou collective, Kwan Baba—the given nickname meaning "father"—had signed contracts to buy thousands of these elevators, sell them to the building collectives and bring in Russian technicians to install them. He had every reason to believe that his efforts would change the skylines of China and make him even wealthier than he was.

And why wouldn't he succeed? He wore conformist unisex suits, he attended every CCP rally he possibly could, he had *guanxi* throughout the southeast and his cooperative was one of the most successful in the province of Fujian, sending a cascade of yuan to Beijing.

But his career was doomed. And the reason for this was simple: a solid, humorless soldier-turned-politician named Mao Zedong, whose capricious 1966 Cultural Revolution incited students across the country to rise up and destroy the four olds: old culture, customs, ideas and habits.

The house of the Ghost's father in an elegant part of Fuzhou was one of the first targets of the rampaging young men who took to the streets, practically shivering with idealism, on the orders of the Great Helmsman.

"You are part of the old," the leader raged. "Do you repent? Do you confess to clinging to the old values?"

Kwan Baba had met them in his living room, which had shrunk to the size of a prison cell due to the number of shouting youths surrounding the family, and had gazed at them not only in fear but in bewilderment too; he honestly hadn't been able to see the evil in what he'd done.

"Confess and seek reeducation and we will spare you!" another cried.

"You are guilty of old thought, old values, old culture. . . .

"You have built a lackey's empire on the backs of the people!"

In fact, the students had no idea what Kwan Baba did for a living or whether the cooperative he headed was based on the purest principles of J. P. Morgan capitalism or Marxist-Leninist-Maoist communism. They knew only that his house was nicer than theirs and that he could afford to buy art from an abhorred "old" era—art that did nothing to inform the people's struggle against the oppressive forces of the West.

Kwan and his wife, along with the twelve-year-old Ang and his older brother, stood speechless before the seething crowd.

"You are part of the old . . ."

Much of that night was a terrible, confused blur to young Ang.

But one part was permanently branded into his memory and he thought of it now, standing in his luxurious high-rise overlooking the harbor, awaiting the Changs' betrayer.

The tall student leader of the cadre stood in the middle of the living room, wearing black-rimmed glasses, lenses slightly askew because they'd been made at one of the local collectives. Spittle flying from his mouth, he engaged in a furious dialectic with young Kwan Ang, who hovered meekly beside the kidney-shaped coffee table on which his father had taught him to use the abacus years before.

"You are part of the old," the student raged into the boy's face. "Do you repent?" For emphasis, with every line he spoke he swung the thick baton—heavy as a cricket bat—to the floor between them; it landed with a loud thud.

"Yes, I repent," the boy said calmly. "I ask the people to forgive me."

"You will reform your decadent ways."

Thud.

"Yes, I will reform my ways," he said, though he didn't know what "decadent" meant. "The old ways are a threat to the collective good of the people."

"You will die if you retain your old beliefs!"

Thud.

"Then I will reject them."

Thud, thud, thud . . .

So it continued for endless minutes—until the blows the student rained down finally stole the life from what the student had been striking with the iron-tipped baton: The Ghost's parents, who lay bound and gagged on the floor at their feet.

The boy gave not a single glance at the bloody forms as he recited the catechism the students thirstily sought to hear. "I repent my ways. I reject the old. I regret that I have been seduced by unbeneficial and decadent thought."

He was spared, but not his older brother, who fled to the gardener's shed and returned with a rake—the only weapon the foolish boy could find. Within minutes the students reduced him to a third bloody pile on the carpet, as lifeless as his parents.

The fervent youngsters took loyal Kwan Ang with them, welcoming the young boy into the heart of the Glorious Red Banner Fuzhou Youth Brigade, as they spent the rest of the night ferreting out more of the pernicious old.

None of the students noticed that the next morning Ang slipped away from their impromptu headquarters. It seemed that with so much reform to perpetrate none of them even remembered him.

He, however, remembered them. His short time as an old-despising Maoist revolutionary—no more than a few hours—had been spent quite productively: memorizing the names of the youths in the cadre and planning their deaths.

Still, he bided his time.

Naixin . . .

The boy's sense of survival was strong and he escaped into one of his father's junkyards near Fuzhou. He lived there for months. He would prowl through the huge place, hunting rats and dogs for food, tracking them through the skeletons of machinery and mounds of trash with a homemade spear and a club—a rusty shock absorber from a wrecked Russian truck.

When he grew more confident and learned that the cadres were not searching for him he began making forays into town to steal food from trash bins behind Fuzhounese restaurants.

Because of their seafaring history and extensive contact with the rest of the world the Fuzhounese have always been among the most independent of Chinese. Teenage Kwan Ang found that the Communist Party and the Maoist cadres steered clear of the waterfront and docks, where snakeheads and smugglers didn't give a shit about downtrodden masses, and spouting ideology was a sure way to get yourself killed. The boy was informally adopted by several of these men and began running errands for them, earning their trust, eventually being allowed to head up some of their smaller schemes, like thefts from the docks and extorting protection money from businesses in town.

He killed his first man at thirteen—a Vietnamese drug dealer who had robbed the snakehead Ang was working for. And at fourteen he finally tracked down, tortured and killed the students who'd robbed him of his family.

Young Ang was not a fool; he looked around him and realized that the thugs he worked with tended to rise only so far—largely because of their poor education. He knew that he needed to master business, accounting and English—the coming language of international crime. He would sneak into the state schools in Fuzhou, which were so crowded that the teachers never knew that one of the students was not officially enrolled.

The boy worked hard amassing money, learning which crimes to avoid (stealing from the state and importing drugs, each of which would assure that you were the headline act at the well-attended Tuesday morning executions in the local football stadium) and which crimes were acceptable: stealing from the foreign businesses that were stumbling obliviously into the Chinese market, dealing in guns and human smuggling.

His experience on the waterfronts had given him an expertise in smuggling, extortion and money laundering, and these were the areas in which he made his money, first in Fuzhou then in Hong Kong and expanding throughout China and the Far East. He made a fetish of staying out of the limelight, of never being photographed, going to desperate lengths never to be spotted, much less arrested. He was thrilled when he learned that some local public security bureau officer had dubbed him Gui, the Ghost. He immediately adopted the nickname.

He was successful because the money itself was not what excited him. Rather it was the challenge itself. To lose was to be shamed. To win was glorious. The driving force in his life was the hunt. In gambling dens, for instance, he would play only games of skill. He was contemptuous of the fools who would pay money for a chance at a wheel of fortune or a lottery.

Challenges . . .

Like finding the Wus and the Changs.

He wasn't displeased with how the hunt was going. The Ghost had learned from his sources that the Wus were in a special safehouse—not an INS one but a facility run by the NYPD—which he never would have expected. Yusuf had talked to a colleague who would check out the place, see what the security was like and perhaps even kill the Wus if he had an opportunity.

As for the Changs—they'd be dead by nightfall, betrayed by their own friend, this Tan fellow, whom the Ghost would, of course, kill after the man revealed the family's address.

He was also pleased to hear from his source that the police weren't having much success tracking him down. The FBI side of the case was stalling and most of the case had fallen to the city police department. His luck was changing.

These meditations were interrupted by a knock on the door.

The betrayer had arrived.

The Ghost nodded toward a Uighur, who pulled his gun out of his waistband. He opened the door slowly, pointing his pistol toward the visitor.

The man in the hallway said, "I am Tan. I am here to see the man who is called the Ghost. Kwan is his real name. We have a business matter. It's about the Changs."

"Come in," the Ghost said, stepping forward. "Do you want some tea?"

"No," the old man replied, hobbling inside, looking around. "I won't be here long."

Chapter Thirty-two

With his still eyes, beneath drooping lids, Chang Jiechi surveyed the men in the room: the Ghost himself, then two men from some Chinese minority—Uighurs or Kazahks. Like many older Han Chinese, Chang Jiechi thought of them by the word "barbarians."

The old man continued farther into the room, thinking: What a journey it had been to come here to this place that would be the site of his death. Thinking too about his son, Sam Chang, who, he hoped, was still unconscious from the tea Chang Jiechi had given him, generously laced with some of the old man's morphine.

"What is the only reason that a man would do something like you are about to do—something foolhardy and dangerous?"

"For the sake of his children."

No father, of course, would willingly let a son go to his death. Chang Jiechi had decided as soon as Sam had returned from Chinatown last night that he himself would drug his son and come here in his stead. Sam had a half a life span ahead of him here in the Beautiful Country. He had his sons to raise and now—miraculously—the daughter that Mei-Mei had always wanted. Here was freedom, here was peace, here was a chance for success. He would not let his son miss out on these things.

As the drugged tea had taken effect and his son's lids fell heavily and the cup dropped from his hand Mei-Mei had risen, alarmed. But Chang Jiechi had told her about the morphine and what he intended to do. She tried to stop him but she was a woman and she was his daughter-in-law; she acquiesced to his wishes. Chang Jiechi had taken the gun and some money and, embracing Mei-Mei and touching his son's forehead one last time, left the apartment, with instructions not to wake William under any circumstances. He'd found a taxi and used the church van map to show the driver where he wished to go.

Now he walked stiffly into the Ghost's elegant apartment. The barbarian with the gun hovered close and Chang Jiechi understood that he would have to put the men at ease before he would have a chance to pull out his own pistol and put a bullet into the heart of the snakehead.

"Do I know you?" the Ghost asked, eyeing him curiously.

"Perhaps," Chang Jiechi replied, making up something he believed was reasonable and would make the Ghost less suspicious. "I'm involved in the tongs here in Chinatown."

"Ah." The Ghost sipped his tea.

The barbarian remained nearby, looking suspiciously at the old man. The other young man, dark and brooding, sat down in the back of the apartment.

As soon as the thug that was closest turned his attention away, Chang Jiechi would shoot the Ghost.

"Sit down, old man," the Ghost said.

"Thank you. My feet aren't well. Dampness and heat in my bones."

"And you know where the Changs are?"

"Yes."

"How do I know I can trust you?"

Chang Jiechi laughed. "Regarding trust, I think I have more to worry about than you do."

Please, he prayed to the spirit of his own father, a man gone from this earth for forty-six years and the primary god in Chang Jiechi's pantheon, higher even than the Buddha: Father, make that man put his gun away and give me five seconds. Let me save my family. Give me the chance for one bullet—that's all I ask. I'm only three meters away, I cannot miss.

"How do you know the Changs?" the Ghost asked.

"Through a relative in Fuzhou."

"You know I wish them harm. What reason do you have to betray them?"

"I need the money for my son. He is not well. He needs doctors."

The Ghost shrugged and said to the barbarian, "Search him. Let me see any papers he has on him."

No! thought Chang Jiechi in alarm.

The barbarian stepped forward, blocking his view—and aim—of the Ghost.

Chang Jiechi held up a hand and stopped the barbarian. "Please. I am an old man. I deserve your respect. Don't touch me. I will give you my papers myself."

The barbarian glanced back at the Ghost with a raised eyebrow. And when he did, Chang Jiechi drew the pistol from his pocket and, without hesitation, shot the barbarian in the side of the head. He dropped hard and lay motionless, sprawled on a footstool.

But the Ghost reacted immediately and leapt behind a heavy couch as Chang Jiechi fired again. The bullet snapped through the leather but he had no idea whether or not he'd hit the snakehead. He turned toward the second barbarian in the back of the apartment but the man had already raised his gun and was aiming it. Chang Jiechi heard a shot and felt a huge fist strike his thigh as the heavy bullet spun him around and he landed on his back on the floor. The barbarian hurried toward him. The old man might have fired at the man and possibly hit him. Instead, he turned to the couch and repeatedly fired his gun toward where the Ghost was hiding.

Then he realized that the weapon had stopped firing.

He was out of bullets.

Had he hit the Ghost?

Oh, please, Guan Yin, goddess of mercy . . . Please!

But a shadow grew on the wall. The Ghost rose from behind the couch, unhurt, his own pistol in his hand. Breathing heavily, he pointed the black muzzle toward Chang Jiechi and walked around the furniture. A glance at the dead barbarian.

"You're Chang's father."

"Yes, and you're the devil who's on his way back to hell."

"But not," the Ghost said, "on your ticket."

The other barbarian, moaning and whispering hysterically in a language that Chang Jiechi did not understand, hovered over the body of his countryman. He then rose and started toward the old man, pointing the gun at him.

"No, Yusuf," the Ghost said impatiently, waving him back. "He'll tell us where the rest of them are."

"Never" was the defiant response.

The Ghost said to his confederate, "We don't have much time. Somebody will have heard the shots. We'll have to leave. Use the stairs. Not the elevator. Have the van waiting by the back door."

The agitated man continued to stare at Chang Jiechi with wide eyes, hands shaking in rage.

"Did you hear me?" the Ghost raged.

"Yes."

"Then go. I'll join you in a minute. Go!"

Chang Jiechi began to crawl desperately toward the closest doorway, which led to a dim bedroom. He glanced back. The Ghost was in the kitchen, taking a long filleting knife from a drawer.

Just ahead of Amelia Sachs, driving her bee-yellow Camaro at seventy miles an hour, was the building that contained the Ghost's safehouse apartment. The structure was huge, though, many stories tall and wide. Finding which apartment was the Ghost's would be a chore.

A sharp crackle in her Motorola speaker.

"Be advised, all RMP units in the vicinity of Battery Park City, we have a ten-thirty-four, reports of shots fired. Standby. . . . All units, further to that ten-thirty-four. Have a location. Eight-oh-five Patrick Henry Street. All units in area respond."

The very building she was now bearing down on. The Ghost's. Was it a coincidence? She doubted it, though. What had happened? Did he have the Changs inside the building? Had he lured them there? The families, the children . . . She pushed the accelerator farther down and depressed the button of her mike, pinned to her windbreaker. "Crime Scene Five Eight Eight Five to Central. Approaching scene of that ten-thirty-four. Anything further, K?"

"Nothing further, Five Eight Eight Five."

"No apartment number, K?"

"Negative."

"K."

A few seconds later, Sachs's Camaro was up on the curb, leaving room for the ambulances and other emergency vehicles, which would soon be converging on the building.

As she ran inside, minding the slick, rosy marble floors, she noted that the flower beds near the front door overflowed with mulch, which was scattered on the sidewalks—undoubtedly the source of the trace that they'd found at the earlier scene.

There was no security guard or doorman station in the building but several people were standing in the lobby, looking uneasily at the elevators.

Sachs asked a middle-aged man, wearing workout clothing, "Did you report the shots?"

"I heard something. I don't know where from, though."

"Anybody?" Sachs asked, glancing at the other tenants.

"I think it was west," an elderly woman said. "High up, but I'm not sure where."

Two other responding RMPs pulled up out front and the uniformed officers ran inside. Sellitto, Li and Alan Coe were behind them. An ambulance appeared and then two Emergency Services Unit trucks.

"We heard the ten-thirty-four," Sellitto said. "This's his building, right? The Ghost's?"

"Yep," Sachs confirmed.

"Jesus," the homicide detective muttered. "There've gotta be three hundred units here."

"Two hundred seventy-four," the elderly woman said.

Sellitto and Sachs conferred. The name on the apartment directory would be fake, of course. The only way to find the Ghost would be a dangerous, door-to-door search.

Crewcut Bo Haumann strode into the lobby with more ESU officers. "We've sealed all the exits," he said.

Sachs nodded. "What floor?" she asked the elderly woman.

"I was on nineteen. West wing. They seemed awfully close."

A young man in a business suit had joined them. "No, no, no," he said. "I'm sure they were from fifteen. South. Not west."

"You sure?" Haumann asked.

"Absolutely."

"I don't think so," the woman offered in gentle disagreement. "They were higher. And it was definitely the west wing of the building."

"Great," Haumann muttered. "Well, we've gotta move. We could have injureds. We'll search everywhere."

Sachs's Motorola clattered again. "Central to Crime Scene Five Eight Eight Five."

"Go ahead, Central."

"Landline patch."

"Go ahead, K."

"Sachs, are you there?" Lincoln Rhyme's voice said.

"Yeah, go ahead. I'm here with Lon and Bo and ESU."

"Listen," the criminalist said, "I've been talking to dispatch and corre-
lating the reports from the people in the building who called nine-one-
one. It looks like the shots came from either the eighteenth or nineteenth
floors, somewhere in the middle of the west side of the building."

The speaker was a squawk box, not a headset; anyone nearby could
hear the transmission. "Okay, you all hear that?" Haumann asked his officers.

They nodded.

"We're going to sweep, Rhyme," she said. "I'll call you back."

Haumann divided his officers into three teams, one for each floor—
eighteen and nineteen—and one to divide up further and sweep the stair-
wells.

Sachs noticed Coe nearby. He was checking his own pistol—the large
Glock with which he was a proven bad shot—and had sidled over to one
of the ESU teams. She whispered to Haumann, "Keep him off the entry.
He's trouble in a tac situation."

Sachs had some credibility with the head of ESU—he'd seen her
under fire—and Haumann agreed. He walked over to Coe and spoke
with him. Sachs didn't hear the exchange but since this was an NYPD
operation, Haumann must've pulled jurisdictional rank and ordered the
agent to stand down. After a moment of heated discussion, the INS
agent's face was nearly as red as his hair. But Haumann had never lost the
will—and demeanor—of the drill sergeant he had once been and Coe
soon gave up his futile protests. He turned away and stormed out the
front door, pulling out his cell phone, undoubtedly to lodge a protest with
Peabody or somebody at the Federal Building.

The ESU head left a small team to guard the lobby then he, Sachs and
a group of officers stepped into one of the elevators and started up to the
eighteenth floor.

They crowded away from the door when it opened and one officer
looked out with a metal mirror attached to a wand. "Clear."

Out they stepped, moving cautiously along the carpet, trying to remain
quiet though their equipment rang like mountain climbers'.

Haumann gave the hand signals that meant to spread out. Two officers, armed with MP5 machine guns, joined Sachs and together they

deployed to start the search. Bracketed by the two large cops, machine guns ready, Sachs picked a door and knocked.

There was an odd sound from inside, a faint clunk, as if something heavy was being set down next to the door. She glanced at the ESU officers, who leveled their weapons at the doorway. With a satisfying zip of Velcro, Sachs drew her pistol from her holster and stood back slightly.

Another clunk from inside, a scraping of metal.

What the hell was that noise?

A chain rattled.

Sachs put a few pounds of nervous pressure on the trigger guard of her weapon, though not on the trigger itself, and tensed as the door opened.

A tiny, gray-haired woman looked up at them. "You're the police," she said. "You're here about those firecrackers I complained about." She stared at the large machine guns the ESU officers carried. "Oh. Well. Look at this."

"That's right, ma'am," Sachs said, noticing that the clunking sound had been a stool, which the woman had apparently set on the floor to be able to look out through the security peephole.

She grew wary. "But you wouldn't have those guns if they were just firecrackers, right?"

"We're not sure what they were, ma'am. We're trying to find out where the sounds came from."

"I think it's 18K, up the hall. That's why I thought they were firecrackers—because an Oriental man lives there. Or Asian, or whatever you're supposed to say nowadays. They use firecrackers in their religion. They're supposed to scare away dragons. Or maybe it's ghosts. I don't know."

"Are there any other Asians on this floor?"

"No, I don't believe so."

"Okay, ma'am, thank you. Could you go back inside and lock your door. Whatever you hear, don't open it."

"Oh, dear." She looked at the men with the guns again and nodded uncertainly. "Could you tell me—"

"Now, please," Sachs said, smiling, but in a firm voice. She pulled the woman's door shut herself. She called in a whisper to Haumann, "Think it's 18K."

Haumann gave hand signals to his team, directing them to the apartment.

He knocked hard on the door. "Police, open the door!"

No response.

Again.

Nothing.

Haumann nodded to the officer who'd lugged the team's large battering ram with him. He and another cop took hold of the handles on the sides of the thick metal tube and looked at Haumann, who nodded.

The officers eased the ram back and then swung it forward hard into the door near the knob. The lock gave way immediately and the door slammed inward. They dropped the ram, chipping the marble floor. A half-dozen officers, guns to their shoulders, raced into the room.

Amelia Sachs moved in fast too, though behind the others, who sported full body armor, Nomex hoods, helmets and visors. Weapon in hand, she paused in the entryway and looked over the luxurious apartment, painted in subtle grays and pinks.

The ESU entry team fanned out and checked every room and any possible hiding places a human being might fit into. Their gruff voices began reverberating through the place. "Clear here . . . clear . . . Clear in the kitchen. No back entrance. Clear . . ."

The Ghost was gone.

But, just like at Easton Beach yesterday, he'd left death in his stead.

In the living room was the body of a man who bore a resemblance to the one she'd shot outside the Wus' apartment last night. Another Uighur, she assumed. He'd been shot at close range. He lay near a leather couch that had been riddled with bullets. A street gun—a cheap chrome automatic with the serial number etched out—lay on the floor in front of the couch.

The other body was in the bedroom.

He was an elderly Chinese man, lying on his back, his eyes glazed. There was a bullet wound in his leg but the slug had missed the major arteries and veins; it hadn't bled much. Sachs could see no other wounds, even though a long kitchen knife lay near his side. She pulled on rubber gloves and felt his jugular. No pulse.

Emergency Medical Services technicians arrived and checked the man over, verifying that he was dead.

"What's the COD?" one of the techs mused.

Sachs studied him. Then leaned forward. "Ah, got it," she said, nodding at the man's hand, in which was clutched a brown bottle. Sachs worked it out of his fingers. The characters on the label were in both Chinese and English. "Morphine," she said. "Suicide."

This might have been one of the immigrants on the *Fuzhou Dragon*—perhaps Sam Chang's father, who'd come here to kill the Ghost. She speculated about what had happened: The father had shot the Uighur but the Ghost had jumped for cover behind the couch and the old man had run out of ammunition. The Ghost took the knife and was going to torture him to learn where the rest of the family was but the immigrant had killed himself.

Haumann listened into his headset and reported that the rest of the building was clear; the Ghost had escaped.

"Oh, no," she muttered.

Crime Scene arrived—two techs carrying large metal suitcases into the hallway outside the apartment. Sachs knew them and nodded a greeting. She opened the cases, donned the Tyvek suit and then announced to the ESU team, "I need to process the room. Could I have everybody out of here please?"

For a half hour she worked the scene and though she collected some evidence none of it gave an obvious indication of where the Ghost might have gone to.

As she finished the search Sachs was aware of cigarette smoke. She looked up to see Sonny Li standing in the doorway, surveying the room. "I know him from boat," Li said, shaking his head with a sadness in his eyes. "That Sam Chang's father."

"I figured. Why'd he try it? One old man against the Ghost and the others?"

"For family," Li said quietly. "For family."

"I suppose you want to run the scene too?" she asked without any irony. Li's correct prediction about Jerry Tang and his surprise appearance at the Wus' apartment yesterday had bolstered his credibility as a detective.

"What you think I doing now, Hongse? I walking grid."

She laughed.

"Loaban and me talk last night. He tell me about walking grid. Only I walk grid in my mind now."

Sort of like Rhyme does, Sachs reflected. "You finding anything good?"

"Oh, plenty, I'm saying."

She turned back to the more tangible evidence and wrote out the chain of custody cards and packaged the evidence for transport.

In the corner of the room she noticed a small altar and several statues of Chinese gods. The words from the woman up the hall echoed in her mind.

They use firecrackers in their religion. They're supposed to scare away dragons.

Or maybe it's ghosts.

Chapter Thirty-three

Dozens of flashing lights surrounded the high-rise. The Ghost turned and looked back at them. Yusuf, the silent Turk, drove along Church Street away from the place. He was grim and badly shaken from the loss of yet another comrade but he drove calmly and was careful not to draw attention to the stolen Windstar van.

After the old man had killed himself, without revealing anything (he had nothing in his pockets either), the Ghost had fled down the stairs and sprinted into the parking lot just as he'd heard sirens in front of the building. He was now still struggling to catch his breath and to calm his heart.

The police had arrived too quickly to be responding to the sound of the gunshots; they'd *known* that he was there. How? Gazing absently at the people on the morning streets, he considered this. The safehouse had absolutely no connection to him. Finally he decided that they had probably tracked the place down through phone calls to and from the Uighur center in Queens. That had given the police his cell phone number and they'd traced the location of the safehouse. Probably there was other evidence too; his intelligence about this Lincoln Rhyme suggested that he was fully capable of making a deduction like that—but he was troubled that he'd gotten no advance warning that the police were on their way there. He'd thought his *guanxi* was better than this.

Yusuf said something in his native Turkic and the Ghost said in English, "Repeat."

"Where you go?"

The Ghost had several other safehouses in the city but only one nearby. He gave him directions. Then the Ghost handed the man another five thousand in one-color. "Go find somebody else to help us. You'll do that?"

Yusuf hesitated.

"I'm sorry about your friends," the Ghost said, masking the contempt in his voice with as much faux sympathy as he could add. "But they were careless. You're not careless. I need you to help me. There'll be another ten thousand for you. Cash to you alone. You don't have to split it."

He nodded.

"Okay, go find someone else. But not at the Uighur center. Don't go back there. The police will be watching it. And get another cell phone. Call me on mine and give me your new number." He recited the number of his new mobile phone—another one he'd kept in the high-rise and had taken with him, along with the money, when he'd escaped a few minutes before.

"Drop me on the corner, up there."

The Turk rolled to a stop at Canal Street, not far from where they had nearly killed the Wus yesterday. The Ghost climbed out then leaned down and had the Turk reiterate his instructions in English, made sure that he remembered the number of the Ghost's new cell phone.

The van sped off.

The Ghost stretched, his eyes following a Chinese teenager in a tight knit blouse, short skirt and implausibly high heels, which gave her a stuttering gait.

He watched her disappear in the crowd. He wasn't the only man watching her though the Ghost suspected that only he wanted to hurt her very badly before he fucked her.

Turning the opposite way, he started down disheveled Canal Street. He still had a long walk to get to his other safehouse—it was nearly a kilometer east. As he walked he considered what he needed to do: Foremost was a new gun—something big, a SIG or a Glock. It seemed this was going to be a neck-and-neck race to see who got to the Changs first, he or the police, and if it came to a shoot-out he wanted good firepower. He also needed some new clothes. A few other things as well.

The battle was growing more and more challenging. He thought of the days of his youth when he'd hide from Mao's cadres in the junkyard, patiently stalking rats and vicious dogs for food. He thought too of the search for his father's killers in the youth brigade. Those times had taught him a lot about the art of hunting and one lesson he learned was this: The stronger adversary expects you to seek out and exploit his weakness and he prepares his defense accordingly. But the only effective way to prevail against such an enemy is to use his *strength* against him. And this is what the Ghost now intended to do.

Naixin? he asked himself.

No. The time for patience was over.

Chang Mei-Mei set a cup of tea in front of her groggy husband.

He blinked at the pale green cup but his attention, as was that of his wife and sons, was wholly on the television set.

The news story, they learned with the translation assistance of William, was about two men found dead in Lower Manhattan.

One of the men was a Chinese-Turkestan immigrant from Queens.

The other was a sixty-nine-year-old Chinese national, believed to have been a passenger on the *Fuzhou Dragon*.

Sam Chang had wakened from his heavy sleep, cotton-mouthed and disoriented, a half hour ago. He'd tried to stand but fell, crashing to the floor, bringing the children and his wife running. As soon as he noticed the gun was gone he'd understood what his father had done and stumbled toward the door.

But Mei-Mei had stopped him. "It's too late," she'd said.

"No!" he'd cried, falling back onto the couch.

He'd turned to her. His loss and sorrow tipped him into fury and he raged at her, "You helped him, didn't you? You knew what he was going to do!"

The woman, holding Po-Yee's toy kitten, looked down at it. She said nothing.

Chang had made a fist and drawn back to strike her. Mei-Mei had squinted and turned away, anticipating the blow. William shifted from one foot to the other, Ronald cried. But then Chang had lowered his hand. Thinking, I've taught her and my children to respect their elders, my father most of all. Chang Jiechi would have ordered her to help him and she would have obeyed.

As the pernicious effects of the powerful medicine had worn off, Chang had then sat for a time, racked by worry, hoping for the best.

But the television report confirmed that the worst had come to be.

The Turkestan had been shot to death, the reporter explained, by the elderly man, who had then died of an overdose of morphine, apparently a suicide. The apartment was believed to have been a hideout for Kwan Ang, the human smuggler wanted in connection with the sinking of the *Fuzhou Dragon* early yesterday. Kwan had escaped before the police arrived and was still at large.

Ronald continued to cry and looked back and forth from the TV to his mother then his father. "Yeye," he said. "Yeye . . ."

Sitting cross-legged, rocking back and forth anxiously, William bitterly spat out the translation of the pretty newscaster's words. By coincidence the reporter was Chinese-American.

The story concluded and, as if the televised confirmation of Chang Jiechi's death signaled the moment, Mei-Mei rose and went into the bedroom. She returned with a sheet of paper. She handed it to her husband then hefted Po-Yee on her hip and wiped the girl's face and hands.

Numb, Sam Chang took the folded piece of paper and opened it. The letter had been written in pencil, not a brush charged with rich ink, but the characters were beautifully drawn; a true artist, the old man had taught his son, can excel in any medium, no matter how base.

> *My son:*
> *My life has been full beyond my hopes. I am old and I am sick. Seeking a year or two more of life on earth gives me no comfort. Rather, I find solace in my duty to return to the soul of Nature at the hour inscribed for me in* The Register of the Living and the Dead.
> *And that moment is now.*
> *I could say many things to you, summarize for you all the lessons of my life, all that I have learned from my father and from your mother and from you, son, as well. But I choose not to do so. Truth is unwavering but the path to truth is often a maze that we each must struggle to find on our own. I have planted healthy bamboo and it has grown well. Continue your journey away from the earth and toward the light and nurture your own young crops. Be vigilant, as any farmer, but give them space. I have seen the stock of the plant; they will grow straight.*
> *—Your father*

Sam Chang was seized with bottomless anger. He rose fast from the couch and, groggy from the drug, struggled to stay upright. He flung the teacup against the wall and it shattered. Ronald shied away from his enraged father.

"I am going to kill him!" he screamed. "The Ghost is going to die!"

His tirade started the baby crying. Mei-Mei whispered something to her sons. William hesitated but then nodded toward Ronald, who hefted Po-Yee. Together they walked into the bedroom. The door closed.

Chang said to her, "I found him once and I'm going to find him again. This time—"

"No," Mei-Mei said firmly.

He turned to face his wife. "What?"

She swallowed and looked down. "You will not."

"Don't speak to me like that. You're my wife."

"Yes," she said to him, her voice quavering, "I *am* your wife. And I'm the mother of your children. And what will happen to us if you die? Have you thought about that? We'd live on the street, we'd be deported. Do you know what life in China would be like for us when we returned? A widow of a dissident with no property, no money? Is that what you want for us?"

"My father is dead!" Chang raged. "The man responsible for that has to die."

"No, he doesn't," she replied breathlessly, working up her courage once again. "Your father was an old man. He was sick. He was not the center of our universe and we must move on."

"How can you say that?" Chang raged, shocked at her impudence. "He's the reason I exist."

"He lived a full life and now he's gone. You live in the past, Jingerzi. Our parents deserve our respect, yes, but nothing more than that."

He realized that she'd used his Chinese given name. He didn't think she'd done so in years—not since they'd been married. When she addressed him, she always used the respectful *zhangfu*, "husband."

In a steadier voice now Mei-Mei said, "You won't avenge his death. You'll stay here with us, in hiding, until the Ghost is captured or killed. Then you and William will go to work at Joseph Tan's printing company. And I'll stay here and teach Ronald and Po-Yee. We'll all study English, we'll make money. . . . And, when there's another amnesty, we'll become citizens." She paused for a moment and wiped her face, from which tears streamed. "I loved him too, you know. It's my loss as well as yours." She resumed cleaning up.

Chang fell onto the couch and sat for a long time in silence, staring at the shabby red and black carpet on the floor. Then he walked to the bedroom. William, holding Po-Yee, stared out the window. Chang began to speak to him but changed his mind and silently motioned his younger son out. The boy warily stepped into the living room and followed his father to the couch. They both sat. After a moment Chang composed himself. He asked Ronald, "Son, do you know the warriors of Qin Shi Huang?"

"Yes, Baba."

These were thousands of full-size terra-cotta statues of soldiers, charioteers and horses built near Xi'an by China's first emperor in the third century B.C. and placed in his tomb. The army was to accompany him to the afterlife.

"We're going to do the same for Yeye." He nearly choked on his sorrow. "We're going to send some things to heaven so your grandfather will have them with him."

"What?" Ronald asked.

"Things that were important to him when he was alive. We lost everything on the ship so we'll draw pictures of them."

"Will that work?" the boy asked, frowning.

"Yes. But I need you to help me."

Ronald nodded.

"Take some paper there and that pencil." He nodded toward the table. "Why don't you draw a picture of his favorite brushes—the wolf-hair and the goat. And his ink stick and well. You remember what they looked like?"

Ronald took the pencil in his small hand. He bent over the paper, began his task.

"And a bottle of the rice wine he liked," Mei-Mei suggested.

"And a pig?" the boy asked.

"Pig?" Chang asked.

"He liked pork rice, remember?"

Then he was aware of someone behind him. And he turned to see William looking down at his brother's drawing. Somber-faced, the teenager said, "When grandmother died, we burned money."

It was a tradition at Chinese funerals to burn slips of paper printed to look like million-yuan notes, issued by the "Bank of Hell" so that the deceased would have money to spend in the afterworld.

"Maybe I can draw some yuan," William said.

Chang was swept with emotion at his words but he didn't embrace the boy, as he wanted desperately to do. He said simply, "Thank you, son."

The lean boy crouched down beside his brother and began to draw the bills.

When the children had finished their drawings Chang led his family outside into the backyard of their new home and, as if this were Chang Jiechi's actual funeral, he set two burning incense sticks in the ground to mark the spot where the body would have lain and then, setting afire the pictures their sons had drawn, they watched the smoke disappear into the gray sky and the ash melt into black curls.

Chapter Thirty-four

"Somebody made another move on the Wus," Sellitto said, glancing up at Rhyme from his cell phone.

"What?" Sachs asked, astonished. "In our Murray Hill safehouse?"

Rhyme wheeled around to face the detective, who said, "Dark-complected man, slight build, wearing gloves, was spotted on one of the security cameras in the alleyway. He was checking out one of the rear windows. Coincidence, you think?"

Sonny Li laughed bitterly. "With Ghost, there not coincidences."

With a concurring nod, Rhyme asked, "What happened?"

"Two of our people went after him but he got away."

The criminalist then asked, "How the hell did the Ghost find out where they were?"

"Who'd know?" Sellitto asked.

Sachs considered this. "After the shoot-out on Canal Street, one of his *bangshous* could've followed me to the clinic then followed the Wus to the safehouse. Hard to do but possible." She walked to the whiteboard and tapped an entry. "Or how 'bout this?"

· *Ghost is reported to have gov't people on payroll.*

"A spy, you thinking?" Sellitto asked.

She said, "Nobody at the bureau knew we sent them to Murray Hill.

Dellray had left by the time I thought of it. That leaves somebody at the INS or NYPD."

"Well," Sellitto said, "we damn well can't keep the Wus there anymore. I'll call the U.S. Marshals and have them taken to a witness protection facility upstate." He looked at the team around him. "And *that* information doesn't leave this room." He placed the call and arranged to have the Wus transported in a bulletproof van.

Rhyme was growing impatient. "Somebody check with the bureau. Where the hell is Dellray's replacement? Eddie, make the call."

Deng got in touch with bureau's ASAC. It turned out that there'd been some delay with the magical "powwow" that was supposed to result in additional agents to work GHOSTKILL.

"They said everything'll be in place this afternoon."

"What's *'everything'?*" Rhyme asked caustically. "And what fucking *place* does it have to be in before we get the agents? Don't they know there's a killer out there?"

"You want to call them back?"

He snapped, "No. I want to look at the evidence."

Sachs's search of the crime scene at the Ghost's safehouse on Patrick Henry Street had mixed results. One discouraging fact was that the cell phone that had been instrumental in tracking down the Ghost had been abandoned in the high-rise. Had he still been using it, they might have been able to trace him. Moreover, the fact he'd left it meant that he'd probably figured out that this was how they'd found him and would now be far more careful when calling on mobiles.

Unlike the shooter killed on Canal Street, the Uighur in the safehouse did have some identification on him, a driver's license and a card with the address of the Turkestan cultural center in Queens. But Bedding and Saul and a team of tactical agents were at the center now and the head of the organization had said only that he'd heard that some unidentified Chinese man had hired a few people in the neighborhood to move furniture. He didn't know anything else. They would continue to lean on him, the Twins assured, but their assessment was that he'd rather go to jail than dime out the Ghost.

The name on the lease of the Ghost's apartment didn't help either: Harry Lee. His social security number and references were fake and the certified rental check came from a bank in the Caribbean. "Lee" was the equivalent of "Smith" in English, Deng reported.

The body of the old man found dead from the morphine overdose, though, did reveal some clues. He'd carried in his wallet an ID card, very blurred from the seawater, that identified him as Chang Jiechi. They also found a very old scrap of paper hidden behind the ID. Deng smiled sadly. "Look at that. It's an autograph from Chiang Kai-shek, the nationalist leader. The inscription thanked Chang Jiechi for his efforts to resist the communists and keep the Chinese people free from dictatorship."

Rhyme's gaze then slipped to the row of pictures below the ones of the old man's corpse. They were close-ups of his hands. The criminalist moved his own finger slightly and eased the Storm Arrow up to the board.

"Look at that," he said. "His hands."

"I shot them because of the blotches," Sachs said.

Chang Jiechi's fingers and palms were covered with blue-black stains. Paint or ink. Clearly not the purple shade of post-mortem lividity—which in any case wouldn't've occurred so soon after death.

"The fingers!" Rhyme called. "Look at the fingers."

She squinted and walked close. "Indentations!" She pulled the print-out of Sam Chang's fingerprints off the wall and held it close to that of the father's hand. The palms and digits were different sizes—and the old man's were far more wrinkled—but the indentations Rhyme had spotted on Sam Chang's fingers and thumb were similar to the lines clearly evident on his father's.

They'd assumed that the marks on Sam Chang's fingers were from an injury of some kind. But clearly that wasn't the case.

"What's it mean?" Mel Cooper asked. "Genetic?"

"No, can't be," Rhyme said, his eyes scanning the picture of the old man's hand. He closed his eyes for a moment and let his mind fly—like one of the peregrine falcons lifting off from its bedroom window perch. Ink on his hands, indentations . . . Then his head jerked back in the chair and he looked at Sachs. "They're painters! Father and son're both artists. Remember the logo of The Home Store on the van? One of them painted it."

"No," Li said, looking at the photo. "Not painters. *Calligraphers*. Calligraphy in China lots important. Hold brush like this." He grabbed a pen and held it perfectly vertical, gripped firmly in a triangle formed by the thumb and his first two fingers. When he released it and held his hand up, the red indentations in his fingers and thumb were identical to those in the hands of Chang and his father. Li continued, "Calligraphy considered art in China. But during Proletarian Revolution, artists persecuted bad. Lots calligraphers got jobs printing and sign painting. Doing useful things. Good for society. On boat Chang tell us he dissident and got fired from teaching job. Nobody hire him at schools. Make sense for him do printing, sign painting."

"And at the clinic Wu said that Chang had a job here lined up already," Sachs reminded.

"We know the Changs're in Queens," Rhyme said. "Let's get as many Chinese-speaking officers from the Fifth Precinct as we can to start calling quick-print, printing or sign-painting companies that've just hired somebody illegal."

Alan Coe laughed—apparently at Rhyme's naïveté. "They're not going to cooperate. No *gaunxi.*"

"Here's some fucking *auanxi,*" Rhyme snapped. "Tell them if they lie about it and we find out, the INS is going to raid their shop and—if the Changs are killed—we'll book them for accessory to murder."

"Now you think like Chinese cop," Sony Li said with a laugh. "Using Historically Unprecedented People's Ox Prod."

Deng pulled out his cell phone and made a call to his headquarters.

Mel Cooper had run some of the trace from the safehouse on Patrick Henry Street through the gas chromatograph. He studied the results. "Something interesting here." He glanced at the bag that Sachs had marked with a felt-tip pen.

"It was on Chang's father's shoes. Nitrates, potassium, carbon, sodium . . . Biosolids. In significant amounts too."

This caught Rhyme's attention. "Biosolid" was a term undoubtedly invented by some public relations expert who was clever enough to know that the marketing potential of the product would be severely limited if the stuff was sold under its real name: processed human shit.

The fourteen waste treatment plants in New York City produced more than a thousand tons of biosolids a day and sold it throughout the country as fertilizer. For there to be significant amounts on the victim's shoes meant that the Changs were probably living quite close to one of the plants.

"Can we search house by house near the treatment plants?" Sellitto asked.

Rhyme shook his head. There were a number of treatment plants in Queens and given the fickle winds in the New York City area, the Changs could be living in a several block radius around any of them. Without narrowing the search down further—by finding the print shop where Sam Chang would be working, say—a door-to-door search would take forever.

The rest of the evidence didn't help much. The morphine that the man had killed himself with had come from a clinic in China and therefore was of no use to them forensically.

"Morphine can kill you?" Sellitto asked.

"The rumor is that's how the writer Jack London killed himself," pointed out Lincoln Rhyme, whose knowledge of suicide techniques was as extensive as his command of historical criminal trivia. "Besides, in the right dosage, *anything* can kill you."

Sachs then added that the old man had no subway transfers or other receipts on him to suggest where he might've come from.

But, Rhyme was soon reminded, Amelia Sachs was not the only cop to have run the crime scene in the Ghost's high-rise.

Sonny Li said, "Hey, Loaban, I found things too when I search Ghost's place. You want to hear?"

"Go ahead."

"Got some good stuff, I'm saying. Okay, there a statue of the Buddha across from door, facing it. No stereos or red color in his bedroom. Hallway painted white. Bookcases had doors on them. Had statue of eight horses. All mirrors very tall so they not cut off part of head when you look in them. Had brass bells with wooden handles—he keep them in western part of room." He nodded at the apparent significance of this. "Figure it out, Loaban?"

"No," Rhyme snapped. "Keep going."

Li patted his shirt for his cigarettes then let his arms fall to his side. "Over my desk at security bureau office in Liu Guoyuan I got sign."

"Another expression?"

"*Ju yi fan san.* It mean: learning three things from one example. From Confucius saying: 'If I show man corner of object and he not able to figure out what other three corners look like, then I not bother to teach him again.'"

Not a bad motto for a forensic detective, Rhyme reflected. "And you deduced something *helpful,* something we can *use* from a statue of eight horses and brass bells?"

"Feng shui, I'm saying."

"Arranging furniture and things for good luck," Thom said. When Rhyme glanced at him he added, "It was on a show on the Home and Garden Channel. Don't worry—I watched it on my own time."

Impatient Rhyme said, "So he lives in a good-luck apartment, Li. What's the *evidentiary* point?"

"Hey, congratulations, Sonny," Thom said. "You got the last-name treatment. He saves that for his really good friends. Note that *I'm* only 'Thom.'"

"Speaking of which, *Thom*, I believe you're here merely to write. Not to editorialize."

"The point, Loaban? Pretty clear to me," Li continued. "The Ghost *hire* somebody to arrange his room and guy he hire do fuck good job. Know his stuff. Maybe know other places the Ghost has apartments."

"Okay," Rhyme said. "*That's* useful."

"I go check feng shui men in Chinatown. What you think?"

Rhyme caught Sachs's eye and they laughed. "I need to write a new criminalistics text book. This time I'll add a woo-woo chapter."

"Hey, know what our leader Deng Xiaoping say. He say it not matter if cat black or white, so long as it catches mouse."

"Well, go catch yourself a mouse, Li. Then come on back here. I need some more *baiju*. Oh, and Sonny?"

The Chinese cop glanced at him.

"*Zaijian*," Rhyme carefully pronounced the word he'd learned on a Chinese language translation website.

Li nodded. "'Goodbye.' Yes, yes. You even pronounce good, Loaban. *Zaijian*."

The Chinese cop left and they returned to the evidence. But the team made no headway and an hour went by without any word from the officers who were canvassing the quick-print shops in Queens.

Rhyme stretched his head back into the pillow. He and Sachs gazed at the charts, Rhyme feeling a too-familiar sensation: the desperate hope that evidence long picked over would yield just one more nugget even though you knew there was nothing else for it to reveal.

"Should I talk to the Wus again, or John Sung?" she asked.

"We don't need more witnesses," Rhyme murmured. "We need more *evidence*. I need something concrete."

More goddamn evidence . . . They needed—

288 / Jeffery Deaver

Then his head swiveled fast toward the map—the original one: of Long Island. He looked at the tiny red dot about a mile off the coast of Orient Point.

"What?" Sachs asked, seeing him squint.

"Goddamn," he whispered.

"What?"

"We have another crime scene. And I forgot all about it."

"What?"

"The ship. The *Fuzhou Dragon.*"

GHOSTKILL

Easton, Long Island, Crime Scene	Stolen Van, Chinatown	Jerry Tang Murder Crime Scene
· Two immigrants killed on beach; shot in back.	· Camouflaged by immigrants with "The Home Store" logo.	· Four men kicked door in and tortured him and shot him.
· One immigrant wounded—Dr. John Sung.	· Blood spatter suggests injured woman has hand, arm or shoulder injury.	· Two shell casings—match Model 51. Tang shot twice in head.
· "Bangshou" (assistant) on board; identity unknown.	· Blood samples sent to lab for typing.	· Extensive vandalism.
· Assistant confirmed as drowned body found near site where *Dragon* sank.	· Injured woman is AB negative. Requesting more information about her blood.	· Some fingerprints.
· Ten immigrants escape: seven adults (one elderly, one injured woman), two children, one infant. Steal church van.	· Fingerprints sent to AFIS.	· No matches except Tang's.
· Blood samples sent to lab for typing.	· No matches.	· Three accomplices have smaller shoe size than Ghost, presumably smaller stature.
· Injured woman is AB negative. Requesting more information about her blood.		· Trace suggests Ghost's safehouse is probably downtown, Battery Park City area.
· Vehicle awaiting Ghost on beach left without him. One shot believed fired by Ghost at vehicle. Request for vehicle make and model sent out, based on tread marks and wheelbase.		· Suspected accomplices from Chinese ethnic minority. Presently pursuing whereabouts.
· Vehicle is a BMW X5.		· Uighurs from Turkestan Community and Islamic Center of Queens.
· Driver—Jerry Tang.		· Cell phone calls lead to 805 Patrick Henry Street, downtown.
· No vehicles to pick up immigrants located.		
· Cell phone, presumably Ghost's, sent for analysis to FBI.		
· Untraceable satellite secure phone. Hacked Chinese gov't system to use it.		
· Ghost's weapon is 7.62mm pistol. Unusual casing.		
· Model 51 Chinese automatic pistol.		
· Ghost is reported to have gov't people on payroll.		
· Ghost stole red Honda sedan to escape. Vehicle locator request sent out.		
· No trace of Honda found.		
· Three bodies recovered at sea—two shot, one drowned. Photos and prints to Rhyme and Chinese police.		
· Drowned individual identified as Victor Au, the Ghost's *bangshou*.		
· Fingerprints sent to AFIS.		
· No matches on any prints but unusual markings on Sam Chang's fingers and thumbs (injury, rope burn?)		
· Profile of Immigrants: Sam Chang and Wu Qichen and their families, John Sung, baby of woman who drowned, unidentified man and woman (killed on beach).		

Canal Street Shooting Crime Scene	Safehouse Shooting Crime Scene
· Additional trace suggesting safehouse is in Battery Park City area.	· Fingerprints and photos of Chang Jiechi's hands reveal father—and son Sam—are calligraphers. Sam Chang might be doing printing or sign painting. Calling stores and companies in Queens.
· Stolen Chevrolet Blazer, untraceable.	
· No match on prints.	
· Safehouse carpet: Arnold company's Lustre-Rite, installed in past six months; calling contractors to get list of installations.	
· Location of installations determined: 32 near Battery Park City.	· Biosolids on deceased's shoes suggest they live in neighborhood near sewage treatment plant.
· Fresh gardening mulch found.	· Ghost uses feng shui practitioner to arrange his living space.
· Body of Ghost's accomplice: ethnic minority from west or northwest China. Negative on prints. Weapon was Walther PPK.	
· Details on immigrants:	
· The Changs: Sam, Mei-Mei, William and Ronald; Sam's father, Chang Jiechi and infant, Po-Yee. Sam has job arranged but employer and location unknown. Driving blue van, no make, no tag number. Changs' apartment is in Queens.	
· The Wus: Qichen, Yong-Ping, Chin-Mei and Lang.	

Chapter Thirty-five

Lon Sellitto said, "But the evidence on the ship'd be messed up, wouldn't it, Linc? Because of the water."

Sachs said, "'Although submersion in water may destroy or degrade certain types of evidence, such as water-soluble chemicals, other forms of physical evidence, even trace, may be preserved and readily discovered, depending on the currents and the depth of and temperature of the water. Indeed, some may be better preserved than had the scene been on dry land.' How'd I do, Rhyme?"

"Good, Sachs. I'm impressed." The passage was from Rhyme's textbook on criminalistics.

"Somebody call the Coast Guard, patch me through to whoever's in charge of the rescue out there."

Sellitto finally got through and put the call on speakerphone.

"This is Fred Ransom speaking. I'm captain of the *Evan Brigant*." The man was shouting; the wind whistled loudly over the mouthpiece of his radio mike.

"This is Detective Sellitto, NYPD. I talked to you before?"

"Right, sir. I recall."

"I'm here with Lincoln Rhyme. Where are you now?"

"Just above the *Dragon*. We're still looking for survivors but haven't had any luck."

Rhyme asked, "What's the status of the ship, Captain."

"She's on her starboard side about eighty, ninety feet down."

"What's the weather like now?"

"Lot better'n it was. Ten-foot seas, wind about thirty knots. Light rain. Visibility, probably two hundred yards."

"You have divers available who can check out the interior?" Rhyme asked.

"Yessir."

"Can they dive in that weather?"

"Conditions aren't the best but they're acceptable. You know, sir, we've already scanned for survivors. Negative on that."

"No, I'm talking about searching for evidence."

"I see. We could send some folks down. The thing is, though, that my divers've never done that. They're S and R."

Search and Rescue Rhyme recalled.

The captain asked, "Could somebody walk them through what to do?"

"Sure," Rhyme said, though he was discouraged at the idea of explaining a lifetime of crime scene investigation to a novice.

Then Amelia Sachs's voice interrupted. "I'll search it."

Rhyme said, "I'm talking about the ship itself, Sachs."

"I understand that."

"It's ninety feet underwater."

She bent down and said into the speakerphone, "Captain, I can be down in Battery Park in thirty minutes. Can you have a chopper get me out to your location?"

"Well, we can fly in this weather. But—"

"I'm open-water certified—PADI." Meaning she had her scuba diving license from the Professional Association of Diving Instructors. Rhyme knew that she and her former boyfriend Nick had taken the course together and gone on a number of dives. Not surprisingly, though, speed-lover Sachs had found cigarette boats and jet-skiing more to her liking.

"But you haven't been diving for years, Sachs," he pointed out.

"Like riding a bike."

"Miss . . ."

"That'd be Officer Sachs, Captain," she said.

"Officer, there's a big difference between recreational dives and what it's like down there today. My people've been diving for years and I wouldn't feel real comfortable sending *them* into an unstable wreck under these conditions."

"Sachs," Rhyme said, "you can't. You're not trained for that."

"No way," she said.

"There're a million things they'd miss. You know that. They'd be the same as civilians. All respect, Captain."

"Understood, Officer. But my vote is it's too risky."

Sachs paused and then said, "Captain, you have children?"

"I'm sorry?"

"You have a family?"

"Well," he said, "yes, I do."

"This perp we're after is the man who sank that ship and killed most of the people inside. And right now he's trying to kill some immigrants who escaped—a family with two children and a baby. I'm not going to let that happen. There may be some evidence inside that ship that could tell us where he is. My expertise is finding clues—under all conditions."

Sellitto said, "Use our divers." Both the NYPD and the city's fire department had experienced scuba divers.

"They're not Crime Scene," Sachs argued. "They're just S and R too." She looked at Rhyme, who hesitated for a long moment. But then nodded, indicating that, yes, he'd back her up.

"Will you help us out here, Captain?" Rhyme asked. "She needs to be the one who goes down."

Through the wind the captain said, "Okay, Officer. But tell you what, we'll set the chopper down at the Hudson River helipad. That'll save some time. It's closer than Battery Park. You know it?"

"Sure," she said. Then added, "One thing, though, Captain?"

"Yes'm?"

"On a lot of those dives I did in the Caribbean?"

"Right."

"Afterward, when we were sailing home, the crew made rum punch for everybody—it was included in the cost of the dive. You have anything like that on Coast Guard cutters?"

"You know, Officer, I think we may be able to rustle something up for you."

"I'll be at the pad in fifteen minutes."

They hung up and Sachs glanced at Rhyme. "I'll call you with what I find."

There was so much he wanted to say to her and yet so little he was able to. He settled for "Search well—"

"—but watch my back."

She stroked his right hand—the one whose fingers couldn't feel any sensation whatsoever. Not yet, at any rate. Maybe after the surgery.

He glanced at the ceiling, toward his bedroom, where the god of detectives, Guan Di, presently sat with his evaporating cup of sweet wine. But Lincoln Rhyme, of course, restrained himself from sending a prayer to a folk deity wishing Sachs a safe journey and sent that message directly—though tacitly—to her.

Learning three things from one example . . .

Confucius, hm? I like that, thought Lincoln Rhyme. He said to his aide, "I need something from the basement."

"What?"

"A copy of my book."

"I'm not sure where they are," Thom replied.

"Then you better start looking, don't you think?"

With a loud sigh, the aide vanished.

Rhyme was referring to a hardcover book that he'd written several years ago, *The Scenes of the Crime*. In it, he'd examined fifty-one old crime scenes in New York City, some solved, some not. The book included a cross section of the more notorious crimes in the city, ranging from mayhem in the Five Points section of town, considered in the mid-1800s one of the most dangerous places on earth, to architect Stanford White's love triangle murder in the original Madison Square Garden, to Joey Gallo's unfortunate last meal at a Little Italy clam house, to John Lennon's death. The illustrated book had been popular—though not popular enough to keep it from being remaindered; the surplus copies had been sloughed off to "bargain books" shelves in bookstores around the country for discounted sales.

Still, Rhyme was secretly proud of the book; it was his first tentative venture back into the real world after his accident, an emblem that, despite what had happened to him, he was capable of doing *something* beyond lying on his ass and bitching about his state.

Thom returned ten minutes later, his shirt streaked with dirt and his handsome face dotted with sweat and dust. "They were in the farthest corner. Under a dozen cartons. I'm a mess."

"Well, I'd think if things were better organized down there, it might've taken less work," Rhyme muttered, eyes on the book.

"Maybe if you hadn't said to pack them away, you never wanted to see them again, you hated the quote fucking things, it might not have taken so much work either."

"Say, is the cover torn?"

"No, the cover's fine."

"Let me see," Rhyme ordered. "Hold it up."

The weary aide brushed some dirt off his slacks and then offered the book for inspection.

"It'll do," the criminalist said.

Rhyme looked around the room uneasily. His temples were pounding, which meant his heart, which he couldn't feel, was pumping blood hard.

"What, Lincoln?"

"That touchpad. Do we still have it?"

A few months ago, Rhyme had ordered a touchpad attachment for the computer, like a mouse, thinking that he could use his extant finger—his left ring finger—to control the computer. He hadn't shared with Thom or Sachs how important it had been for him to make the pad work.

But he hadn't been able to. The range of motion for the digit was too limited to move the cursor in any helpful way, unlike the touchpad controller that operated his Storm Arrow, which was specifically made for people in his condition.

The failure had, for some reason, devastated him.

Thom left the room for a moment and returned with the small gray unit. He hooked up the system and placed it under Rhyme's ring finger. "What are you going to do with it?" Thom asked.

Rhyme grumbled, "Just hold it still."

"All right."

"Command, cursor down. Command cursor stop. Command, double click." A drawing program popped up on the screen. "Command, line draw."

Surprised, Thom asked, "When did you learn that?"

"Quiet. I need to concentrate." Rhyme took a deep breath and then he started to move his finger on the pad. A shaky line appeared on the screen. Sweat popped out on his forehead from the tension.

Breathing hard, riddled with anxiety, as if he were dismantling a bomb, Rhyme said through clenched teeth, "Move the pad to the left, Thom. Carefully."

The aide did and Rhyme continued giving him directions.

Ten minutes of agony, ten minutes of exhausting effort . . . He gazed at the screen, finally satisfied with the result. He rested his head on the back of the chair. "Command, print."

Thom walked to the printer.

"You want to see your handiwork?"

"Of course I want to see it," Rhyme barked.

Thom picked up the sheet and held it in front of Rhyme.

To my friend, Sonny Li —
From Lincoln

"I think that's the first thing you've written since the accident. In your actual handwriting."

"It's a goddamn schoolchild's scrawl," Rhyme muttered, feeling exhilerated at the accomplishment. "Hardly legible."

"You want me to paste that in the book?" Thom asked.

"If you would, yes. Thank you," Rhyme said. "Then set it aside and we'll give it to Li when he gets back."

"I'll wrap it up," the aide said.

"I don't think we need to go *that* far," Rhyme snapped. "Now, let's get back to the evidence."

Chapter Thirty-six

Okay, I can do this.

Amelia Sachs stood on the rippled metal floor of the Coast Guard's Sikorsky HH-60J helicopter fifty feet above the whipping antenna of the cutter *Evan Brigant* and let the crewman fit the harness around her.

It had never occurred to her when she'd requested the helicopter ride out to the ship that the only way to get onto the ship would be by winching down to a bobbing deck.

Well, what did she expect, she now reflected, an escalator?

The chopper pitched in the fierce wind and beneath them, through the mist, she could see the gray water breaking around the cutter in ragged white ridges.

Encased in an orange vest and battered helmet, Sachs gripped the handhold near the open doorway and thought again, *Okay, I can do this.*

The crewman shouted something she didn't hear and she shouted back for him to repeat it—a request he apparently didn't hear, for he took her words to be an acknowledgment. Then a hook was attached to the harness and the rig double-checked. The crewman shouted something else. Sachs pointed to herself, then out the door and received a thumbs-up.

Okay . . .

I can do this.

Her essential fear was claustrophobia, not heights, but still . . .

Then out she went, holding the cable, even though she thought she'd

298

been told not to. She swung wildly from the momentum of stepping out the door. In a moment the motion slowed and she started down, buffeted by the wind and the powerful downdraft from the rotor blades.

Down, down . . .

A shroud of fog suddenly enveloped her and she was disoriented. She found herself hanging in space, not able to see either the chopper above or the ship below. Rain spattered her face and she was blinded. Vertigo consumed her and she couldn't tell if she was swinging like an out-of-control pendulum or dropping toward the ship at a hundred miles an hour.

Oh, Rhyme . . .

But then the cutter grew visible beneath her.

The *Evan Brigant* bobbed up and down and rocked but whoever was at the helm held the vessel perfectly in position despite waves that were so huge that they seemed fake—something created by a special-effects team for a movie. Her feet touched the deck but just as she hit the quick-release button on the harness the ship dropped to the bottom of a wave and she fell four feet to the deck, hitting hard, her arthritic legs screaming in pain. As two seamen ran to help her up she reflected that this was probably what the crewman on the chopper had been warning her about.

Boating is not a sport for arthritics, Sachs recalled; she had to flex her knees continually for stability as she made her way to the bridge. She had an imaginary conversation with Dr. John Sung, reporting to him that Chinese medicine had yet to score serious points over Percoset and anti-inflammatories.

On the bridge the improbably young-looking captain, Fred Ransom, greeted her with a smile and a handshake. He welcomed her to the ship and led her to the chart table. "Now, here's a picture of the vessel and where she's laying."

Sachs concentrated on the image of the ship. Ransom told her where the bridge was and where the cabins were located—on the same deck but down a lengthy corridor toward the stern.

"Now, one thing, Officer, just to warn you," he said delicately. "We understand there are about fifteen bodies inside and there'll be some sea-life activity regarding them. It could be pretty grim. Some of my crew have sort of a tough time . . ."

But his voice faded as he looked into her eyes.

Sachs said, "Appreciate the warning, Captain. But I do run crime scenes for a living."

"Sure, Officer, understood. All right, let's get you into your gear."

Another trek outside into the rain and wind. They made their way to the stern of the ship. In a small shed, open to the rear, she was introduced to two other officers, a man and a woman, both wearing yellow and black wet suits and boots. They were the chief dive officer on board the ship and his second in command.

"Understand you did PADI?" the man asked. "How many dives?"

"I'd guess twenty-five or so."

This relieved them somewhat.

"And the last time was?"

"Make it a few years."

This response had the opposite effect.

"Well, we're going walk you through all the steps again," the male officer said, "like you're a novice."

"I was hoping you would."

"Your deepest?" the woman dive officer asked.

"Eighty feet."

"That's about the same as here. The only difference is that it'll be murkier. The currents're stirring up the bottom."

The water wasn't that cold, they explained, still retaining much of the summer's heat but to be under for any length of time would deplete her body heat quickly and so she needed to wear a wetsuit, which insulated her not only with the rubber but, as the name suggested, a thin layer of water between her skin and the shell of the suit.

Behind a screen she stripped and then struggled to put the suit on.

"Are you sure this isn't a child's size?" she called, gasping from the effort of pulling the tight rubber over her hips and shoulders.

"We hear that a lot," the woman dive officer responded.

Then they suited her up with the rest of the equipment: weights, mask and the air tank attached to the BCD—buoyancy control device, a vest that you inflated or deflated with a control near your left hand, which made you rise or sink in the water.

Also attached to the air tank was a primary regulator—the one that she'd breathe through—and then a secondary one, nicknamed the octopus, that could be used by a fellow diver to breathe off her tank if the buddy's air supply was cut off. They also fitted a head-mounted spotlight to her hood.

They ran through the basic hand signals for communicating with dive partners.

A lot of information, important information, and she struggled to keep it in her mind.

"How 'bout a knife?" she asked.

"You've got one," the dive chief said, pointing to her BCD. She drew the weapon only to find that it didn't have a point.

"You're not going to be stabbing anything," the woman said, seeing Sachs's concern. "Only cutting. You know, wire or something that entangles you."

"Thinking more about sharks, actually," she said.

"Rarely see sharks in these waters."

"Hardly ever," the other officer echoed. "Not big ones anyway."

"I'll take your word for it," Sachs said, replacing the knife. Wasn't the movie *Jaws* set here?

The dive chief handed Sachs a large mesh bag for stowing any evidence she found. Into these she placed what she'd brought for evidence collection—plastic bags. Then he and his assistant donned their equipment and, carrying their flippers, all three walked unsteadily to the very stern of the heaving ship.

Shouting over the noise of the wind the dive chief said, "Too choppy to go off the deck. We'll get into the raft, put our flippers on and then fall backward into the water. Hold your mask and regulator to your face. Other hand on your weight-belt release."

She tapped the top of her head—the hand signal for okay.

He did the same.

They climbed into the yellow raft, which was already in the water and reared up and down like a bucking horse. They sat on the side and checked their equipment.

Twenty feet away was an orange buoy. The dive chief pointed to it and said, "There's a line from there that goes straight down to the vessel. We'll swim over to that and follow the line down. What's your plan for the search?"

She called back, "I want to get samples of the explosion residue from the hull and then search the bridge and cabins."

The other divers nodded.

"I do the inside alone."

This was a breach of the fundamental scuba rule that you be able to swim to your buddy on one breath. The dive chief frowned.

"You're sure?"

"Have to."

"Okay," he said uneasily. Then he continued, "Now, sounds don't work well underwater—hard to tell where they're coming from—but if you're in trouble bang on your tank with the knife and we'll search for you." He held up her SPG—submersible pressure gauge—which showed how much air was in her tank. "You've got three thousand pounds of air. You'll burn it fast because you're going to be pumped up on adrenaline. We leave the bottom with five hundred. No less than that. That's an iron-clad rule. No exceptions. We come up slow—no faster than the bubbles from our regulator and we pause for three minutes fifteen feet down."

Otherwise, Sachs knew, there was a risk of decompression sickness—the bends.

"Oh, and what's the most important rule in scuba?"

Sachs remembered it from her course years ago. "Don't ever hold your breath underwater."

"Good. Why?"

"Otherwise your lungs could explode."

Then they started her air and she pulled on her fins then mask, gripped the regulator fiercely in her teeth. The dive chief gave the other "okay" sign—middle finger and thumb in a circle—and she responded the same way. She pumped some air into her BCD to allow her to float on the surface. They gestured for her to roll backward.

She gripped the mask and regulator so they wouldn't be torn off by the entry and she held her weight-belt release so that if her buoyancy device failed and she dropped toward the bottom she could dump the weights and swim to the surface.

Okay, Rhyme, here's one for Guinness: the record for searching the most submerged crime scene.

One, two, three . . .

Backward into the churning water.

By the time she righted herself the others were in the water beside her and gesturing toward the buoy. In a few minutes they'd swum to it. Okay signs all around. Then a thumbs-down, which meant descend. Then they took their BCD control in their left hand and deflated the vests.

Immediately, noise became silence, motion became stillness, heavy became weightless and they drifted downward placidly along the thick rope toward the bottom.

For a moment Sachs was struck by the absolute peace of life underwater. Then the serenity was broken as she looked below her and saw the dim outline of the *Fuzhou Dragon*.

The image was more unsettling than she'd expected. The ship on her side, a black gash in the hull from the explosion, the rust, the peeling paint, the encrusting barnacles on the plates. Dark and jagged and foreboding—and containing the bodies of so many innocent people.

A coffin, she thought, with a clenched heart. It's a huge, metal coffin.

Sharp pain in her ears; she pinched her nose through the soft plastic portion of the mask and blew to equalize the pressure. They continued downward. As they got closer to the ship she began to hear the noises— grating and moaning as the ship's thick metal plates scraped on the rocks.

Hate that noise. Hate it, hate it. It sounded like a huge creature dying.

Her escorts were diligent. They'd stop the descent occasionally and check on her. Okay signs were exchanged and they continued downward.

At the bottom she looked up and found that the surface didn't seem as far away as she'd expected, though she recalled that water has the effect of acting like a lens and magnifying everything. A glance at her depth gauge. Ninety feet. A nine-story building. Then a glance at her pressure gauge. Jesus, she'd already used 150 pounds of air on the effortless descent.

Amelia Sachs pumped air into the BCD to neutralize her buoyancy— so that she floated level. She first pointed toward the gash in the hull and together the threesome swam toward it. Despite the pitching surface above them the currents here were gentle and they could move easily.

At the site of the explosion Sachs used her blunt knife to scrape residue from the outwardly curled metal. She placed some of the black ashy material into a plastic bag, sealed it and put that in the mesh collection bag.

She looked at the dark windows of the bridge forty feet away. Okay, Rhyme, here we go. They swam toward it.

And the pressure gauge gave her its emotionless message: 2350 pounds.

At 500 they left the bottom. No exceptions.

Because the ship was on its side the bridge door now opened upward, toward the surface. It was metal and very heavy. The two Coast Guard officers struggled to lift it and Sachs swam through the opening and down into the bridge. They lowered the door into the closed position. It clanked shut with chilling boom and Sachs realized that she was now trapped inside the ship. Without her companions she probably couldn't open the door herself.

Forget it, she told herself, reached up to the light mounted on her wetsuit hood and clicked it on. The beam offered her faint comfort. She turned and swam away from the bridge down a dark corridor that led to the cabins.

Faint motion too from the dimness. Coming from what? Fish, eels, squid?

I don't like this, Rhyme.

But then she thought about the Ghost searching for the Changs, about the baby, Po-Yee, the Treasured Child.

Think about that, not about the darkness or confinement. Do this for her, for Po-Yee.

Amelia Sachs swam forward.

She was in hell.

No other word described it.

The black hallway was filled with sooty debris and refuse, scraps of cloth, paper, food, fish with piercing yellow eyes. And overhead, a shimmering, like ice: the thin layer of air trapped above her. The sounds were harrowing: the scraping and groaning, moans. Squeals like human voices in agony, pings and snaps. The clank of metal on metal.

A fish, gray and sleek, darted past. She gasped involuntarily at the motion and turned her head to follow it.

She found herself looking at two dull human eyes in a white lifeless face.

Sachs screamed through her regulator and jerked back. The body of a man, barefoot, his arms above his head, like a perp surrendering, floated nearby. His legs were frozen in the position of a runner's and, as the fish sped past, the small wake turned him slowly away from her.

Clank, clank.

No, she thought. I can't do this.

Already the walls were closing in on her. Plagued all her life by claustrophobia, Sachs couldn't stop thinking of what would happen if she got caught in one of these tiny passages. She'd go mad.

Two deep breaths of dry air through the regulator.

She thought of the Chang family. She thought of the toddler.

And she swam on.

The gauge: 2300 pounds of pressure.

We're doing fine. Keep going.

Clank.

That damn noise—like doors closing, sealing her shut.

Well, ignore it, she told herself. Nobody's closing any doors.

The rooms above her—on the side of the *Dragon* facing the surface—were not, she deduced, the Ghost's: two didn't appear to have been occupied on the voyage and one was the captain's; in this one she found seafaring memorabilia and pictures of the bald, mustachioed man she recognized as Captain Sen from the pictures tacked up on Lincoln Rhyme's wall.

Clank, clank, clank . . .

She swam downward to check out the rooms on the other side of the narrow corridor—facing the bottom.

As she did, her tank caught on a fire extinguisher mounted to the wall and she froze in position. Trapped in the narrow corridor she was seized with a flash of panic.

It's okay, Sachs, Lincoln Rhyme's voice said to her in that deep, lulling voice he always fell into when speaking to her through her headset at crime scenes. *It's okay.*

She controlled the panic and backed up, freeing herself.

The gauge told her: 2100 pounds.

Three of the cabins below her hadn't been occupied. That left only one more—it had to be the Ghost's.

A huge groan.

More clanks.

Then a moaning so loud she actually felt it in her chest. What was happening? The whole ship was buckling! The doors would be jammed. She'd be trapped here forever. Suffocating slowly . . . Dying alone . . . Oh, Rhyme . . .

But then the moaning stopped, replaced by more clanking.

She paused at the entrance to the Ghost's cabin, below her feet.

The door was closed. It opened inward—well, downward. She gripped the knob and twisted. The latch released and the heavy wooden door eased downward. Looking beneath her into the darkness. Things were swimming around inside the room. Jesus . . . She shivered and remained where she was, hovering in the narrow corridor.

But Lincoln Rhyme's voice, as clear as if he'd been speaking through her headphones, sounded in her thoughts. *"It's a crime scene, Sachs. That's all it is. And searching crime scenes is what we do, remember? You grid it, you search it, you observe it, you collect evidence."*

Okay. Rhyme. But I could live without eels.

She let some air out of the BCD and dropped slowly into the room.

Two sights made her gasp.

In front of her a man floated in the black space, eyes closed, his jaw down as far as it could go, arms outstretched, his coat billowing out behind him. His face was white as paper.

The second thing she saw was less macabre but far stranger: what must have been a thousand hundred-dollar bills floated in the water, filling the room, like flakes in a plastic souvenir snowball.

The bills explained the man's death. His pockets were filled with money and she deduced that as the ship started to go down he'd run to the cabin to get as much of the Ghost's cash as he could but he'd been trapped here.

She eased farther into the room, the bills swirling in her wake.

The money soon proved to be a major pain in the ass. It stuck to her, it obscured the scene like smoke. (Add this to your book, Rhyme: excessive money at the crime scene can make searches extremely difficult.) She couldn't see more than a few feet past the cloud of bills. She grabbed several handfuls of the money for evidence and put them in her collection bag. Kicking her way to what was now the top of the room—originally the side—she noticed an open attaché case floating in the thin air pocket. She found more currency inside—Chinese, it seemed. A handful of these bills went into the collection bag.

Clank, clank.

Jesus, this is spooky. Darkness around her, unseen things caressing the wetsuit. She could see only a few feet in front of her—the tunnel of dim illumination cast by the tiny spotlight on her head.

She then located two weapons: an Uzi machine pistol and a Beretta

9mm. She examined them closely and found that the Uzi's serial number had been etched out. She let this weapon drop to the bottom. There was a number on the Beretta, though, which meant it might yield some traceable connection to the Ghost. She slipped it into her evidence bag. A glance at her pressure gauge: 1800 pounds of air. God, she was going through it fast. Breathe slowly.

"Come on, Sachs, concentrate."

Right, sorry, Rhyme.

Clank, clank, clank.

I hate that fucking sound!

She searched the body of the corpse. No wallet or ID.

Another shiver. Why was this scene so horrible, so eerie? She'd processed dozens of bodies. But then she realized: the corpses at those scenes had always lain like broken toys on the ground, pulled, inanimate, to the concrete or grass or carpet by gravity. They weren't real. But this man wasn't still at all. As cold as the heartless water around him, white as snow, he moved like an elegant dancer in slow motion.

The stateroom was very small and the body would interfere with her search. So, with a respect that she wouldn't have felt anywhere outside of this horrible mausoleum, she eased the body upward into the corridor and pushed him away. Then she returned to the Ghost's cabin.

Clank, clank . . . clank.

Ignoring the spooky moans and the clanking, she looked around her. In a tiny room like this, where would one hide things?

All the furniture was attached to the walls and floors. And there was only one small dresser. Inside were Chinese-brand toiletries, nothing that yielded any obvious evidence.

She looked for anything hidden in the closet but found only clothes.

Clank, clank . . .

What do we think, Rhyme?

"I think you've got, let's see, about fourteen hundred pounds of air left. I'd say if you don't find something soon, get the hell out."

I'm not going anywhere yet, she thought. Hovering, she looked slowly around the room. Where would he hide things? He left his guns, he left the money. . . . that means the explosion took him by surprise too. There *has* to be something here. She glanced again at the closet. The clothes? Maybe. She kicked toward it.

She began to go through them. Nothing in any of the pockets. But she kept searching and—in one of his Armani jackets—found a slit he'd made in the lining. She reached in and extracted an envelope containing a document. She trained the light on it. Don't know if it's helpful or not, Rhyme. They're in Chinese.

"That's for us to find out back home. You find it, Eddie'll translate it, I'll analyze it."

Into the bag.

Twelve hundred pounds of pressure. But don't hold ever, ever, ever hold your breath.

Why was that again?

Right. Your lungs'll explode.

Clank.

Okay, I'm outta here.

She made her way out of the small stateroom and into the corridor, the treasures of evidence stashed in the bag tied to her belt.

Clank clank clank . . . clank . . . clank . . . clank.

She turned back down the endless corridor—the route by which she could escape from this terrible place. The bridge seemed miles away down the black corridor.

The longest journey, the first step . . .

But then she stopped, gripping the doorway. Jesus, Lord, she thought.

Clank clank clank . . .

Amelia Sachs realized something about the eerie banging she'd been hearing since she'd entered the ship. Three fast bangs, three slow.

It was Morse code for *S-O-S*. And it was coming from somewhere deep within the ship.

Chapter Thirty-seven

S-O-S.

The universal distress call.

S-O . . .

Somebody was alive! The Coast Guard had missed a survivor. Should she go find the other divers? Sachs wondered.

But that would take too long; Sachs imagined from the uneven pounding that the trapped air the survivor was breathing was nearly gone. Besides, the sound seemed to be coming from nearby. It should take only minutes to find the person.

But where were they exactly?

Well, obviously it hadn't come from the direction of the bridge, through which she'd entered the ship. It wasn't coming from the cabins here either. It had to be one of the holds or the engine room—in the lower part of the ship. Now, with the *Dragon* on its side, those areas were level with her, on her left.

Yes, no?

For this she couldn't ask Lincoln Rhyme's advice.

There was no one to help her here.

Oh, Jesus, I'm really going to do this, aren't I?

Less than 1200 pounds of air left.

So you better get your butt going, girl.

Sachs glanced at the faint illumination where the bridge was, then she turned away from it toward the darkness—and the claustrophobia—and kicked hard. Following the clanking.

S-O-S.

But when she came to the end of the black corridor, from which she thought she heard the code, Sachs found no way to get into the interior of the ship. The corridor just ended. She pressed her head against the wood, though, and could distinctly hear the clanging.

O-S.

Training the light on the wall she discovered a small door. She opened it and gasped as a green eel swam leisurely past her. She let her heart calm and gazed inside, looking to her left, into the bowels of the ship. The shaft was a dumbwaiter, presumably to cart supplies up to the cabin deck and the bridge from the lower decks. It measured about two feet by two feet.

Confronting the thought of swimming into the narrow space, she now thought about going back for help. But she'd already wasted too much time finding the doorway.

Oh, man . . .

One thousand pounds of air.

Clank, clank . . .

She closed her eyes and shook her head.

Can't do it. No way.

S-O-S.

Amelia Sachs, calm as tea when she hit 130 miles per hour in her Camaro SS, would wake up sobbing after dreams of herself imprisoned in chambers and tunnels and mine shafts.

Can't do it! she thought again.

Then sighed through her regulator and pulled herself into the narrow space, turned left as best she could and kicked her way deeper into hell.

God, I hate this.

Nine hundred pounds of pressure on her gauge.

She eased forward, moving along the shaft that was just wide enough to accommodate her and her tank. Ten feet. Her tank suddenly caught on something above her. She fought down the shiver of panic, clamping her teeth furiously on the mouthpiece of her regulator. Rotating slowly she found the wire that had snagged her and she freed herself. She turned back and found another blue-white face protruding through another doorway of the dumbwaiter shaft.

Oh, my Lord . . .

The man's eyes, opaque as jelly, stared in her direction, glowing in the bright light. His hair rose outward from his head like the coat of a porcupine.

Sachs eased forward and kicked slowly past the man, struggling to ignore the chilling sensation of the crown of his head brushing her body as she swam past.

S . . .

The sound, though still feeble, was louder here.

O . . .

She continued down the shaft to the very bottom of the dumbwaiter and, pushing aside the panic as she neared the exit, she forced herself to move calmly through the doorway into what was the galley of the *Dragon.*

S . . .

The black water here was filled with trash and flecks of food—and several bodies.

Clank.

Whoever was signaling couldn't even make an entire letter now.

Above, she saw the shimmering surface of a large air pocket and a man's legs in the water, dangling downward. The feet, in socks, moved slightly, almost a twitch. She swam quickly toward them and burst to the surface. A bald man with a mustache was clinging to a rack of shelves that were bolted to the wall—now the ceiling of the kitchen—turned away with a cry of shock and undoubtedly from the pain of the blinding light shooting into his eyes.

Sachs squinted. She recognized him—why? Then realized that she'd seen his picture on the evidence board in Rhyme's town house—and the one she'd seen in the cabin just a few minutes before. This was Captain Sen of the *Fuzhou Dragon.*

He was muttering incoherently and shivering. He was so blue he looked cyanotic—the color of an asphyxia victim. She spit the regulator out of her mouth to breathe the air that was trapped in the pocket and save her own store of oxygen but the atmosphere was so foul and depleted that she felt faint. She grabbed the mouthpiece again and began to suck the air from her own supply.

Pulling the secondary regulator off her vest, she stuck it into Sen's mouth. He breathed deeply and began to revive somewhat. Sachs pointed downward into the water. He nodded.

A fast glance at the pressure gauge: 700 pounds. And two of them were using her supply now.

She released air from the BCD and, with her arm around the limp man, they sank to the bottom of the galley, pushing aside the bodies and cartons of food that floated in their way. At first she wasn't able to locate the doorway to the dumbwaiter shaft. She felt weak with panic for a moment, afraid that the moaning she'd heard meant the ship was settling and buckling and the doorway was now sealed off. But then she saw that the body of a young woman had floated in front of it. She gently pulled the corpse aside and opened the dumbwaiter doorway wide.

They couldn't both fit into the shaft side by side so she eased the captain in before her, feet first. Eyes squeezed shut, still shivering violently, he gripped the black hose of his regulator desperately with both hands. Sachs followed him, imagining all too clearly what might happen if he panicked and ripped the regulator from her mouth or tore her mask or the light off: trapped in this horrible narrow place, thrashing in panic as she breathed the foul water into her lungs . . .

No, no, stop thinking about it! Keep going. She kicked hard, moving as quickly as she could. Twice the captain, floating backward, became jammed and she had to free him.

A glance at the gauge: 400 pounds of pressure.

We leave the bottom with five hundred. No less than that. That's an iron-clad rule. No exceptions.

Finally they got to the top deck—where the cabins were located and the corridor that led to the bridge and, beyond that, precious Outside, with its orange rope that would take them to the surface and a boundless supply of sweet air. But the captain was still dazed and it took a long minute to maneuver him through the opening first while making certain that he kept the regulator in his mouth.

Then they were out of the dumbwaiter and floating into the main corridor. She swam beside the captain and grabbed him by his leather belt. But as she started to kick forward she braked suddenly to a stop. The knob on her air tank was snared. She reached back and found it was caught by the jacket on the body that'd been in the Ghost's stateroom.

The gauge: 300 pounds of pressure.

Goddamn, she thought, pulling fiercely at the snag, kicking. But the body was jammed in a doorway and the tail of his jacket had wound tightly around the tank knob. The harder she pulled the more snugly she was held.

The needle of the pressure gauge was now below the redline: 200 pounds remained.

She couldn't reach the snag behind her.

Okay, nothing to do . . .

She ripped open the Velcro of the BCD vest and slipped out of it. But as she turned to focus on the tangle the captain went into seizure. He kicked out hard, struck her in the face with his foot. The spotlight went out and the regulator popped from her mouth. The blow pushed her backward.

Darkness, no air . . .

No, no . . .

Rhyme . . .

She made a grab for the regulator but it floated somewhere behind her, out of reach.

Don't hold your breath.

Well, I fucking have to . . .

Blackness all around her, spinning in circles, groping desperately for her regulator.

Where were the Coast Guard baby-sitters?

Outside. Because I told them I wanted to search alone. How could she let them know she was in trouble?

Fast, girl, fast . . .

She patted the evidence bag and reached in desperately. Pulled out the Beretta 9mm. She pulled the slide to chamber a round and pressed the muzzle close to the wooden wall, where she knew she wouldn't hit Sen, and pulled the trigger. A flash and loud explosion. The blowback and recoil nearly broke her wrist and she dropped the weapon through the cloud of debris and gunpowder residue.

Please, she thought . . . Please . . .

No air . . .

No . . .

Then lights burst on silently as the dive chief and his assistant kicked fast into the corridor. Another regulator mouthpiece was thrust between her lips and Sachs began to breathe again. The dive chief got his secondary regulator into the captain's mouth. The stream of bubbles was faint but at least he was breathing.

Okay signs were exchanged.

Then the foursome made its way out of the bridge and to the orange rope. Thumbs-up. Calmer now that the risk of confinement was gone, Sachs concentrated on ascending leisurely, no faster than her bubbles, and breathing, deep in, deep out, as they left behind the ship of corpses.

Sachs lay in the cutter's sick bay, breathing deeply; she'd opted for nature's air, turning down the green oxygen mask the corpsman offered her—it would, she was afraid, only increase her sense of confinement, having something else pressed close against her body.

As soon as she'd climbed onto the bobbing deck she'd stripped off the wetsuit—the tight outfit itself had become another carrier of the pernicious claustrophobia—and wrapped the thick government-issue blanket around her. Two sailors escorted her to the sickbay to check out her wrist, which turned out not to be badly injured at all.

Finally, she felt well enough to venture up top. She popped two Dramamine and climbed the stairs to the bridge, observing that the helicopter was back, hovering over the cutter.

This ride wasn't for Sachs, however, but was to evacuate unconscious Captain Sen to a Long Island medical center.

Ransom explained how they'd probably missed the captain during their search for victims. "Our divers did a long search, banging on the hull, and didn't get any response. We did a sound scan later and that came back negative too. Sen must've wedged himself in the air pocket, passed out, then come to later."

"Where's he going?" she asked.

"Marine station in Huntington, part of the hospital. They have a hyperbaric chamber there."

"Is he going to make it?"

Ransom said, "Doesn't look good. But if he survived twenty-four hours under these conditions then I guess anything's possible."

Slowly the chill subsided. She dried off and dressed once more in her jeans, T-shirt and sweatshirt and then hurried to the bridge to call Rhyme. Neglecting to share some of her underwater adventures, she told him that she'd found some evidence. "And maybe a wit."

"A *witness?*"

"Found somebody still alive in the ship. The captain. Looks like he got some of the people trapped in the hold into the galley after the ship went down. But he was the only one who survived. If we're lucky he'll be able to give us some leads to the Ghost's operation in New York."

"Did he say anything?"

"He's unconscious. They're not even sure he's going to make it— hypothermia and decompression sickness. The hospital'll call as soon as they know something. Better have Lon send baby-sitters for him too. The Ghost'll come after him if he finds out he's still alive."

"Hurry back, Sachs. We miss you."

The royal we, she knew, coming from Lincoln Rhyme, really meant "I."

She assembled the evidence she'd found underwater, drying the letter she'd found in his jacket with paper towels from the cutter's galley. This would contaminate it some but she was worried that more exposure to seawater would deteriorate the paper so much it couldn't be read. Crime scene work, Rhyme had often told her, was always a compromise.

Captain Ransom walked onto the bridge. "There's another chopper on the way here for you, Officer." He carried two large Styrofoam coffee cups, covered with lids. He handed her one.

"Thanks."

They peeled the lids off. His contained steaming black coffee.

She laughed. In *her* cup was fruit juice that was mixed, she could smell, with a generous slug of rum.

Chapter Thirty-eight

Feng shui, which literally means wind and water, is the art of trapping good energy and luck and repelling bad.

It's widely practiced around the world but because of the astonishing number of rules and the rarity of the ability to assess the dynamics of good and evil there are very few truly talented feng shui practitioners. It entails far more than just arranging furniture, as Loaban's assistant had suggested, and the Ghost's apartment had clearly been done by a master. Sonny Li knew plenty of feng shui practitioners in China but he had no idea who here in New York could have prepared the Ghost's apartment so expertly.

But rather than race around like Hongse in her yellow car to track down someone who could help him, Li remained true to his Taoist way.

The way to use life is to do nothing through acting, the way to use life is to do everything through being . . .

And so Detective Sonny Li went into the fanciest bubble tea shop he could find in Chinatown, sat down at a table and slouched back in the chair. He ordered a cup of the odd beverage: tea sweetened with sugar and lightened with milk. In the bottom of the tall cup were large chewy black pearls of tapioca that you sucked up through a wide straw and ate. Like the famous (and equally expensive) foaming iced tea popular in Fuzhou, this was a Taiwanese creation.

Sonny didn't much care for the tea but he kept it in front of him to buy the right to sit here for what might be a long time. He studied the chic room, which had been planned by some too-clever designer. The chairs were metal and purple leather, the lighting was subdued and the wallpaper fake Zen. Tourists would breeze into the place, drink down their tea and then hurry off to see more Chinatown sights, leaving behind huge tips, which Sonny Li at first thought was their forgotten change; tipping is rare in China.

Sitting, sipping . . . Thirty minutes passed. Forty-five.

Do everything through being . . .

His patience was finally rewarded. An attractive Chinese woman in her early forties walked into the tea shop, found a seat near him and ordered a tea.

The woman wore a beautiful red dress and high, narrow heels. She read the *New York Times* through stylish reading glasses with narrow rectangular lenses and blue frames no thicker than a pencil line. Most of the Chinese women shopping here in Chinatown carried cheap plastic bags wrinkled from many uses. But this woman carried one made of flawless white paper. Inside was a box tied with a gold cord. He deciphered the name on the side of the bag: SAKS FIFTH AVENUE.

She was exactly the sort of woman Sonny Li wanted yet knew he would forever be denied. Sleek, stylish, beautiful, hair shiny and dense as a crow's black pelt, a lean face with some Vietnamese features beautifully sharpening the Han Chinese, keen eyes, bright red lips and Dowager Empress nails to match.

He looked over her dress again, her jewelry, her sprayed hair and decided, Yes, she's the one. Li picked up his tea, walked to her table and introduced himself. Li sat, though the chair he chose was near but not actually *at* her table, so that she wouldn't be threatened by his presence. He casually struck up a conversation with her and they talked about the Beautiful Country, about New York, about bubble tea and about Taiwan, where she'd been born. He said casually, "The reason I troubled you— forgive me—but perhaps you can help. The man I work for? He has bad luck. I believe it is because of how his apartment is arranged. You obviously have a good feng shui man."

He nodded at the emblems that had told him that she indeed followed feng shui diligently: an ostentatious bracelet of nine Chinese coins, a pin in the likeness of the homely goddess Guan Yin and a scarf with black fish on it. This was why he had selected her—on this evidence, and because she was obviously rich, which meant that she would go to only the best practitioners of the art, men of the sort that the Ghost too would hire.

He continued, "If I could give my boss the name of someone good to arrange his home and office he might think more of me. It might help me keep my job and raise myself in his view." With these words Li lowered his head but kept his eyes on her face and was pierced by what he saw: pity generated by his shame. What was so wrenching to him about that look, though, was that the phony shame emanating from Sonny Li the undercover cop was virtually identical to the true shame that Sonny Li the man felt daily from his father's cascade of criticism. Perhaps, he reflected, this is why she believed him.

The beautiful woman smiled and dug into her purse. She wrote out a name and address—on a slip of paper not bearing her own name or phone number, of course. She slipped it to him and withdrew her hand quickly before he could touch her palm and grasp it in desperation and hunger, which in fact he was close to doing.

"Mr. Wang," she said, nodding at the card. "He is one of the best in the city. If your employer has money he will help him. He is most expensive. But he will do a good job. He helped me marry well, as you can see."

"Yes, my boss has money."

"Then he too can change his fortune. Goodbye." She stood, gathered her glossy bag and purse and strode out of the shop on her immaculate heels, leaving her check sitting prominently on the table for Sonny Li to pay.

"Sachs!" Rhyme looked up from the computer screen. "Guess what the Ghost blew the ship up with?"

"Give up," she called, amused to see the look of pleasure accompanying this gruesome question.

Mel Cooper answered, "Grade A, brand-new Composition 4."

"Congratulations."

This had put Rhyme in a good mood because C4—despite being movie terrorist's staple for bombs—was actually quite rare. The substance was available only to the military and a few select law enforcement agencies; it wasn't used in commercial demolition. This meant that there were relatively few sources for high-quality C4, which in turn meant that the odds of finding a connection between that source and the Ghost were far better than if he'd used common TNT, Tovex, Gelenex or any of the other commercially available explosives.

More significantly, though, C4 is so dangerous that by law it must contain markers—each manufacturer of the material adds inert but distinctive chemicals to its version of the explosive. Analysis of the trace at the scene of an explosion will reveal which marker was present and this tells investigators who manufactured it. The company, in turn, must keep detailed records of whom its products were sold to, and the purchasers must keep detailed files on where the explosive was stored or used.

If they could find the person who sold the Ghost this batch of C4, he might know where the snakehead had other safehouses in New York, or other bases of operation.

Cooper had sent the trace results to Quantico. "Should hear back in the next few hours."

"Where's Coe?" Sachs asked, looking around the town house.

"Down at INS," Rhyme said then added acerbically, "Don't jinx it by mentioning his name. Let's hope he stays there."

Eddie Deng arrived from downtown. "Got here as soon as you called, Lincoln."

"Excellent, Eddie. Put your reading specs on. You've got to translate for us. Amelia found a letter in the Ghost's sports coat."

"No shit," Deng said. "Where?"

"A hundred feet underwater. But that's another story."

Deng's eyes were fine—no reading glasses were required—but Mel Cooper did have to set him up with an ultraviolet reading hood to image the ink on the letter; the characters had been bleached out by the seawater and were barely visible.

Deng hunched over the letter and examined it.

"It's hard to read," Deng murmured, squinting. "Okay, okay . . . It's to the Ghost. The man who wrote is named Ling Shui-bian. He's telling the Ghost when the charter flight will be leaving Fuzhou and when and where to expect it at the Nagorev military base outside of St. Petersburg. Then he says he's wiring the money into an account in Hong Kong—no number or bank. Then it describes the cost of the airplane charter. It then says part of the money is enclosed—in dollars. Finally, there's a list of the victims—the passengers on the *Dragon*."

"That's all?"

"I'm afraid so."

"Have some of our people in China check out that guy—Ling," Rhyme told Sellitto. Then the criminalist asked Mel Cooper: "Trace in the paper?"

"Just what you'd expect," the lab man said. "Salt water, sea-life excrement, pollution, plant particles, motor oil, diesel fuel."

"How much money was there, Sachs?" Rhyme asked.

"A lot. Maybe a thousand. But it's hard to tell when you're swimming around in it."

The U.S. bills she'd collected were all in hundred-dollar denominations, freshly printed.

"Forged?" Rhyme asked.

Cooper examined one. "Nope."

The yuan she'd found—the Chinese paper currency—were faded and crumpled. "There were about thirty packs this size," she explained. Eddie Deng totaled the amount in this packet. "Thirty stacks, given the exchange rate," the young detective estimated, "equals about twenty thousand dollars U.S."

Sachs continued, "I also found an Uzi and a Beretta but he'd taken the serial number off the Uzi and I lost the Beretta on the ship."

"Knowing the Ghost," Rhyme said, "any gun of his, even with serial numbers, is going to be untraceable."

"Thom! We need our scribe! Thom!"

The criminalist looked toward the hallway.

The harried young man entered the room. He wrote down the information that Rhyme had dictated about the explosives, the letter and the trace on it, the guns.

There was an electronic trill as a cell phone rang and—typical nowadays—everyone looked down to see if it was his or hers ringing. Sachs was the winner and she pulled the unit off her belt.

"Hello?"

"Amelia?"

She recognized John Sung's voice. Her stomach did a little flip at the memory of last night.

"John."

"How are you?"

Been for one hell of a swim, she thought, but aside from that, doing okay. "Fine," she said. "Kind of busy right now."

"Of course," the doctor said. What a voice, she thought. Pure bedside manner. "Any luck finding Sam Chang and his family?"

"Not yet. We're working on that right now."

"I was just wondering if you might have some time to stop by later."

"I think that'll work out. But can I call you in a bit, John? I'm at Lincoln's right now and it's a little crazy."

"Of course. I'm sorry to interrupt."

"No, no, I'm glad you did. I'll call you later."

She hung up and started to return to the evidence. But she glanced up and saw Lon Sellitto looking at her with what could only be described as a glare.

"Detective," she said to him, "can I talk to you outside for a minute?"

Gruffly Sellitto said, "What's there to—"

"Now," she snapped.

Rhyme glanced at them for a moment but lost interest in the curious exchange and returned to examining the evidence boards.

Sachs walked into the corridor and Sellitto followed, his feet pounding heavily on the floor. Thom had noticed something was wrong. "What's going—" But the aide's voice was lost as Sachs swung the door shut angrily. They continued down the hallway to where she gestured—the back of the town house—and they entered the kitchen.

She spun around, hands on her narrow hips. "Why've you been on my case for the past two days, Detective?"

The big man pulled his belt up over his belly. "You're crazy. It's your imagination."

"Bullshit. You have something to say to me, say it to my face. I deserve that."

"Deserve it?" he asked in a snide tone.

"What *is* all this?" she snapped.

There was a pause while he looked at the butcher block, where Thom had set a half-dozen tomatoes and a pile of basil. Finally he said, "I know where you were last night."

"Yeah?" she asked.

"The baby-sitters outside of Sung's apartment told me you went there after you left here and you didn't leave till one forty-five."

"My personal life is my own business," she said coldly.

The burly cop looked around and then whispered vehemently, "But it's *not* just your business anymore, Amelia. It's *his* business too."

She frowned. "His? Who?"

"Rhyme. Who d'you think?"

"What're you talking about?"

"He's tough. Tougher than anybody I know. But the one thing that'll break him into little pieces is you—if you keep going the way you're headed."

She was bewildered. "Headed?"

"Look, you didn't know him back then—that woman he was in love with, Clare. When she died, it took him forever to get over it. He came to work, he did his job, but it took a year for that light to come back in his eyes. And his wife . . . They had some fights, sure—I'm talking MGM Grand kind of fights. It wasn't the greatest marriage in the world but, after the accident, when he knew it wasn't going to work and he got divorced, that was hard for him, real hard."

"I don't know where you're going with this."

"You don't? It's pretty clear to me. You're the center of his life. He's let down all his defenses with you. You're going to break him. And I'm not going to let that happen." His voice dropped even further. "Just think about—if you keep seeing this guy it's going to kill Rhyme. It's . . . What the hell're you laughing at?"

"You're talking about me and John Sung?"

"Yeah, the guy you've been sneaking off to see."

Sachs's hands rose to her face and she began shaking with the laughter."Oh, Lon . . ." Then she turned away quickly away from the detective because a moment later—as she'd suddenly known would happen—the laughter turned into tears.

"I've got to talk to you about something."

"You're looking like it's bad news, Doctor."

"Why don't we sit down over there in the corner?"

"Jesus," Sellitto said, starting forward. Then stopping, hands at his side, awkward. "Amelia, what . . ."

She held up a hand and turned away.

"What's going on?"

Finally she caught her breath, wiped her face and turned back to the detective. "It's not what you're thinking, Lon."

Another tug of his belt. "Go on."

"You know Rhyme and I've talked about having kids."

"Yeah."

She gave a sour laugh. "It didn't work. It's not like we were trying that hard but I wasn't getting pregnant. I was worried that there was something wrong with Lincoln. So a few weeks ago we went in and we both had checkups."

"Yeah, I remember he went to the doctor."

She thought back to that day in the waiting room.

"Ah, Ms. Sachs. Here you are."

"Hello, Doctor."

"I've just been meeting with Lincoln Rhyme's physician."

"Yes?"

"I've got to talk to you about something."

"You're looking like it's bad news, Doctor."

"Why don't we sit down over there in the corner?"

"Here's fine. Tell me. Let me have it straight."

"Well, Lincoln's doctor tells me that the results of his fertility workup are well within normal levels. A slightly diminished sperm count, which is typical of someone in his condition, but nowadays that's a very slight hurdle to pregnancy. I'm afraid, though, that you have a more serious problem."

"Me?"

Staring at the butcher block next to her, she now told Sellitto about this conversation with the doctor. Then she added, "I've got something called endometriosis. I've always had problems but I never believed it was as bad as what the doctor told me."

"Can they cure it?"

Sachs shook her head. "No. They can operate, do hormonal therapy but it wouldn't really help the fertility thing."

"Jesus, I'm sorry, Amelia."

She wiped her face again. A sad smile blossomed on it. "Dryness and heat in the kidney."

"What?"

Sachs offered a hollow laugh. *"That's* what I was doing at John Sung's. Dryness and heat in the kidney—those're the reasons for infertility, according to Chinese medicine. Last night he examined me and gave me an acupressure treatment. And he's getting some herbs that he thinks'll help. That's what he just called about. Wait here." Sachs walked to hallway, dug into her purse and returned with what Sung had just given her when she'd seen him last night. She handed the book to the detective. The title was *Herbal Treatments and Acupressure Techniques to Assist Fertility.*

"It turns out a lot of Western doctors recommend that women with endometriosis use Chinese medicine to treat it. Last night, when I took Lincoln upstairs we talked about it. He thought it was pretty silly but he'd noticed how upset I've been lately because of this. He's right—he said I've been distracted. It's even bothering me when I'm running scenes. So we decided I'd go ahead and see what Sung could do for me." She fell silent. Finally she said, "There's so much death around me, Lon . . . my father, my relationship with my boyfriend, Nick—when he went off to prison it was like he died. Then all the crime scenes I run. I wanted to have some *life* around us, Lincoln and me. I wanted so badly to fix what's wrong inside me."

Whatever it takes, look out for yourself first. If you're not whole, you'll never be able to take care of anybody else.

Sung's treatment, she hoped, was a way to do this—to make herself whole.

Lifting his palms, Sellitto said, "I didn't know. You were real secret about it."

Angrily she said, "Because it's nobody's business but Lincoln's and mine." She nodded toward Rhyme's room. "Don't you know what he and I are to each other? How could you think I'd do something like that?"

The disorderly detective couldn't hold her gaze. "With Betty leaving and everything, I was just thinking about what happened to me." The big cop's marriage had broken up some years before. No one knew the details of Sellitto's divorce but it was a well-known fact that being married to a cop was tough and many a spouse had gone looking for a more attentive alternate. She supposed Betty had had an affair. "I'm sorry, Officer. I shoulda thought better." He extended his hand and she reluctantly shook his huge palm.

"Will that do any good?" He nodded at the book.

"I don't know," she answered. Then smiled wistfully. "Maybe."

"Back to work?" Sellitto asked.

"Sure." She wiped her eyes a final time and they returned to Rhyme's living room.

Easton, Long Island, Crime Scene	Stolen Van, Chinatown	Jerry Tang Murder Crime Scene
· Two immigrants killed on beach; shot in back.	· Camouflaged by immigrants with "The Home Store" logo.	· Four men kicked door in and tortured him and shot him.
· One immigrant wounded—Dr. John Sung.	· Blood spatter suggests injured woman has hand, arm or shoulder injury.	· Two shell casings—match Model 51. Tang shot twice in head.
· "Bangshou" (assistant) on board; identity unknown.	· Blood samples sent to lab for typing.	· Extensive vandalism.
· Assistant confirmed as drowned body found near site where *Dragon* sank.	· Injured woman is AB negative. Requesting more information about her blood.	· Some fingerprints.
· Ten immigrants escape: seven adults (one elderly, one injured woman), two children, one infant. Steal church van.	· Fingerprints sent to AFIS.	· No matches except Tang's.
· Blood samples sent to lab for typing.	· No matches.	· Three accomplices have smaller shoe size than Ghost, presumably smaller stature.
· Injured woman is AB negative. Requesting more information about her blood.		· Trace suggests Ghost's safehouse is probably downtown, Battery Park City area.
· Vehicle awaiting Ghost on beach left without him. One shot believed fired by Ghost at vehicle. Request for vehicle make and model sent out, based on tread marks and wheelbase.		· Suspected accomplices from Chinese ethnic minority. Presently pursuing whereabouts.
· Vehicle is a BMW X5.		· Uighurs from Turkestan Community and Islamic Center of Queens.
· Driver—Jerry Tang.		· Cell phone calls lead to 805 Patrick Henry Street, downtown.
· No vehicles to pick up immigrants located.		
· Cell phone, presumably Ghost's, sent for analysis to FBI.		
· Untraceable satellite secure phone. Hacked Chinese gov't system to use it.		
· Ghost's weapon is 7.62mm pistol. Unusual casing.		
· Model 51 Chinese automatic pistol.		
· Ghost is reported to have gov't people on payroll.		
· Ghost stole red Honda sedan to escape. Vehicle locator request sent out.		
· No trace of Honda found.		
· Three bodies recovered at sea—two shot, one drowned. Photos and prints to Rhyme and Chinese police.		
· Drowned individual identified as Victor Au, the Ghost's *bangshou*.		
· Fingerprints sent to AFIS.		
· No matches on any prints but unusual markings on Sam Chang's fingers and thumbs (injury, rope burn?)		
· Profile of Immigrants: Sam Chang and Wu Qichen and their families, John Sung, baby of woman who drowned, unidentified man and woman (killed on beach).		

Canal Street Shooting Crime Scene	Safehouse Shooting Crime Scene	Fuzhou Dragon Crime Scene
· Additional trace suggesting safehouse is in Battery Park City area.	· Fingerprints and photos Chang Jiechi's hands reveal father— and son Sam—are calligraphers. Sam Chang might be doing printing or sign painting. Calling stores and companies in Queens.	· Ghost used new C4 to blow up ship. Checking origin of explosive through chemical markers.
· Stolen Chevrolet Blazer, untraceable.		· Large quantity new U.S. bills found in Ghost's cabin.
· No match on prints.		
· Safehouse carpet: Arnold company's Lustre-Rite, installed in past six months; calling contractors to get list of installations.	· Biosolids on deceased's shoes suggest they live in neighborhood near sewage treatment plant.	· Approx. $20,000 in used Chinese yuan found in cabin.
· Location of installations determined: 32 near Battery Park City.	· Ghost uses feng shui practitioner to arrange his living space.	· List of victims, air charter details and bank deposit information. Checking name of sender in China.
· Fresh gardening mulch found.		· Captain alive but unconscious.
· Body of Ghost's accomplice: ethnic minority from west or northwest China. Negative on prints. Weapon was Walther PPK.		· Beretta 9mm, Uzi. Unable to trace.
· Details on immigrants:		
· The Changs: Sam, Mei-Mei, William and Ronald; Sam's father, Chang Jiechi and infant, Po-Yee. Sam has job arranged but employer and location unknown. Driving blue van, no make, no tag number. Changs' apartment is in Queens.		
· The Wus: Qichen, Yong-Ping, Chin-Mei and Lang.		

Chapter Thirty-nine

"Fred," Rhyme said as Dellray—now wearing the orangest shirt that the criminalist had ever seen—walked into his living room laboratory.

"Hey," Sachs said to the agent. "They let you wear shirts like that? Say, is that a real color?"

"You gave us a hell of a scare," Rhyme said.

"'Magine what I *myself* was feelin', settin' my ass down on a few sticks of Mr. *N*oble's creation." He looked around the room. "Where Dan?"

"Dan?" Rhyme asked.

"The SSA?"

Noting the blank stares, Dellray continued, "The supervisin' agent, the guy who took over for me. Dan Wong. From our San Francisco office. Wanna thank him for takin' over."

Rhyme and Sachs looked at each other. The criminalist said, "Nobody took over for you. We're still waiting."

"Still *waitin'*?" Dellray whispered in disbelief. "I talked to Dan myself last night. He's the man you need. Run dozens of human smuggling cases. He's some kinda expert in snakeheads and Chinese culture. He was gonna call you an' be out here on a army jet this morning."

"No word."

Dellray's expression of astonishment turned to anger. "What about SPEC-TAC?" he asked suspiciously. "They *are* here, ain't they?"

"Nope," Sachs said.

With a snarl he pulled his phone off his belt as if he were quick-drawing his weapon. One speed-dial button later he was connected. "This's Dellray . . . Put him on. . . . Don't care. Want him now. . . . Like I said, which mebbe you din't hear. I. Want. Him. Now. . . ." A disgusted sigh. "Well, have him call me. An' *you* tell me—what happened to Dan Wong?" He listened for a long moment then snapped the phone off without a farewell.

"Dan got some emergency assignment in Hawaii. Word came from Washington, so it got priority over our li'l pissy insig*nifi*cant case here. *Somebody* was s'posed to call me—and you—but it fell through the cracks."

"And SPEC-TAC?"

"The SAC's calling me back. But if they ain't here by now something's fucked up in a big way."

Rhyme said, "They told us it was on the 'scroll' for a meeting today."

"Hate that crappy way they talk," Dellray snapped. "I'ma get it taken care of when I get back to the office. No excuse for this."

"Thanks, Fred. We need the help. We've got half the Fifth Precinct trying to find the print shop or painting company where Sam Chang works and we're coming up with zilch."

"This ain't good."

Sellitto asked, "Where're you with the bomb investigation?"

"That's th'other reason I came by. Simon says zip . . . Can't make a baby step of headway. My CIs, they're scouring Brighton Beach but they ain't turning up anything. Not. A. Peep. And I run dozens of skels there."

"You're sure the device's Russian?"

"When're we sure 'bout anyfuckin'thing?"

That much was true. Rhyme nodded at a paper bag he carried. "What've you got?"

He dug out a plastic bag containing the bright yellow stick of explosive and tossed it across the room to Sachs.

She caught it one-handed. "Holy Mother, Fred," she called.

"S'only dynamite. And if it din't go off with a detonator it sure ain't gonna go bang with a little lob to left field. Hey, Aye-melia, you wanna play softball on the bureau team? That was a good catch."

She examined the stick of dynamite.

"Friction ridges?" Sellitto asked.

"Wiped clean. No prints."

She held it up for Rhyme, who noticed numbers printed on the side. "What'd the lot numbers turn up?" he asked Dellray.

"Nothin'. Our boys said it was too old to trace. 'Nother dead end."

"One man's dead end is another man's door," Rhyme said, reminding himself to share this saying, which he'd just made up, with Sonny Li when the Chinese cop returned. "Did they test it for markers?"

"Nup. Said it was too old for marker additives too."

"Probably is. But I want to test it anyway." He shouted to Mel Cooper, "Get it over to the lab ASAP. I want it analyzed. The works."

Chromatography—the analytical process of choice to test the dynamite—usually required that the samples be burned. But Rhyme wasn't about to set fire to a piece of explosive in his town house. The NYPD lab downtown had special equipment for doing so.

Mel Cooper called one of his technicians downtown and made arrangements for the test then handed the stick back to Dellray, giving him instructions on where to drop it off.

"We'll do what we can, Fred."

Then Cooper looked over a second bag Dellray handed him. It contained a Duracell battery, wires and a switch. "All generic, nothing helpful. It's your tract housing of bombs," the tech announced. "Detonator?"

A third bag appeared. Cooper and Rhyme examined what was left of the scorched piece of metal. "Russian, military grade," Rhyme said.

A detonator was basically a blasting cap, which contained a core of fulminate of mercury or similar explosive and wires, which heated up when an electrical charge was sent through them and set off the primer explosive, which in turn set off the main charge.

There wasn't much of this one left; it was the only part of the bomb that had actually gone off when Dellray sat on the device. Cooper put it under the compound microscope. "Not much. A Russian letter *A* and *R*. Then the numbers one and three."

"And nobody's database has a record of that?"

"Nope—and we checked ever-body: NYPD, ATF, DEA and Justice."

"Well, we'll see what the lab comes up with."

"I owe you, Lincoln."

"Pay me back by getting somebody from your shop to work GHOSTKILL, Fred."

. . .

Four blocks from the bubble tea house Sonny Li found the address of Mr. Wang, which the woman in red had given him.

The storefront showed no indication of what the occupant did for a living but in the dusty front window sat a shrine, illuminated by a red light-bulb and sticks of incense long burnt away. The faded letters said, in Chinese, FORTUNES TOLD, TRUTH REVEALED, LUCK PRESERVED.

Inside, a young Chinese woman behind a desk looked up at Li. On the desk in front of her were both an abacus and a laptop computer. The office was shabby but the diamond Rolex watch on her wrist suggested that the business was successful. She asked if he was here to hire her father to arrange his home or office.

"I was pleased to see an apartment I believe your father did. Can you tell me if it was his work?"

"Whose apartment?"

"It was an acquaintance of another friend, who sadly has gone back to China. I don't know his name. I do know the address, though."

"And that is what?"

"Five-oh-eight Patrick Henry Street."

"No, no," she said. "My father does not work there. He does no work south of Midtown. Only for uptown people."

"But your office is here."

"Because people expect it to be here. All of our clients are on the Upper East and Upper West Sides. And only a portion of them are Chinese."

"And you don't live in Chinatown?"

She laughed. "We live in Greenwich, Connecticut. Do you know it?"

"No," he said. Disappointed, Li asked, "Can you tell me who might've arranged this apartment. It was very well done."

"This friend, he is wealthy?"

"Yes, very wealthy."

"Then I would say Mr. Zhou. He does many of the rich places downtown. Here's his address and name. He has an office in the back of a grocery and herb store. It's about five blocks from here." She wrote the name on another slip of paper and jotted down the directions.

He thanked her and she turned back to the computer.

Outside, for luck, Sonny Li waited until a taxi speeding down the street was three meters away then jumped in front of the car. The driver cursed and extended his middle finger.

Li laughed. He'd cut the demon's tail very close and rendered him powerless. Now, blessed with invulnerability, he would find the Ghost.

He glanced at the slip of paper once more and started down the street toward the Lucky Hope Shop.

The Ghost, wearing his windbreaker to conceal his new Glock 36, a .45 caliber model, was walking down Mulberry Street, sipping the milk out of a whole coconut he'd bought at the corner. A short straw protruded from the opening the vendor had hacked into the top with a cleaver.

He'd just gotten the news from the Uighur that Yusuf had hired to break into the special NYPD safehouse where the Wu family was being kept in the Murray Hill section of the city. But the security was better than he'd expected and the guards had spotted him. They'd nearly caught him but the Turk had escaped. Undoubtedly the police had moved the family already. A brief setback but he'd eventually find out where they were.

He passed a store selling statues and altars and joss sticks. In the window was an effigy of his protector, the archer god Yi. The Ghost bowed his head slightly and then continued on.

As he walked, he asked himself: Did he believe in spirits?

Did he believe that the dragons inhabited hills?

He doubted that he did. After all, Tian Hou, the goddess of sailors, might have shaken her finger at the tempestuous sea and calmed it but she'd done so only in a myth. In reality she hadn't saved the piglets trapped in the hold of the *Fuzhou Dragon*.

And his own prayers to the goddess of mercy, Guan Yin, had gone unanswered years ago—she hadn't stopped the hand of the pimply student from beating his parents and brother to death for the ambiguous crime of being part of the old.

On the other hand, the Ghost certainly believed in qi—the life energy that flows through everyone. He had felt this force a thousand times. He felt it as the transfer between him and the woman he was fucking, felt it as the power of victory the instant he killed an enemy, felt it as a warning that he should avoid going into this room or meeting with that businessman. When he'd been sick or endangered he'd felt his qi impaired.

Good qi and bad qi.

And that meant you could channel the good force and divert or block the bad.

Down one alley, then down another, then across a busy street. Into yet another dim cobblestoned alley.

Finally he arrived at his destination. He finished the milk in the coconut and tossed the shell into a trash can. Then he carefully wiped his hands on a napkin and walked through the doorway, waving hello to his feng shui expert, Mr. Zhou, who sat in the back of the Lucky Hope Shop.

Sonny Li lit another cigarette and continued down a street called The Bowery.

Li knew snakeheads and he knew that they had money and a fierce sense of survival. The Ghost would have other safehouses in the area, and, since feng shui was such a personal matter, if the Ghost was satisfied with the work that Zhou had done on Patrick Henry Street he would have used the man for these other locations too.

He felt good. Good omens, good power.

He and Loaban had made their sacrifices to Guan Di, the god of detectives.

He'd been cutting demons' tails.

And he had a loaded German automatic pistol in his pocket.

If this feng shui man knew he was working for one of the most dangerous snakeheads in the world, he might be reluctant to talk about him. But Sonny Li would get him to.

Judge Dee—the fictional detective, prosecutor and judge in old China—conducted investigations very differently from Loaban. The techniques were similar to those used in modern-day China. The emphasis was on interrogation of witnesses and suspects, not on physical evidence. The key in criminal investigations, like so much else in Chinese culture, was patience, patience, patience. Even the brilliant—and persistent—Judge Dee would reinterview the suspect dozens of times until a crack was found in his alibi or explanation. The Judge would then tear apart upon the man's story until the suspect delivered the all-important goal of criminal investigation in China: not a jury verdict, but a confession, followed by the equally important vow of contrition. Anything that could elicit a confession was fair—even torture (though in Judge Dee's day if you tortured a suspect and it later turned out that he was innocent the judge himself would be tortured and put to death).

Sonny Li was the namesake of a great American gangster, Sonny

Corleone, son of the Godfather Vito Corleone. He was a senior officer and detective in the First Prefecture, People's Public Security Bureau, Liu Guoyuan, Fujian Province, a world traveler and the friend of *loaban* Lincoln Rhyme. Li would extract the Ghost's other addresses from the feng shui expert no matter what it took.

He continued along the street, past the bustling crowds, the fish markets in front of which were baskets of scrabbling blue crabs and bins of ice containing clams and fish—some of them sliced open, their tiny black hearts still beating.

He came to the Lucky Hope Shop, a small place but packed with merchandise: jars of twisted ginseng root, packs of dried cuttlefish, Hello Kitty toys and candies for children, noodles and spices, dusty bags of rice, bins of melon seeds, star noodles, tea for the liver and kidney, dried croaker, oyster sauce, lotus, jelly and gums, frozen tea buns and packs of tripe.

In the back he found a man sitting at a desk, smoking, reading a Chinese-language newspaper. The office was, as Sonny Li had expected, perfectly arranged: convex mirrors to trap the bad energy, a large translucent jade dragon (better than wood or ceramic) and—important for successful business—a small aquarium against what would be the north wall. In it swam black fish.

"You are Zhou?"

"Yes, that's right."

Li said, "I'm honored to meet you, sir. I was at the apartment of a friend at 508 Patrick Henry Street. I believe you arranged it."

Zhou's eyes narrowed a millimeter then he nodded cautiously. "A friend."

"That's right, sir. Unfortunately, I need to get in touch with him and he is no longer at that apartment. I was hoping you could tell me where he might be. His name is Kwan Ang."

Another faint, faint contraction of the man's brows.

"I am sorry, sir. I don't know anyone of that name."

"That's unfortunate, Mr. Zhou. Because if you did know him and you were to direct me to any other places he might be found, there would be a lot of money in it for you. It's important that I find him."

"I can't help you."

"You know that Kwan Ang is a snakehead and a murderer. I suspect you do know that. I can see it in your eyes." Sonny Li could read faces the way Loaban could read evidence.

"No, you are mistaken." Mr. Zhou began to sweat. Beads appeared on his scalp.

"So," Li continued, "any money he has paid you has blood on it. The blood of innocent women and children. Does that not trouble you?"

"I cannot help you." Zhou gazed down at a sheaf of papers on his desk. "Now I must get back to work."

Tap, tap . . .

Li was gently striking the desktop with his pistol. Zhou stared at it fearfully. "So you must be considered a confederate of his. Perhaps you are his partner. You are a snakehead too. I think that is so."

"No, no. I honestly don't know who you mean. I am simply a practitioner of feng—"

"Ah," Li sneered. "I'm tired of this. I'll call the INS and let them take over from here. They can deal with you and your family." He nodded toward a cluster of family pictures on the wall. Then he turned toward the door.

"There's no need for that!" Zhou said quickly. "Sir. . . . You mentioned money before?"

"Five thousand one-color."

"If he—"

"Kwan will never learn about you. You'll be paid in cash by the police."

Zhou wiped his face with his shirt sleeve. His eyes swept the desktop as he debated.

Tap . . . tap . . . tap . . .

Finally Zhou blurted, "I am not sure of the address. He and his associate picked me up here and drove me to the apartment through alleyways. But if you want him, I will tell you this—he was here not five minutes ago. He left just before you walked in."

"What? Kwan Ang himself?"

"Yes."

"Which way did he go?"

"Outside the store I saw him turn left. If you hurry you can find him. He's carrying a yellow bag with my store's name on it. He— Wait, sir. My money!"

But Li was sprinting out of the store.

Outside, he turned to the left and jogged down the street. He looked around frantically. Then, about a hundred meters away he saw a man of medium build, with short, dark hair, carrying a yellow shopping bag. His gait was familiar; Li remembered it from the ship. Yes, Li thought, his heart stuttering with excitement, it's the Ghost.

He supposed he should try to call Loaban or Hongse. But he couldn't risk the man's escaping. Li started after him, gripping the pistol in his pocket.

Sprinting, breathless, he closed the distance quickly. He was gasping loudly and as he got nearer, the Ghost paused. As he started to look behind him Li ducked behind a Dumpster. When he looked out again the snakehead was continuing through the deserted alley.

In Liu Guoyuan, Sonny Li had a pale blue uniform, white gloves and a hat with a patent-leather brim. But here he looked like a busboy. He had nothing on him to indicate that he was working with the New York Police Department and Lincoln Rhyme. He was concerned that if someone saw him arrest the Ghost they would think that he himself was an attacker, a bandit, and the police would arrest *him*, and the snakehead would escape in the confusion.

And so Li decided to take the man here, in the deserted alley.

When the Ghost turned down one more alley, Li made certain that no one was around and simply sprinted forward as fast as he could run, the pistol outstretched in his hand.

Before the snakehead realized he was being pursued, Sonny Li was on him, grabbing his collar and shoving his gun into the man's back.

The killer dropped the yellow bag and started to reach under his shirt. But Li pressed his gun against the Ghost's neck. "Don't move." He took a large pistol from his prisoner's belt and slipped it into his own pocket. Then he roughly spun the snakehead around to face him. "Kwan Ang," he intoned then recited the familiar incantation: "I'm arresting you for violation of the organic laws of the People's Republic of China."

But as he was about to continue the litany and present the particular offenses Li's voice faded. He glanced at the neck of the Ghost's shirt, which had been tugged open as he'd reached for his pistol.

Li saw a white bandage taped to the man's chest.

And dangling from a leather cord around the Ghost's neck was a soapstone amulet in the shape of a monkey.

Chapter Forty

His eyes wide in shock, Sonny Li stepped back, holding the pistol level at the Ghost's face.

"You, you . . ." he stammered.

His thoughts were jammed as he tried to figure out what was happening. Finally he whispered, "You killed John Sung at the beach and you took his papers and the stone monkey. You've been pretending to be him!"

The Ghost looked at him carefully. Then he smiled. "We've both been doing some masquerading, it looks like. You were one of the piglets on the *Fuzhou Dragon*." He nodded. "Waiting to get me on U.S. soil to arrest me and turn me over to the police here."

Li understood what the man had done. He'd stolen the red Honda from the restaurant on the beach. Loaban and the police assumed he'd driven it to the city. But, no, he'd stuffed Sung's body into the trunk and hidden it near the beach—where no one would think to look for it. Then he'd given himself a superficial wound with his own gun and swum back into the ocean, awaiting rescue by the police and the INS, who helpfully transported him into the city themselves—first to the hospital and then to the immigration hearing officer.

Ten judges of hell, Li thought again. Hongse had no clue that the "doctor" was the snakehead himself. "You were using the policewoman to find out where the Changs and the Wus were."

He nodded. "I needed information. She was happy to provide it." The Ghost now examined Li more closely. "Why did you do this, little man? Why did you come all the way after me?"

"You killed three people in Liu Guoyuan, my town."

"Did I? I don't remember. I was there a year ago, I think. Why did I kill them? Maybe they deserved it."

Sonny Li was appalled that the man didn't even remember the deaths. "No, you and a little snakehead started shooting. You killed three bystanders."

"Then it was an accident."

"No, it was murder."

"Well, listen, little man, I'm tired and I don't have much time. The police are close to finding the Changs and I have to get there first and then get out of this country and go home. So, one hundred thousand one-color," the Ghost said. "I can give it to you in cash right now."

"I'm not like most of the security bureau officers you're used to."

"You mean you're *more* greedy? Then two hundred thousand." The Ghost laughed. "You would have to work for a hundred years to make that much money in Liu Guoyuan."

"You are under arrest."

The smile on the Ghost's face faded, realizing that he was serious. "This will go badly for your wife and children if you don't let me go."

Li growled, "You will lie down on your belly. Now."

"All right. An honorable and honest security bureau officer. I am surprised. . . . What's your name, little man?"

"My name is not your concern."

The Ghost knelt on the cobblestones.

Li decided to use his shoelaces to tie the Ghost's wrists. He then—

Suddenly Li realized in shock that the shopping bag was between them and that the Ghost's right hand had disappeared behind it.

"No!" he shouted.

The Lucky Hope Shop bag exploded toward Li as the Ghost fired through it with a second gun he had hidden in an ankle holster or his sock.

The bullet zipped past Li's hip. He raised his hand in an automatic gesture, flinching. But by the time he was thrusting his own pistol forward the snakehead had knocked it from his hand. Li grabbed the

Ghost's wrist and tried to pull the Model 51 from his fingers. Together they tumbled to the slick cobblestones and this gun too fell to the ground.

Desperately, they clutched at each other, clawing and striking when they could but mostly wrestling and trying to reach one of the weapons that lay on the cobblestones near them. The Ghost slammed his palm into Li's face and stunned him then spun away, struggling to pull the Glock from the cop's pocket.

Li recovered quickly and tackled the Ghost, knocking this weapon too to the ground. The cop's knee struck the killer's back and knocked the breath out of him. Still facing away from Li, the Ghost, gasping and moaning in pain, struggled to his knees. Li's arm remained around the snakehead's throat in a choke hold.

Unstoppable, the Ghost struggled toward the pistol.

Stop him, stop him, Li raged to himself. He's the man who would kill Hongse, the man who would kill the Changs.

Who would kill Loaban too.

Stop him!

He seized the leather thong around the Ghost's neck, the one that held the stone monkey amulet and began to pull hard. The leather tightened. The Ghost's hands flailed uselessly and from his throat came a gurgling noise. The snakehead began to quiver. His heels were nearly off the ground.

Let go, Sonny Li told himself. Arrest him. Don't murder him.

But he didn't let go. He pulled harder and harder.

Until the leather snapped.

The monkey figurine fell to the ground and shattered. Li stumbled backward, falling hard into the alley, striking his head on the cobblestones. He nearly passed out.

Judges of hell . . .

The cop could faintly see the Ghost, also on his hands and knees, gasping and coughing, holding his throat with one hand as his other patted the ground for a weapon.

An image came into Li's mind: His stern father reprimanding him for some foolish comment.

Then another one: The bodies of the Ghost's victims in Li's town in China, lying bloody on the sidewalk in front of the café.

And he pictured another terrible sight, one that had not yet happened:

Hongse dead, lying in darkness. Loaban too, his face as still in death as his body had been in life.

Sonny Li rolled to his knees and began crawling toward his enemy.

The crime scene bus left twenty-foot skid marks on the Chinatown street, which was slick with runoff from the melting ice from bins at a nearby fish market.

Amelia Sachs, her face grim, jumped out, accompanied by INS agent Alan Coe and Eddie Deng. They ran through the pungent alleyway toward the cluster of uniformed officers from the Fifth Precinct. The men and women stood casually, looking as matter-of-fact as police always did at crime scenes.

Even scenes of homicides.

Sachs slowed and gazed down at the body.

Sonny Li was lying on his stomach on the filthy cobblestones. Eyes partially open, palms flat beside him, level with his shoulders, as if he were about to start a series of push-ups.

Sachs paused, filled with the desire to drop to her knees and grip the man's hand. She'd walked the grid many times in the years she'd worked with Rhyme, but this was her first scene involving a fellow cop—fellow cop and, she could now say, friend.

A friend too of Rhyme's.

Still, she resisted the temptation toward sentiment. This was, after all, a crime scene no different from any other and, as Lincoln Rhyme often pointed out, one of the worst contaminants at scenes was careless cops.

Look past it, ignore who the victim is. Remember Rhyme's advice: Give up the dead.

Well, that'd be damn tough to do. For both of them. But for Lincoln Rhyme especially. Sachs had noticed that in the past two days Rhyme had formed an improbable bond with this man, as close as he'd come to a friendship since she'd known him. She was now aware of the painful silence of a thousand conversations never to occur, of a thousand laughs never to be shared.

But then she thought of someone else: Po-Yee, soon to be another victim of the man who'd committed this crime, if they didn't find him. And so Sachs put the pain away, the same way she closed and locked the storage box in which her Colt .45 competition shooting pistol rested.

"We did what you wanted," said another officer, a detective in a gray suit. "Nobody got closer'n this. Only the EMS tech was in." A nod toward the body. "He's DCDS."

Cop initials perfunctorily signifying the category of lifelessness: deceased confirmed dead at the scene.

Agent Coe walked slowly up to her. "I'm sorry," the agent said, running his hand through his scarlet hair. There seemed to be little genuine sadness in his voice, however.

"Yeah."

"He was a good man."

"Yes, he was." She said this bitterly, thinking: And he was a hell of a better cop than you are. If you hadn't fucked up yesterday we'd've gotten the Ghost. Sonny would still be alive and Po-Yee and the Changs would be safe.

She motioned to the cops. "I've got to run the scene. Could I have everybody out of here?"

Oh, man, she thought, dismayed at what she now had to do—though she was anticipating not of the difficult and sad task of searching the scene but of something far more arduous.

She pulled her headset on and plugged it into her radio.

Okay. Just go ahead. Do it.

She made the call to Central and was patched through to the phone.

A click.

"Yes?" Rhyme asked.

She said, "I'm here."

A pause then: "And?"

She sensed him trying to keep hope out of his voice.

"He's dead."

The criminalist gave no response for a moment. "I see."

"I'm sorry, Lincoln," she said softly.

Another pause and he said, "No first names, Sachs. Bad luck, remember?" His voice nearly caught. "All right. Get going. Run the scene. Time's running out for the Changs."

"Sure, Rhyme. I'm on it."

She quickly dressed in the Tyvek suit and went about processing the scene. Sachs did the fingernail scrapings, the substance samples, the ballistics, the footprints, the shell casings, the slugs. She took the pictures, she lifted prints.

But she felt she was just going through the motions. Come on, she snapped at herself. You're acting like you're some damn rookie. We don't have time to just collect evidence. Think about Po-Yee, think about the Changs. Give Rhyme something he can work with. Think!

She turned back to the body and processed it more carefully, considering everything that she found, demanding in her mind that every bit of evidence explain itself, offer an explanation of where it had come from, what it might mean.

One of the uniformed officers walked up to her but seeing her stony face he retreated quickly.

A half hour later she'd finished bagging everything, written her name on the chain of custody cards and assembled the evidence.

She made another call to the criminalist.

"Go ahead," Rhyme said grimly. How it hurt to hear the pain in his voice. For years she'd heard so much flat emotion, so much lethargy, so much resignation. That had been tough but it didn't compare to the pain now in Rhyme's voice.

"He was shot three times in the chest but we've got four casings. One casing's from a Model 51, probably the one we saw before. The others are .45. He was killed with that one, it looks like. Then I found the Walther that Sonny was carrying. There was trace on his leg—yellow paper flecks and some kind of dried plant material. And there was a pile of the same material on the cobblestones."

"What's your scenario, Sachs?"

"I think Sonny spots the Ghost leaving a store, carrying something in a yellow bag. Sonny follows him. He collars him in the alley here and gets the Ghost's new gun, the .45. He assumes that's his only weapon. Sonny relaxes and tells the Ghost to get onto the ground. But the Ghost pulls out his backup—the Model 51—and shoots through the bag, spattering the plant material and flecks of paper on Sonny. The bullet misses but the Ghost jumps him. There's a fight. The Ghost gets the .45 and kills Sonny."

"Because," Rhyme said, "the yellow paper and the plant material were on Sonny's legs—meaning the Ghost had the Model 51 in an ankle holster and fired low. The gunshot residue was high on his body—from the .45."

"That's what it looks like."

"And how do we *use* that scenario?"

"Wherever the Ghost bought that stuff that was in the bag, a clerk might know him and have an idea where he lives."

"You want to canvass all the stores near there to see who has yellow bags?"

"No, that'd take too long. It'd be better to find out what the plant material is first."

"Bring it in, Sachs. Mel'll run it through the chromatograph."

"No, I've got a better idea," she said. A glance at Sonny Li's body. She forced herself to look away. "It's probably herbs or spices. I'm going to stop by John Sung's apartment with a sample of it. He should be able to tell me right away what it is. He only lives a few blocks from here."

V

All in
Good Time

———◆◆◆———

Wednesday, the Hour of the Rooster, 6:45 P.M.,
to Monday, the Hour of the Monkey, 3 P.M.

To effect capture . . . the opponent's men must be
entirely encircled without any adjacent places vacant. . . .
Exactly as in war, when a post is surrounded, the soldiers are taken prisoner by the enemy.

　　　　　　　　　　　　　　　—The Game of Wei-Chi

Chapter Forty-one

He stared out the window at the gray dusk, premature because of the lingering storm. His head drooped forward, heavy, heavy, immobile. This wasn't from damaged fibers of nerve but from sorrow. Rhyme was thinking of Sonny Li.

When he'd run the forensic unit he'd had the chance to hire dozens, probably hundreds of employees and to finagle—or bully—onto his staff men and women from other assignments because he knew they were damn good cops. He couldn't tell exactly what appealed to him about these people. Oh, sure they had the textbook qualifications: persistence, intelligence, patience, stamina, keen powers of observation, empathy.

Yet there was another quality. Something that Rhyme, for all his rational self, couldn't define, though he recognized it immediately. There was no better way to say it than the desire—even the joy—of pursuing a prey at all costs. Whatever else Sonny Li's failings—his cigarettes at crime scenes, his reliance on omens and the woo-woo factor, he had this essential aspect. The lone cop had traveled literally to the ends of the earth to collar his suspect. Rhyme would've traded a hundred eager rookies and a hundred cynical veterans for one cop like Sonny Li: a small man who wanted nothing more than to offer to the citizens on his beat some retribution for the harms done to them, some justice, some comfort in the aftermath of evil. And for his reward Li was content to enjoy a good hunt, a challenge and, perhaps, just a little respect from those he cared about.

He glanced at the book he'd inscribed to Li.

To my friend . . .

"Okay, Mel," he said evenly. "Let's put this one together. What've we got?"

Mel Cooper was hunched over the plastic bags the patrolman had raced here from the crime scene in Chinatown. "Footprints."

"We sure it was the Ghost?" Rhyme asked.

"Yep," Cooper confirmed. "They're identical." Looking at the electrostatic prints that Sachs had taken.

Rhyme agreed they were the same.

"Now the slugs." He was examining the two bullets, one flattened, one intact, both bloody. "Check the lands and grooves."

This referred to the angular marks left in the soft lead bullet by the rifling in the barrel of the gun—the spiral grooves that spin the slug to make it go faster and more accurately. By examining the number of grooves and the degree of the twist, a ballistics expert can often determine the type of gun the shooter used.

Cooper, wearing latex gloves, measured the undamaged slug and the marks cut in the side from the rifling. "It's a forty-five ACP. Octagonal profile on the lands and grooves, right-hand twist. I'm guessing one complete twist every fifteen, sixteen inches. I'll look that up and—"

"Don't bother," Rhyme said shortly. "It's a Glock." The unsexy but dependable Austrian pistols were increasingly popular throughout the world, among criminals and police alike. "What's the wear on the barrel?"

"Sharp profile."

"So it's new. Probably the G36." He was surprised. This compact but extremely powerful handgun was expensive and wasn't widely available yet. In the United States you found it mostly among federal agents.

Useful, useful? he wondered.

Not yet. All it told them was the type of gun, not where the weapon or the ammunition had been purchased. Still, it was evidence and it belonged on the board.

"Thom . . . Thom!" Rhyme shouted. "We need you!"

The aide appeared immediately. "There're other things I need—"

"No," Rhyme said. "There *aren't* other things. Write."

The aide must have sensed Rhyme's despondency over the death of Sonny Li and said nothing in response to the sharp command. He picked up the marker and walked to the whiteboard.

Cooper then opened Li's clothes over a large sheet of clean, blank newsprint. He dusted the items of clothing with a brush and examined the trace that had fallen onto the paper. "Dirt, flecks of paint, the yellow paper particles that probably were from the bag and the dried plant material—spices or herbs—that Amelia mentioned," Cooper said.

"She's checking out the plant stuff right now. Just bag them and put them aside for the time being." Rhyme, who over the years had grown immune to the horror of crime scenes, nonetheless felt a pang as he looked at the dark blood on Li's clothing. The same clothing he'd worn in this very room not long ago.

Zaijian, Sonny. Goodbye.

"Fingernail scrapings," Cooper announced, examining the label on another plastic bag. He mounted the trace on a slide in the compound microscope.

"Project it, Mel," Rhyme said and turned to the computer screen. A moment later a clear image appeared on the large flat screen. What do we have here, Sonny? You fought with the Ghost, you grabbed him. Was there anything on his clothes or shoes that was transferred to you?

And if so, will it send us to his front door?

"Tobacco," the criminalist said, laughing sadly, thinking of the cop's addiction to cigarettes. "What else do we see? What are those minerals there? What do you think, Mel? Silicates?"

"Looks like it. Let's run some through the GC/MS."

The gas chromatograph/mass spectrometer would determine exactly what the substance was. Soon the results came back—magnesium and silicate.

"That's talc, right?"

"Yep."

The criminalist knew that talcum powder was commonly used by some people as a deodorant, by workers who wore tight-fitting rubber gloves for protection and by those who engaged in certain sexual practices using latex clothing. "Go online and find out everything you can about talc and magnesium silicate."

"Will do."

As Cooper was typing madly, Rhyme's phone rang. Thom answered it and put the call on the speaker.

"Hello?" he asked.

"Mr. . . . Rhymes please."

"Rhyme is the name, yes. Who's this?"

"Doctor Arthur Winslow at Huntington Medical Center."

"Yes, Doctor?"

"There's a patient here, a Chinese man. His name is Sen. He was medevaced to us after the Coast Guard rescued him from a sunken ship off the North Shore."

Not *exactly* the Coast Guard, Rhyme thought. But he said, "Go ahead."

"We were told to contact you with any news about him."

"That's right."

"Well, I think there's something you ought to know."

"And what would that be?" Rhyme asked slowly, though his meaning was really: Get to the point.

He sipped the bitter coffee even though he hated it.

Seventeen-year-old William Chang sat in the back of the Starbucks not far from the family's apartment in Brooklyn. He wanted Po-nee tea— made the way his mother prepared it, brewed in an old iron pot—but he kept drinking the coffee as if he were addicted to the muddy, sour drink. Because that is what the pompadoured *ba-tu* across from him was now sipping; for William to drink tea would seem like a weakness.

Wearing the same black leather jacket he'd been in yesterday, the kid—who'd identified himself only as Chen—finished his conversation on a tiny Nokia phone and clipped the unit back onto his belt. He made a point of checking the time on his gold Rolex.

"What happened to the gun we sold you yesterday?" he asked in English.

"My father found it."

"Asshole." He leaned forward ominously. "You didn't tell him where you got it?"

"No."

"If you told anyone about us we'll kill you."

William Chang, hardened by his life as a dissident's son, knew not to give an inch with people like this. "I didn't fucking tell anybody anything. But I need another gun."

"He'll find that one too."

"No, he won't. I'll keep it with me. He won't frisk me."

Chen eyed a long-haired Chinese girl nearby. When he saw she was reading what seemed to be a college textbook he lost interest. He looked William up and down and then asked, "Hey, you want a DVD player? A Toshiba. It's sweet. Two hundred. A flat-screen TV? Eight hundred."

"I want a gun. That's all I want."

"And why don't you get some better clothes. You look like shit."

"I'll get clothes later."

"Hugo Boss, Armani. I can get you whatever you want. . . ." Sipping the coffee, he studied William closely. "Or you can come with us some night. We're going to a warehouse in Queens next week. They're getting a shipment in. Can you drive?"

"Yeah, I can drive." William looked out the front window. He saw no sign of his father.

The *ba-tu* asked, "You got balls, don't you?"

"I guess."

"Your triad hijack anything in Fujian?"

William didn't exactly have a triad, just some friends who would occasionally steal cars and shoplift liquor and cigarettes from time to time.

"Hell, we hit dozens of places."

"What was *your* job?"

"Lookout, getaway."

Chen thought for a moment then asked, "Okay, we're inside a warehouse and you're on guard, you know. You see a security guard coming toward us. What would you do? Would you kill him?"

"What is this, a fucking test?"

"Just answer. You have the balls to kill him?"

"Sure. But I wouldn't."

"Why not?"

William sneered. "Because only an idiot would get executed over some clothes."

"Who said clothes?"

"You did," William replied. "Armani, Boss."

"Well, there's a guard. Answer me. What the fuck would you do?"

"I'd come up behind him, take his gun away and I'd keep him on his belly till you had all the clothes in the get-away wheels. Then I'd piss on him."

Chen frowned. "Piss on him? Why?"

"Because the first thing he'd do was go change his clothes—before he called the police. So the cops wouldn't think he'd peed his pants. That'd give us time to get away. And he never got hurt so the cops couldn't get us for assault."

This is what William had heard that some gang by the waterfront near Fuzhou had done once.

Chen wouldn't allow himself to be impressed. But he said, "You'll come to Queens with us. I'll meet you here tomorrow night. I'll bring some people."

"I'll see. I have to get back now. My father'll notice I'm gone." He took a wad of dollars from his pocket, flashed it at the *ba-tu*. "What do you have?"

"I sold you the only good one I had," Chen said. "That chrome baby."

"It was a piece of shit. I want a real gun."

"You *do* have balls. But you got a mouth too. You better watch it. All I've got is a Colt .38. Take it or leave it."

"Loaded?"

Chen fiddled with the gun inside the bag.

"Three rounds."

"That's all?" William asked.

"Like I said—take it or leave it."

"How much?"

"Five hundred."

William laughed harshly. "Three or I walk."

Chen hesitated then nodded. "Only 'cause I like you."

Both young men glanced around the Starbucks. The bag was exchanged for the money.

Without a word William rose. Chen said, "Tomorrow. Eight. Here."

"I'll try."

Chen laughed. "'Piss on him.'" He turned back to his coffee.

Outside, William started quickly down the sidewalk away from Starbucks.

The figure stepped out of the alley, moving quickly toward him.

William stopped, startled. Sam Chang walked up to his son.

The boy started walking again, fast, head down.

"Well?" Chang asked, falling into place beside the boy.

"I got it, Baba."

"Give it to me," his father said.

He passed his father the bag, which disappeared into the man's pocket. "You didn't tell him your name?"

"No."

"You didn't mention the Ghost or the *Dragon?*"

"I'm not stupid," William snapped. "He doesn't have any idea who we are."

They walked in silence for a few minutes.

"Did he charge you all the money?"

William hesitated and began to say something. Then he dug into his pocket and handed his father back the remaining hundred dollars of the cash his father had given him for the gun.

As they approached the house he said to his son, "I'm going to put it in the front closet. We'll use it only if the Ghost tries to get inside. Never take it with you anywhere. Understand?"

"We should each get one and carry it."

"Do you understand?" Chang repeated firmly.

"Yes."

Chang touched his son's arm. "Thank you, son. It was a brave thing to do."

You do *have balls.* . . .

"Yeye would be proud of you," his father added.

William nearly said, Yeye would be still be alive if it weren't for you. But he remained silent. They arrived at their front door. Chang and William looked around. No one had followed them from the coffee shop. They pushed quickly inside.

As Chang hid the gun on the top shelf of the closet—where only he and William could reach it—the boy dropped into the couch next to his brother and the baby girl. He picked up a magazine and thumbed through it.

But he paid little attention to the articles. He was thinking about what Chen had asked him. Should he meet with the other members of the triad tomorrow night?

He didn't think he would. But he wasn't sure. It was never a bad idea, he'd learned, to keep your options open.

Chapter Forty-two

John Sung had changed clothes. He was wearing a turtleneck sweater—which seemed odd in the heat, though it made him look pretty stylish—and new workout pants. He was flushed and he seemed distracted, out of breath.

"Are you all right?" Amelia Sachs asked.

"Yoga," he explained. "I was doing my exercises. Tea?"

"I can't stay long." Eddie Deng had gone back to the Fifth Precinct but Alan Coe was waiting for her downstairs in the crime scene bus.

He held up a bag. "Here's what I wanted to give you. The fertility herbs I told you about last night."

She took the bag absently. "Thank you, John."

"What's wrong?" he asked, scanning her troubled face. He motioned her inside and they sat on the couch.

"That police officer from China, the man who helped us? He was found dead about an hour ago."

Sung closed his eyes for a moment and sighed. "Was it an accident? Or did the Ghost get to him?"

"The Ghost."

"Oh, no, I'm sorry."

"I am too." She said this brusquely, dismissing the emotion in the best spirit of Lincoln Rhyme. She reached into her pocket and withdrew a plastic bag of the plant material she'd found at the scene. "We found this where he was murdered."

"Where?" he asked.

"In Chinatown. Not far away. We think it's some herbs or spices that the Ghost bought. Rhyme was hoping if we can figure out what it is we might find the store where he bought it. Maybe one of the clerks might know where the Ghost lives."

He nodded. "Let me see it." Sung opened the bag, then shook some out onto the counter. He bent down, inhaled the aroma and examined the substance. She thought Lincoln Rhyme would use a gas chromatograph and mass spectrometer to do exactly the same thing, separating a mixture into its component parts and identifying them.

Finally he said, "I smell astragalus, ginger, poria, maybe some ginseng and alisma." He shook his head. "I know you'd like me to tell you it's sold in only one or two stores. But I'm afraid you can buy it at any herbalist, drugstore or grocery in China. I would suppose it's the same here."

Discouraged, she thought of something else. "What do they do?" Maybe the Ghost was suffering from some sickness or injury and they could trace him through other doctors as they'd done with Wu Qichen's wife.

"It's more of an over-the-counter tonic than a medicine. It improves resistance, tonifies your *qi*. Many people use it to heighten the sexual experience. Supposedly it helps men stay erect longer. It's not meant to treat a specific illness."

So much for that theory, Sachs thought glumly.

"You could check the stores closest to where the policeman was killed," Sung suggested. "But I suppose you've thought of that."

She nodded. "That's what we'll have to do. Maybe we'll get a break." She started to stand and winced as pain shot through her shoulder—a muscle she'd pulled on the *Fuzhou Dragon*.

"Taking your medicine?" he asked, chiding her.

"Yeah, I am. But you know how disgusting it tastes?"

"You can drink beer for pleasure. Here, sit down again."

She hesitated and lowered herself painfully to the couch. He moved close behind her. She could sense his proximity from the way the ambient noise in the room grew mute. Then she felt his hands on her shoulder as they began squeezing—softly at first then harder, more probing.

His face was near the back of her head, his breath caressing her neck. The hands moved up and down her skin, pressing hard but just short of the point of pain. It was relaxing, yes, but she felt momentarily disconcerted when the palms and fingers nearly encircled her throat.

"Relax," he whispered in that calm voice of his.

She tried to.

His hands slid to her shoulders then down her back. They moved forward along her ribs but stopped before he touched her breasts and returned again to her spine and neck.

Wondering if there really was something he could do for her—to improve the chance of her and Rhyme's having children.

Dryness in the kidneys . . .

She closed her eyes and lost herself in the powerful massage.

She felt him shift closer to her, getting better leverage, it seemed. He was only inches away. His hands moved up her spine to her neck once more, encircling them. His breathing was coming quickly—from the effort, she supposed.

"Why don't you take off that gun belt of yours?" he whispered.

"Bad karma?" she asked.

"No." He laughed. "It's interfering with your circulation."

She reached for the buckle and started to undo it. She felt his hand close around the thick nylon strap to help her remove it.

But then a harsh sound interrupted them—her cell phone ringing. She eased away from him and pulled the unit off her belt. "Hello? This is—"

"Sachs, get ready to roll."

"What do you have, Rhyme?"

There was no answer for a moment as she heard someone else in his room speaking to the criminalist.

A moment later he came back on the line. "The captain of the ship, Sen, is conscious. Eddie Deng's on the other line, interviewing him. . . . Hold on." Voices, shouts. Rhyme's commanding: "Well, we don't *have* time. Now, now, now! . . .Listen, Sachs, the captain spent some time in the hold of the *Dragon*. He overheard Chang talking with his father. Looks like some relative or friend arranged for an apartment and job for the family in *Brooklyn*."

"Brooklyn? What about Queens?"

"Sam Chang's the clever one, remember? I'm sure he said Queens to lead everybody off. I narrowed down the area where I think they are— Red Hook or Owls Head."

"How do you know?"

"How else, Sachs? The trace on the old man's shoes, biosolids.

Remember? There're two waste treatment facilities in Brooklyn. I'm leaning toward Owls Head. It's more residential and's closer to Sunset Park, the Chinese community there. Eddie Deng's having his people from the Fifth Precinct call printing companies and sign painters in Owls Head. Lon's putting ESU on alert. And the INS's getting together a team too. I want you over there. I'll let you know as soon as I have an address."

She glanced up at Sung. "John, Lincoln's found the Changs' neighborhood. I'm going over there now."

"Where are they?"

"In Brooklyn."

"Oh very good," he said. "They're safe?"

"So far."

"May I come? I can help translate. Chang and I speak the same dialect."

"Sure." Sachs said into the phone, "John Sung's coming with me and Coe. He's going to translate. We're on our way, Rhyme. Call me when you have an address."

They hung up and Sung stepped into the bedroom. A moment later he came out, wearing a bulky windbreaker.

"It's not cold out," Sachs said.

"Always keep warm—important for the *qi* and blood," he said.

Then Sung looked at her and took her by the shoulders, Sachs responding with a smile of curiosity. With sincerity in his voice he said, "You have done a very good thing, finding those people, Yindao."

She paused and looked at him with a faint frown of curiosity. "Yindao?"

He said, "It's my pet name for you in Chinese. 'Yindao.' It means 'close friend.'"

Sachs was very moved by this. She squeezed his hand. Then stepped back. "Let's go find the Changs."

On the street in front of his safehouse the man of many names—Ang Kwan, Gui, the Ghost, John Sung—reached his hand out and shook that of Alan Coe, who was, it seemed, an INS agent.

This gave him some concern, for Coe, he believed, had been part of a group of Chinese and American law enforcers pursuing him overseas. The task force had gotten close to him, troublingly close, but the Ghost's *bangshou* had done some investigating himself and learned that a young woman who'd worked in a company that the Ghost did business with had been giving the INS and the police information about his snakehead operations. The *bangshou* had kidnapped the woman, tortured her to find out what she'd told the INS and then buried her body in a construction site.

But apparently Coe had no idea what the Ghost looked like. The snakehead recalled that he'd been wearing the ski mask when they'd tried to kill the Wus on Canal Street; no one would have gotten a look at his face.

Yindao explained what Rhyme had learned and the three of them got into the police station wagon—Coe climbing into the back before the Ghost could take that strategically better seat, as if the agent didn't trust an illegal alien to be sitting behind him. They pulled away from the curb.

From what Yindao was telling Coe, the Ghost understood that there would be other cops and INS agents present at the Changs' apartment. But he'd already made plans to get a few minutes alone with the Changs. When Yindao had come to his apartment a few moments ago, Yusuf and another Uighur had been there. The Turks had slipped into the bedroom before the Ghost had opened the outer door and, later, when he'd gone to get his gun and windbreaker he'd told them to follow Yindao's police car. In Brooklyn the Turks and the Ghost together would kill the Changs.

Glancing back, he noticed that Yusuf's Windstar was close behind them, several cars away.

And what about Yindao? He might have to wait until tomorrow for their intimate liaison.

Naixin, he reflected.

All in good time.

Images of fucking her now filled his thoughts: he quickly lost himself in his continuing fantasies about Yindao, which had grown ever more powerful since he'd first seen her on the beach—swimming out to save him. Last night he'd given her only a chaste acupressure treatment, accompanied by some mumbo jumbo about it helping fertility. Their *next* get-together would be very different. He would take her to a place where he could play out all the fantasies that had been reeling through his thoughts.

Yindao, pinned beneath him, writhing, whimpering.

In pain.

Screaming.

He was now powerfully aroused and used the excuse of turning around to speak to Coe to hide the evidence of his desire. He began a conversation about the INS's guidelines for political asylum. The agent was blunt and rude and clearly disdainful, even of the man he thought the Ghost to be: a poor widower doctor, a dissident who loved freedom, seeking a better home for his family, harmless and willing to work hard.

Keep the piglets out of the country at all costs, the agent was saying. The message beneath his words was that they weren't fit to be Americans. The politics and morality of illegal immigration meant nothing to the Ghost but he wondered if Coe knew that there were proportionately fewer Chinese-Americans on welfare than any other nationality, including native-born whites. Did he know that the level of education was higher, the incidence of bankruptcy and tax evasion far lower?

It would give him pleasure to kill this man and he was sorry that he couldn't take the time to make it a long death.

The Ghost glanced at Yindao's legs and felt the churning low in his belly again. He recalled their sitting together in the restaurant yesterday, sharing his honest assessment of himself.

Break the cauldrons and sink the boats . . .

Why had he opened up to her in this way? It was foolish. She might have caught on as to who he was, or at least grown suspicious. He'd never been that frank with anyone in describing his philosophy of life.

Why?

The answer had to be more than his desire to possess her physically. He'd felt passion for hundreds of women but had kept most of his inner feelings to himself before, during and after the act. No, there was something else about Yindao. He supposed that it was this: he recognized something of his own soul within her. There were so few people who understood him . . . whom he could talk with.

But Yindao was this sort of woman, he believed.

As Coe was rambling on ad nauseam about the necessity of quotas and the burden on the social welfare rolls due to illegal immigration, even citing facts and figures, the snakehead was thinking about how sad it was that he couldn't take this woman back with him to show her the beauties of Xiamen, walk with her around Nanputou Temple—a huge Buddhist monastery—and then take her for peanut soup or noodles near the waterfront.

But there was no doubt that he wouldn't hesitate to do what he'd planned—take her to a deserted warehouse or factory and spend an hour or so fulfilling his relentless fantasy. And kill her afterward, of course. As Yindao herself had told him, she too would break the cauldrons and sink the boats; after she learned he was the Ghost she would not rest until she had killed or arrested him. She had to die.

The Ghost glanced back at Coe with a smile, as if acknowledging whatever the man was talking about. The snakehead focused past the agent. Yusuf and the other Uighur were staying right with the police car. Yindao had not noticed the van.

The Ghost turned back. His eyes swept over her. He then muttered a few words.

"What was that?" Yindao asked him.

"A prayer," the Ghost said. "I am hoping that Guan Yin will help us find the Changs' home."

"Who's that?"

"She's the goddess of mercy," was the answer, though it came not from the Ghost but from helpful Agent Alan Coe in the backseat.

Chapter Forty-three

Ten minutes later Lon Sellitto's phone rang.

Rhyme and Cooper stared at it rapt in anticipation.

The detective took the call. Listened. Then his eyes closed and he broke into a smile.

"They found the Changs' address!" he shouted and hung up. "That was one of the patrolmen down at the Fifth. He found a guy in Owls Head who owns two quick-print shops. Name's Joseph Tan. Our guy gave him the line about the family'd be dead in a couple hours if we didn't find out where they were. Tan broke down and admitted he'd gotten Chang and his kid a job and set 'em up in an apartment."

"He have an address?"

"Yep. Two blocks from the sewage treatment plant. God love crap, what can I say?"

Rhyme thought of Sonny Li's equally irreverent plea to the god of cops. *Guan Di, please let us find the Changs and catch the fuck Ghost.*

He wheeled into position in front of the whiteboards. He gazed at the chart, the pictures of evidence.

Sellitto said, "I'll call Bo and the INS and get everybody going."

But the criminalist said, "Hold on a minute."

"What's the matter?"

"An itch," Rhyme said slowly. "I have an itch." His initial exhilaration at locating the Changs faded.

Rhyme's head moved slowly from side to side as he took in Thom's careful jottings and photographs and other bits of evidence from this case—each adding to the whole grim story, like hieroglyphs in ancient Egyptian tombs.

He closed his eyes and let this information speed through his mind as fast as Amelia Sachs in her Camaro.

Here's the answer, Rhyme thought, opening his eyes once again and staring at the entries.

The only problem is that we don't know the question.

Thom appeared in the doorway. "Time for some ROMs," the aide said.

Range of motion exercises were important for quads. They kept the muscles from atrophying, they improved the circulation, they had a beneficial psychological effect too—which Rhyme publically disavowed. Still, his sessions were partially based on the premise that there would come a day when he himself would use his muscles again.

And so while he groused and complained and gave Thom hell when the aide expertly performed the ROMs then measured the results, he secretly looked forward to the daily exercises. Today, however, Rhyme cast a strong glance at the aide and the young man got the message. He retreated to the hallway.

"What're you thinking?" Sellitto asked.

Rhyme didn't answer.

Engaged in its own range of motion exercises, his mind, unlike his lifeless limbs, was limited by nothing. Infinite height, infinite depth, past and future. The criminalist now mentally followed the trails of evidence that they had collected while working the GHOSTKILL case, some of them as wide as the East River, some as narrow and frail as thread, some helpful, some as seemingly useless as the broken nerves that ran from Lincoln Rhyme's brain south into his still body. But even these he didn't neglect.

GHOSTKILL

Easton, Long Island, Crime Scene

· Two immigrants killed on beach; shot in back.

· One immigrant wounded—Dr. John Sung.

· "Bangshou" (assistant) on board; identity unknown.

   · Assistant confirmed as drowned body found near site where *Dragon* sank.

· Ten immigrants escape: seven adults (one elderly, one injured woman), two children, one infant. Steal church van.

· Blood samples sent to lab for typing.

   · Injured woman is AB negative. Requesting more information about her blood.

· Vehicle awaiting Ghost on beach left without him. One shot believed fired by Ghost at vehicle. Request for vehicle make and model sent out, based on tread marks and wheelbase.

   · Vehicle is a BMW X5.

   · Driver—Jerry Tang.

· No vehicles to pick up immigrants located.

· Cell phone, presumably Ghost's, sent for analysis to FBI.

   · Untraceable satellite secure phone. Hacked Chinese gov't system to use it.

· Ghost's weapon is 7.62mm pistol. Unusual casing.

   · Model 51 Chinese automatic pistol.

· Ghost is reported to have gov't people on payroll.

· Ghost stole red Honda sedan to escape. Vehicle locator request sent out.

   · No trace of Honda found.

· Three bodies recovered at sea—two shot, one drowned. Photos and prints to Rhyme and Chinese police.

   · Drowned individual identified as Victor Au, the Ghost's *bangshou*.

· Fingerprints sent to AFIS.

   · No matches on any prints but unusual markings on Sam Chang's fingers and thumbs (injury, rope burn?)

· Profile of Immigrants: Sam Chang and Wu Qichen and their families, John Sung, baby of woman who drowned, unidentified man and woman (killed on beach).

Stolen Van, Chinatown

· Camouflaged by immigrants with "The Home Store" logo.

· Blood spatter suggests injured woman has hand, arm or shoulder injury.

· Blood samples sent to lab for typing.

   · Injured woman is AB negative. Requesting more information about her blood.

· Fingerprints sent to AFIS.

   · No matches.

Jerry Tang Murder Crime Scene

· Four men kicked door in and tortured him and shot him.

· Two shell casings—match Model 51. Tang shot twice in head.

· Extensive vandalism.

· Some fingerprints.

   · No matches except Tang's.

· Three accomplices have smaller shoe size than Ghost, presumably smaller stature.

· Trace suggests Ghost's safehouse is probably downtown, in Battery Park City area.

· Suspected accomplices from Chinese ethnic minority. Presently pursuing whereabouts.

   · Uighurs from Turkestan Community and Islamic Center of Queens.

· Cell phone calls lead to 805 Patrick Henry Street, downtown.

Canal Street Shooting Crime Scene	Safehouse Shooting Crime Scene	*Fuzhou Dragon* Crime Scene	Sonny Li Murder Crime Scene

· Additional trace suggesting safehouse is in Battery Park City area.
 	
· Stolen Chevrolet Blazer, untraceable.
 	
· No match on prints.
 	
· Safehouse carpet: Arnold company's Lustre-Rite, installed in past six months; calling contractors to get list of installations.
 	
  · Locations of installations determined: 32 near Battery Park City.
 	
· Fresh gardening mulch found.
 	
· Body of Ghost's accomplice: ethnic minority from west or northwest China. Negative on prints. Weapon was Walther PPK.
 	
· Details on immigrants:
 	
  · The Changs: Sam, Mei-Mei, William and Ronald; Sam's father, Chang Jiechi and infant, Po-Yee. Sam has job arranged but employer and location unknown. Driving blue van, no make, no tag number. Changs' apartment is in Queens.
 	
  · The Wus: Qichen, Yong-Ping, Chin-Mei and Lang.
	· Fingerprints and photos Chang Jiechi's hands reveal father—and son Sam—are calligraphers. Sam Chang might be doing printing or sign painting. Calling stores and companies in Queens.
	
	· Biosolids on deceased's shoes suggest they live in neighborhood near sewage treatment plant.
	
	· Ghost uses feng shui practitioner to arrange his living space.
		· Ghost used new C4 to blow up ship. Checking origin of explosive through chemical markers.
		
		· Large quantity new U.S. bills found in Ghost's cabin.
		
		· Approx. $20,000 in used Chinese yuan found in cabin.
		
		· List of victims, air charter details and bank deposit information. Checking name of sender in China.
		
		· Captain alive but unconscious.
		
		  · Regained consciousness, now in INS detention.
		
		· Beretta 9mm, Uzi. Unable to trace.
			· Killed by new Glock 36, .45 caliber. (Gov't issue?)
			
			· Tobacco.
			
			· Flecks of yellow paper.
			
			· Unidentified plant material (herbs, spices, drugs?).
			
			· Magnesium silicate (talc) under fingernails.

The highway took a sweep around the Brooklyn Army facility and Yindao steered the police station wagon onto an exit ramp, about as fast as the Ghost himself would have taken the turn in his BMW or Porsche, and descended into a pleasant neighborhood of tidy yards and red-brick buildings.

The Ghost glanced into the side mirror casually and noticed that Yusuf was still behind them.

Then he looked at Yindao, the profile of her beautiful face, her shimmery red hair pinned into a bun, the outline of her breasts beneath her black T-shirt.

He was startled by the blare of the woman's phone ringing again.

She answered it.

"Rhyme . . . yeah, we're in the neighborhood. Go ahead." She fell silent. "Excellent!" She turned to the Ghost and Coe. "He's found them. A friend of Chang's got him an apartment and a job near here. It's not that far away." She turned her attention back to the phone. As she listened to what Rhyme was saying, though, the expression on her face grew momentarily dark. It seemed to the Ghost that she had tensed in reaction to whatever the man was now telling her. The Ghost wondered if Rhyme had learned something about him. He grew vigilant.

"Sure, Rhyme," she said finally. "Got it."

Yindao disconnected the call.

"Damn," Coe said. "I never thought he'd really be able to do it."

The Ghost looked at her. "So he got the exact address."

She didn't answer for a moment. Finally she said, "Yeah."

Then she began talking, just chatting like a schoolgirl, about her life in Brooklyn. The Ghost saw at once that this wasn't her nature and he grew even more suspicious. Whatever Rhyme had told her at the end of their conversation, he now understood, had nothing to do with the Changs.

He noticed her hand slip to her leg, which she scratched absently. She left her hand near her hip and he realized that the gesture was merely an excuse to move her hand to her gun.

With his eyes still on the road, the Ghost's hand now slipped casually to his side and then curled behind his back until it was touching the grip of his Glock pistol, which rested in the waistband of his workout slacks under the windbreaker.

Silence in the car as they drove for some minutes through residential streets. It seemed to the Ghost, though, that Yindao was merely driving in circles. He grew even more tense and cautious.

Another turn and, looking at the house numbers, she pulled up to the curb, put the car in park and set the brake. Pointing to a small brownstone apartment building.

"That's it."

The Ghost glanced quickly but kept his attention wholly on Yindao.

"Not the shithole I was expecting," Coe said cynically. "Let's go get this over with."

Yindao said casually, "Wait." And she turned to her right to look at Coe over the seat.

The Ghost could see easily that it was a feint. She moved fast—far faster than the Ghost had expected. Before the snakehead could even close his fingers around his own pistol, Yindao had swept hers from her holster and was swinging the gun toward him.

Chapter Forty-four

The Ghost involuntarily flinched, half-expecting Yindao to shoot him without warning—which is what he, of course, would have done had the circumstances been reversed.

But the muzzle of the black weapon traveled past him in a blur and came to rest on the man in the backseat.

"Not an inch, Coe. Don't move an inch. Keep your hands where I can see 'em."

"What . . . What is this?" Coe asked, rearing back in shock.

"Don't move," she snapped. "One hand disappears and you're dead."

"I don't—" The agent blinked.

"You understand me?"

"Yes, I fucking understand you," he spat out angrily. "You better tell me what this is all about."

"On the phone a minute ago? Lincoln had a little more to tell me than just directions to the Changs. He looked over the evidence a second time and made some phone calls. You thought you covered it up pretty well, didn't you?"

"Put that down, Officer! You can't—"

"He knows all about it. How *you're* the one working for the Ghost."

The agent swallowed. "Are you out of your fucking mind?"

"You're his guardian angel. You're protecting him. That's why you fired that shot at the Wus' place on Canal Street: you weren't trying to hit him.

You were trying to *warn* him. And you've been feeding him information—you told him the Wus were in the Murray Hill safehouse."

Coe looked around nervously, glancing outside. "This's bullshit."

The Ghost struggled to control his breathing. His hands shook. He was sweating furiously. He wiped his palms on his slacks.

"Don't worry, John," Yindao said to him. "He's not going to hurt anybody else." She continued speaking to the agent, "And you got the Ghost a nice new gun—a Glock. A new .45. Which happens to be the issue weapon in the INS."

"You're crazy, Officer."

"We've had reports all along that the Ghost was bribing people in the government over here. We just never thought it'd be an INS agent. Why all the trips to China, Coe? According to Peabody, none of the other field agents travel over there as much as you do. Sometimes apparently on your own nickel too. You were meeting your boss's snakeheads."

"Because my informant disappeared over there and I wanted to get the asshole who did it."

"Well, Rhyme's contacting the Fuzhou security bureau right now. He wants to look over the evidence in *that* case too."

"You're saying I killed my own informant? A woman with children?"

"We'll look at the evidence," she said coolly.

"If anybody said they ever saw us together, the Ghost and me, they're lying."

"That doesn't mean anything. He's not going to meet anybody in person who could testify against him. He's got intermediaries who do that."

"You're dreaming, Officer."

"No, we're just examining *evidence*," Yindao said. "Rhyme just ran your cell phone call record. A half dozen calls to a dead-letter answering service in New Jersey in the past two days."

"Oh, bullshit. I use that for my local CIs."

"You never mentioned running informants before."

"Because it didn't have anything to do with this case."

Yindao snapped, "Were you going to call the Ghost when we got to the Changs' apartment? Or were you just going to kill them yourself? . . . And us too?"

Coe swallowed. "I'm not saying another word to you. I want to talk to a lawyer."

"You'll have plenty of time for that. Now, right hand on the door handle. It moves off by one inch, I'll park one in your arm. Understand me?"

"Listen—"

"*Understand* me?"

The Ghost looked at her flinty eyes and felt a chill himself. He wondered if she hoped the man would reach for his gun so that she could shoot him.

"Yes," Coe muttered, furious.

"Left hand, thumb and index finger only, on your weapon, grip first. Move real slow."

Disgust on his face, Coe carefully removed the weapon and handed it to her.

Yindao pocketed it and then said, "Out of the car." She opened her door and stepped out. Then she opened his, the pistol unerringly targeted on the agent's chest. "Slow."

He followed her out. She gestured him around to the sidewalk.

"Face down."

The Ghost's heart—which had been pounding like a bird trapped in a glass case—calmed slowly.

Afraid, you can be brave . . .

This was the height of irony, he reflected. He did indeed have Americans on the take, even within the INS—a hearing officer included, which is why he'd been released so fast and easily yesterday morning. But he didn't know the names of everyone his agents had bribed here. And, as Yindao had just explained to Coe, he rarely had direct contact with any of them. As for knowing the location of the Wus' safehouse in Murray Hill— Yindao herself had given that information away when she'd asked if he wanted to join them there.

Since Coe was apparently working for him, should he now try to save the man?

No, better to cut him off. The arrest would be a good diversion. And Yindao and the others would be less cautious thinking they'd caught the traitor.

He watched as, on the sidewalk, she expertly cuffed the agent, holstered her weapon, then pulled Coe roughly to his feet. The Ghost rolled down his window and nodded toward the apartment. "Do you want me to talk to the Changs?"

"That's not their place," Yindao said. "It's still a few blocks from here. I lied—I had to keep Coe off guard. I picked it because there's a police precinct house around the corner. They're going to hold him for the FBI to pick up."

The Ghost looked Coe over and added a dismayed tone to his voice as he said, "You were going to tell the Ghost where they were. Those children . . . you were going to let him kill those children. You're despicable."

The agent stared back angrily for a moment—until Yindao roughly led him to the corner, where she was met by three uniformed officers, who took him into custody. The Ghost glanced behind him and saw, at the end of the block, Yusuf's van idling at the curb.

Five minutes later Yindao returned, climbed in the car, fired up the engine. They resumed their drive. She looked at the Ghost and shook her head with a grim laugh. "I'm sorry. Are you all right?" Although the incident had shaken her some, she now seemed more like herself. Relaxed and confident.

"Yes." The Ghost laughed too. "You handled that perfectly. You're quite an artist at your profession." His smile faded. "A traitor within the INS?"

"All that crap about the Ghost killing his informant. He suckered us." She picked up her cell phone and made a call. "Okay, Rhyme, Coe's in custody at the precinct. . . . No, no problems. John and I are going on to the Changs' now. . . . Where're the teams? . . . Okay, I'll be there in three minutes. We're not going to wait for ESU. The Ghost could be on his way there right now."

He could indeed, the snakehead reflected.

Yindao hung up.

So they would be there before everyone else. His liaison with Yindao would not have to wait after all. He'd kill the Changs, get Yindao into the Turks' van and escape. The Ghost's hand went to her shoulder and squeezed it. He felt his erection grow even more powerful.

"Thanks for coming along, John." She smiled at him. "What do I say, for 'friend,' *Yindao*'?"

He shook his head. "That's what a man would say to a woman. You would say, '*Yinjing.*'"

This was the word for male genitals.

"*Yinjing,*" she said.

"I'm honored," he said, bowing his head slightly. He looked over her red hair, her pale skin, her long legs . . . "Your friend Rhyme is quite a detective. I would like to visit him after all this is over."

"I'll give you a card. I have one in my purse."

"Good."

Rhyme would have to die too. Because the Ghost knew that he also was a man who would never stop until he'd defeated his enemies. *Po fu chen zhou. . . .* Break the cauldrons and sink the boats. Too dangerous to stay alive. She'd told him that he was paralyzed. How could one torture him, the Ghost wondered. His face, eyes, tongue . . . There would be ways, depending on how much time he had. Fire was always good.

Yindao turned abruptly down a one-way street and stopped. She examined the address numbers and then continued halfway down the block. She double-parked and left a police ID on the dashboard.

"That's the house there." She pointed to a three-story, redbrick house several doors away, the lights on in the ground-floor apartment. Modest but, the Ghost reflected, far more luxurious than the yellow-and-beige clapboard or cinder-block houses for which so many Chinese have Mao to thank.

They climbed out of the car and walked to the sidewalk, paused. "Stay out of sight," she whispered and led him close to a line of boxwood hedges. The Ghost glanced back. Yusuf had parked and, through the faint dusk light, the Ghost could just see him and the other Turk.

He leaned close and smelled scented soap on her skin and sweat. He found his arousal unabated and he pressed against her arm and hip as she examined the house. She nodded at the bay window in front. "We'll go through the back door—if it's unlocked. They'd be able to see us from the front and might run."

She gestured him to follow her around the back of the house nearest them, then together they cut through the backyards to the Changs'. They moved slowly, so they wouldn't knock into anything in the near-dark and announce their presence.

At the back door of the piglets' apartment they paused and Yindao looked into the window—at a small kitchen. No one was inside. "Always look through the back window first," she whispered. "My new police tactical rule." She smiled wistfully at this—though she didn't explain why.

"Come on," she said. "Move slow. Don't startle them. Tell them right away we're here to help. We want to protect them from the Ghost. And tell them there's a good chance for asylum."

The Ghost nodded and tried to imagine what their reaction would be when Sam Chang and his wife saw who the police translator was.

Yindao tried the door. It was unlocked. She pushed it open quickly—so it wouldn't squeak, he supposed.

How should he handle this? he wondered. He realized that he should probably debilitate Yindao immediately. She was too much of a risk merely to threaten. The best thing to do, he decided, was to shoot her in the leg—the back of her knee would be ironic, he decided, considering her arthritis. He and the Turks would kill the Changs. Then back to the Windstar. They would speed to a safehouse or a deserted warehouse somewhere, for his hours with Yindao.

They walked silently through the small, stifling kitchen.

On the stove a pot of water was heating. Half an onion sat on a cutting board, a bunch of parsley nearby. What, he wondered, had Mrs. Chang been making for dinner?

Yindao walked through the kitchen. She paused at the doorway of the corridor that led to the living room, gestured that he stop.

The Turks, he noticed, were outside, in the alley beside the house. Yindao's back was to him and he motioned them around to the front. Yusuf nodded and the two men moved off.

The Ghost decided that he would let Yindao precede him. Give her a minute or so inside the living room with the Changs to put them at ease and to give the Turks a chance to get in position at the front door. Then he would push inside and shoot her, which would be a signal for the Turks to break in and help him finish off the family.

Hanging back, the Ghost reached under his windbreaker and pulled his gun from the waistband of his workout slacks.

Alone, Yindao began to walk slowly into the dark corridor.

Chapter Forty-five

A sound nearby.

A footstep? wondered Sam Chang, sitting on his couch, next to his youngest son.

In the front? In the back?

They sat in the dim living room of their apartment, clustered around the television on which a talk show was playing. The volume was up but still Chang had clearly heard a noise.

A snap.

Yes, a footstep.

What *was* it?

A phoenix rising from ashes, a dragon angered that this heavy house had been built on his home?

The spirit of his father returning here to comfort them?

Perhaps to warn them.

Or maybe it was Gui, the Ghost himself, who had found them.

It's my imagination, Chang thought.

Except that he looked across the room and saw William, where he'd been reading a year-old auto magazine. The boy was sitting up, his neck lifted, head swiveling slowly, like a heron trying to identify the source of danger.

"What is it, husband?" Mei-Mei whispered, now seeing both their faces. She pulled Po-Yee to her.

Another click.

A footstep. He couldn't tell where it came from.

Sam Chang was on his feet quickly. William joined him. Ronald started to rise but his father waved the young boy into the bedroom. A firm nod at his wife. She gazed into his eyes for a moment then slipped into the bedroom with the toddler and youngest son and shut the door silently.

"Do what I told you, son."

William took his position beside the doorway that led to the back of the apartment, holding an iron pipe Chang had found in the backyard. Together father and son had planned what they would do if the Ghost came for them. Chang would shoot the first person through the door— either the Ghost or his *bangshou*. Hearing the shot, the others would probably hang back, giving William time to grab the fallen man's pistol, so he too would have a weapon.

Chang then shut off two of the lights in the living room so that he would not be so evident a target but could see the assailant in the doorway in silhouette. He'd shoot for the head; from here he couldn't miss.

Sam Chang crouched down behind a chair. He ignored his exhaustion from the ordeal on the ship, exhaustion from the loss of his father, exhaustion from the erosion of his soul in these two short days, and with his steady, calligrapher's hands, pointed the weapon at the doorway.

Inside the town house Amelia Sachs stepped forward slowly into the dark corridor.

"Wait here a minute, John," she whispered.

"Yes" came the faint reply.

She stepped into the corridor. Hesitated only a moment and then called, "Now."

"What?" the Ghost asked, hesitating.

But instead of responding she spun back toward him, raising her own pistol so quickly that the motion of the black weapon was a gray blur. The abyss of the muzzle settled steadily on the Ghost's chest before he could even lift his own Glock.

Sachs's utterance hadn't been directed to the Ghost at all, but to the half-dozen men and women in full combat gear—Bo Haumann and other Emergency Services Unit tactical cops—who pushed into the small kitchen. They rushed in from the back door and past her from the living room, guns pointed at the shocked Ghost's face, screaming their deafening litany, "Down, down, down, police, drop your weapon, on the floor, down!"

His pistol was torn from his hand and he was flung facedown to the floor and cuffed and frisked. He felt a tug at his ankle and the Model 51, his lucky gun, was lifted away, then his pockets emptied.

"We've got the subject down," an officer shouted. "Scene clear."

"Outside, we've got two, both down and locked." Meaning on their bellies with cuffs or plastic restraints on their wrists. These were the two men in the Windstar Sachs had spotted following them. More of the Uighurs from the cultural center in Queens, she'd assumed.

"Any other minders?" Sachs bent down and whispered harshly into the Ghost's ear.

"Any—"

"We've got the two men who were following us. Anybody *else*?"

The Ghost didn't answer and Sachs said into her radio, "I only noticed the one van. That's probably it."

Then Lon Sellitto and Eddie Deng joined her from upstairs, where they'd been waiting, out of the way of the takedown team. They looked the Ghost over as he lay on the floor, breathless from the shock and the rough treatment. Amelia Sachs thought he looked harmless—just a handsome but diminutive Asian man with slightly graying hair.

Sellitto's radio blared with the message, "Snipers One and Two to Base. Okay to stand down?"

He turned the squelch down on his Motorola and said, "Base to Snipers. That's a roger." The big detective added to the Ghost, "They had you in their sights from the minute you stepped out of the station wagon. If you'd aimed your weapon in her direction you'd be dead now. Lucky man."

They dragged the Ghost into the living room and pushed him into a chair. Eddie Deng read him his rights—in English, Putonghua and Minnanhua. Just to make sure.

He confirmed that he understood, with surprisingly little emotion, Sachs observed, considering the circumstances.

"How're the Changs?" Sachs asked Sellitto.

"They're fine. Two INS teams're at their apartment. It almost got ugly. The father'd got his hands on a gun and was ready to shoot it out but the agents spotted him through a window with a nightscope. They got the apartment's phone number and called to tell them that they were surrounded. As soon as Chang realized it was a legit INS team and not the Ghost he gave it up."

"The baby?"

"She's fine. Social worker's on the way. They're going to keep them at their place in Owls Head until we're through with this piece of shit." Nodding toward the Ghost. "Then we can go over there and debrief them."

The town house in which they now stood, about a mile from the Changs' was a neatly decorated place, full of flowers and tchotchkes: a surprise to Sachs, considering that it was inhabited by one of the city's best homicide detectives.

"So this's *your* house, Lon?" she asked, picking up a porcelain Little Bo Peep statuette.

"It's my better other's," he answered defensively, using the cop's pet name for Rachel, his girlfriend (he'd combined "better half" and "significant other," in a rare display of levity). They'd moved in together several months ago. "She inherited half of this stuff from her mother." He took the figurine from Sachs and replaced it carefully on the shelf.

"This was the best we could do for a takedown site on such short notice. We figured if we drove too far from Owls Head, the prick'd start to get suspicious."

"It was all fake," the Ghost said, amused. It seemed to Sachs that his English was better than the dialect he'd affected when he'd been portraying John Sung. "You set me up."

"Guess we did."

Lincoln Rhyme's call—as they'd been driving through Brooklyn, on their way to the Changs' real apartment in Owls Head—had been to tell Sachs that he now believed the Ghost was masquerading as John Sung. Another team of INS and NYPD cops was on their way to the Changs' real apartment to detain them. Sellitto and Eddie Deng were setting up a takedown site at Sellitto's house, where they could collar him without the risk of bystanders' getting killed in a shoot-out with the homicidal snakehead and capture any *bangshous* with him. Rhyme assumed that they would be following Sachs from the safehouse in Chinatown or else would be summoned by the snakehead via cell phone when they arrived at the Changs'.

As she'd listened to Rhyme's voice, it had taken all of Sachs's emotional strength to nod and pretend that Coe was working for the Ghost and that the man who was supposedly her friend, her doctor, the man sitting two feet from her and undoubtedly armed, wasn't the killer they'd been seeking for the past two days.

She thought too of the acupressure session last night—coming to him with her secret, with her desperate hope of being cured. She shivered with repulsion at the memory of his hands on her back and shoulders. She thought too with horror that she'd actually mentioned to him the location of the safehouse where the Wus were staying when she'd asked him if he wanted to join them.

The Ghost asked, "How did your friend, this Lincoln Rhyme, know that I wasn't Sung?"

She picked up the plastic bag containing the contents of the Ghost's pockets. Inside were the fragments of the shattered monkey amulet. Sachs held it close to his face.

"The stone monkey," she explained. "I found some trace under Sonny Li's fingernails. It was magnesium silicate, like talc. Rhyme found out that it came from soapstone—which is what the amulet's carved out of." Sachs reached out and roughly tugged down Ghost's turtleneck, revealing the red line from the leather cord. "What happened? He ripped it off your neck and it broke?" She released the cloth and stepped away.

The Ghost nodded slowly. "Before I shot him he was clawing the ground. I thought he was begging for mercy but then he looked up and smiled at me."

So Li had scraped some of the soft stone under his nails intentionally to tell them the Ghost was actually Sung.

Once Cooper's report on magnesium silicate told them that the substance might be soapstone Rhyme remembered the contamination on Sachs's hands yesterday. He realized that it might've come from Sung's amulet. He'd called the officers who'd guarded Sung's apartment and they'd confirmed that there was back entrance to the place, which meant that the Ghost had been able to come and go without their seeing him. He'd also asked if there was a gardening shop near the place—the likely source for the mulch that they'd found—and was told about the florist on the ground floor of the apartment building. Then he checked calls to Sach's cell phone; the number of the cell that'd been used to call the Uighur center showed up in her records.

The real John Sung had been a doctor and the Ghost was not. But, as Sonny Li had told Rhyme, everyone in China knew something about Eastern medicine. What the Ghost had diagnosed about Sachs and the herbs he'd given her were common knowledge among anyone who'd been treated regularly by a Chinese doctor.

"And your friend from the INS?" the Ghost asked.

"Coe?" Sachs replied. "We knew he didn't have any connection with you. But I had to pretend Coe was the spy—we needed to make sure you didn't think we were on to you. And we needed him out of the way. If he'd found out who you were he might've gone after you again—like he did on Canal Street. We wanted a clean takedown. And we didn't want him to go to jail for killing someone." Sachs couldn't resist adding, "Even you."

The Ghost merely smiled calmly.

When she'd handed Coe over to the three cops from the precinct house, she'd explained to him what was going on. The agent, of course, had been shocked to have been sitting inches from the man who'd killed his informant in China and had begun to complain angrily that he wanted to be part of the takedown. But the order to keep him in protective custody had been issued by One Police Plaza and he wasn't going anywhere until the Ghost was in custody.

Then she looked him over. Shook her head in disgust. "You shot Sung, hid the body, then shot yourself. And swam back into the ocean. You nearly drowned."

"I didn't have much choice, did I? Jerry Tang abandoned me. There was no way I was going to escape from the beach without masquerading as Sung."

"What about your gun?"

"Stuffed it into my sock in the ambulance. Then I hid it in the hospital and picked it up after the INS officer released me."

"INS officer?" she mused, nodding. "You *did* get released awfully fast." The Ghost said nothing and she added, "Well, that's something else we'll look into." Then she asked, "Everything you told me about John Sung . . . you made it up?"

The Ghost shrugged. "No, what I told you about him was true. Before I killed him I made him tell me about himself, about everyone who was on the raft, about Chang and Wu. Enough so I could make my performance believable. I threw out his picture ID and kept the wallet and the amulet."

"Where's his body?"

Another placid smile was his response.

His serenity infuriated her. He was caught—and was going to jail for the rest of his life and might possibly be executed but he looked as if he were only being inconvenienced by a late train. Fury seized her and she drew back her hand to strike him in the face. But when he gave no reaction—no cringe, no squint—she lowered her arm, refusing to give him the satisfaction of stoically withstanding the blow.

Sachs's ringing phone intruded. She stepped away and answered. "Yes?"

"Everyone having *fun?*" Rhyme's voice demanded sarcastically.

"I—"

"Having a picnic maybe? Taking in a movie? Forgetting about the rest of us?"

"Rhyme, we were in the middle of a takedown."

"I suppose somebody was going to call me *eventually* and let me know what happened. At some point . . . No, I won't, Thom. I'm pissed off."

"We've been a little busy here, Rhyme," she answered.

"Just wondering what was going on. I'm not psychic, you know."

She knew he'd already heard that none of their team was injured—otherwise he wouldn't be riddling her with sarcasm.

She responded, "You can stow the attitude—"

"'Stow'? Spoken like a true sailor, Sachs."

"—because we caught him." She added, "I tried to get him to tell me where John Sung's body is but he—"

"Well, we can figure that out, Sachs, can't we? It *is* obvious, after all."

To some people maybe, she reflected, though she was delighted to hear his characteristic barbs, rather than the flat-line voice of earlier.

The criminalist continued, "In the trunk of the stolen Honda."

"And that's still out on the eastern end of Long Island?" she asked, understanding finally.

"Of course. Where else would it be? The Ghost stole it, killed Sung and then drove *east* to hide it—we wouldn't look that direction. We'd assume he headed west—into the city."

Sellitto hung up his phone and pointed to the street.

Sachs nodded and said, "I've got to go see some people, Rhyme."

"See some people? See, you *are* treating this like a goddamn picnic. Who?"

She considered for a moment and said, "Some friends."

Chapter Forty-six

She found the family standing outside a run-down house near Owls Head Park. The smell of sewage was heavy in the air—from the treatment plant that had both betrayed them and saved their lives.

None of the family was in handcuffs and Sachs was pleased at that. She was also pleased that two uniformed NYPD police were chatting good-naturedly with the boy who must've been the Changs' youngest son.

His father, Sam Chang, stood with his arms crossed, grim and silent, head down, as an Asian-American man in a suit, an INS agent, she assumed—talked with him, jotting notes.

At his side was an unhappy, stolid woman in her forties, holding the hand of Po-Yee. Sachs felt a huge thud within her when she saw the Treasured Child. The toddler was adorable. A round-faced girl with silky black hair cut in bangs and short on the sides. She wore red corduroy jeans and a Hello Kitty sweatshirt that was about two sizes too big for her.

A detective recognized Sellitto and walked up to him and Sachs. "The family's fine. We're taking them to INS detention in Queens. It looks like with Chang's record of dissident activity—he was at Tiananmen and has a history of persecution—he's got a good shot at asylum."

"You have caught the Ghost?" Sam Chang asked her in unsteady English as he joined them. He would have heard the news but understandably couldn't get enough reassurance that the killer was in fact safely in custody.

"Yes," she said, her eyes not on the man she was speaking to, though, but on Po-Yee. "He's in custody."

Chang said, "You were important with his capture?"

Sachs smiled. "I was at the party, yep."

"Thank you." The man seemed to want to add more but the English was perhaps too daunting. He thought for a moment and then asked, "I may ask you? The man, old man killed in Ghost's apartment building? Where is body?"

"Your father?"

"Yes."

"At the city morgue. Downtown in Manhattan."

"He must have proper funeral. Is very important."

Sachs said, "I'll make sure he's not moved. After you're through with the INS you can arrange to have a funeral home pick him up."

"Thank you."

A small blue Dodge with a City of New York seal pulled up to the scene. A black woman in a brown pants suit got out, carrying an attaché case. The woman spoke to the INS agent and Sachs. "I'm Chiffon Wilson. I'm a social worker with Children's Services." An ID card was flashed.

"You're here for the baby?"

"Right."

Chang looked quickly at his wife. Sachs asked, "You're taking her?"

"We have to."

"Can't she stay with them?"

Wilson shook her head sympathetically. "I'm afraid not. They have no claim to her. She's an orphaned citizen of another country. She'll have to go back to China."

Sachs nodded slowly then gestured the social worker aside. She whispered, "She's a girl. You know what happens to baby girl orphans in China?"

"She'll be adopted."

"Maybe," Sachs said dubiously.

"I don't know about that. I just know that I'm following the law. Look, we do this all the time and we've never heard about any problems with the kids who go back to the recipient country."

Recipient country . . . The phrase troubled her as much as Coe's harsh "undocumenteds." Sachs asked, "Do you ever hear *anything* at all after they go back?"

Wilson hesitated. "No." She then nodded to the INS agent, who spoke in Chinese to the Changs. Mei-Mei's face went still but she nodded and directed the baby to the social worker. "She will . . ." Mei-Mei said. Then frowned, trying to think of the English words.

"Yes?" the social worker asked.

"She will be good take care of?"

"Yes, she will."

"She very good baby. Lost mother. Make sure she good take care of."

"I'll make sure."

Mei-Mei looked at the girl for a long moment then turned her attention back to her youngest son.

Wilson picked up Po-Yee, who squinted at Sachs's red hair and reached out to grip a handful of the strands with curiosity. When she tugged hard, Sachs laughed. The social worker started for her car.

"*Ting!*" came a woman's urgent voice. Sachs recognized the word for "wait" or "stop." She turned to see Chang Mei-Mei walking toward them.

"Yes?"

"Here. There is this." Mei-Mei handed her a stuffed animal toy, crudely made. A cat, Sachs believed.

"She like this. Make her happy."

Wilson took it and gave it to Po-Yee.

The child's eyes were on the toy, Mei-Mei's on the girl.

Then the social worker strapped the child into a car seat and drove away.

Sachs spent a half hour talking to the Changs, debriefing them, seeing if she could learn anything else that might help shore up the case against the Ghost. Then the exhaustion of the past two days caught up with her and she knew it was time to go home. She climbed into the crime scene bus, glancing back once to see the Changs climb into an INS minibus. She and Mei-Mei happened to catch each other's eyes for an instant, then the door closed, the bus pulled into the street and the vanished, the piglets, the undocumenteds . . . the *family* began their journey to yet another temporary home.

Evidence exists independent of perpetrators, of course, and even though the Ghost was in custody Lincoln Rhyme and Amelia Sachs spent the next morning processing the information that continued to arrive regarding the GHOSTKILL case.

An analysis of the chemical markers in the C4 by the FBI had deter-mined that the likely source of the plastic explosive used to blow up the ship was a North Korean arms dealer, who regularly sold weaponry to China.

Recovery divers from the *Evan Brigant* had brought up the bodies of the crewmen and the other immigrants from the *Fuzhou Dragon*, as well as the rest of the money—about $120,000. The cash had been logged into evidence and was being stored in an FBI safe deposit box. They also had learned that Ling Shui-bian, the man who had paid the money to the Ghost and had written him the letter that Sachs found in the ship, had an address in Fuzhou. Rhyme assumed he was one of the Ghost's little snakeheads or partners, and he emailed the name and address to the Fuzhou public security bureau with a note telling them about Ling's involvement with the Ghost.

"You want it on the chart?" Thom asked, nodding at the whiteboard.

"Write, write!" he said impatiently. They still would have to present the evidence to the prosecutors and reproducing the information as it was written on the whiteboards would be the most concise and helpful way to do this.

The aide took the marker and wrote down the information that had just come in.

- Ghost used new C4 to blow up ship. Checking origin of explosive through chemical markers.
  - North Korean arms dealer is source.
- Large quantity new U.S. bills found in Ghost's cabin.
  - Total approximately $120,000.
- Approx. $20,000 in used Chinese yuan found in cabin.
- List of victims, air charter details and bank deposit information. Checking name of sender in China.
  - Ling Shui-bian resides in Fuzhou. Name and address sent to local police.
- Captain alive but unconscious.
  - Regained consciousness, now in INS detention.

As she was writing on the board, Rhyme's computer beeped.

"Command, email," he snapped.

The computer accepted his gruff tone without affront and offered him the list of new messages.

"Command, cursor down. Command, double-click."

He read the message that had just come in.

"Ah," Rhyme announced. "I was right."

He explained to Sachs that the body of John Sung had in fact been found in the trunk of the red Honda that the Ghost had stolen. As Rhyme predicted, the car had been found sunk in a pond only 200 feet from Easton Beach.

So there would be one more murder count to add to the charges against Kwan Ang.

There was another message that interested him. This one was from Mel Cooper, who was back in his office at the NYPD forensics lab in Queens.

> From: M. Cooper
> To: L. Rhyme
> Re: Results of chromatographic and spectrometric analyses of
>   Department of Justice PERT Evidence Sample 3452–02.

The official-sounding heading was in contrast to the informal message below it.

> Lincoln:
> We have met the dynamite and it is phony.
>   Dellray's butt wasn't in any danger. The perp screwed up and used dummy explosive—stuff used for training. I tried to follow up and trace it, but nobody has a database on fake bomb materials. Might be something to think about.

Rhyme laughed. Some arms dealer had scammed Fred Dellray's attacker by selling him the fake explosives. He was relieved that the agent hadn't really been at risk.

The doorbell rang and Thom went down to see who it was.

Heavy footsteps on the stairs. Two sets. He believed they belonged to Sellitto and Dellray—the cop walked with distinctive, heavy footfalls and the agent took the stairs two at a time on his long legs.

For a moment Rhyme, otherwise reclusive, was glad they were here. He'd tell them about the fake bomb. They'd all get a laugh out of it. But then he was aware of something else and an alarm bell went off inside his head. The men had stopped outside the doorway and were whispering. It was as if they were debating between themselves who should deliver bad news.

He was right about whom the steps belonged to. A moment later the rumpled cop and the lanky FBI agent pushed into the bedroom. "Hey, Linc," Sellitto said.

One look at their faces told Rhyme that he was also right about the bad news.

Sachs and Rhyme exchanged a troubled glance.

Rhyme looked from one to the other. "Well, Christ, one of you say something."

Dellray uttered a long sigh.

Finally the detective said, "They took him out of our jurisdiction—the Ghost. He's being sent back to China."

"What?" Sachs gasped.

Angrily Dellray said, "Bein' escorted onto a flight later today." The agent shook his head. "Once it takes off he's free."

Chapter Forty-seven

"Extradited?" Rhyme asked.

"That's the fuzzy little spin they're putting on it," Dellray growled. "But we ain't seen any single solitary arrest warrant for him issued by a Chinese court."

"What does that mean, no arrest warrant?" Sachs asked.

"That his fucking *guanxi*'s saving his ass," Rhyme said bitterly.

Dellray nodded. "'Less the country that wants the extradition shows valid paper, we *never* send nobody back over. No way."

"Well, they'll try him, won't they?" Sachs asked.

"Nup. I talked to our folks over there. The high-ups in China want him back, lemme quote, "'for questioning in connection with irregular matters of foreign trade.' Not a breath 'bout smugglin', not a breath 'bout murder, not a breath. 'Bout. Nothin'."

Rhyme was stunned. "He'll be back in business in a month." The Changs, the Wus and who knew how many others were suddenly at risk again. "Fred, can you do *anything*?" he asked. Dellray was well thought of in the FBI. He had friends at headquarters down on Pennsylvania Avenue and Tenth in D.C. and had a good stockpile of his own *guanxi*.

But the agent shook his head, squeezing the cigarette that rested behind his right ear. "This li'l decision got made in State Department Washington. Not *my* Washington. I got no clout there."

Rhyme remembered the quiet man in the blue suit: Webley from State.

"Goddamn," Sachs whispered. "He knew."

"What?" Rhyme asked.

"The Ghost knew he was safe. At the takedown he was surprised but he didn't look worried. Hell, he told me about killing Sung and taking over his identity. He was *proud* of it. If anybody else'd been collared like that, they would've listened to their rights and shut up. He was goddamn bragging."

"It can't happen," Rhyme said, thinking of the poor people floating dead in the *Fuzhou Dragon* and lying bloody on the sand at Easton beach. Thinking of Sam Chang's father.

Thinking of Sonny Li.

"Well, it *is* extremely happenin'," Dellray said. "He's leaving this afternoon. And there's not a single damn thing we can do."

In the Federal Men's Detention Center in downtown Manhattan the Ghost sat across the table from his lawyer in a private conference room, which the lawyer's handheld scanner had assured them was not bugged.

They spoke in Minnanhua Chinese, quietly and quickly.

When the lawyer was finished telling him about the procedure for his release into the hands of the Fuzhou public security bureau the Ghost nodded and then leaned close. "I need you to find some information for me."

The lawyer took out a pad of paper. The Ghost glanced at it once and frowned. The lawyer put the foolscap away.

"There is a woman who works for the police department. I need her address. Home address. Her name is Amelia Sachs and she lives somewhere in Brooklyn. S-A-C-H-S. And Lincoln Rhyme. Spelled like in poetry. He's in Manhattan."

The lawyer nodded.

"Then there are the two families I need to find." He didn't think it wise to describe them as people he was trying to kill, even in the absence of listening devices, so he said simply, "The Wus and the Changs. From the *Dragon*. They might be in INS detention somewhere but maybe not."

"What are you—?"

"You don't need to ask questions like that."

The slim man fell silent. Then he considered. "When do you need this information?"

The Ghost wasn't sure exactly what awaited him in China. He guessed that he would be back in one of his luxury apartments in three months but it could be less. "As soon as possible. You will keep monitoring them and if the addresses change you will leave a message with my people in Fuzhou."

"Yes. Of course."

Then the Ghost realized that he was tired. He lived for combat, he lived to play deadly games like this. He lived to win. But, my, how tired you got when you broke cauldrons and sank boats, when you simply did not accept defeat. Now he needed rest. His *qi* sorely needed to be replenished.

He dismissed his lawyer then lay back on the cot in the antiseptically clean, square cell, the room reminding him of a Chinese funeral parlor because the walls were blue and white. The Ghost closed his eyes and pictured Yindao.

Lying in a room, a warehouse, a garage, which had been arranged by a feng shui artist in the opposite manner of most practitioners: the nature of his fantasy room would *maximize* anger and evil and pain. The art of wind and water can do this too, the Ghost believed.

Yin and *yang*, opposites in harmony.

The supple woman tied down on the solid floor.

Her fair skin in darkness.

Hard and soft . . . .

Pleasure and agony.

Yindao. . . .

The thought of her would get him through the difficult coming weeks. He closed his eyes.

"We've had our differences, Alan," Rhyme said.

"I guess." INS agent Coe was cautious. He sat in Rhyme's bedroom, in one of the uncomfortable wicker chairs that the criminalist had furnished the room with in hopes that it would discourage visitors from staying for long periods of time. Coe was suspicious about the invitation but Rhyme didn't want there to be any chance of someone's overhearing them. This had to be a completely private conversation.

"You heard about the Ghost's release?"

"Of course I heard about the Ghost," the man muttered angrily.

Rhyme asked, "Tell me, what's your real interest in the case. No bull-shit."

Coe hesitated and then said, "The informant of mine he killed. That's it."

"I said no bullshit. There's more to it, isn't there?"

Coe finally said, "Yeah, there's more."

"What?"

"The woman who was the informant, Julia? We were . . . We were lovers."

Rhyme carefully scanned the agent's face. Although he was a firm believer in the overarching value of hard evidence he wasn't wholly skeptical to messages in faces and eyes. He saw pain, he saw sorrow.

After a difficult moment the agent said, "She died because of me. We should've been more careful. We went out in public some. We went to Xiamen, this tourist city south of Fuzhou. There're lots of Western tourists there and I thought we wouldn't be recognized. But I think maybe we were." There were tears in his eyes now. "I never had her do anything dangerous. Just glance at scheduling calendars from time to time. She never wore a wire, never broke into any offices. But I should've known the Ghost. Nobody could get away with even the slightest betrayal."

I am coming into town on bus, I'm saying. I saw crow on road picking at food. Another crow tried steal it and the first crow not just scare other away—he chase and try to peck eyes out. Not leave thief alone.

"The Ghost got her," Coe said. "She left two daughters behind."

"That's what you were doing overseas during the time you took off?"

He nodded. "Looking for Julia. But then I gave up on that and spent my time trying to get the children placed in a Catholic home. They were girls—and you know how tough a time orphaned girl babies have over there."

Rhyme said nothing at first though he was thinking back to an incident in his own life that was similar to Coe's tragedy. A woman he'd grown close to before the accident, a lover. She was a cop too, a crime scene expert. And she was dead because he'd ordered her into a booby-trapped scene. The bomb had killed her instantly.

"Did it work?" the criminalist asked. "With the girls?"

"No. The state took them and I never saw them again." He looked up and wiped his eyes. "So that's why I go on and on about undocumenteds. As long as people pay fifty thousand bucks for an illegal trip to America we're going to have snakeheads like the Ghost killing anybody who gets in their way."

Rhyme wheeled closer to Coe. "How badly do you want to stop him?" he whispered.

"The Ghost? With my whole soul."

That question had been easy. Rhyme now asked the hard one. "What are you willing to risk to do it?"

But there was no hesitation as the agent said, "Everything."

Chapter Forty-eight

"There may be a problem," said the man's voice through the phone.

Sitting in the middle row of a large INS van en route to Kennedy airport, sweating Harold Peabody nodded as if the caller could see him.

He didn't need problems, not with this case. "Problem. I see. Go ahead."

The man beside Peabody stirred at these words, the quiet man in the navy-blue suit, Webley, who worked for the State Department and who'd made Peabody's life unrefined hell since he'd flown in from Washington the afternoon of the day the *Fuzhou Dragon* sank. Webley turned his head toward Peabody but remained stony-faced, a skill he was extremely good at.

"Alan Coe disappeared," said the caller, the assistant special agent in charge of the FBI's Manhattan office. "We had a report that he was talking to Rhyme. Then he vanished again."

"Okay." Peabody tried to figure out what this meant.

Behind Peabody and Webley were two armed INS agents on either side of the Ghost, whose handcuffs kept clinking as he sipped his Starbucks coffee. The snakehead, at least, seemed untroubled by the talk of problems. "Keep going," Peabody said into the phone.

"We were keeping an eye on Coe, like you said. 'Cause we weren't sure if he'd try to do harm to the subject."

Do harm to the subject . . . What a fucked-up way to talk, Peabody thought.

"And?"

"Well, we can't find him. Or Rhyme either."

"He's in a wheelchair. How hard is it to keep track of him?" Doughy Peabody was drenched. The storm had passed and, though the skies were still overcast, the temperature was in the high 80s. And the government van had government air-conditioning.

"There was no surveillance order," the ASAC reminded calmly. "We had to handle it . . . informally." His equanimity, Peabody realized, put the FBI agent in control of the situation and he reminded himself to try to gin up some more power.

Bureaucracy was such a bitch.

"What's your situational assessment?" Peabody asked. Thinking: How's *that* for jargon, you asshole?

"You know Coe's had a top-of-the-deck priority to get the Ghost himself."

"True. And?"

"Rhyme's the best forensic detective cop in the country. We've been sniffing the thought that he and Coe're planning to take out the Ghost."

How do you sniff a thought? Peabody wondered. "How do you mean?"

"With Rhyme's grip on forensics they might've come up with some way to make it impossible to convict Coe. Manipulate the evidence somehow."

"What?" Peabody scoffed. "Ridiculous. Rhyme wouldn't do that."

These words now brought some emotion to Webley. He frowned.

"Why not?" the ASAC continued. "Ever since his accident he's not the most stable person in the world. He's always had this issue about killing himself. And it sounds like he got pretty close to that Chinese cop. Maybe when the Ghost shot Li it pushed him over the edge."

This sounded crazy, but who knew? Peabody caught people trying to sneak into the country illegally and sent them back home. He didn't know the workings of the criminal mind. In fact he had no experience with psychology whatsoever, except resentfully paying his ex-wife's shrink bills.

As for Coe, well, he *definitely* was unstable enough to try to cap the Ghost's ass. He'd already tried to take him out—at the Wus' apartment on Canal Street.

"What's Dellray say?" Peabody asked.

"He's operational in the field at this time. He's not returning calls."

"Doesn't he work for you?"

"Dellray pretty much works for Dellray," said the ASAC.

"What're you suggesting we do?" Peabody asked, using his wrinkled tan jacket to wipe his face.

"Do you think Coe's following you?"

Peabody glanced around him at the billion cars on the Van Wyck Expressway. "Like I could fucking tell," he answered, giving up entirely on the language of high-level government.

"If he's going to make a move it'll have to be at the airport. Tell your people to look out for him. I'll tell Port Authority security too."

"I just don't see it happening."

"Thanks for the assessment, Harold. But then again it was Rhyme who collared the prick in the first place. Not you." The line went dead.

He turned around and studied the Ghost, who asked, "What was that about?"

"Nothing." Peabody asked one of the agents, "We have body armor in the back?"

"Naw," one answered. Then: "Well, I'm in a vest."

"Me too," said the other agent.

The tone of their voices said that they weren't about to give them up.

Nor would Peabody ask his agents to do so. If Coe made a move on the Ghost and he was successful, well, that was just the way it was. He and Rhyme would have to take the consequences.

He leaned forward and snapped at the driver, "Can't you do anything about the goddamn air-conditioning?"

The shackles binding his wrists felt light as silk.

They would come off as soon as he was at the doorway of the airliner that would carry him back home from the Beautiful Country and, because he knew that, the metal restraints had already ceased to exist.

Walking down the international corridor of JFK airport, he was reflecting on how flying in the Far East had changed. Thinking of the early days when he would fly on the national airline of China: CAAC— which every English-speaking Chinese knew stood for Chinese Airliners Always Crash. Things were different now. Today it would be Northwest Airlines to L.A., then a China Air flight to Singapore with a connection to Fuzhou, business class all the way.

The entourage was a curious one: the Ghost, two armed guards and the two men in charge—Peabody from the INS and the man from the United States Department of State. They were now joined by two armed Port Authority guards, big men, nervous as squirrels, who kept their hands near their weapons as they surveyed the crowd.

The Ghost didn't exactly know what the uneasiness and firepower were all about but he supposed that there'd been death threats against him. Well, that was nothing new. He'd lived with death since the night the Four Olds murdered his family.

Footsteps behind.

"Mr. Kwan . . . Mr. Kwan!"

They turned to see a thin Chinese man in a suit walking quickly toward them. The guards drew their weapons and the approaching man stopped, eyes wide.

"It's my lawyer," the Ghost said.

"You sure?" Peabody asked.

"What do you mean, am I sure?"

Peabody nodded the man forward, frisked him despite the Ghost's protests and let him and the snakehead step to the side of the corridor. The Ghost turned his ear toward the lawyer's mouth. "Go ahead."

"The Changs and the Wus are out on bond, pending the hearing. It looks like they'll be granted asylum. The Wus are in Flushing, Queens. The Changs are back in Owls Head. The same apartment."

"And Yindao?" the Ghost whispered.

The man blinked at the crude word.

The snakehead corrected himself. "I mean the Sachs woman."

"Oh, I have her address too. And Lincoln Rhyme's. Do you want me to write them down for you?"

"No, just tell them to me slowly. I'll remember them."

After only three repetitions the Ghost had memorized them. He said, "You'll find your money in the account." No need to say how much money or which account.

The lawyer nodded and, with a glance at the Ghost's guards, turned and left.

The group continued down the corridor. Ahead of him the Ghost could see the gate, the pretty clerks behind the check-in counter. And through the window he caught a glimpse of the 747 that would soon take him west, like Monkey making his pilgrimage, at the end of which he found enlightenment and contentment.

His boarding pass was protruding from his shirt pocket. He had 10,000 yuan in his wallet. He had a U.S. government escort. He was going home, to his apartments, his women, his money.

He was free. He—

Then sudden motion . . .

Somebody was moving toward him fast and the guards were pulling him aside, their weapons coming out of their holsters again. The Ghost, gasping at the shock, thought that he was going to die. He muttered a fast prayer to his guardian, Yi the archer.

But the attacker stopped short. Breathing unsteadily, the Ghost began to laugh.

"Hello, Yindao."

She was wearing jeans, T-shirt and windbreaker, her badge around her neck. Hands on her hips, one of which rested very close to her pistol. The policewoman ignored the Ghost and glanced at the nervous, young INS agents. "You better have a damn good reason for drawing down on me."

They started to reholster their weapons but Peabody gestured for them not to.

The Ghost focused past Yindao. Behind her was a tall black man in a white suit and noisy blue shirt. The fat cop who'd arrested him in Brooklyn was here as well, as were several uniformed city policemen. But the one person in this retinue who captured his full attention was a handsome dark-haired man about the Ghost's age, sitting in a complicated, bright red wheelchair, to which his arms and legs were strapped. A trim young man— his aide or nurse—stood behind the chair.

This was, of course, Lincoln Rhyme. The Ghost studied the curious man—who'd miraculously discovered the location of the *Fuzhou Dragon* at sea, who'd found the Wus and the Changs and who had actually succeeded in capturing the Ghost himself. Which no other policeman in the world had ever been able to do.

Harold Peabody wiped his face with his sleeve, surveyed the situation and motioned the guards back. They put their weapons away. "What's this all about, Rhyme?"

But the man ignored him and continued to study the snakehead carefully. The Ghost felt a tickle of unease. But then he mastered the sensation. He had *guanxi* at the highest level. He was immune, even to the magic of Lincoln Rhyme, whom he asked bluntly, "Who exactly are you? A consultant? A private detective?"

"Me?" the cripple responded. "I'm one of the ten judges of hell."

The Ghost laughed. "So you inscribe names in *The Register of the Living and the Dead*?"

"Yes, that's exactly what I do."

"And you've come to see me off?"

"No," he answered.

Peabody said cautiously, "And what *do* you want?"

The State Department bureaucrat said impatiently, "All of you, now—just clear on out of here."

"He's not getting on that airplane," Rhyme said.

"Oh, yes, he is," said the dour official. He stepped forward, plucking the Ghost's ticket from his pocket and striding toward the gate agent.

"You take one more step toward that airplane," the fat policeman said to him, "and these officers're authorized to arrest you."

"Me?" Webley muttered angrily.

Peabody gave a sharp laugh and looked at the black agent. "Dellray, what is this crap?"

"Probably oughta listen to my friend here, Harold. In your best interest, believe you me."

Peabody said, "Five minutes."

A regretful frown crossed Lincoln Rhyme's face. "Oh, I'm afraid it may take a little longer than that."

Chapter Forty-nine

The snakehead was far smaller and more compact than Lincoln Rhyme had expected. This was a phenomenon he recalled from his days running the NYPD forensics unit; the perpetrators he pursued took on disproportionate stature in his mind and when he saw them in person for the first time—usually at trial—he was often surprised at how diminutive they were.

The Ghost stood shackled and surrounded by law enforcers. Concerned, yes, but still in control, serene, shoulders and arms relaxed. The criminalist understood immediately how Sachs could have been suckered by him: the Ghost's eyes were those of a healer, a doctor, a spiritual man. They would dole out apparent comfort and invite sharing confidences. But, knowing the man now, Rhyme could see in the placid gaze evidence of a relentless ego and ruthlessness.

"Okay, sir, what's this all about?" asked Peabody's friend—Webley from State, as Rhyme now thought of him, echoing the man's own pompous identification of himself in Rhyme's living room the other day.

Rhyme said to the two men, "You know what happens sometimes in our line of work, gentlemen? I mean, forensic science."

Webley from State started to speak but Peabody waved him silent. Rhyme wouldn't have let anyone rush him anyway. Nobody hurried Lincoln Rhyme when he didn't wish to be hurried.

"We sometimes lose sight of the big picture. All right, I admit *I'm* the one who loses sight more than, say, my Sachs here. She looks at motive, she looks at *why* people do what they do. But that's not my nature. My nature is to study each piece of evidence and put it where it belongs." He glanced at the Ghost with a smile. "Like placing a stone on a *wei-chi* board."

The snakehead who had brought so much sorrow to so many lives said nothing, gave no acknowledgment. The gate agent announced preboarding of the Northwest Airlines flight to Los Angeles.

"We figured out the clues just fine." A nod toward the Ghost. "After all, here he is, caught, right? Thanks to us. And we've got enough evidence to convict him and sentence him to death. But what happens? He's going free."

"He's not going free," Peabody rejoined. "He's going back to stand trial in China."

"Free from the jurisdiction where he's committed a number of serious felonies in the past few days," Rhyme corrected sharply. "Do we *have* to squabble?"

This was too much for Webley from State. "Get to the point or I'm putting him on that plane."

Rhyme continued to ignore the man. He had the stage and wasn't relinquishing it. "The big picture . . . big picture . . . I was thinking how bad I felt. Here, I'd found out where the *Fuzhou Dragon* was and sent the Coast Guard after her but—what happens?—he scuttles it, killing all those people."

Peabody shook his head. "Of course you'd feel bad," he said with some sympathy. "We all felt bad. But—"

Rhyme kept steaming forward. "Big picture . . . Let's think about it. It's Tuesday, just before dawn, on board the *Dragon*. You're the Ghost, a wanted man—wanted for capital offenses—and the Coast Guard is a half hour away from interdicting your smuggling ship. What would you have done?"

The gate agent continued with the boarding of the flight.

Peabody sighed. Webley from State muttered something sotto voce; Rhyme knew it was not complimentary. The Ghost stirred but he remained silent.

Since no one was helping him out Rhyme continued, "*I* personally would've taken my money, ordered the *Dragon* back out to sea full speed ahead and escaped to shore in one of the life rafts. The Coast Guard and cops and INS would've been so busy with the crew and immigrants I could easily've gotten to land and been halfway to Chinatown before they realized I was gone. But what'd the Ghost do?"

Rhyme glanced at Sachs, who said, "He locked the immigrants in the hold, sank the ship and then hunted down the survivors. And he risked getting caught or killed to do it."

"And when he didn't kill them all on the shore," Rhyme took over the narrative, "he followed them to the city and tried to murder them there. Why on earth would he do that?"

"Well, they were witnesses," Peabody said. "He *had* to kill them."

"Ah, *why*? That's the question that nobody's asking." Rhyme asked, "What would it gain him?"

Peabody and Webley from State were silent.

Rhyme continued, "All that the passengers on the ship could do is to testify in one case of human smuggling. But there were already a dozen warrants against him for smuggling around the world. Homicide charges too—look at the Interpol Red Notice. It made no sense to go to all that trouble to murder them just because they were witnesses." He paused a histrionic few seconds. "But killing them makes perfect sense if the passengers were his *intended* victims."

Rhyme could see two different reactions in their faces. Peabody was perplexed and surprised. In Webley from State's eyes there was a different look. He knew exactly where Rhyme was going.

"'Victims,'" Rhyme continued. "That's a key word. See, my Sachs found a letter when she went for her little swim in the *Dragon*."

The Ghost, who'd been staring at Sachs, turned slowly toward Rhyme when he heard this.

"A letter?" Peabody asked.

"It said, more or less, here's your money and a list of the victims you'll be taking to America. . . . Are we catching on to the big picture, gentlemen? The letter didn't say 'passengers' or 'immigrants' or 'piglets'—or your own indelicate term, Peabody, 'undocumenteds.' The letter said quote 'victims.' I didn't realize at first when I had the letter translated that that was the exact word the writer used. And the big picture becomes a lot clearer when we look at who those victims were—they were all Chinese dissidents and their families. The Ghost isn't just a snakehead. He's also a professional killer. He was hired to murder them."

"This man is crazy," the Ghost snapped. "He's desperate. I want to leave now."

But Rhyme said, "The Ghost was planning all along to scuttle the *Dragon*. He was only waiting until the ship was close enough to shore so that he and his *bangshou* could make it to land safely. But a few things went wrong—we found the ship and sent the Coast Guard in, so he had to act sooner than he'd planned; some of the immigrants escaped. Then the explosive was too powerful and the ship sank before he could get his guns and money and find his assistant."

"That's absurd," muttered Webley from State. "Beijing wouldn't hire anybody to kill dissidents. It's not the 1960s anymore."

"Beijing *didn't* do it," Rhyme responded, "as I suspect *you* probably know, Webley. No, we found out who sent the Ghost his instructions and his money. Ling Shui-bian is his name."

The Ghost glanced desperately at the boarding gate.

Rhyme continued, "I sent the Fuzhou police an email with Ling's name and address and told them that I thought he was one of the Ghost's partners. But they sent back a message saying I must be mistaken. His address was a government building in Fuzhou. Ling is the Fujian governor's assistant in charge of trade development."

"What's that mean?" Peabody asked.

"That he's a corrupt warlord," Rhyme snapped. "Isn't it obvious? He and his people're getting millions in kickbacks from businesses all along the southeastern coast of China. He's probably working with the governor, but I don't have any evidence about that. Not yet, anyway."

"Impossible," offered Webley though with much less bluster than he'd displayed earlier.

Rhyme said, "Not at all. Sonny Li told me about Fujian Province. It's always been more independent than the central government likes. It has the most connections with the West and Taiwan—more money too. And the most active dissidents. Beijing is always threatening to crack down on the province, nationalize businesses again and put its own people in power. If that happens, Ling and his boys lose their income stream. So, how to keep Beijing happy? Kill the most vocal dissidents. And what better way to do it than by hiring a snakehead? If they die en route to another country it's their own fault, not the government's."

"And more likely than not," Sachs said, "nobody'd even know that they died. They'd be just one more shipload of the vanished." Nodding at Webley from State, she reminded, "Rhyme?"

"Oh, right. The last piece of the puzzle. Why's the Ghost going free?"

He said to Webley, "You're sending him back to keep Ling and his people in Fujian happy. To make sure our business interests aren't affected. Southeast China is the biggest site for U.S. investment in the world."

"That's bullshit," the man snapped in reply.

The Ghost said, "This is ridiculous. It's the lie of a desperate man." Nodding toward Rhyme. "Where's the proof?"

"Proof? Well, we have the letter from Ling. But if you want more . . . Remember, Harold? You told me that other shiploads of the Ghost's immigrants disappeared in the past year or so. I checked the statements from their relatives in the Interpol database. Most of those victims were dissidents from Fujian too."

"That's not true," the Ghost said quickly.

"Then there's the money," Rhyme said, ignoring the snakehead.

"Money?"

"The smuggling fee. When Sachs went for her little paddle in the Atlantic she found 120,000 U.S. dollars and maybe 20,000 worth of old yuan. I invited a friend of mine from the INS over to my place to help me look at the evidence. He—"

"Who?" Peabody asked sharply. Then he understood. "Alan Coe? It was him, wasn't it?"

"A friend. Let's leave it at that." In fact, the friend *was* Agent Coe, who'd also spent the day stealing classified INS files, which would probably cost him his job, if not earn him a jail sentence. This was the risk that Rhyme had referred to earlier—and that Coe had been only too happy to assume.

"The first thing he noticed was the money. He told me that when immigrants contract with snakeheads they can't pay the down payment in dollars—because there *are* no dollars in China, not enough to pay for transit to the U.S. anyway. They always pay in *yuan*. With a shipload of twenty-five or so immigrants, that means Sachs should've found at least a half million in *yuan*—just for the down payment. So why was there so little Chinese money on board? Because the Ghost charged next to nothing—to make sure that the dissidents on the hit list could afford to make the trip. The Ghost was making his profit from the fee to kill them. The 120,000? Well, *that* was the down payment from Ling. I checked the serial numbers on some of the bills and, according to the Federal Reserve, that cash was last seen going into the Bank of South China in Singapore. Which happens to be used regularly by Fujianese government ministries."

More rows were boarding. The Ghost was truly desperate now.

Peabody had fallen silent and was considering all this. He seemed to be wavering. But the State Department official was resolute. "He's getting on that plane and that's all there is to it."

Rhyme squinted and cocked his head. "How high are we now on the ladder of evidence, Sachs?"

"How about the C4?"

"Right, the explosive used to blow up the ship. The FBI traced it to a North Korean arms dealer, who regularly sells to—guess who? People's Liberation Army bases in Fujian. The *government* gave the Ghost the C4." Rhyme closed his eyes for a brief moment. They sprang open. "Then there's the cell phone that Sachs found at the beach. . . . It was a government-issue satellite phone. The network he used was based in Fuzhou."

"The trucks, Rhyme," Sachs reminded. "Tell them about the trucks."

Rhyme nodded, never able to resist delivering a lesson in his craft. "Interesting thing about crime scene work—sometimes what you *don't* find at a scene is as important as what you *do* find. I was looking at our evidence board and I realized that something was missing: Where was the evidence of the trucks for the *immigrants*? My INS friend told me that ground transport is part of the smuggling contract. But there weren't any trucks. The only vehicle at the beach was Jerry Tang's—to pick up the Ghost and his *bangshou*. Well, why no trucks. Because the Ghost knew the immigrants would never get to shore alive."

The line of boarding passengers was shrinking.

Webley from State leaned down and whispered viciously into Rhyme's face, "You're in way over your head here, mister. You don't know what you're doing."

Rhyme gazed back at him in mock contrition. "Nope, I don't know a thing. Not about world politics, not about *les affaires d'etat* . . . . I'm just a simple scientist. My knowledge is woefully limited. To things like, say, fake dynamite."

Which shut up Webley from State instantly.

"This's where I come in," Dellray said. "Unfortunately for you folks."

Peabody cleared his throat uneasily. "What are you talking about?" he asked—but only because the script called for him to pose the question, the answer to which was the last thing in the world he wanted to hear.

"The bomb in Fred's car? Well, the results came back from the lab about the dynamite. Interesting—it wasn't dynamite at all. It was sawdust mixed with resin. Fake. Used for training. My INS friend told me that Immigration has its own bomb squad and bomb training facility in Manhattan and he stopped by the place this morning. They have dummy explosives on hand to teach rookies recognition and handling. The sticks in Fred's car match the samples from there. And the numbers on the detonator are similar to some he found in an INS evidence locker—they were confiscated last year when some agents arrested a dozen illegal Russian nationals in Coney Island."

Rhyme enjoyed the flicker of horror in Peabody's eyes. The criminalist was surprised that Webley from State could still manage to look so indignant. "If you're suggesting that anyone in the federal government would hurt a fellow agent—"

"Hurt? How could a small detonator hurt anyone? It was just a firecracker, really. No, the important criminal charge *I'd* think of would be felonious interference with an investigation—because it would *seem* to me that you might've wanted Fred off the case temporarily."

"And why?"

"'Cause," white-suited Dellray took over, stepping forward, driving Webley from State against the wall, "I was makin' waves. Gettin' together the SPEC-TAC team. Who woulda taken the Ghost out no nonsense, not pissin' around like the INS folk were doing. Hell, I think that's why *I* was on the case in the first place. I din't know beans 'bout human smugglin'. An' when I arranged for an expert—Dan Wong—to take over the case, next thing we know his butt's on a plane headin' west."

Rhyme summarized, "Fred had to go—so you could dispose of the Ghost the way you'd planned— catching him alive and getting him safely out of the country as part of a deal between the State Department and Ling in Fujian." A nod toward the plane. "Just like what's happened."

"I didn't know anything about killing dissidents," Peabody blurted. "That was never expressed to me. I swear!"

"Watch it," Webley from State muttered threateningly.

"All they said was that they needed to keep the Justice Department minimized. There were important national security issues at stake. Nobody mentioned business interests, nobody mentioned—"

"Harold!" Webley from State cracked the whip. Then he turned away from the sweaty bureaucrat to Rhyme and said in a reasonable voice, "Look, if—I'm saying *if*—any of this is true, you have to realize there's a lot more to it than just this one man, Lincoln. The Ghost's cover's been blown. He's not going to be sinking any more ships. Nobody'll hire him as a snakehead after this. But," the diplomat continued smoothly, "if we send him back, that'll keep the Chinese happy. Beijing won't crack down on the provinces and the end result'll be a better economy for the people there. And with more American influence there'll be improved human rights." He lifted his hands, palms up. "Sometimes we have to make hard choices."

Rhyme nodded. "So what you're saying is that it's essentially an issue of politics and diplomacy."

Webley from State smiled, pleased that Rhyme finally understood. "Exactly. For the good of both countries. It's a sacrifice, sure, but it's one that I think has to be made."

Rhyme considered this for a moment. Then he said to Sachs, "We could call it the Historically Unprecedented Great Sacrifice for the Beneficial Good of the People."

Webley from State's face twisted at Rhyme's sarcasm.

"See," the criminalist explained, "politics are complicated, diplomacy is complicated. But crime is simple. I don't like complicated things. So here's the deal: either you hand the Ghost over to us for prosecution in this country or you let him fly back home. And if you do that we go public with the fact you're releasing a perp in a multiple homicide—for political and economic reasons. And that you assaulted an FBI agent in the process." He added flippantly, "Your choice. Up to you."

"Don't threaten us. You're just fucking city cops," said Webley from State.

The gate agent announced the final boarding of the flight. Now the Ghost was scared. Sweat on his forehead, face dark with rage, he walked up to Webley and raised his hands, the shackles jangling. He whispered angrily to him. The bureaucrat ignored him and turned back to Rhyme. "How the hell're you going to go public? Nobody's going to be interested in a story like this. You think it's fucking Watergate? We're sending a Chinese national back to his homeland to stand trial for various crimes."

"Harold?" Rhyme asked.

Miserable, Peabody said, "I'm sorry. There's nothing I can do."

"So *that's* your answer," Rhyme replied, smiling faintly. "That's all I wanted. A decision. You made one. Good." He thought, with both amusement and sorrow, that this was very much like playing a game of *wei-chi*.

"Thom, could you please show him our handiwork?" Rhyme asked his aide.

The young man took an envelope out of his pocket and handed it to Webley from State. He opened it. Inside was a long memo from Rhyme to Peter Hoddins, international desk reporter with the *New York Times*. It described in detail exactly what Rhyme had just told Peabody and Webley.

"Peter and I are good friends," Thom said. "I told him we might have an exclusive about the *Fuzhou Dragon* sinking and that it had implications all the way to Washington. He was very intrigued."

"Peter's a good reporter," Rhyme said then added proudly, "He was short-listed for a Pulitzer."

Webley from State and Peabody looked at each other for a moment. Then they retired to the corner of the now-empty gate area and each made phone calls.

"We must have Mr. Kwan on board the aircraft now," the gate agent said.

Finally the two federal telephones were hung up and a moment later Rhyme had his answer: Webley from State turned without a word and stalked down the corridor to the main lobby.

"Wait!" the Ghost cried. "There was a deal! We had a deal!"

The man kept going, tearing up Rhyme's memo up as he walked, not even pausing as he tossed it toward a trash container.

Sellitto told the gate agent to close the door to the aircraft. Mr. Kwan wouldn't be making the flight.

The Ghost's eyes bored into Rhyme's and his shoulders slumped, a clear flag of defeat. But an instant later it seemed that the despair from this loss was immediately balanced by the hope of future victory, the *yang* was balanced by a surge of *yin*, as Sonny Li might've said. The snakehead turned toward Sachs. He looked her over with a chill smile. "I'm patient, Yindao. I'm sure we'll meet again. *Naixin*. . . . All in good time, all in good time."

Amelia Sachs returned his gaze and said, "The sooner the better."

Her eyes, Rhyme decided, were infinitely colder than his.

The uniformed NYPD cops took custody of the snakehead.

"I swear that I didn't know what this was all about," Harold Peabody said. "They told me that—"

But Rhyme had grown weary of the verbal fencing. Without a word he moved his finger slightly on the touchpad to turn the Storm Arrow away from the bureaucrat.

It was Amelia Sachs who provided the final interaction between the various branches of government regarding Kwan Ang, Gui, the Ghost. She held out her hand to troubled Harold Peabody and asked, "Could you give me the cuff keys, please? If you want the shackles back after he's booked I'll leave them at Men's Detention for you."

Chapter Fifty

Several day later the Ghost had been arraigned and was being held without bail.

The laundry list of offenses was long: state and federal charges for murder, human smuggling, assault, firearms possession, money laundering.

Dellray and his bosses at Justice had pulled some strings at the U.S. Attorney's Office and, in exchange for his testimony against the Ghost, Sen Zi-jun, captain of the late *Fuzhou Dragon*, was given immunity from prosecution on the charges of human smuggling. He would testify at the Ghost's trial and, following that, be deported to China.

Rhyme and Sachs were presently alone in his bedroom and the policewoman was looking herself over in a full-length mirror.

"You look fine," the criminalist called. She was due to make an appearance in court in an hour. It was an important session and she was preoccupied, thinking about her impending performance before the judge.

She shook her head uncertainly. "I don't know." Amelia Sachs, who'd never looked back when she gave up modeling, called her herself a "jeans and sweats girl." Presently she was dressed in a crisp blue suit, white blouse and, my God, Rhyme now observed, a pair of highly sensible navy-blue Joan & David's with heels that boosted her height over six feet. Her red hair was perfectly arranged on top of her head.

Still, she remained his Sachs; her silver earrings were in the shape of tiny bullets.

The phone rang and Rhyme barked, "Command. Answer phone."
Click.

"Lincoln?" a woman's voice asked through the speaker.

"Dr. Weaver," Rhyme said to the neurosurgeon.

Sachs turned her attention away from couture and sat down on the edge of the Flexicair bed.

"I got your phone call," the doctor said. "My assistant said it was important. Is everything all right?"

"Fine," Rhyme said.

"You're following the regimen I gave you? No alcohol, plenty of sleep?" Then she added with some humor, "No, *you* tell me, Thom. Are you there?"

"He's in the other room," Rhyme responded, laughing. "No one's here to blow the whistle on me."

Except Sachs, of course, but she wasn't going to snitch.

"I'd like you to come into the office tomorrow for the final checkup before the surgery. I was thinking—"

"Doctor?"

"Yes?"

Rhyme held Sachs's eye. "I've decided not to have the operation."

"You're—"

"I'm canceling. Forfeiting my room deposit," he joked, "and down payment."

Silence for a moment. Then: "You wanted this more than any patient I've ever had."

"I *did* want it, that's true. But I've changed my mind."

"You'll recall I've told you all along that the risks were high. Is that why?"

He looked at Sachs. He said only, "In the end, I guess, I don't see that much of a benefit."

"I think this's a good choice, Lincoln. It's the wise choice." She added, "We're making a lot of progress with spinal cord injuries. I know you read the literature. . . ."

"I keep my finger on the pulse, true," he responded, enjoying the irony of the metaphor.

"But there're new things happening every week. Call me whenever you like. We can think about options in the future. Or just call me to talk if you want to."

"Yes. I'd like that."

"I'd like it too. Goodbye, Lincoln."

"Goodbye, Doctor. Command, disconnect."

Silence filled the room. Then a flutter of wings and a shadow disturbed the peace as a peregrine falcon landed on his window ledge. They both stared at the bird. Sachs asked, "Are you sure about this, Rhyme? I'm with you a hundred percent if you want to go ahead with it."

He knew that she would be.

But he knew too, without a doubt, that he didn't want the surgery now.

"Embrace your limitations . . . Fate make you this way, Loaban. And make you this way for purpose. Maybe you best detective you can be because of what happen. Your life balanced now, I'm saying."

"I'm sure," he told her.

She squeezed his hand. Then looked out the window again at the falcon. Rhyme watched the oblique, pale light hitting her face with the demure illumination of a Vermeer painting. Finally he asked, "Sachs, are *you* sure you want to do *this?*"

He nodded toward the file on the table nearby, which contained a picture of Po-Yee, a number of affidavits and official-looking documents.

The top sheet of paper was headed: PETITION FOR ADOPTION.

Then she glanced at Rhyme. The look in her eye told him that she too was sure about the decision she'd made.

Sitting in the judge's chambers, Sachs smiled down at Po-Yee, the Treasured Child, who sat beside her in the chair where the social worker had deposited her a few moments before. The girl played with her stuffed kitten.

"Ms. Sachs, this is a rather unorthodox adoption proceeding. But I assume you know that." Justice Margaret Benson-Wailes, a heavyset woman, sat behind her abysmally cluttered desk in the dark monolith of Manhattan Family Court.

"Yes, Your Honor."

The woman bent forward and read some more. "All I can say is in the past two days I've talked to more people from Human Services, Family Services, city hall, Albany, One Police Plaza and the INS than I talk to in month in most placements. Tell me, Officer, how's a skinny girl like you get so much pull in this city?"

"I'm lucky, I guess."

"More to it than that," the judge said, returning to the file. "I hear good things about you."

Apparently Sachs too had good *guanxi*. Her connections reached from Fred Dellray to Lon Sellitto to Alan Coe (who was, far from being fired, taking over early-retiring Harold Peabody's job at the INS). In the space of several days the miles of red tape that accompany most adoptions had been shredded.

The jurist continued, "You understand, of course, that the welfare of this child comes first no matter what and if I'm not convinced that the disposition is in her best interest I will not sign the papers." The woman had the same benevolently gruff air that Lincoln Rhyme had mastered.

"I wouldn't want it any other way, Your Honor."

Like many judges, Sachs had learned, Benson-Wailes was prone to lecture. The woman eased back in the chair and addressed her audience. "Now, the adoption procedure in New York involves taking a home study, undergoing training and spending time with the child and usually a three-month probation period. I spent all morning reviewing papers and reports, talking to the social workers and the law guardian that we appointed for the girl. I've gotten very good reports but this's been moving faster than the Bulls slide after Michael Jordan left. So here's what I'm going to do. I'll grant foster guardianship for a three-month period, subject to supervision by the Department of Social Services. At the end of that time if there are no problems I will grant permanent adoption, subject to the standard three-month probation period. How's that sound to you?"

Sachs nodded. "It sounds fine, Your Honor."

The justice examined Sachs's face carefully. Then, with a glance at Po-Yee, she jabbed her intercom button and said, "Send in the petitioners."

A moment later the door to the justice's chambers opened and Sam Chang and Mei-Mei cautiously entered. Beside them was their attorney, a Chinese man in a light gray suit and a shirt so boldly red that it might've come from Fred Dellray's closet.

Chang nodded to Sachs, who rose, stepped forward and shook his hand then his wife's. Mei-Mei's eyes went wide when she saw the child, whom Sachs handed off to her. She hugged Po-Yee fiercely.

The judge said, "Mr. and Mrs. Chang, do you speak English?"

"I do, some," Chang said. "My wife, not good."

"You are Mr. Sing?" the judge asked the lawyer.

"Yes, Your Honor."

"If you could translate."

"Certainly."

"Usually the adoption process in this country is arduous and complicated. It is virtually impossible for a couple of uncertain immigration status to be given adoptive custody."

A pause while Sing translated. Mei-Mei nodded.

"But we've got some unusual circumstances here."

Another pause and the Chinese rattled explosively off Sing's tongue. Now both Chang and his wife nodded. They remained silent. Mei-Mei's eyes brightened, though, and her breathing was coming fast. She wanted to smile, Sachs could see, but she restrained herself.

"I'm told by Immigration and Naturalization that you've applied for asylum and, because of your dissident status in China, that it will probably be granted. That reassures me that you can bring some stability into the child's life. As does the fact that both you and your son, Mr. Chang, are employed."

"Yes, sir."

"'Ma'am,' not 'sir,'" sternly corrected Justice Benson-Waite, a woman whose orders in court undoubtedly needed to be issued only once.

"I am sorry. Ma'am."

The judge now repeated for the Changs what she'd told Sachs about the probation and adoption.

Their understanding of English was apparently good enough so that they could comprehend the ultimate meaning of the justice's words without the need for complete translations. Mei-Mei began to cry quietly and Sam Chang hugged her, smiling and whispering in her ear. Then Mei-Mei stepped up to Sachs and hugged her. "*Xiexie*, thank you, thank you."

The justice signed a document in front of her. "You can take the child with you now," she said, dismissing them. "Attorney Sing, see the clerk about the disposition of the paperwork."

"Yes, Your Honor."

Sam Chang led his family, now officially increased by one, to the parking lot near the black-stone Family Court Building. This had been his second court appearance today. Earlier Chang had testified at the Wu family's preliminary hearing. Their asylum bid was less certain than the Changs' but their lawyer was guardedly optimistic that they would remain in the U.S.

The Changs and the policewoman now paused beside her yellow sports car. William, who'd been sullen and moody all day, brightened when he saw it. "A Camaro SS," he said.

The woman laughed. "You know American cars?"

"Who'd drive anything else?" he asked derisively. The lean boy examined the sports car closely. "This is fucking sweet."

"William," Chang whispered threateningly and received back a cold, uncomprehending look from his son.

Mei-Mei and the children continued on to their van and Chang remained beside the policewoman. Translating his words slowly, Chang said to the red-haired woman, "Everything you do for us, you and Mr. Rhyme . . . I am not knowing how to thank you. And the baby . . . See, my wife, she has always—"

"I understand, " the woman said. Her voice was clipped and he realized that though she appreciated the gratitude she was uneasy receiving it. She dropped into the seat of her car, wincing slightly from a sore joint or pulled muscle. The engine fired up with a powerful rattling noise and she drove quickly out of the parking lot, spinning the tires as she accelerated.

In a moment the car was out of sight.

The family was due soon at a funeral home in Brooklyn, where the body of Chang Jiechi was being prepared. But Sam Chang remained where he was, gazing at the complex of gray courthouses and office buildings around him. He needed a moment of solitude, this man caught between the yin and the yang of life. How badly he wanted to slough off the hard, the masculine, the traditional, the authoritarian—the aspects of his past life in China—and embrace the artistic, the feminine, the intuitive, the new: all that the Beautiful Country represented. But how difficult it was to do this. Mao Zedong, he reflected, had tried to abolish old customs and ideas with a simple decree and had nearly destroyed his country as a result.

No, Chang reflected, the past was with us always. But he didn't know, not yet, how to find a place for it in his future. It could be done. Look at how close in proximity was the Forbidden Palace with its ancient ghosts to Tiananmen Square with its very different spirits. But he suspected that this reconciliation would be a process that lasted for the rest of his life.

Here he was, half a world away from everything familiar, steeped in confusion and beset by challenges.

And pummeled too by the uncertainty of life in a strange land.

But some things Sam Chang did know:

That at the autumn tomb-sweeping festival he would find comfort in tidying his father's grave, leaving an offering of oranges and conversing with the man's spirit.

That Po-Yee, the Treasured Child, would grow up to become a woman in complete harmony with this remarkable place and time: the Beautiful Country at the start of a new century, easily embracing the souls of both *Hua* and *Meiguo*, China and America, yet transcending each.

That William would eventually get a room of his own and discover something other than his father to be mad about but that little by little his anger would lift away like a phoenix rising from cooling ash and he too would find a balance.

And that Chang himself would work hard at his job, continue his efforts as a dissident and on his days off would enjoy modest pleasures— strolling with Mei-Mei through their neighborhood, visiting parks and art galleries and passing hours in places like The Home Store, where they would make their purchases or just walk up and down the aisles, examining the bounty on the shelves.

Finally Sam Chang turned away from the tall buildings and returned to the van, summoned by his desire to be with his family again.

Still dressed for her undercover work as a Manhattan businesswoman, Amelia Sachs strode into the living room.

"So?" the criminalist asked, wheeling to face her.

"A done deal," she answered, disappearing upstairs. She returned a few minutes later, as jeans and sweats as she could be.

He said, "You know, Sachs, you could've adopted the baby yourself if you'd wanted." He paused. "I mean, *we* could've done that."

"I know."

"Why didn't you want to?"

She considered her answer then said, "The other day I laid some brass on the deck with a perp in a Chinatown alleyway, then I went swimming ninety feet underwater, then was point on a takedown team . . . I can't *not* do things like that, Rhyme." She hesitated as she thought of how best to summarize her feelings then laughed. "My father told me there're two kinds of drivers—those who check their blind spot when they change lanes and those who don't. I'm not a checker. If I had a baby at home I'd be looking over my shoulder all the time. That wouldn't work."

He understood exactly what she meant. But he asked playfully, "If you don't check your blind spot aren't you worried about an accident?"

"The trick is just to drive *faster* than everybody else. That way there's no chance anybody'll *be* in your blind spot."

"When you move they can't getcha," he said.

"Yep."

"You'd be a good mother, Sachs."

"And you'll be a good father. It'll happen, Rhyme. But let's give it a couple of years. Right now we've got a few other things to do with our life, don't you think?" She nodded at the whiteboard, on which were written Thom's charts for the GHOSTKILL case, the same whiteboard that had been covered with notations from a dozen prior cases and would be filled with those from dozens of future ones.

She was, of course, right, Lincoln Rhyme reflected; the world represented by these notes and pictures, this place on the edge that they shared, was *their* nature—for the time being, at least.

"I made the arrangements," he said to her.

Rhyme had been on the phone, making plans to have Sonny Li's body shipped back to his father in Liu Guoyuan, China. The arrangements were being handled by a Chinese funeral home.

There was one more task attendant to the death that Rhyme needed to do. He called up a word processing program. Sachs sat down next to him. "Go ahead," she said.

After a half hour of writing and rewriting he and Sachs finally came up with this:

> *Dear Mr. Li:*
> *I am writing to express my heartfelt condolences at the death of your son.*
>
> *You should know how thankful my fellow police officers and I are for the privilege of having been able to work with Sonny on the difficult and dangerous case that resulted in the loss of his life.*

He saved many lives and brought a vicious killer to justice—an accomplishment we alone could not have achieved. His actions have brought the highest honor to his memory and he will always have a place of great respect within the law enforcement community of the United States. I truly hope you are as proud of your son for his courage and sacrifice as we are.

Lincoln Rhyme, Det. Capt., NYPD (Ret.)

Rhyme read it and grumbled, "It's too much. Too *emotional*. Let's start over."

But Sachs reached down and hit the print key. "Nope, Rhyme. Leave it. Sometimes too much is a good thing."

"You sure?"

"I'm sure."

Sachs set the letter aside for Eddie Deng to translate when the young cop arrived later in the day.

"Want to get back to the evidence?" Sachs asked. Nodding toward the whiteboards. There was much preparatory work that needed to be done for the Ghost's trial.

But Rhyme said, "No, I want to play a game."

"Game?"

"Yeah."

"Sure," she said coyly. "I'm in the mood to win."

"You wish," he chided.

"What game?" she asked.

"*Wei-chi*. The board's over there. And those bags of stones."

She found the game and set it up on the table near where Rhyme was parked. She glanced at his eyes, which were examining the grid of the board, and said, "I think I'm being hustled, Rhyme. You've played this before."

"Sonny and I played a few games," he said casually.

"How few?"

"Three is all. I'm *hardly* an expert, Sachs."

"How'd you do?"

The criminalist said defensively, "It takes a while to get the feel for a game."

"You lost," she said. "All of them."

"But the last one was close."

She looked over the board. "What'll we play for?"

With a cryptic smile Rhyme replied, "We'll think of something." Then he explained the rules and she leaned forward, raptly taking in his words. Finally he said, "That's it. . . . Now, you've never played so you get an advantage. You can make the first move."

"No," Sachs answered. "No advantages. We'll flip a coin."

"It's customary," Rhyme assured her.

"No advantage," Sachs repeated. Then dug a quarter out of her pocket. "Call it," she said.

And tossed the coin into the air.

Acknowledgments

My thanks to Kim Arthur and the folks at Invacare and to Cheryl Lehman for their extremely helpful insights on care of and equipment available for spinal cord injury patients. And, as always, to Madelyn.

About the Author

Former journalist, folksinger and attorney Jeffery Deaver's novels have appeared on a number of bestseller lists around the world, including the *New York Times*, *London Times* and *Los Angeles Times*. The author of seventeen novels, he's been nominated for four Edgar Awards from the Mystery Writers of America and an Anthony Award, is a two-time recipient of the Ellery Queen Reader's Award for Best Short Story of the Year, and won last year's Thumping Good Read Award in the United Kingdom. His book *A Maiden's Grave* was made into an HBO movie starring James Garner and Marlee Matlin, and his novel *The Bone Collector* was a feature release from Universal Pictures, starring Denzel Washington and Angelina Jolie. Turner Broadcasting is currently making a TV movie of his novel *Praying for Sleep*. His most recent novels are *The Blue Nowhere*, *The Empty Chair* and *Speaking in Tongues*. He lives in Virginia and California. Readers can visit his website at *www.jefferydeaver.com* or the website for *The Blue Nowhere* at *www.thebluenowhere.com*.